# Pushed to the Edge of EXISTENCE

BILL CONRAD

First Edition

interviewingimmortality.com

bill@interviewingimmortality.com

www.facebook.com/Interviewingimmortality/

www.goodreads.com/author/show/17088207.Bill_Conrad

www.amazon.com/Bill-Conrad/e/B074FFPZX9

Cover art by Payton Braun



Printed and bound in the United States of America.

eBook ISBN: 978-1-7340387-3-6

Print ISBN: 978-1-7340387-4-3

# TABLE OF CONTENTS

# ONE

Wednesday, May 10, 2017. Newlyweds Kim and Gabe Alexander arrived at their house in Miramar, Florida, after a long Alaskan flight. Kim unlocked the door and started to enter, but Gabe stopped her. He scooped her up in his arms and carried her through the doorway. "Welcome home, wife."

"That's the first time you've called me your wife."

"True."

"Does being married feel different?"

"Not really."

"Good," Kim said with a big grin.

"It is strange speaking to you. I'm used to communicating mentally. Want to switch?"

"I enjoy hearing your voice," Kim answered, nudging Gabe.

"A nice compliment."

"Our wedding vows stipulated two compliments per day."

"The real number is fifty for the husband and twenty for the wife. Read the fine print next time."

"You're too much."

Kim needed six more credits to get her master's degree in design, business, and math at Nova Southeastern University. While she enjoyed school, her dry-cleaning business, Harrington Enterprises, required significant time. They had recently expanded to 35 locations and employed 91 staff members. Kim had hired two excellent people for the main office. Boyd worked on logistics and accounting, while Ellen handled marketing and human resources.

Kim diverted some dry-cleaning profits to help Gabe start his semiconductor business, KimSemi. The month before, they had begun selling a disk controller for Linux servers. Profits were initially low but increased due to marketing and financial assistance from the owners of Gabe's prior companies, Silicon Serpent and Pacific Progressive Peripherals. Initial customer feedback was excellent, and the company was on track to become self-sufficient in two months.

After unpacking and a quick nap, Gabe and Kim sat down for dinner. Their housekeeper, Anna, had been one of Kim's classmates, and she loved to cook. This evening, she made the South American dish *arroz con pollo y coco*, or rice with chicken and coconut milk.

"When will you tell your mother that we got married?" Kim asked between bites.

"Umm."

Kim slid his cell phone across the table and said, "She's going to be livid at not getting a wedding invite."

"I know," Gabe said with a sigh. "I'm kind of ashamed of not inviting her. It seemed like getting married right then was the best choice."

"Your sister is going to beat you bloody."

"I know."

"You need to tell them something else."

"What?"

"I'm pregnant," Kim answered with a bashful smile.

"But we only had sex three days ago," Gabe protested. "That's not enough time for the test strips to get an accurate reading."

Kim stared at Gabe for a moment. Then he stood and hugged Kim, mentally sending warm emotions to her mind. "Sometimes my brain can get in the way," he admitted.

"I noticed."

"I'm thrilled!" Gabe said with a tighter hug.

"Me too."

"You are going to be a terrific mother."

"Only with your help."

"We should celebrate," Gabe suggested, pulling Kim out of her chair.

"Being with you is all I need."

"That's nice, but we should do something. How about Friday night, we go to that fancy restaurant? What is it? Blue Ginger something? Or we could go to that expensive day spa near the mall. What's it called?"

"Anything is fine, as long as it's with you," Kim answered. "Hey, you're still not off the hook. Call your family."

"After dinner. I promise."

Gabe kissed Kim, sat, and asked, "When did you know?"

"Since gaining our mental ability, I understand more about my body. On Friday morning, I felt something different. It took me a while to put things together. Now, I'm sure."

"Do you know the sex?"

"My body tells me it's a girl."

"Wow, that's amazing."

"You're not disappointed?" Kim asked.

"What do you mean?"

"In your last marriage, you had daughters. Don't you want a son?"

"Daughters are great. I should know."

•

After dinner, Gabe called his mother. "Hi, Mom-O."

"All these years, and I'm Mom-O, not Mother?"

"An old habit," Gabe admitted. "Hey, there is something important I have to tell you."

"You married Kim?"

"What?"

"A mother knows these things. Is she pregnant?"

"Um, yes. I found out a few minutes ago."

"And you did not see fit to invite me to the wedding?"

"We got married in Alaska by the same judge who sentenced me," Gabe solemnly answered.

"Interesting choice," Mrs. Alexander commented.

"It seemed fitting."

"When can I see the new couple?"

"Any time you like."

"Does Bridget know?"

"I'm calling her next," Gabe quickly answered.

"Good. I'm happy for the two of you. Kim is an incredible woman who made a better man out of you. Do right by her."

"I will."

"I mean it!" Mrs. Alexander demanded.

"I know," Gabe said, and winced.

"I have something in the oven."

"You always use that excuse. When was the last time you even turned that thing on? We have a lot more to talk about."

"Call your sister."

"Will do. Love you, Mom-O."

"Love you right back," Mrs. Alexander said, then hung up.

Kim had been listening to the one-sided conversation and commented, "Your mom hates talking to you on the phone."

"I know. She talks to my sister for hours. But get her in person, and she'll talk your ear off."

"Why?" Kim wanted to know as she twisted strands of her long black hair.

"I never figured that out."

"Better call your sister."

Gabe nodded at Kim, then dialed and got a busy signal. "Bridget doesn't have voicemail?" Kim asked.

"She doesn't even have a cell phone," Gabe answered with a groan. "Her husband's anti-technology."

"Ooo. It must be fun when you two talk," Kim said with a laugh.

"It's a riot!"

•

The two finished their chores and were getting ready for bed when Gabe's phone rang. A voice with a strong Texas accent yelled, "You jerk! You married Kim, and she's prego?"

"You talked to Mom?" Gabe asked his sister, Bridget.

"For the last two hours. That woman doesn't know the meaning of silence."

"She never talks to me like that."

"What's with that? 'I have something in the oven.' It's always the same excuse."

"I never figured that out. Hey, I am guessing Mom brought you up to speed?"

"No wedding invite for your sis?"

"It kind of worked out that way," Gabe admitted while feeling guilty.

"Well, you two are inseparable. So, it stands to reason you two would go off and get hitched. When's she due?"

"The traditional nine months."

"Sex?"

"Girl."

"Great. Hey, wait. How do you know the sex already? You need an ultrasound for that. Trust me, I've had enough of them."

"Kim knows, and that is all there is to it."

"That girl is as smart as they come."

"No arguments here," Gabe said with pride.

"Hey, I got that picture you all sent. What's the deal? You look like you are twenty-something. What's Kim feeding you, and how can I get some?"

After their Alaskan adventure, Gabe appeared younger. However, due to their arrangement with the mysterious Jason, he agreed not to discuss the topic and pleasantly replied, "Healthy living."

"You're up to something. I can always tell. Now, spill it! What's your secret?"

"Good food," Gabe answered in a cagey voice.

"Tell me, or I will wrestle you to the ground like when we were kids!"

"Remember the Patersons' car? Please drop this."

At age fourteen, Bridget and her boyfriend stole their neighbor's car. They got into a wild police chase and crashed the car into the local gymnasium. The police searched the surrounding area but were unable to locate the car thieves. When Bridget returned late that night, Gabe told her he had watched the theft from his bedroom window. She begged him not to turn her in. Gabe loved Bridget and agreed on one condition. She would never commit another crime. This arrangement lasted for a month, when the police caught her shoplifting. However, Gabe had made a promise and kept her secret.

"Bringing out the big guns?" Bridget asked with a sigh. "You never told me what you two did in Alaska. This is the same topic. Right? Alright, I get it. Mum's the word."

"Thanks," Gabe said with relief.

"In all these years, you have never peeped about what you saw that night. So, this thing must be super hush-hush."

"It's important."

"Well, alright. Next time we talk, I am getting you drunk, and then you will spill your guts like when I made you try vodka. Remember that?"

"Actually, I no longer drink," Gabe admitted.

"Really?"

"Yes."

"That girl is improving you big-time," Bridget observed with pride.

"True."

"Bro!"

"What?"

"You know, Kim is the best thing that ever happened to you."

"I used to be married to a wonderful woman, and we had two amazing daughters."

"Lydia's eggs were drying up like the Sahara Desert, and she knew it. So, she dug her hooks into the first nice man who looked her way. Kim's a different breed. She respects you."

"I know."

"Do everything she says. No matter what!" Bridget demanded.

"I will."

"Well, as soon as little Brian is old enough, we'll fly out and see you-all."

"Looking forward to it."

"I am happy as heck for you three," Bridget said with glee.

"Thanks."

"Hugs and kisses."

"Love ya, sis."

After he hung up, Kim said, "You don't spend enough phone time with your family. You need to work on that."

"True."

"Did she say when she wanted to come by?"

"I'm thinking August. When you're finished with school."

"Sounds good. Goodnight, hubby."

•

Twenty-two-year-old Kim is a striking blend of her diverse heritage from Tanzania, Spain, Jamaica, and Cuba. Standing five foot eight, she possessed an athletic build with long, shapely legs, an ample bust, and a trim waistline. Kim's straight, jet-black hair complemented her golden-bronze skin, thin nose, pucker lips, picturesque brown eyes, and high cheekbones. Her trademark confident expression conveyed both charm and self-assurance. Kim's expert application of makeup always struck the perfect balance between sophistication and allure.

After interacting with the white box gifted to them by the alien race known as the Veronn, Kim and Gabe learned how to mentally communicate words and emotions with each other from over ten feet away. It also provided them with the tools to better understand the human mind.

It was now possible to interpret some emotions in other people's minds. On rare occasions, Kim could telepathically understand (without the white box) a word or two. She had utilized this ability to assist her accountant, Boyd, with his marital and inner-office communication challenges.

Unfortunately, the more Kim meddled, the more uncomfortable he became. This intrusion came to a head one morning when she confronted Boyd about his "mentally undressing" a coworker. Boyd felt humiliated, and he resigned. This was an incredible blow to Kim and the company.

•

Thirty-nine-year-old Gabe was a man of quiet strength. Standing six foot two, his thick, chestnut-brown hair added a touch of rugged charm, tousled just enough to give him a casual yet polished look. Gabe could trace his lineage to England and Hungary, but grew up in Killeen, Texas.

Gabe's chiseled jaw and strong profile complemented his broad shoulders. Recently, he gained a newfound level of muscle definition through dedicated yoga and regular workouts at their home gym. Gabe's updated hairstyle further stressed this change— a short pompadour suggested by Kim. The subtle alteration reflected his willingness to embrace his wife's expert fashion sense.

Like Kim, Gabe's new mental ability was also an issue with KimSemi employees. He knew he should ignore his telepathic insights, but this inside knowledge confused him, and ignoring nonverbal facts was often impossible. This insight led to illogical or inappropriate questions and awkward situations. As a result, Gabe's coworkers kept him at a distance.

Unfortunately, their new ability hindered their relationship despite Kim's best efforts to discuss problems. The most hurtful incident occurred when she revealed her family's cancer history. Gabe thought with no consideration, <Cool. I can start dating again.>

Kim felt justifiably hurt, and Gabe profusely apologized for his inappropriate thought. She understood this thought was random and did not represent his true feelings. However, Kim often recalled the incident, and when Gabe experienced her pain, it saddened him.

The incident inspired a new rule. To mitigate future unwanted mental intrusions, Gabe suggested they use a flat hand gesture to indicate "Get out of my thoughts" and a thumbs-up for "Let's swim." (Swimming was their term for mental communication.) This simple solution improved their relationship, but misunderstandings still occurred.

Two weeks after returning from their vacation, the pair discussed using the white box to avoid misunderstandings. The box was three inches long, a quarter inch high by an inch wide, with no controls or seams. They had only used it five times because the experience was mentally overwhelming. This was because the white box conveyed vivid emotions along with information (thought content).

That evening, they took comfortable positions in the fitness room while Kim gingerly held the white box. As in the previous experience, her mind opened to a vast mental picture. This time, Kim had more control and found a menu listing functions, databases, and controls. It took several minutes to maneuver her thoughts to activate the "mental analyzer." This mode allowed her to examine her mind from an abstract perspective, and the device revealed the region responsible for mental interaction.

Several minutes later, Kim thought to Gabe with intense emotions, <Wow, this is amazing.>

<Your thoughts feel superfluid,> Gabe responded with great joy.

<I am going to guide your mind to its 'fur-mow.' That's the region responsible for thought control.>

<Fur-mow? That sounds like part of a cat,> Gabe thought, smiling, and said, "Meow, meow."

<Funny. According to the white box, most humans have a fur-mow but do not have access to it. I also learned that the Veronn enhanced our fur-mow so they could comprehend our thoughts. Here, let me guide you, Kim thought cautiously. <It's over here. Like this.>

<I feel something,> Gabe thought with wonder.

<Alright. You found it. See this area on the left? That is the power level. Place emphasis there, like squeezing your fist, and you will feel the mental image of me fade or increase. Feel this.>

Gabe experimented with his fur-mow and unflexed it. Kim's mental impression faded. Then he flexed it, and her mental image sharpened. <I get it now,> he thought. <It feels like moving my finger. Wow, it will be nice to stay out of people's minds. This is really cool.>

<True. Hey, what are you doing?> Kim asked with hesitation.

<Nothing. I wanted to keep it simple.>

<I felt that. You want me to navigate to the section about semiconductors.>

<Oops,> Gabe admitted with embarrassment.

<Hon!>

<Sorry, babe. I'll behave.>

<Let's finish up,> Kim thought with happiness. <And then I want to jump you.>

<You behave,> Gabe thought with humor.

<I'm glad you still get excited when you see me.>

<Babe! I will always be attracted to you. You know that.>

<I know,> Kim admitted with embarrassment. <I think this pregnancy is messing with my head.>

<I've been told that can occur,> Gabe thought.

<You can be funny when you want to be. Now, let's put the white box away, and then I will rock your world!> Kim challenged.

<OK.>

<Just OK? Hon, stop feeling so intimidated.>

<Sorry, babe,> Gabe admitted with regret.

<You need to enjoy stuff more.>

<True.>

<Alright, Mr. Confidence. How do you propose to please me?>

<I felt some tension in your neck. How about I start by working some of it out?>

<You know, you have a lot of confidence for a man with no confidence.>

Kim giggled, and the pair left their fitness room. After returning the white box to its hidden location, they undressed and got into bed. Kim rolled onto her stomach, and Gabe began working on her neck muscles. <You still have a delicate touch,> she commented with warm emotions.

<I try,> Gabe admitted, while working to hold back his excitement.

<Those are lusty thoughts.>

<You have a nice butt.>

<Thanks,> Kim thought with some misgivings.

<Hey, stop feeling like that,> Gabe told her. <We're married, and it is legally permissible to admire your fantastic body.>

Kim rolled over and thought, <You still think I have a nice body?>

Gabe began caressing Kim's ample chest and thought, <I knew you had a perfect body the first second I saw you.>

<That was a long time ago,> Kim admitted with embarrassment.

<Not that long, and you still have a perfect body.>

Kim grasped Gabe and thought with desire, <You have a studly body too.>

<Thanks,> Gabe thought with deep pleasure.

<Just thanks?>

<Thanks, my wonderful wife.>

<That's better,> Kim challenged with sexual intent.

<You are obviously ready,> Gabe thought with desire as he savored Kim's intense emotions.

<As are you.>

<You know the rules. Let's stop swimming. It will be a lot easier now.>

<Not this time. Stay in my mind,> Kim responded.

<You're the boss,> Gabe thought with humor and joy.

<I will show you who's boss!> Kim challenged Gabe with great sexual intent. She placed Gabe inside and thought, <Ooo. That was a rush. You liked that.>

<You also loved that first push,> Gabe thought as he experienced Kim's deep mental pleasure.

<Move to the left. Yeah, like that. A little more. Like that. That's good.>

The pair began moving in passion, and a moment later, Gabe sensed sharp negative emotions and thought with great concern, <What's wrong?>

<Something's off.>

<I'll stop,> Gabe replied.

<No, you're close.>

<Your happiness is much more important.>

<Keep going. A little more,> Kim said a little less confidently. Their intense passion increased, and she thought, <Stop!>

Gabe pulled out and thought with deep regret, <I'm so sorry.>

<Stop apologizing.>

<Sorry.>

<Hon!> Kim chided

<Oops.>

<Stop automatically feeling guilty. I loved what you did.>

<What did I do wrong?> Gabe needed to know.

<Assuming you made a mistake is your go-to response. Stop that.>

<I'll try,> Gabe admitted with embarrassment. <Do you know what the issue is?> he said to change the subject, then realized Kim had picked up on it.

<I'm not sure. Let me put it together.>

Gabe held Kim's hand and stroked her face until she thought, <It's the baby.>

<I don't understand.>

<It's strange. Our daughter is aware we're having sex.>

<Really?> Gabe asked with surprise.

<Yup.>

<That's creepy.>

<Exactly.>

<No sex for a while?> Gabe thought while trying to suppress his disappointment.

<I can always please you. You know that.>

Gabe lightly squeezed Kim's arm and asked, <What did I tell you so long ago?>

<That we're in this together,> Kim thought with relief.

<Yes.>

<The student has become the master. Relax with me.>

<You're one of a kind.>

The pair held each other until they drifted off to sleep.

# TWO

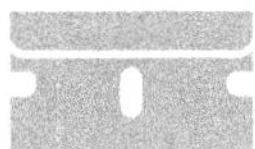

The couple discussed baby names and chose Emma after Kim's mother, Emelia. Three months later, she had matured enough to communicate basic emotions, strengthening the mother-daughter bond. Gabe swam in his daughter's mind while resting his head against Kim's belly. Emma could not form words or mental pictures, but she felt comforted by her parents' presence.

At Kim's first pediatric visit, she informed the doctor about her child's sex and the exact development stage with confidence. The doctor was impressed with her insight, but still scheduled an ultrasound. "If you think it is necessary," Kim commented. "Emma knows how well she's doing."

•

While the Alexander household had many positives, Kim and Gabe had health problems. Gabe experienced sudden itching, stomach cramps, dizziness, and headaches. At the same time, Kim had headaches, dizziness, muscle aches, and difficulty comprehending the passage of time. They had visited several doctors but could not obtain a firm diagnosis.

The pair used the white box to investigate their health issues in more detail. Kim concluded their brains were "misaligned." She searched for more information in the extensive white box health database, but failed to understand the problem. Kim commented to Gabe, <I get the feeling we're missing something super obvious. But for the life of me, I cannot discover what the heck's going on.>

•

Gabe got a call from his former boss, Al Horne. They had worked together at Silicon Serpent to develop a disk controller for Computix Systems. Unfortunately, when Gabe went missing in Alaska, his unpleasant coworker, Sato Tonegawa, claimed Gabe's work as his own.

Gabe exposed the lie, which led to Sato's termination. As an act of revenge, Sato and a woman named Jenna Cox instigated a massive online campaign involving many people to discredit Gabe and Kim. In response, Kim hired Russian hackers to commit several drug and computer theft crimes, which were made to appear as if the thirty most prolific slanderers were responsible. The accused did not cooperate during the trials and were all convicted, ending the vilification.

Six months later, Al informed Gabe on the phone call that while serving his sentence (for the crimes the Russian hackers instigated), Sato wrote a long letter to the president of Computix Systems. In it, he claimed Gabe stole Computix Systems' disk controller technology. Now, Computix Systems was threatening to sue Silicon Serpent and KimSemi.

Al hired a corporate lawyer, who spoke to the Computix Systems lawyers. Neither company wanted the negative publicity, so they agreed to meet at Computix Systems headquarters in New York to settle their differences amicably.

That night, Gabe told Kim the bad news, and she had some bad news of her own. A friend messaged her about a Facebook post. The ringleader of the harassment campaign, Jenna Cox, received a pardon from the Alaskan governor. Over 100 people "liked" the post, and several replied with detestable comments about the couple.

Gabe wanted to discuss the topic mentally, but Kim felt it prudent to verbalize her feelings so she could express her anger without unsettling him. "I will take care of Jenna," Kim coldly began. "You deal with Sato. Also, we're not playing games."

"Agreed."

"I'll contact the Russian hackers. Hopefully, they can help."

"Any ideas on our overall plan?" Gabe asked.

"We're going to deal with everybody at once."

"I like it."

"What about Sato?" Kim asked. "He's still in prison."

"My goal will be to separate him from his computer."

"Break his hands!" Kim said with a scowl. "That will stop him from typing."

"Hey, hey, let's dial it back. How about we frame him for something? They can lock him up in solitary confinement."

"Hmm. I guess that could work," Kim said in an unsure voice.

"I am attending a meeting in New York to get KimSemi back on track. How about afterward, I talk to my prison buddies? I'm sure they'll have ideas for handling problem inmates."

"That sounds like a plan."

"What about Jenna and that other lady? Teresa, was it?"

"That's my problem," Kim retorted. "Don't worry about it."

"Are you sure?"

"I don't want you to be involved. This is my thing, and if it goes sideways, you need to raise our daughter while I'm in jail."

"How is she?" Gabe asked, trying to change the subject.

"She is curious about what we're doing."

"Wow!" Gabe exclaimed.

"I sense her desire to learn. She gets that from her mother," Kim said with a smile. "Only a few months until we see her pretty face."

"She will get that from her mother as well."

"Thanks. You've been a great husband."

"I try."

"Stop being so modest and take the compliment," Kim chided.

"Alright."

"I can tell you want to rub my feet because it has been a bad day."

"You figured this out without swimming?" Gabe asked in a coy voice.

"I know you. But I don't need to have my feet rubbed every day."

"Not true. I recall a wedding vow that specifies one foot massage per day. So, put 'em up, wonderful wife."

Kim snickered while Gabe massaged her feet, and they watched the evening news.

•

Promptly at 8:50 a.m. on Monday, Gabe met his former Silicon Serpent coworker, Gustavo, and owner, Al Horne, in a lavish Computix Systems conference room. Al's lawyer was also in attendance, and the four had briefly chatted before the meeting. The disk controller division manager, Nick Stanley, began, "Gentleman, I'm upset."

"We didn't steal your designs," Al challenged through gritted teeth. "I can prove that!"

"I am about to present ten technical intellectual theft allegations. We will discuss each one at length."

Nick displayed the first presentation slide, and the two groups argued. Occasionally, the lawyers interrupted with legal opinions. Half an hour later, they had reached the third slide. Sensing a fruitless debate, Nick verbally outlined a lofty payment plan for Silicon Serpent and KimSemi. Al was visibly unimpressed and demanded to see Sato's evidence. He was "tired of salad and wanted meat and potatoes."

While the discussion raged, Gabe swam. He admired Al's brilliance and ability to interact with the assembled people while remaining composed. Gustavo worked hard to suppress his anger and struggled to stay silent. Gabe mentally felt Gustavo pressing a pen into his leg to suppress rage. He wondered if his pants would have an ink stain.

The lawyers all thought about billable hours and how they would spend the money they were making. Gabe found Nick to be a curious individual, and he discovered that he had orchestrated a brilliant move to cover up unrelated problems.

Gabe then focused on one man who had remained silent while diligently studying the other people. He was in his late sixties and wore a spotless pinstriped suit with a thin blue tie. Gabe sensed deep complexity, focus, and intelligence.

Gabe's attention broke when Nick began pounding his fists on the table. He demanded, "Justice for all!" Gabe thought this was absurd because they were not in a courtroom, but the Computix Systems employees nodded in approval.

However, the man with the blue tie was frowning, and Gabe again entered his mind. Clearly, the man did not like Nick's grandstanding. Gabe suddenly realized this man must be in charge, which gave him hope that they could reach an agreement.

Nick sat and let a Computix Systems lawyer take over the discussion, even though he had only made it to the fifth slide. Gabe returned to Nick's mind, hoping he could find a solution. He suddenly felt a vivid thought: <I'm so relieved we're not talking about the Dolphin server schedule. This lawsuit will save my job.>

Now, Gabe knew what was happening and looked at Al with raised eyebrows. Al knew he was onto something and nodded. Gabe turned to the man with the blue tie and said, "Sir, I don't believe we've met."

"Blake Wade," the man answered, and Al nodded to him.

"Nice to meet you," Gabe said calmly, sensing caution. "Let me first say that these allegations are groundless, but that doesn't matter."

"Why?" Blake challenged as Gabe sensed curiosity.

"A big lawsuit will not solve your problem. In the best case, it will be a whirlwind of bad publicity."

Gabe sensed surprise at the word "publicity" and realized Nick had not discussed this topic beforehand.

"My problem?" Blake asked with concern.

"Your Dolphin server is far behind schedule."

"How the heck did you know that?"

Gabe froze and lied, "It's common industry knowledge."

"I see. What's your proposal?" Blake asked.

"I see several opportunities."

"Such as?"

"Let's start with Silicon Serpent. Al put me in charge of the RAID 5 project four years ago. Things were going well, and Nick liked our progress. Personally, I thought our teams worked well together. Then, right before the prototype was ready for fabrication, Sato became the project manager. Unfortunately, he changed the project focus and made poor decisions. To make matters worse, I vacationed in Alaska at the height of this setback."

"Wait a minute," Nick interrupted. "You are that Kuiu Island guy. They put you in jail for killing that twelve-year-old girl!"

Gabe knew Nick had planned to bring this topic up at the perfect time to cause the most damage, but hearing the lie still angered him. He took a deep breath to calm down while staring daggers at Nick and continued through gritted teeth, "You have some misinformation. Kim was seventeen at the time, not twelve. Together, we survived a sinking cruise ship and the harsh Alaskan wilderness. We developed a strong friendship, but it was not intimate. To answer your allegation, I pleaded guilty so she wouldn't have to testify. I did so because I did not want her to be publicly crucified."

Gabe sensed relief in Blake and deep fear in Nick. To deflect the conversation, Nick blurted out, "She killed four bears with a rock."

"Kim bravely killed a single bear with a rusty fishing knife," Gabe corrected.

"That's not what the news reported," Nick countered while being relieved that the conversation had changed.

"Let's get back to the topic at hand. While I was fighting for my life in Alaska, Sato modified one of my test articles and claimed it was a functional design. He was too inept to realize that it had no real guts. When I returned, I showed everybody the truth."

"Al informed us that the team had to start from the beginning," Blake said as Gabe perceived renewed interest.

"Sato wiped the servers and backup drives."

"And that's why the project took so long?" Blake asked.

"Yes."

"Why is Sato in prison?"

"Al fired him for what he did, and then he could not find employment. This ticked him off, and he attacked us online. That's where the public got this nonsense.

"Anyway. Because Sato could not find legitimate work, he hacked into government computers and tried to sell the files. The authorities caught him red-handed and sent him to jail. There, he devised a new plan to discredit his former employer. This brings us to today."

"Wow! That's a wild story," Blake said with a big nod.

"True."

"What's your plan?"

"I have a good understanding of the RAID 5 project, and with Gustavo's help, I'm sure we can make it work in 30 days. I'll do my part for free as a gesture of good faith."

"Is that all?"

"No. Also, as a gesture of good faith, I will show you the technology behind KimSemi's product. Then, it will be apparent that no intellectual theft has occurred. But I require a non-disclosure agreement."

Gabe sensed Blake's surprise and asked, "Can you give me a baseline difference?"

"Of course. The RAID 5 is a simple controller that is optimized for cost. My product uses brand-new technology that simultaneously executes 32 disk commands. It also has interactive memory buffering."

Blake nodded and asked, "What about the Silicon Serpent's intellectual property theft allegations? Sato claimed Al sold our design to our competitor."

"The only other company that makes a similar product is the 1085 series from Lance Microsystems. As you know, they released that product ten years ago and have not announced any new revisions since then. Plus, I know Al. He's honest and would never risk his reputation for a few bucks."

"Hmm. I'm satisfied," Blake said after some consideration, and Gabe knew he felt good about his proposed solution. "Getting this project back on track is the most critical path. Thirty days? Let's make this happen."

Nick looked surprised and nodded.

•

Gabe arrived at the Fairbanks Correctional Facility the following day and met with his former inmates. They enjoyed seeing their friend and talking about old times. Gabe explained his Sato issue, and they offered several ghastly solutions involving paying prisoners to murder him or threatening his family. He did not like their heavy-handed approach and asked for more realistic options.

One of Gabe's former students, Tuk Tuk, had been quiet during the discussion. He cut an imposing figure at six feet three, his towering frame accentuated by bulging muscles. As an Alaska Native, Tuk Tuk possessed a quiet dignity that emanated from deep within. He was a man of few words, his calm demeanor often masking keen observation skills.

Despite his reserved nature, those who crossed paths with Tuk Tuk immediately regretted their mistake. They became friends when Gabe helped him pass his high school equivalency exam.

"I read you got back together with that girl," Tuk Tuk began in a friendly voice.

"I married Kim, and we're expecting our first child."

"And this guy is bothering you that much?"

"He is trying to put my company out of business and spreading awful lies about my wife. I have to stop him, no matter the cost," Gabe said with a sharp nod.

"Do you love her?"

"She means everything to me."

Tuk Tuk thought deeply and said, "You know all about my past. I cannot undo what I've done, but you helped me become a better person."

"I'm glad you let me help."

"You know what revenge does to a man. Look at the cons around here."

"I know what happens when someone goes down the wrong path."

"Do you really need to stop this guy?" Tuk Tuk needed to know.

"I must free my family from his lies. This isn't about revenge."

Tuk Tuk studied Gabe for a long moment and said, "I will help you, but you are taking a one-way trip to hell. You know that. Is there no other way?"

"This man won't listen to reason."

"Where is he locked up?"

"The prisoner database listed Lompoc Federal Correctional Institution in California."

"Hang out for a while."

Gabe spoke to the other inmates, and two hours later, Tuk Tuk returned. "Here's a phone number. They will do the job for fifty grand, but these men are sharks. So take every possible precaution."

"I owe you big-time. Is there anything I can do for you?"

Tuk Tuk shook his head and answered, "Gabe, you dragged me out of the gutter. I am the one in your debt."

"I don't see it that way. May I at least buy you another Kindle book reader?"

"Wow. You would do that?"

"Of course. Anything for a friend," Gabe said with a smile.

"That means a lot."

That night, Gabe called the number from a payphone. The gruff male voice provided specific instructions and hung up. Gabe then called Kim from his hotel room and explained what the man requested.

The following morning, Gabe ate a tasty breakfast at a nearby café and then returned to retrieve an overnight package from the hotel's front desk. It contained a USB drive and an encouraging note from Kim.

That evening, Gabe flew to Los Angeles, rented a car, and stayed at a small hotel. The following morning, he drove to a Denny's Restaurant in a sketchy Baldwin Park shopping center. The caller had asked Gabe to wear a red hat and sit at a specific booth at 1:00 p.m. At 3:30, four motorcycles roared up. Two men got off their bikes while two stared directly at Gabe. The men on the bikes intentionally moved their leather vests to reveal large revolvers.

After looking around, the two entered the restaurant, and one man sat at a booth in the back. The other man eased into Gabe's booth and stared him down. This imposing biker stood a towering six foot four and weighed at least 300 pounds.

His long, greasy brown hair hung in unkempt tangles around his broad shoulders, framing a face etched with rugged lines and a menacing expression. Violent tattoos adorned his arms, each mark telling a story of strength and turmoil. A foul body odor clung to the man, speaking of long nights spent in the shadows and dark deeds.

He was clad in a dirty black shirt emblazoned with an evil skull and a well-worn black leather biker vest adorned with the ominous emblem of "Death's Avengers" in bold red letters. The man's eyes glinted with a dangerous intensity, scanning his surroundings with a predatory instinct for survival.

Gabe did his best to remain calm and kept his hands visible. Then, after a long moment, the man began, his voice deep and quiet, with extreme intent, "I understand you have a problem."

"Prisoner number 45298-319, Sato Tonegawa," Gabe answered with his most confident voice.

"What's your beef with him?"

"He's terrorizing my family."

"How'd you get my number?"

"An Alaskan gang member made the introduction," Gabe answered, realizing he had a shaky voice.

"The con's name?"

"You know the rules. No names."

"You spent time in the hole?" the man guessed with a nod.

"Two years."

"For?"

"I got together with a seventeen-year-old woman."

"You mess her up?"

"I would never harm a woman."

"Hmm. As we agreed, the fee is fifty gees."

Gabe had been counting on his swimming ability to provide a decisive edge, as it had in the business meeting. However, when he read this man's mind, it was clear he had no intention of making a deal. Instead, the man visualized getting the money and then signaling the man in the back to slice Gabe's neck open on the way out. He now understood the magnitude of his failure.

Gabe's mind raced to find a solution, but he could only sense the man's intense greed. Suddenly, he realized this greed could be the solution and said with maximum fake confidence, "I know how this works."

"How what works?" the man asked with a chuckle.

"After I give you the money, that big guy will ice me. What's the signal? One finger down?"

"Hmm," the man murmured with raised eyebrows.

"There's a better way."

"Listening," the man said with concern.

"What are you going to do with the fifty gees?"

"Whatever I want," the man answered with a chuckle and a dismissive hand gesture.

"Why not make it half a mil?"

"Five hundred gees?" the man asked with raised eyebrows.

"Everybody knows *product* is worth ten times more on the inside."

"Agreed."

"The problem with so much *product* is that somebody will get caught. Probably one of your guys."

"What are you saying? Make this Sato the fall guy?"

"That and more."

"And more?"

Gabe leaned forward and said, "The people on the inside have all the time in the world to come up with a big sting. What they need is seed money to get things rolling. If you do this correctly, you can make it look like Sato controls several people. Including your rival groups."

"My *rival groups*?" the man asked with concern.

"Your *competitors*."

"Hmm."

Gabe had been choosing every word based on the man's mental reactions to ensure he did not push him too hard. Finally, he sensed amusement and lied, "There are forty-two people outside of prison who are harming my family. I don't want them iced. I only need somebody to send them a strong message. If this first job goes well, there will be future work."

"Forty-two?"

"Yes," Gabe confirmed with a sharp nod, even though he had made up the number. "Forty-two *easy jobs*."

"That will require a lot of dough."

"My business is growing."

"What do you want done to Sato?"

"I want him to spend the rest of his life behind bars and never touch a computer."

"You don't want him roughed up?" the man asked in surprise.

"That isn't necessary. Just set up the right situation to keep him quiet."

"Hmm. Show me the cash."

"I'm going to remove something from my sock. Is this alright?"

"With your left hand," the man cautioned him. "Keep your right hand on the table. Move slowly."

Gabe extracted the USB drive, wiped it with his napkin, and passed it to the man.

"Is this a bank account number?" the man guessed.

"That is fifty gees of Bitcoin."

"What's a Bitcoin?"

"Electronic currency. Untraceable and safer than cash. There are instructions on the device for converting the Bitcoin to money."

"And you have forty-two more people lined up?" the man demanded with narrow eyes.

"Yes."

"You seem confident that I will not signal my boy."

Gabe leaned back momentarily, thinking about how his former wife would handle confident people. Then he recalled a discussion in which she convinced an insurance agent to give them a better rate, and he modified her technique. "Let me ask you this. You're a badass biker. Right? This means you party hard and do whatever the heck you want. But what I want to know is: what makes you happy?"

"Money," the man said with a wave of his hand.

"I disagree, though I think you enjoy making money. Tell me. Which is a better story to tell your brothers? You iced an unarmed guy who tried to protect his family? Or that you came up with this fantastic scheme that saved his family, took out your rivals, and made a gigantic pile of cash?"

"Why not skip Sato and screw over somebody else?"

"There's no hero in that story. All badass biker stories need heroes."

The man narrowed his eyes in deep thought, and Gabe's swimming revealed a shifting greed. Finally, he adopted a wicked smile and said, "You're an interesting man."

"Thanks."

"Forty-two?"

"Forty-two."

"Hmm."

The man stood and then pointed his finger up. Gabe turned to see the man in the back of the restaurant raise his eyebrows, nod, and walk to them. The first biker asked Gabe again, "Forty-two?"

"Forty-two."

"We're doing this thing?" the other biker asked.

"Dude has a fun plan."

The first biker left the restaurant, and the remaining biker commented, "I do not know what you said to Wilbert, but this is a first."

The second biker walked out to join his companions while Gabe breathed a massive sigh of relief. *What kind of hard-core biker name is Wilbert?* he wondered.

•

Gabe flew home and met Kim at the airport. After hugging, she said, "I missed you."

"Missed you too."

"Make any progress?"

"I think so," Gabe answered with hesitation. "The biker guy looked mean as heck. I'm not sure we can trust him."

"I've made a lot of progress."

"But first, how is Emma?"

"She's doing well. I get the impression that her eyes are forming."

"That's amazing," Gabe said with a smile.

"To answer your question, the hackers identified 28 people who are actively trying to destroy our reputation. Jenna is running it, and Teresa is her second-in-command, even though she is in jail. I took care of everything."

"Really? How?" Gabe wanted to know.

"A new member joined the Kuiu Saviors. She is a rich newspaper owner and wants to fly them to Florida for an all-expenses-paid strategy conference."

"The Kuiu Saviors?" Gabe asked with a chuckle. "Like the island in Alaska?"

"I know. It's an awful name."

"What's going to happen when they arrive?"

"We will introduce ourselves, explain that what they are doing is wrong, and show them what will happen to them if they continue."

"What about Jenna and Teresa?" Gabe asked.

"I told you I would handle them."

"Going to keep me in the dark?"

"I want to keep you in the clear. Understood?"

"I guess," Gabe answered, as Kim's cold determination surprised him.

•

Three weeks later, the Kuiu Saviors exited an eye-catching charter bus after spending the night at a five-star hotel, which had been paid for by their new supporter. They walked into an elegant office complex located outside of Tampa. Security guards in crisp uniforms escorted them to a conference room with a banner that read "Welcome, Kuiu Saviors." In the front was an imposing lectern, and they spoke excitedly to each other about the new direction their group would be taking.

Unexpectedly, one of the security guards walked up to the lectern and began speaking, "Do you know who I am?"

The room became quiet, and heads shook. "My name is Gabe Alexander," the security guard answered. "The woman back there is Kim Alexander, my wife."

Kim was dressed in security gear and nodded.

"Raise your arms! Now!" Gabe said.

The other security guards all put their hands on their guns. The assembled people looked at each other and began complying. "Good," Gabe continued. "You can follow directions. Well, all of you have taken it upon yourselves to—"

A man in the front row interrupted. "We don't have to take this!"

Gabe drew his gun and walked over to the man. He pressed the barrel into the man's forehead and said, "I will shoot you dead! Right here. Right now! Sit your dumbass down!"

The man looked at the assembled security guards, seeing their angry expressions. He also noticed three had taken their guns out of their holsters. Kim sensed the members still needed convincing. She drew her weapon and put the barrel against the back of a woman's head while glaring at the man.

The man sat and raised his arms. Gabe holstered his weapon and returned to the lectern. "No more interruptions!" he ordered. "Now, all of you messed with our lives. You spread wild rumors and harass our friends, family, coworkers, and customers. The first time this happened, we sent a bunch of you to prison. That obviously didn't work, so we're giving you an ultimatum.

"But first, let's rewind the clock. You convinced yourself that I abused my daughters and struck my former wife so hard that she needed surgery to put her eyeball back in. On top of that, I stole from work and sexually abused my coworkers. Let's think about this. All my misdeeds occurred without a single incident being documented in a human resources write-up, hospital record, or arrest report. How is it possible for one man to get away with so many serious crimes?"

The assembled people kept their hands up, looking confused. Gabe then asked a woman dressed in a pink dress, "Yvette. You called my coworkers several times. What did they say about me?"

Yvette remained silent, and Gabe ordered, "Answer or take a bullet! What?"

Gabe again drew his gun, walked over to Yvette, and pressed the barrel against her forehead. She looked at him in horror and mumbled, "They said you were a great boss and to stop calling them."

"Every time you called, they said that?"

"Um. Yes."

"Alright, we're making progress. Now, let's talk about my prison time. Does anybody know why I pled guilty? Earl. Answer!"

Gabe approached a tall man in a gray suit. Earl answered in a shaky voice, "Because you were guilty."

"Did you read the courtroom testimony? Every paper had it." Nobody responded, and Gabe asked, "Not one of you read it?"

Gabe returned to the lectern and said, shaking his head, "You are pathetic! All of you! Well, I have the article right here. Let me read:

> Gabriel: Just like in a war, we had to put aside the rules. With that in mind. I had the great privilege of making Kimberly happy. I will stop at nothing to ensure she remains safe. Therefore, I am pleading guilty to prevent her from enduring any negative publicity.
>
> Judge Gibbs: Do you feel remorse over your actions?
>
> Gabriel: Your Honor, remorse isn't the right word. Kimberly's father spoke to me once. He struck me as an honorable man. I think he would want me to use the word "responsible."

"I pleaded guilty to prevent the woman I loved from experiencing the pain of testifying. I would do anything for her. This includes killing every single one of you."

Two guards looked concerned when Gabe said "killing."

"Now, let's look at the woman you are attacking," he continued. "She is supposed to be a casualty of my tyrannical abuse. If you use your own logic, you are attacking the victim. In doing so, you made three massive mistakes. The first is the assumption that Kim is too naïve to understand what happened to her. Let's dispel this silliness right now. Kim is only 22 and is about to complete her master's degree in design, business, and math. Plus, she's in charge of a thriving business.

"Your second mistake is underestimating her drive. Who do you think came up with the idea of bringing you here? Who organized this? Who paid for your tickets? Kim did. Kim did it all. And finally. Your biggest mistake is thinking Kim is weak. That's the worst misjudgment possible. Ask anybody who knows her. They will tell you the same thing. She's a fighter. That woman right there is the most dangerous person you will ever encounter. I'm done with you. All of you!"

The people looked at each other with wide eyes. Then Kim approached the lectern and yelled, "You sicken me! Posting all your lies behind closed doors like you were on a crusade to save the world. You're pathetic. Well, it's time for your punishment. Take off your clothes!"

Kim saw Gabe's surprised expression. She suppressed her smile and continued, "Get going. You there, dumbass. Strip. Now!"

The people looked at each other, and Kim motioned to the guards. They drew their weapons but looked unsure. Soon, the people began undressing, and Kim said, "That's better. Next to the door, you'll find envelopes with your names. Inside, you will see every scrap of information available about you and the people you care about.

"We towed your rental cars, emptied your hotel rooms, and canceled your flights. I gave all your information to the best identity thieves in the world. They sold your houses and emptied your bank accounts. Every one of you is up to your eyeballs in debt. This afternoon, hundreds of people are entering this country using your names, and it will take years to rebuild your pathetic lives.

"But that's not what is important. Right now, you are breathing. But that can change in an instant. Notice somebody is missing? Jenna's gone. Gone for good."

Kim looked at Gabe; he raised his eyebrows, and she continued, "This will be the last time we meet. There will be no third chance. Your new job is to delete every lie you posted. If I see a single new one, I will pick up an envelope and terminate you and every family member on that list. And don't get any bright ideas. I have a one-hundred-million-dollar bank account and standing instructions with scary people to do bad things if I kick it. Are we clear?"

The people looked at each other, and Kim yelled, "I didn't hear a 'yes.'"

"Yes," the people mumbled.

"Leave!"

Most people had undressed to their underwear. Kim again took out her gun and pointed it at a bald man in the first row. He removed his boxers, covered his genitalia, and walked to the door. The man briefly turned to the others, found his envelope, and exited.

The woman beside him looked at Kim in horror and removed her remaining clothing. The rest of the group followed suit. Some sobbed as they left, and others faked bravery as the sunlight struck their naked bodies.

The guards picked up the clothes, and they exited the building. At the charter bus, everybody boarded. As the driver closed the doors, Gabe took a picture of the naked group with his cell phone, inspiring Kim to laugh.

"What the heck, lady?" one security guard asked.

"Don't worry. You'll get your five hundred dollars," Kim answered with a big grin.

"The Craigslist job posting promised a ten-minute security gig. It said nothing about forcing people to take their clothes off."

"It lasted ten minutes, and you get to keep your uniforms."

"What about that woman you killed?"

"Don't be silly," Kim said with a fluttering gesture. "She has a long walk home through the swamp."

"What about our guns? Can we keep them?"

"I already told you they are movie prop guns, and the answer is no."

"Did you speak the truth?" another guard asked. "Are you the two Kuiu Island people? Like in the news?"

"We are."

"And those naked people messed with you?"

"Yeah, we wanted to send them a clear message to stop harassing us. Thanks for the help."

"That rocked."

"I liked it too," Kim said with a laugh.

The bus returned to the meeting point, and the guards put their prop guns into a box. Kim gave each one a thousand dollars and explained there was an extra five hundred to keep quiet. When the guards departed, Gabe asked, "What happened to Jenna?"

Kim took out a cell phone Gabe had never seen before and showed him a video. He saw a woman with red hair facing away from the camera. Her wrists were bound, and she had many bruises. An unseen person pushed her toward the water with a rifle barrel. The woman turned to look at the camera, and Gabe recognized Jenna Cox. The unseen person then pushed Jenna into the water. It violently churned, and two alligators began attacking her. She fought for her life and screamed as the alligators mauled her. The thrashing lasted a full minute until they pulled Jenna's body under. The camera moved closer to focus on a leg stump surrounded by bloody water.

Kim turned off the video and said, "I sent this to Teresa's daughter with the message, 'Tell your mother to stop what she is doing or this will happen to you.'"

"Wow! Um—" Gabe stammered, then his voice trailed off.

"Do you understand why I had to do this?"

"You killed a woman. That's not how we do things."

<Do you remember all the lies?> Kim mentally asked with concern.

<Of course.>

<What lie hurt the most?>

<I didn't appreciate the one about abusing my daughters,> Gabe admitted sorrowfully.

<How about the lies about me?>

<Those were awful.> Gabe thought with pain.

<Relax. There's no danger. Think. The lies about me?>

<I hated the one where I forced myself on you so hard that I broke your arms.>

<How did that make you feel?>

<Like the worst person in the world. I would never hurt the woman I love.>

<I sense your anguish. The lie I hated the most was about you killing my sister. Do you feel my pain?>

<It's deep,> Gabe admitted sorrowfully.

<You feel my pain even though I never had a sister?>

<Yes,> Gabe answered while being close to tears from directly experiencing Kim's anguish.

<How would you feel if they made up lies about Emma? What kind of life would she have? I had to stop this madness before Emma is born.>

Gabe looked down as Kim continued. <You realize what's next? They're going to make up a lie that you killed Emma's sister.>

Gabe considered Kim's logic for a long moment and thought, <I'm sorry.>

<It's alright. I will always be here for you. No matter what,> Kim thought, encouraging him.

•

Later that month, authorities searched the Lompoc Federal Correctional Institution, resulting in fifteen charges for heroin distribution. Additionally, the local police executed search warrants at four nearby residences, resulting in six arrests. The article in the newspaper mentioned Sato Tonegawa.

Meanwhile, Gabe worked with Silicon Serpent on their RAID 5 product, and the project was back on track. The company had additional good news. The designers and managers at Computix Systems studied Gabe's design and quickly concluded it was vastly superior to theirs. They were so impressed that they agreed to use this KimSemi product in one of their new servers.

Gabe also shared his initial specifications for what he called "a server on a chip" with Computix Systems. This new processor would significantly reduce the cost of a low-end file server and deliver improved performance. Computix Systems signed a contract based on the estimated specifications to purchase the first ten thousand units.

Kim's business continued to expand, and she hired two people to fill the void left by Boyd. Dan took over business operations, and Sally became responsible for accounting and inventory. Unfortunately, Boyd posted on Facebook that he was getting a divorce. The news saddened Kim, but she managed to get his resume in front of the hiring manager at a shipping company. While Boyd interviewed poorly, he still got the job.

Three months later, a visibly pregnant Kim attended her college graduation. Gabe now had a deep connection to his unborn daughter and found it amusing that she enjoyed country music. When the subject came up, Kim always said with a laugh, "Your daughter. Not mine."

Ten days after her graduation, Kim's water broke. In the delivery room, Gabe put his hand on Kim's belly and his forehead on her forehead. <This is the big day.>

<Are you excited to see your daughter?>

<Of course! Hey, stop that. No anxiety. Everything will be fine.>

<Does this remind you of your first child?>

<Yes and no,> Gabe answered.

<What's different?>

<I'm experiencing a birth from your perspective.>

<Few husbands get to do that.>

<I'm probably the first.> The thought made Gabe swell with pride.

The anesthesiologist moved Kim on her side, inserted the epidural, and injected painkillers.

<Emma is ready,> Gabe thought to Kim as he experienced the slight pain of the needle in her back.

<We both are. My body tells me it will be around fifteen minutes.>

Gabe said without looking up, "It's going to be fifteen minutes. Please get ready."

"What?" the delivery nurse asked.

"Emma will arrive in fifteen minutes."

"I've done this over a hundred times. The birth is at least an hour away."

"Well, either way, please get ready."

The delivery nurse shook her head. Confident in her judgment, Kim thought, <Relax, hon, I'm fine.>

<Emma feels anxious.> Gabe was concerned as his forehead continued touching Kim's forehead.

<She's not scared.>

<My brave daughter takes after my brave wife.>

<True,> Kim admitted with cautious pride.

Gabe smiled, and seven minutes later, Kim began pushing.

"Um, wow," the delivery nurse said. "I see the head."

"We know," Gabe replied while his head still touched Kim.

"You know what?" the delivery nurse asked.

"Put more lube around her head. She feels uncomfortable," Gabe instructed.

"Um. Wait, what? Who's uncomfortable?"

"Apply the lube. It hurts."

"Working on it."

Gabe continued to look into Kim's eyes as he experienced everything she and Emma did. As she pushed, he shared her exhaustion and desire to give birth. Gabe also felt Emma's fear and extreme discomfort from being pushed. Three minutes later, he knew Emma would come out in one push.

<Ready for this?> Kim asked.

Gabe sensed Kim's fear. <Yes,> he answered, convinced everything would be alright.

<When Emma comes out, I want you right there. Hold her hand. She needs to know you are there. Don't worry about me. Got that?>

Encouraging Kim, Gabe answered, <Yes, babe. I love you.>

<I love you, too.>

"Ready?" Gabe asked.

The delivery nurse replied, "Wow, this is fast. Three more pushes, Mom. One, two, three."

Kim pushed once, and Emma slid right into the nurse's hands. Gabe raised his head from Kim's and held Emma's hand while looking at her with great pridc.

"Sir, let us do our job!" the nurse instructed.

Emma's eyes adjusted to the light for the first time, and she looked at her father with a curious expression. "Hello, Emma. Welcome to the world," he said softly.

The nurse shook her head and cleared Emma's nose with a suction syringe. Gabe pushed her chest with two fingers, and Emma took her first breath.

"That's the darndest thing," the nurse commented while cleaning Emma. She cut the umbilical cord and wrapped her in a fluffy pink blanket. Gabe continued to hold her hand while looking into her eyes with a big smile. Emma smiled back, and the nurse commented to the anesthesiologist, "She didn't cry a peep."

"She likes her father," the anesthesiologist said.

The nurse began moving Emma to a warming table, and Gabe said, "My daughter wants to be with her mother."

"Um, only for a short while. She needs to conserve body heat."

The nurse bundled Emma in a blanket and brought her to Kim. Emma looked into Kim's eyes and, fifteen minutes later, began falling asleep while Kim held her.

# THREE

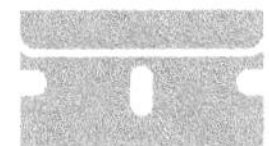

The happy family arrived home two days later, and Emma became the center of attention. Kim spent two weeks recovering before returning to work. However, there was a significant issue. Emma refused to be separated from her parents, and the only solution was to take her to work with them. Fortunately, she behaved like an angel and enjoyed quietly observing her surroundings.

Eight weeks later, Kim arrived home to see an unfamiliar car in the driveway and the front door open. Because of the Kuiu Saviors, she carried a nine-millimeter Beretta handgun in her purse. With Emma safely in the car, Kim cautiously approached the front door, drew her gun, and clicked the safety off. She peeked inside and saw a man in black jeans with a suit jacket sitting on their sofa.

It was the secretive Jason Becker who arranged for Gabe to get a light prison sentence for keeping quiet about the Alaskan incident. He stood five foot eight, with short, curly, gray-black hair. Gabe and Kim thought he looked like the comedian Dennis Miller. Jason was holding a Heineken beer bottle and reading their newspaper. Then, Jason looked up and said, "Why don't you bring Emma in so we can talk?"

Kim stared deeply into Jason's cold and confident eyes. Sensing there was no danger, she clicked the safety on and put the gun back in her purse. Then, Kim brought Emma inside and placed her in a bassinet.

Jason found Emma's angry expression perplexing as she glared at him while drinking her bottle. "I remembered you like beer," Jason said with a smile. "Want one? I put a six-pack in your fridge to chill down."

"Our house is alcohol-free," Kim answered with a scowl.

"I hope you don't mind that I'm having one now."

"It's fine. You know, our house has a sophisticated alarm."

"I noticed," Jason said with a grin.

"How did you disable it? The alarm company told me that's impossible."

"I called them, and they turned it off."

"I don't believe you," Kim said as she folded her arms.

"An old habit."

"Now what?"

"Will Gabe be home in about ten minutes?" Jason sidestepped.

"Yes."

"Wonderful," Jason said with a grin, then leaned back. He turned to Emma and said, in an uplifting voice, "Congratulations are in order. Your daughter looks beautiful and healthy."

"Thanks."

"I see that both of your businesses are flourishing."

"We work hard," Kim tersely replied as she folded her arms tighter and narrowed her glare.

"I also see the two of you have had your hands full with those unpleasant people."

"We're handling them."

"Nice alligator video," Jason said with a wicked smile and a chuckle.

Kim had taken the video from Jenna's phone, and she wondered how Jason had managed to intercept it. "Thank you," she said cautiously.

"We learned from your health records that you two are having some issues, especially Gabe. How severe is it?"

Kim was angry because Jason had obtained her private health information, and she replied coldly, "He has headaches and tremors. My headaches aren't bad, but my balance gets out of whack."

"Do you know what's going on?"

"From what we can tell, our brains are misaligned. I know that's not a medical term, but it is what we call it. The doctors don't have an explanation."

"Can Gabe function?" Jason asked.

"Some mornings, he has to sit for a while before he can drive. Otherwise, he's good to go."

"I'm aware of a new drug that might help. A sample will be in the mail."

"Do you know what's causing our health problems?" Kim asked.

Jason pursed his lips, deep in thought, then answered, "I'm not sure."

"Do you have access to medical resources that are not available to normal people?"

"At a later date, I might offer something," Jason answered with a twinkle in his eye. Then, after looking at Kim for a long moment, he continued, "You two kept your word."

"As promised."

"That means a lot."

"We know," Kim said with a nod.

"I read a funny transcript of a call between Gabe and his sister. He told her to stop asking questions or he would spill the beans about the neighbor's stolen car. That impressed me."

"You know about the stolen car conversation?" Kim asked, surprised.

"We keep tabs on you two."

"Hmm."

Kim heard Gabe's car entering the driveway. <Jason's here.>

<What does he want?>

<His thoughts are jittery. He wants something important.>

<Any danger?> Gabe asked, his heart pounding.

<Not yet.>

<On my way.>

Gabe entered. "Jason," he said in a controlled voice.

"I would offer you a brewski, but Kim told me you two are off the sauce."

"We're no longer compatible with alcohol," Gabe answered, frowning.

"That's acting healthy. Well, let's get to it. How about some background? Hmm. I'm not used to being this honest. Here it is. The, ahh— incident you two were part of was big. Bigger than any other incident that my, ahh— department has encountered. We had to bring in people from all over to clean up the mess. Even with the extra help, we had to go in fast and sloppy. What does this mean? Quite simply, we killed every person who knew the truth."

"That's awful!" Kim exclaimed.

"We had no other options. Now, ahh— here's the hard part. You two were, ahh— part of that cleanup. Remember when I invited you into my car? You two sat on hypodermic needles. Kim, they ordered me to give you a full dose of incurable strep. And, Gabe, you got a deadly shellfish virus. We took this drastic step to keep the secret. That order came straight from the top."

Gabe looked at Kim in horror.

Jason cleared his throat before continuing. "Now, that's when our little plan ran into a snag. Ahh— you two came away squeaky clean. Not even a cough. When something like that happens, there can only be one conclusion. When a person gets taken, ahh— er—" Jason lowered his voice. "Off-world, there are— er, *precautions* taken by the ahh— er— *outsiders* to keep them from getting Earth diseases. A side effect of these *precautions* is that the human body will become great at killing the little buggers that make us sick. You survived because these precautions obliterated my poisons."

Jason paused and then continued at a normal volume. "A side effect of these precautions is that you age more slowly. Gabe, that's why you look twenty-something. Oh, big plus. You will also live longer.

"Now, straight up. Going off-world is a major no-no. Every nation has the same strict laws. Unless permitted beforehand, we will put a person down. No exceptions. We cannot afford a virus outbreak from some off-world bug.

"I didn't put two and two together until long after our meeting. Now, here is where things got interesting. You two did your best to lead quiet lives. But, in reality, you became massive beacons for the conspiracy nuts. They focused all their efforts on that crucible theory that Gabe made up. Fantastic name, by the way. Quite catchy. And, boy, oh boy, did the media eat it up. And convincing the world that the Air Force HAARP project was responsible for setting the atmosphere on fire and killing everybody on Kuiu Island? I loved it. Stick it to those flyboys.

"When all the hubbub died down, I talked to my bosses, and they agreed to spare your lives. This is the only exception to off-world law that has ever occurred."

Kim scowled. "You are making an ends-justify-the-means argument."

"Hmm. I suppose. I never really thought of it that way."

"What changed? Why are you here?" Gabe demanded.

"Well, you two began doing all that yoga stuff— some of that mental hoo-ha rubbed off on your yoga friends at the prison and here in Florida. We started getting all kinds of reports about people completing each other's sentences. This set off our alarms."

Gabe shook his head and asked, "What the heck is wrong with completing a sentence?"

"Rapidly completing a sentence requires telepathy. Some humans have this mild ability, but it's harmless. However, completing lots of sentences is a sign of advanced telepathy. My department cannot allow this."

"Why is having telepathy so bad?" Kim asked.

"How do I put this? Hmm. I work with many, er— ahh— *individuals*, and they have a lot of ahh— *experience* with how societies develop. There is a natural progression. You know, the Stone Age leads to the Bronze Age and then all the way to the Computer Age. If you plot this development, it shows a flat slope with a few humps. A hump is what we call a 'reasonable expected advancement.' An example is the telegraph, which brought people closer.

"Human bodies have a similar developmental line, but the changes occur more slowly. For example, walking upright was a 'reasonable expected advancement.'

"Getting back to the issue at hand. Your yoga friends are passing along telepathy to their families. This must stop."

"Why? They are learning," Kim countered.

"How do I explain this? Hmm. Imagine somebody transported Emma back in time two thousand years. While she would not have your knowledge, she would grow up taller, smarter, faster, and healthier than everybody else. Emma's offspring would dominate the world. More to the point, mental development must grow hand in hand with society. This means each generation is slightly better."

"I am getting the sense there is something you are not saying about Emma." Kim's eyes narrowed with suspicion. "You used her as an example for a reason."

"You picked up on that?" Jason asked, realizing he had underestimated Kim.

"Yes."

"Hmm. You're correct."

"But you cannot say anything about it?" Kim guessed.

"Very perceptive."

"Why are you here?" Gabe demanded again.

"I need you to turn off those yoga people's mental ability at the prison. And Kim needs to work on her yoga friends here."

"Hey, we kept our word and did not say a thing to anybody. You have no right to ask that of us." Kim protested.

Jason leaned back, nodded, and thought for a moment. "I respect your position," he said. "Let me explain my position. If we do not nip this thing in the bud, there is strong, er– *historical evidence* to show that billions will die in telepathic wars. Now, how do *we* fix this?

"My department has two options. One: kill everybody we suspect has telepathic ability and those around them. This solution has many problems. The big one is publicity. The lesser problem is that a few would escape, making the situation far worse.

"Two: a surgical strike to deprogram one person at a time. Now, here's where our situation gets complex. The– *telepathic* individuals in my department would not, er– *blend in.* That leaves you two. And Kim cannot go into a men's prison, which leaves Gabe.

"Now, this is where we face the issue. Gabe, you're an engineer. You understand all about positive and negative feedback. People respond quicker to negative but better to positive. Let's start with the negative. You have a wonderful family; I will say no more. And, yes, you could fight back by going public. Also, if I make a bunch of threats, our relationship will never recover.

"Now for the positive. You two already make beaucoup bucks, and I don't have the financial means to reward you. Plus, you've seen my car."

Kim grinned, and Gabe smiled. "I might be able to help with your health issues," Jason continued. "In addition, I will tell you that behind the scenes, we work very hard to deflect nasty people away from you. That will continue.

"Now, it may seem that I'm not offering a lot, but trust me, I am. So, you two should probably mentally communicate about my request."

"Wait a sec," Gabe interrupted. "I do not know if what you are asking is possible."

"My ahh– *friends* informed me that these people are at the beginning stages of telepathy. They say a person with your advanced ability can deprogram a novice telepath."

"I don't even know where to start," Gabe said, throwing up his hands.

"You're a bright guy. You'll figure this out."

"Maybe Kim could help in the prison. She has better intuition."

"It must be you," Jason said. "She has her work cut out here."

<He has us,> Gabe thought to Kim.

<We must think of what's best for Emma.>

<Agreed.>

"When do I leave?" Gabe asked.

"Wow!" Jason exclaimed. "Thanks for the quick decision."

"You're right. The only card we can play is to go public, and media attention is the last thing we want."

"I appreciate your cooperative attitude. That makes my job easier."

"You brought us beer."

"True."

"What's next?"

"Here's Donna Parks's card. She's our admin and will arrange a flight to Alaska, accommodations, and volunteer you as a prison yoga instructor. Incidentally, from now on, you are to inform Donna when you travel."

"Why?" Kim needed to know.

"Things have changed, and that's all I can tell you," Jason answered.

"Does this mean we are prisoners without walls?"

"Everything will be fine if you play by the rules. Gabe, I need this handled ASAP. Provide Donna with a status update every morning, and immediately call me with any issues. Kim, you do the same with your friends here."

"And then we're out. Right?" Gabe asked intently.

Jason sighed, drank the last of his beer, stood, got another, and sat. He looked at Kim and then at Emma. She finished her milk, made a little fist, and then pointed to him. "Emma doesn't like me," Jason said with a grin.

"She's an excellent judge of character," Kim said with a smirk.

"Funny! I like that. Alright. How about this? What do you think really happened in Alaska?"

"We were on a cruise. Aliens called the Veronn attacked our ship, and we survived. Then, while we were walking around, we noticed these aliens following us. So, we confronted them and saved everybody," Kim answered confidently.

"And then what?"

"They set up an Alaskan memorial center, and the crazy people believed Gabe's government cover-up story. Nothing more."

"Who cleaned up the real mess, and what price did society pay?"

"I don't understand."

"How many people died?" Jason asked as he sat forward.

"The papers said 13,451."

"No. I mean, how many people did my department terminate because of what they knew?"

Kim shook her head. "Two hundred and fifty-one, my dear," Jason answered. "What do you think my job is?"

"I'm not sure. From what you say, you seem to place a low value on human life."

Jason took a long sip of beer and pointed the bottle at Kim. "On that point, you're mistaken. I'm the one who must make the tough choices. Today, everybody is happy. We blissfully go about our lives without a second thought. Why? Everybody knows a big meteor caused the deaths in Alaska, and if they do not buy that, they have Gabe's crucible theory.

"If we didn't have this confidence, the already fragile economy would fail, and millions would starve.

"Kim, my job is hard. Because of technology, news travels faster than wildfire. Therefore, it's up to me to prevent all harmful information from reaching its intended audience. And in almost every circumstance, I only have one deadly option. If I fail, then humanity fails. It's that simple."

“Why not tell the truth?” Kim suggested.

“People can never be told the truth about what I see and do. They would panic. Now, look. I’ve already said far more than I should have. To answer your question, I’m not sure what your future holds. You two have unique skills. And right now, the world needs Gabe to go to Alaska. Can I count on you?”

“Of course,” Gabe quickly answered.

“Good.”

“Will Emma be safe from your wrath?”

“Yes.”

“Forever?” Gabe insisted.

“Yes.”

“Promise?”

“You have my word.”

“Good,” Kim said with a nod.

Jason smiled at Emma. She made another little fist with a stern expression. “Wow, you really don’t like me,” Jason said. “Someday, I hope you understand I’m looking out for you.”

“Please put your beer bottles in the outside recycling bin,” Kim requested.

“Will do.”

Jason retrieved the other bottle, smiled, and walked out the front door.

<Strange,> Kim thought while rubbing her lower lip.

<Not how I expected my day to go. I’d hoped we got rid of that guy.> Gabe chuckled and continued. <I guess I’m off to Alaska, and you get to play with your yoga friends.>

<Yup.> Kim thought, apprehensive.

<Life with you is an adventure.>

<Gabe?>

<Wow, that was a sexy thought. Are you all healed down there?>

<My down there misses you.> A mix of conflicting emotions swarmed through Kim.

<My down there misses you even more.>

<When Emma is asleep, I’m going to rock your world.>

<I will add ‘get jumped by my wife’ to the schedule after I clear it with Donna.>

<Hon!> Kim grinned.

Later in the evening, Gabe brushed his teeth and waited for Kim to put Emma to sleep. Ten minutes later, she guided him toward their bed and removed his pajamas, maintaining firm eye contact. Then Kim pushed Gabe down, straightened his legs, and kneeled on top of him. When she determined the best moment, she passionately entered his mind.

Gabe felt her intense presence and made a great effort not to look into his beloved wife's eyes, lest he oggle her chest. This effort lasted an astounding 30 seconds before his gaze slid down.

Kim liked Gabe's excitement over her body and the fact that, despite great effort, he could not control himself. She used one finger to tilt his head back, which moved his gaze back to her eyes. Kim then used the same finger to make swirls on his chest.

When Kim sensed Gabe's mind had the right intensity, Kim undressed and returned to kneeling on top of him. She reveled in his excitement, which furthered their passion. Kim again lifted his gaze with her finger and returned to making swirls on his chest. Her confidence entranced Gabe with a new level of arousal.

Kim maintained eye contact and, when she felt Gabe at his peak, placed her hands on his chest. He experienced a tremendous rush of excitement as she continued to force eye contact with her finger.

When Kim sensed the right level of passion, she placed Gabe inside while holding his gaze. He instantly appreciated the sexual rush of entering his wife while continuing to be entranced by her confidence. Kim took pleasure in the moment and waited for Gabe's anticipation to build. Then, she began moving her hips to maximize his experience.

Gabe could not believe this new level of sexual bliss and used every ounce of strength to hold back. However, Kim sensed his efforts and sped up, which induced an intense orgasm.

As Gabe's pleasure subsided, Kim allowed herself to climax and experienced many sensual waves roll through her body as she pushed against Gabe.

The pair rested in each other's arms as their passion gently subsided. They exchanged many warm thoughts about the moment and how fortunate they felt to be together. Finally, they fell asleep in a tight embrace.

# FOUR

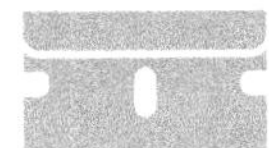

Gabe spent the next day preparing for his trip and working with Donna to make travel arrangements. This included buying two prepaid cell phones so he could talk to Kim without the government eavesdropping. After packing, Kim drove him to the airport. As he exited the car, Emma realized her father was leaving and began crying.

"Emma, my sweet," Gabe said. "I'm sorry, I must leave. But I will be back as soon as possible."

Emma cried harder and reached out her hands. Gabe held her for several minutes while whispering encouragement. Finally, when her crying turned to sniffles, he said, "Mommy will be with you all day. I love you very much."

Emma began moving her lips, and she said, "Gaayybb aah."

Gabe shrieked, "She said, 'Gabe!' That's her first word! She's only six weeks old!"

"Wow!"

"Daaaa-dee," Emma spoke again.

"We're so proud of you."

The pair hugged Emma, and she beamed with a toothless smile. "I need you to do something important," Gabe said. "I need you to take care of mommy. Will you do that for me?"

Emma looked at Gabe for a long moment and reached out to Kim. Kim moved Emma into her arms. "Gh-bi Gaabee," she said.

"Goodbye, my sweet daughter. I'm so proud of you. Remember to take care of mommy. I love you very much."

"Have a safe flight, and text me when you land," Kim said, holding back tears. "Love you, hon."

"Love you right back, wonderful wife."

•

Eleven hours later, Gabe landed in Fairbanks, Alaska. His rental was a blue Jeep with worn tires, rust everywhere, a cracked windshield, and a big dent in the right door. Gabe only cared about a working heater, but seeing an open field on the way to the apartment Donna had arranged inspired his inner child. The Jeep effortlessly bounded through big snowdrifts while Gabe's smile set a world record.

Two hours later, Gabe arrived at the Glenn Ivy apartment complex and met the apartment manager, Joey. He explained that no other apartments were available because a nearby oil field had started a new operation.

Joey commented that the other tenants were "entertaining," with a wink. The gesture made Gabe feel as if he had missed something basic, and he began unloading.

Ten minutes later, Gabe drove to a nearby restaurant. While the portions were large, the shepherd's pie he ordered tasted bland. This lonely experience reminded him how much he missed his family, and he hoped his trip would be short.

Back at the apartment, Gabe unpacked and read emails for an hour. He was about to shower when somebody softly knocked on his door. Gabe cautiously opened the door to find himself face-to-face with an attractive woman. She wore a sleek, black, low-cut shirt with sensual curves and form-fitting gray jeans that accentuated her slender frame. The giant loop earrings dangling from her ears added a bold touch to her ensemble, while tall black boots completed her suggestive look.

The woman's deep blue eyes sparkled with a hint of mischief, and her blond-brown hair cascaded in loose waves around her shoulders. Every detail seemed meticulously curated, from flawless makeup to well-manicured nails.

Gabe was taken aback and managed to mutter, "Hello?"

"You're new here?" the woman asked in a seductive voice with a slight Russian accent.

"Yes."

"No other places available?"

"There is a new oil field, and they need workers," Gabe cautiously answered, wondering what the woman wanted.

"What do you do for a living?"

This woman's forward attitude took Gabe aback. "I'm a yoga instructor."

"Does that mean you bend in great ways?"

"Kind of," Gabe admitted.

"Anything else?" she asked in a seductive voice.

"I'm an electrical engineer by trade."

"Does that mean you can fix sinks? Joey promised to fix my sink three times this week."

"It's kind of late, but I can look."

The woman led him three doors down to her apartment. When Gabe entered, her choice of decor seemed out of place. Tiny red lights bounced off the ceiling, creating an intimate and cozy feel in the living room. Gabe suspected this woman was a romance author, and the atmosphere helped her get into the writing mood.

They walked to the bathroom, and the woman turned on the sink. The water did not flow down the drain. Gabe turned off the tap, opened the under-sink doors, and reached behind the drainpipe to undo the screw that connected the pivot rod to the stopper. He then pulled out the stopper to reveal a long tangle of hair. "Do you have a bag or something?" Gabe asked.

"Icky! I'll get a trash bag."

Gabe put the foul-smelling mass into the bag. The woman tied the bag shut, and then Gabe reassembled the stopper. He tested the sink, and the water flowed down rapidly. "Well, that should be fine," Gabe announced with a big grin.

"How much?" the woman asked with a wink.

"How much what?"

"Do I owe you?"

"Nothing, of course."

The woman nodded, then quickly took off her shirt. Underneath, she wore a frilly, satin red push-up bra.

"Wait, wait, wait," Gabe stammered. "What the heck are you doing, lady?"

"My job. But for you, this is free," the woman answered, putting her hands on Gabe's shoulders.

"What? No! Put your top back on," Gabe yelled as he pushed her hands off him.

The woman looked at him strangely and asked, "What gives? You gay or something?"

"I'm happily married!"

"Why should that matter? I could be your girlfriend— for a reasonable rate."

"No, thank you," Gabe said, crossing his arms.

"Suit yourself. Wait. Don't you know about this place?"

"Know what?"

"Everybody here turns tricks," the woman confidently answered.

"I don't understand. What does 'turn tricks' mean?"

The woman laughed and answered, "Honey, I didn't know they still made men like you. I'm a prostitute, dear."

"Oh. I have never met a, um— a prostitute."

"Well, now you have.

"Now, let's get your pants off, and I'll show you the time of your life."

"What? No, no, no!" Gabe protested.

"I'm kidding. I respect a man who stays true to his wife. Anyway, thanks for the help."

"Yeah, sure, I guess."

"You need to relax," the woman said as she touched Gabe's arm.

"That's what my wife keeps telling me."

"Lucky woman."

"Lucky man."

The woman laughed and walked Gabe to his door. "Molly," she said with a grin.

"Gabe."

"Nice meeting you."

Molly winked at Gabe. Then he closed the door and called Kim, "Hi, babe."

"It's good to hear your voice, hon."

"Hey, I have to tell you something important."

"What?"

"I'm sort of staying at a brothel."

"Really?" Kim asked with a laugh.

"Why are you laughing?"

"I trust you. You know that."

"A woman already propositioned me. She even took her top off, and I saw her red bra. I think she even wanted to have sex with me. I felt so embarrassed."

"Did she have nice boobs?" Kim asked with another laugh.

"What? Babe, this is serious!"

"What are her rates? Start with fifty bucks."

"I'm in a real bind here. This is serious!" Gabe protested.

"Hon, what is the first thing you do when you see me?"

"Say hi?" Gabe guessed.

"You smile. Every time. You smile even when you're upset."

"But—"

"Hon, I know you better than you know yourself," Kim interrupted. "I trust you. Now it's your turn to trust yourself. The fact that you called proves your deep commitment to our marriage. So, relax. Get a good night's rest and hit the ground running. I want you home soon so I can be the one to make you uncomfortable. Alright?"

"Yes, my love," Gabe said with relief.

"Now, Emma wants to talk to you."

Kim moved the phone, and Gabe said, "Hi, Emma."

Gabe heard a rustling sound, and Kim said in the distance, "That's Daddy. Say hi."

"Hi, my little sweet. Daddy loves you."

"Emma is becoming fidgety," Kim said. "Love you, my big hunk of a man."

"Love you, my fantastic wife."

The call ended, and Gabe felt a great sense of relief that his beloved wife trusted him despite his living arrangements.

Gabe took a shower and then tried to sleep. Unfortunately, his headaches had returned and, combined with an uncomfortable bed, falling asleep took a long time.

•

The alarm clock blared, and Gabe realized he had company. An attractive Asian woman lay next to him.

"Morning, stud," she said in a seductive voice.

"What the heck!" Gabe yelled.

"I'm Sue."

"I do not care what your name is! What are you doing in my bed?"

"Whatever you want, jackhammer," Sue purred.

"Please leave!"

"If that's what you want, cuddles. Otherwise—"

"How the heck did you get in here?" Gabe demanded.

"Oh, you poor man."

"What?"

"Picking locks is a skill of the trade, dearie. A girl never knows where she's going to wake up."

"Leave, now!" Gabe again demanded.

"I'm only five doors down, good-looking."

Sue got out of bed, and Gabe noticed she wore a translucent silk nightgown with nothing underneath. She looked back with a seductive smile, winked, and walked away, her hips swaying in exaggerated movements. Gabe immediately called Kim, and she answered in a sleepy voice, "Hello?"

"Nothing happened! I swear, nothing. You must believe me! I swear on my life. Please believe me!"

"What?" Kim asked with a yawn.

"I woke up, and there was this woman in bed with me. She told me her name. She said it was Sue. She told me that she had picked the lock on my door. But nothing happened. I swear that nothing happened! Honestly. You've got to believe me. Oh, please believe me. I would never cheat on you. Never. No matter what. I swear!"

"You woke with some girl, and nothing happened. Thanks for the update. Emma kept me awake past three."

"But the woman?" Gabe pleaded.

"Put a bigger lock on the door or something. I'm going back to sleep."

"But what if she tries to bribe me or something? She might have a picture of us. Together. I might already be all over the YouTube."

"*The YouTube*?" Kim asked with a chuckle. "Is that what you call it? Look, if this bothers you, get her info, and I'll take care of it. Love you."

The call ended with a click. Gabe wanted to call Kim back to reiterate his innocence. But, as he pressed the icon, he had a profound revelation. *Wow, she trusts me. That's amazing. Now, all I have to do is trust myself. I can do that. Right? What the heck? Of course I can do that, because I already did.* The knowledge lifted Gabe's spirits, and he got dressed.

•

At precisely 9:00 a.m., Gabe entered Warden Randal Clayford's office at the Fairbanks Correctional Center. His thinning pepper-gray hair was meticulously combed, adding a touch of sophistication. Yet there was a certain disheveled charm to how his hair seemed to rebel against its neat confines.

Draped over Randal's tall frame was a tan suit that, though well-tailored, seemed ill-suited to his proportions. The jacket strained at the seams, hinting at the breadth of his broad shoulders, while the trousers pooled at his ankles. Despite its mismatched nature, the ensemble had an air of elegance. Randal smiled pleasantly and began in a warm baritone voice, "Morning, Gabe."

"Good morning, Warden Clayford."

"You're no longer an inmate. It's alright to call me Randy."

"Thank you, Randy," Gabe said with a smile.

"I'm to understand you're volunteering to be a yoga instructor. Most unusual. Most unusual."

"That's about the size of it."

"I did a bit of investigating. You have a successful business. Very successful."

"Not successful enough," Gabe admitted. "We have razor-thin profits and dodged a huge lawsuit by an inch."

"Your wife also runs a wonderful business. Wonderful business."

"She's doing great. I'm super-proud of her."

"Oh, that was the other thing. Congratulations on having a daughter."

"You know about that?" Gabe asked in bewilderment.

"I'm friends with your wife on Facebook. We both like John Coltrane music."

"I need to get into that Facebook craze," Gabe admitted with a chuckle.

"Very true. Now, let's get down to brass tacks. Why are you really here? I need to know."

Gabe thought momentarily and answered, "I'm trying to give back to the community."

"Your answer does not seem sincere."

Gabe sighed and said, "My wife keeps telling me I'm a rotten liar."

"She's correct," Warden Clayford said with a smile.

"Do you remember when I first came here and got placed into protective custody?"

"Of course."

"And now you've got another crazy request for me to be a yoga instructor?"

"Both requests came right from the top."

"Randy, I need to tell you something," Gabe said, briefly turning away.

"Proceed."

"Before I answer, please understand that I greatly respect you."

"But?" Warden Clayford asked, gesturing for further communication.

"I answer to powerful government people."

"You're here against your will?"

Gabe did not answer. "I see," Warden Clayford concluded and then sighed.

"Please don't ask questions. I will do my best to be here for the shortest possible time and do anything you ask. You can count on that."

"You know, I investigated what occurred on Kuiu, and like many people, I don't believe the official report."

"I survived that entire mess. Trust me, that island got hit by a big meteor, and that is all there is to it."

"Hmm. Well, you've proven yourself trustworthy, and I see no reason not to trust you now."

"Thank you. This means a lot," Gabe said with a smile.

"We now have three yoga classes, and I will arrange for you to start tomorrow morning at ten. After that, there is an afternoon class at one, and an evening class at six. The classes run Monday through Saturday. I assume you want to lead them all?"

"Please."

"I will arrange that. However, there may be an issue. The six o'clock class is Muslim. They will disapprove of a nonbeliever in their presence, and I cannot do anything about that."

"I'll figure something out," Gabe said with a nod.

"Good, good. Well, this has been entertaining. Here is your pass and a list of students."

"Thank you, Randy."

"Off you go."

Gabe left the prison and drove to a nearby Sears. Unfortunately, his warm clothing was not warm enough, and his "waterproof" shoes leaked. In the hardware section, Gabe purchased their best door hasp and the tools to install it. Afterward, he ate a tasty roast beef sandwich at a family restaurant.

Back at the apartment complex, Gabe stopped at Joey's door and found it open. After knocking on the door frame, he walked inside, calling Joey's name. Then, Gabe noticed a file cabinet and realized that Sue's information might be inside.

Gabe respected people's privacy, but being faithful to his wife outweighed his concerns. After locating her apartment rental file and taking a picture with his phone, he returned the file. On the way out, he ran into Joey. "I looked, and you weren't home," Gabe said, hoping Joey had not seen him near the filing cabinet.

"Yeah, I was patching the stupid roof again. What a pain. Anyway, Molly said you fixed her sink. She has been bugging me about that. So, thanks."

"No problem. Hey, listen. I had an incident this morning, and I need to install one of those door lock hasps on the inside. I bought one at Sears and will remove it when I leave.

"Sue told me about running into you. Wow, she's a handful. So, yeah, you can install one of those thingies. The locks the builders put in are a joke."

"Thanks."

"Did you have her?" Joey slyly asked.

"What?"

"Did you have a piece of Sue?"

"I love my wife!" Gabe answered in a raised voice.

"So?"

"Being faithful matters."

"You know the girls have a little bet on you."

"What?" Gabe asked, confused.

"In the winter, there isn't a lot to do. It's TV, dope, and screw. Sometimes, all three at once. When a new fish arrives, the girls put a hun-ski into a pool to see who bangs him first."

"What? A sex bet over me? This is outrageous!"

"We make our own entertainment," Joey said with a laugh.

"I don't want to be a part of it!"

"That makes it more interesting."

"I need to find another place to live," Gabe said, throwing up his hands.

"Not going to happen, bud. Trust me. There's no other place for miles. People have offered me double my rates."

"Gahh! I need to do something."

"No way, no how. That's not going to happen. Not in this town."

"Well, thanks for letting me put in the hasp."

Joey smiled and went inside. A deflated Gabe walked to his apartment and sent Sue's apartment application picture to Kim. "In a meeting," she texted back. "I'll handle this."

Gabe spent the rest of the afternoon installing the hasp and ensuring the windows were secure. That night, he ate salty microwaved lasagna that came out much worse than the enticing picture on the box. Afterward, he answered KimSemi emails and watched the one working television channel. An hour later, he fell asleep exhausted.

Gabe headed out of the building the following day while reading a text message. Sue walked by in the other direction. "Joey told you about our bet?" she asked with a wink.

"I would appreciate it if you would end your wager."

"Listen, sweetie. I've never lost a bet and don't intend to start."

"Are you sure? I can give you the cash you already invested."

"Honey, you cannot afford me. This bod makes three grand an evening in the high season."

"You don't know who I am?"

"Only a poor yoga teacher, snookums," Sue answered with a big grin.

"Yoga is my second job."

"Whatever, honey."

In her mid-twenties, Sue possessed a radiant beauty that drew attention. With its smooth complexion and delicate features, her flawless face was accentuated by tasteful makeup. Sue stood five foot six and held herself with great poise. Her long, jet-black hair cascaded down her back with vibrant blue tips. Sue's well-toned arms hinted at her dedication to fitness and self-care. Completing her look was a pair of pink boots adorned with fluffy blue fur and oversized triangle earrings.

Sue's forward attitude reminded him of his former wife, Lydia. He took a moment to muster his confidence and said in a calm voice, "You've underestimated somebody."

"I have been in this business a long time. Trust me, nothing gets by me, sugar. I've seen them come, and I've seen them go. You're exactly the type of man I mold into whatever shape I want. Trust me. The cold will drive you into my arms, and you can't do a thing about it. So no, you are underestimating me, cutie-pie."

"I'm not referring to myself," Gabe continued, narrowing his eyes.

"Then who?"

"Look up Kuiu Island and the name Kim. See you around, Zhang Tu from Rhode Island."

Gabe's remark took Sue aback. "You know my real name?" she asked, stunned.

"That's not important. My wife knows, which means you stepped into a world of hurt."

Gabe left the bewildered Zhang/Sue standing in the hallway.

•

Gabe arrived at the Fairbanks Correctional Center at 9:30 a.m. The guards searched him at the entrance and then waved him through. Then Gabe changed into loose yoga clothes and headed for his first class. The students were happy to see their old friend and began an advanced routine.

Due to his recent long days at KimSemi, Gabe had not exercised regularly and had lost some of his flexibility. However, he pushed through the pain and did his best to smile. He briefly entered their minds during this time and discovered they all had rudimentary telepathic skills. Gabe probed further in the strongest student's mind and felt a communication challenge so shocking that he coughed to suppress his surprise.

Thirty minutes later, Gabe imparted the positive message, "Laugh when you can, apologize when you should, and let go of what you can't change."

Gabe then allowed a student to run the second half of the class. When the session finished, the students warmly shook his hand and thanked him. In the parking lot, Gabe called Jason. "I'm not afraid to admit when I am wrong. The guys here are advanced."

"It's a bad time. Make it quick!" Jason demanded.

"Large problem identified, working on a fix."

"Got it."

The call ended abruptly, leaving Gabe staring at the parking lot. He returned to the prison and rounded up some friends. They talked about old times, and Gabe handed his former student, Tuk Tuk, a new Kindle book reader loaded with books.

Tuk Tuk thanked Gabe several times. The conversation turned to Gabe's flirtatious neighbors, and everybody knew about the oil field workers. "I might be able to arrange a place," Tuk Tuk offered.

"Really?" Gabe asked. "Where?"

"It's an old servant's quarters. Nice, though."

"That's twice you saved me."

"It's you who saved me. Plus, you got me a new Kindle."

"Anything for a friend."

"Did that California thing work out?"

"After I convinced the bikers not to kill me, they came through."

"I got a message about forty-two more jobs," Tuk Tuk warned him.

"I bluffed those guys."

"They are expecting more work."

"I'll have to figure out a way to pay them off."

"Sooner would be better than later," Tuk Tuk recommended.

"Thanks for the advice."

"I will talk to my friend about renting the room."

"That would be amazing."

At 1:00 p.m., Gabe led the second yoga class. These students were not as advanced, and only a few had telepathic abilities. Gabe was relieved and spent the rest of the afternoon in the prison library. He ate an uneventful mass-prepared chicken dinner at the prison cafeteria and arrived at the 6:00 p.m. yoga class.

The assembled Muslim men glared at Gabe as he took the lead. He took a deep breath to center himself and put his hands together in a welcome gesture. "Gentlemen," he began. "I would like to thank you for the privilege of leading this class. I understand you likely have misgivings over my lack of faith in your religion, and I have seriously considered this important matter. With your permission, I would like to share what I've come up with. While here, I will fully respect your Muslim beliefs. As such, I stand before you as a humble servant of Allah and will do my best to follow his teachings. May Allah reward you. Let us begin."

The men seemed intrigued as Gabe took them through yoga moves. He was relieved that the concern over his presence had passed and allowed himself to relax. A few minutes later, Gabe entered their minds and sensed that six men had telepathic abilities. To his dismay, three individuals strongly challenged him to communicate. He continued the routine and, toward the end, held a Vriksasana pose.

Gabe had researched the Quran the previous evening and written a passage on his arm. He read pleasantly, "Do they not see the birds controlled in the atmosphere of the sky? None holds them up except Allah. Indeed, in that are signs for a people who believe."

Gabe held the position for a moment. "What a beautiful quote," he observed. "I interpret this message from Allah to mean the signs of something greater than myself are everywhere. For example, the warmth of the sun on a chilly day."

Gabe changed to a forward bend and held it. "Silently, I ask each of you to reflect upon this kindhearted expression."

He held the position, then led the class through cool-down moves. Gabe bowed and discreetly read another passage on his other arm, "All the praises are due to Allah. How free from imperfections is Allah. Gentlemen, thank you for the honor of being in your presence."

The students looked at Gabe with interest and silently left the room. One stayed behind. "I'm opposed to your leading our class," he flatly stated.

"I'm sorry that my presence upsets you. Please understand that I'm trying to help."

"I permitted one lesson as a favor to Tuk Tuk."

"Thank you for this opportunity."

The student turned to leave and then turned back. "Do you follow the Quran?" he asked with concern.

"I'm finding the subject intriguing and am trying to absorb the positive message."

The student studied Gabe for a long moment. During this time, Gabe swam and sensed thoughts of hope. "You don't lie," the student observed.

"You deserve the truth."

"You show respect."

"Only because you have earned my respect."

"What have I done to earn your respect?" the student challenged.

"You're trying to better your life, and this location hinders your worthy quest."

"Indeed," the student said with a nod. "I noticed our holy words written on your arm. Do you expect to gain my respect by cheating?"

"I wanted to make sure that I correctly recited the quote. My goal was to avoid disrespecting your faith."

"Why are you risking the wrath of Allah to teach us yoga?"

"It's complicated," Gabe admitted. "My best answer is that I'm trying to give something back."

"A worthy cause. Tell me. Did you speak the words of the Quran from the writing on your arm or from your heart?"

"I researched the best quote that applied to this situation. When I read it, I fully believed in the positive message," Gabe answered.

"You're an intriguing man. I welcome you to teach another class."

"Thank you for that great honor. I will do my best to act respectfully and learn from the wisdom contained in the Quran."

The student nodded and walked away. Gabe was relieved that the incident had passed and left the prison. He changed at the apartment and found a restaurant with a salad bar.

While eating, Gabe's headaches returned, and this pain made it challenging to drive. All the lights were off when he turned down the street to his apartment. Gabe parked and used the light from his cell phone to make his way up the stairs.

Joey met him halfway and said, "Some dumbass oil worker smacked his car into the transformer. This was the first time he ever drove on snow."

"I saw the electrical crew down thc block."

"They told me it would take several hours to fix."

"Will there be hot water for a shower in the morning?" Gabe asked.

"Maybe? I dunno."

Joey shrugged and continued down the stairs. Gabe entered his apartment and turned on the prepaid cell phone. Kim picked up on the first ring. "Hello?" she asked in a sleepy voice.

"Wow, you sound really out of it."

"Yeah, I haven't been getting much sleep," Kim admitted in a distant voice.

"I'm so sorry that I'm not there to help."

"I know."

"Babe. I have some bad news. This thing is going to take a while."

"How long?" Kim yawned.

"A few weeks, maybe more. Plus, I have not figured out how to do the job. Any luck at your end?"

"Not really."

"Jason texted that you weren't at last night's yoga class."

"I went in the side door," Kim said after a long pause.

"What's up? Is everything alright?"

"Oh, I don't know."

Gabe knew Kim was not acting like herself and probed. "How are you feeling? Are you sick?"

"Something's bothering me."

Gabe suspected Kim had changed the subject to avoid his question. This was the first time she'd ever deflected their conversation. "What, babe?" he asked cautiously.

"That thing about wanting to date again if I died from cancer."

"Oh, that. Well, I acted insensitively, and there's no excuse."

"You behaved so rudely!"

The bold statement took Gabe aback, and he closed his eyes in shame. Then, a long moment later, he spoke quietly. "I agree, and I'm sorry. But I think something else is going on. What is it? What's on your mind? Tell me."

"I don't know. I guess I miss you," Kim admitted.

"I miss you too. Look. I acted like a jerk, and it will never happen again. But please understand that there were strange circumstances at play. Normal people don't swim. You get to see what's behind the magician's curtain. There were bound to be surprises."

"I'm still upset."

"Your anger is fully justified. The important thing is that I understand my error and will try hard in the future. I am sure it was a one-time incident."

"It better be!" Kim warned.

"It's good that we're talking about this. How can I help us get through this issue?"

"I guess I'm still hurt."

"What can I do to make things right?"

"I don't know," Kim answered with a sigh.

"We need to resolve this in person. How about this? I have Sunday off. I can fly out Saturday night and spend Sunday afternoon with you and Emma. Then fly back. Sound good?"

"I don't know," Kim said in a distant voice.

"Babe, this isn't you. What's going on? Tell me."

"I don't know. I just—" Kim's voice drifted off.

Gabe patiently waited for a response and eventually asked, "Just what?"

"I do not know. I guess I'm still upset," Kim answered with an enormous sigh.

"Please tell me how I can help."

"I wish you understood how I felt."

"Babe! I instantly knew how you felt. My actions were awful, and I deeply regret the incident."

"I'm still upset."

Gabe did not understand why Kim had taken this tangent and was unsure how to resolve the problem. Finally, he became frustrated and said, "Well, I've been in your mind too!"

"So?"

"Well, when trying to get yourself into the mood, you think about the 'dunga-dunga-dunga' guys."

Months ago, a friend had texted Kim a funny X-rated video clip. It had two well-endowed men comically dancing while playing with themselves and singing, "dunga-dunga-dunga." Kim occasionally fantasized about this erotic moment before becoming intimate. "You know about that?" Kim whispered.

"Of course."

"I'm so embarrassed."

"Don't be. Look, babe, it's clear you love me; the core of your soul loves me. Of course, we have our little quirks, and swimming sometimes reveals our inner thoughts. No big deal. Everything's fine."

"You're right. I'm overreacting. Work has been hard, and Emma is a handful."

"That is good to hear," Gabe said with relief.

"I shouldn't take my frustrations out on you."

"I'm so happy that I didn't do something wrong."

"There you go again. I'm the one who should be apologizing. Let's start over. How's it going?"

"I may have arranged a new place to stay. That's the good news. The bad news is that we somehow have to pay off the LA bikers."

"It's only money. Let me figure out the LA thing."

Gabe heard the phone being muffled. "Emma's crying. Got to run," Kim said.

He did not hear any crying and asked, "I would like to speak to Emma."

"Tomorrow."

"You mean the world to me, babe. I am glad we got this issue out in the open. I love you."

"Love you too."

Kim ended the call, leaving Gabe bewildered. He concluded that his absence was the source of the problem and determined that the best course of action was to focus on deprogramming. To expedite the process, Gabe wanted to bring the white box into the prison to better interact with the students. This was risky because Jason would get involved if somebody discovered the white box. In addition, Gabe's sense of reality disappeared when he used it.

Gabe began experimenting with the white box while performing yoga to solve this last issue. Unfortunately, he could only do one or the other. Finally, Gabe lay on his bed, taking deep breaths and established communication with the white box.

Once Gabe was at the main menu, he tried to stand. Unfortunately, he rolled onto the floor with a big thud. Frustrated, Gabe got back into bed and reestablished communications. When he reached the main menu, he opened his eyes and turned to read the alarm clock. It took three tries before he succeeded. Then he attempted to sit, which took six tries.

Encouraged by his success, Gabe moved to the corner of the bed while remaining at the main menu. Then, with great care, he steadied himself and stood. Cautiously, Gabe took a small step forward and then another.

It took Gabe twenty minutes to relearn how to walk. When he was confident, he attempted to sit and touch his toes. With this mastered, he relearned the other yoga poses.

An hour later, Gabe was confident enough to explore semiconductors while doing yoga. This dual effort proved more challenging than he anticipated, and it took over an hour to become proficient.

At one point, Gabe's mind drifted. *I have to stop calling you 'the white box.' What are you called?* As he concentrated, it seemed he should know the proper name, and the white box did not like being called a "white box."

An hour later, Gabe felt comfortable enough to move the white box into his sock. Unfortunately, this added to the difficulty, and it took another hour to achieve the same level of interaction.

The following day, a groggy Gabe woke in a cold, dark room to the sound of his cell phone alarm. He took a near-freezing shower and drove to the prison with the heater on maximum. Gabe led the 10:00 a.m. yoga class and met with Warden Clayford afterward.

"Thanks for seeing me."

"It is I who should thank you," Warden Clayford said with a smile. "The inmates all enjoy your presence. It gives them hope."

"I'm glad."

Warden Clayford could see Gabe's discomfort. "What's up?" he asked.

"I have an unpleasant request."

"They asked me to be as supportive as possible."

"I know, but I don't like putting you in an unethical position. It's not fair."

"What are you asking?"

"I have a small device I would like to take inside. It's the size of a pack of gum."

"Your request would break a lot of rules. Can you make it through a metal detector?"

"I took it through an airport metal detector."

"That should be fine."

"Thank you very much. I assure you it's not dangerous and will never leave my sock."

"What is it?"

"Please don't ask," Gabe cautioned.

"That serious?"

"If somebody got ahold of it— there would be huge consequences."

"I think I understand," Warden Clayford said with a nod. He leaned back briefly and continued, "I see you are continuing your friendship with Tuk Tuk."

"He's been very nice to me."

"Word is that he did you a big favor."

Gabe became uncomfortable and said, "Somebody was after my family, and he helped set them straight. I'm deeply grateful."

"Favors concern me," Warden Clayford said, his eyes narrowing.

"They concern me even more."

"Don't makc it a habit."

"It will never happen again."

"Well, good. I'm glad that we have that cleared up. Thank you for coming to me first about your concerns."

"In matters of this nature, it is best to ask permission far in advance."

"That's why I like you," Warden Clayford said, smiling. "You're an honest man."

"I try my best."

"One of these days, I would like to learn what this is about."

"Randy, I deeply respect you, but hope you never find out. It's a painful weight to carry."

"Hmm."

"My only goal is to lead a quiet life."

"A worthy goal. Now, important things. I watched a Facebook video of Emma saying, 'I want see book' this morning. Quite an accomplishment at seven weeks."

"Wow, I haven't seen that," Gabe admitted. "I don't have a Facebook account."

"You should get one."

"Everybody tells me that."

"Well, off you go."

"Thank you."

Gabe retrieved the white box from under the Jeep's seat and put it in his sock. At the metal detector, he walked through while Warden Clayford watched closely. As Gabe left, he noticed him speaking to the officer who operated the detector.

The yoga class began promptly at 1:00 p.m. Halfway through, Gabe turned the class over to a student. Gabe assumed the student's place, and he entered the white box main menu several yoga positions later.

Gabe felt pain in his arm and then realized he had fallen. Fortunately, the floor had a padded cushion, and he quickly stood. Gabe bashfully explained that he had not had a good night's rest due to a power failure. The students understood, and the routine continued.

Two moves later, Gabe entered the main menu and was happy to be able to continue the yoga routine. Half an hour later, the student leader ended their session. As Gabe was heading to the prison library to relax, he unexpectedly met Tuk Tuk. "Here is the address," he said, as he handed Gabe a slip of paper written in a woman's handwriting. "She's expecting you at eight in the morning. Unfortunately, the servant's house is full of junk, and it needs a good cleaning."

"I could rent a truck."

"You would do that?"

"Of course."

"That would be great."

"No problem."

Tuk Tuk seemed to be uncomfortable and asked, "Hey?"

"Yes?"

"This woman."

"Yes?"

"She means a lot to me," Tuk Tuk admitted.

"Any friend of yours is a friend of mine."

"Good. Well, there is—"

"What?" Gabe asked.

"She's sensitive about her appearance."

"Oh, I understand. I will do my best to be a gentleman."

"You are about to be tested," Tuk Tuk said with a grin.

"Thank you for the opportunity."

"She could use the company."

"I'm looking forward to meeting her."

Tuk Tuk waved goodbye, and then Gabe went to the library. He led the 1:00 class and had a work conference call from his car. Later that evening, Gabe led the 6:00 p.m. yoga class. He recited a Quranic quote at the halfway point, and a student took over. Gabe then attempted to use the white box and accessed the main menu.

Unexpectedly, the lead student said, "The Quran speaks, 'I will cast terror into the hearts of those who disbelieve. Therefore, strike off their heads and strike off every fingertip of them.'" The lead student held his toe-touching yoga pose, then moved into cow pose. "Gabe, how would you interpret this excerpt?"

Gabe thought to himself, *Well, this is the ultimate test. I'm going to answer this question while using the white box.*

The student made two more moves, and Gabe raised his chin slightly. The student held the mountain pose, and Gabe answered.

"Thank you for the opportunity to share my thoughts. Recently, I've been absorbing the wisdom contained within the Quran. What strikes me most is its peaceful approach. With this in mind, I believe I understand the intent of this excerpt. Good Muslims must overcome their peaceful nature and defend themselves if the two parties cannot find a reasonable solution. I think this graphic description serves as a warning to those who do not follow the wise path laid out by Allah."

The student nodded, changed moves, and said, "Let us silently consider this wisdom."

Gabe sighed with relief that the incident had passed. He was also pleased he'd answered a challenging question while using the white box.

Ten minutes later, the students finished class and began leaving. The student who had spoken to Gabe the previous evening lingered. "You provided a thoughtful interpretation," he said.

"It's how I felt."

"Do you own a copy of the Quran?" the student asked, arching an eyebrow.

"I've been using my computer."

The student solemnly handed Gabe a well-used book. "This copy has led many followers to enlightenment."

"I would be deeply honored to accept this precious gift."

The student smiled and departed. On the way out of prison, Gabe left a message for Warden Clayford requesting a day off to move. Afterward, he ate a bowl of spicy chili at a local restaurant and drove to his apartment.

It relieved Gabe to see the lights on, and he walked up to the main entrance. Molly was on her way out, and she smiled at him. "You're looking good," she said with a wink.

"Why, thank you. You look beautiful as well. Have a pleasant evening."

Molly blew Gabe a kiss and got into a big blue pickup truck with giant tires. The male driver glared at him harshly and sped away. Gabe climbed the stairs and met Joey at the top. "Hey, I think I found another place to stay," he said.

"Molly and Sue will miss you." Joey regarded Gabe with an odd look. "Plus, you haven't met Raven. What a honey."

"I cannot risk upsetting my wife."

"A bet is a bet. The girls will still come after you."

"How much do I owe you?" Gabe asked.

"This will be easy. I have a mile-long list of roughnecks who want your place at triple the price. So let me keep the ninety-nine-dollar security deposit and this month's rent. Then we're square."

"Thanks. Also, I haven't checked the place out yet. So, it's not official."

"I can live with that."

Gabe walked to his room, and Sue/Zhang opened her door. She touched his arm with affection and batted her eyes. "Nice to see you," Gabe said in a forced, pleasant voice.

"My door is always open, studmuffin."

"Not going to happen."

"That teeny-weeny lock you installed won't stop me, powerhouse."

"You should be worried about my wife," Gabe cautioned.

"I read all about you two. It's complete crap. You're sooo not the type who would rough up a girl, sweetie-poo."

"Um, I wish other people would figure that out."

"I'm going to win the bet. Count on it, sugar," Sue/Zhang said and raised her flawlessly sculpted eyebrows.

Gabe sighed and asked, "Did you read about the other parts?"

"Killing three bears with a stolen steak knife? I know all about bears. She probably scared them away."

"That's not how it happened," Gabe informed her.

"No worries. I can defend myself against any chick, Mr. Muscles."

"Not Kim."

"A quick lay can be our little secret, cutie-pie."

"No, thank you."

"Keep me in mind, snookie-okie."

"Not going to happen."

Sue/Zhang winked and closed her door. A relieved Gabe entered his apartment, looked up truck rentals, answered emails, and then called Kim. "Hey, babe. How's it going?"

Kim took a while to answer in a sleepy voice. "Alright, I guess."

"Is Emma keeping you awake? You sound tired."

"Mmm, yeah," Kim admitted.

"The warden told me you posted a video of her asking for a book?"

"Even *he* has a Facebook account. You need to get one."

"I know."

"Emma's speech is developing faster than I expected." This statement uplifted Gabe's spirits.

"I miss her so much."

"I can tell."

"How are you feeling? Our last conversation didn't go like the Kim I'm used to."

"I guess I'm fine," Kim answered with a yawn.

"Do you think it is because we're separated? Is there a swimming issue?"

"Yeah, probably."

Gabe didn't understand Kim's distant behavior and uncoordinated speech. "What should we talk about?" he asked. "I would like to take a vacation when I return. Anywhere you like. I have always wanted to visit Jamaica. You have been there many times and could show me around."

After a long pause, Kim asked, "Why do you always stare at my boobs? It's so rude!"

The accusation floored Gabe. He cautiously answered, "My love, since the first moment I bumped into you, I found you sexy. Your body is astounding, and my eyes get naturally drawn to your perfect breasts. I know I have a problem, and I apologize for making you uncomfortable. Please forgive me."

"It's still rude!" Kim countered.

"I will try harder."

"You better!"

"As you know from swimming, I respect you at a deep level."

"How?" Kim demanded.

"My love, you're amazing, smart, talented, creative, funny, and an exceptional mother."

"You think so?" Kim countered, which confused Gabe, and he wondered why she was attacking him.

"You're the smartest woman I've ever met."

"Even with all your semiconductor nerds?"

Gabe did not like the term "nerds," and he took a moment to calm down. He knew Kim understood this distaste and wanted to know why she used this word. Out of this sidetrack, Gabe answered, "Babe. I read your thesis. Trust me. Your mind is astounding. But the best part is that you are amazing in many areas. My love, you are by far the most intelligent woman I've ever met, and the best is yet to come."

A long moment later, Kim said, "I guess that might make it all alright to ogle me."

"I'm sorry if I ever made you uncomfortable. From now on, I'll try much harder to behave."

"You haven't upset me," Kim admitted. "I guess I'm venting. Emma's a handful."

"It's fine. But, in the future, please let me know when you feel down. I'll understand."

"How's it going?" Kim asked in an uplifting voice.

"I have made some progress."

"Ahh! Emma got into the cookies. Got to run."

The call abruptly ended. Gabe wanted to know why their recent conversations had been so harsh. Plus, he knew Emma could not eat cookies because her teeth had not formed, and she was not tall enough to reach the counter. *So, why did Kim say that?*

# FIVE

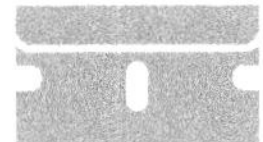

Gabe rented a U-Haul truck the following morning and drove down a dirt road outside Fairbanks. Ten miles later, he turned down another dirt road, and a large two-story house came into view. Gabe could see it had once looked impressive, but had fallen into disrepair. Next to it was a smaller house, barn, and a long storage building with garage doors.

Gabe saw a woman standing at the main house entryway, attentively observing him. He got out of the truck, and as he approached, he recognized her as the woman he had briefly met outside the prison on the day of his release.

As in their previous meeting, the woman looked disfigured, and it took effort not to stare. She stood a modest five foot four with a concerned expression, yet held a steadfast resolve. Her brown eyes, framed by the slight sheen of rimless glasses, held deep intellect and sharp awareness.

She wore her black hair, streaked with strands of gray, tied back with an air of practicality. The woman's attire was unassuming, consisting of a simple combination: a blue sweater over a tan shirt and gray slacks. Adorning her wrists and neck were gold Native Alaskan jewelry pieces, and she completed her ensemble with a pair of flat shoes. Despite the woman's unremarkable appearance, there was an undeniable grace in how she carried herself, a quiet strength that spoke of resilience in the face of adversity. "Hello. It's nice to see you again," Gabe began pleasantly.

"Gabe, the teacher. It's nice to see you, too," the woman answered in a crackly voice. "Please call me Karen."

"Thank you, Karen."

"My brother told me that the Glenn Ivy sisters were giving you a hard time, and you needed a place to stay."

This statement confused Gabe because Tuk Tuk had confessed to killing his parents and only sibling. "They had some sort of sex bet involving me," Gabe said, still wondering who this woman was.

"Those girls are dedicated. That's for sure. Well, you can stay in what I like to call the 'servant's quarters.' Our maid and cook lived there twenty-odd years ago."

"I brought this truck to clear out the trash."

"What a great idea."

The pair walked over to the single-story guest house. Karen took a key from her pocket, opened the door, and they entered. Dusty white sheets covered the furniture, and piles of junk were everywhere. "We can clear all this stuff out," Karen suggested. "I have been wanting to do this for years."

"Can I back the U-Haul up to the door?"

"Sure."

Gabe drove the truck over, lowered a ramp, and began loading. Meanwhile, Karen removed the covers and cleaned. An hour later, she said, "The bed looks good. But, from what I remember, the washer doesn't work, and I cannot find the vacuum cleaner."

"That washer does not look like it's worth fixing, and the dryer's old. I'll get new appliances and a vacuum on my way back from the dump."

"You don't have to do that," Karen said, shaking her head.

"It's the least I can do. Having a peaceful place to stay means more than anything."

"Well, alright."

Gabe disconnected the washer and dryer with a pair of pliers he found in a drawer. Karen brought in a dolly, and he used it to remove the appliances. Gabe then drove to the landfill and afterward went to Sears. He purchased a washer, dryer, vacuum, cleaning supplies, and kitchenware.

By 7:00 p.m., Gabe was exhausted. He took a shower and was ready to drive to a restaurant when Karen met him at the door. "Do you like steak?" she asked.

"That would be amazing."

They walked to the main house. The home's shabby exterior belied its gracious interior, to Gabe's surprise. They passed a roaring fire in an enormous brick fireplace and entered an elegant dining room where Karen had laid out a delightful meal. "Not what you expected?" she asked with a big grin.

"Um, no," Gabe bashfully replied.

"I intentionally keep the outside looking messy."

"Camouflage?" Gabe guessed.

"Exactly."

"Well, it fooled me."

Karen laughed, and they sat to eat. The food was delicious, and in between bites, Gabe asked, "How much do I owe you every month?"

Karen fluttered her hand and replied, "You can stay here as long as you like. Payment is unnecessary."

"Well, how about this? There's a coffee can near the dryer. What if it magically became full of beer money?"

"Beer money?" Karen asked with a crackly laugh. "As I stated, you can stay here as long as you like. I appreciate the company." She paused a moment, thinking. "Let me tell you something about Felix—that's Tuk Tuk's actual name. Incidentally, never, ever call him Felix. He's extremely sensitive.

"When you first met Felix, he was charging like a bull down a hellish road. He wouldn't have survived another year without meeting you. And, well, you took him under your wing and turned his life around. For the first time, somebody believed in him, and we are truly grateful for what you did."

"That's fantastic."

"He even calls me from time to time. He never did that before meeting you."

"Really?" Gabe asked.

"Do you know what we talk about?"

"No."

"You, of course! Teacher Gabe did this today. Teacher Gabe did that. Every time."

"Wow!" Gabe exclaimed.

"You helped him more than you'll ever know."

"Tuk Tuk, I mean Felix, did all the work."

"You encouraged him. He needed that."

"I did my best," Gabe admitted.

"It's alright to stare."

"Oh, I'm terribly sorry." Gabe briefly put his hands over his mouth, then continued. "I behaved rudely, and I'm ashamed of my actions. Please forgive me."

Karen motioned to her face. "I've been dealing with this since I was a teenager," she said, thinly smiling. "Your discomfort will pass. I've seen it happen hundreds of times. Now, I want to hear all about it."

Karen made a pot of orange peel tea, which they sipped from porcelain cups as they sat in comfortable leather chairs in front of the fire.

Gabe revealed his life's story, and Karen asked many questions. She liked how Kim attacked a bear and shot the wolves. Karen also appreciated Gabe's prison sacrifice to spare Kim the agony of testifying. It then brought a tear to her eye when he told her they got back together and had a wonderful daughter. However, Gabe did not mention their telepathic ability or why he returned to Alaska.

"Quite a life," Karen said with a smile. "But you've left out important details."

Gabe became uncomfortable and asked, "Like what?"

"I hear things. Like the fake meteorite story. Plus, everybody knows you got a brief prison sentence for keeping quiet."

"I watched a real meteorite come out of the sky. And trust me, I had a long sentence."

"It's in your expression," Karen said with a wink. "You're not being honest. Plus, everybody knows all about the HAARP experiment. That's the secret government radio base near Gakona Lodge. They did some sort of test and set the atmosphere on fire. The experts call it 'the crucible theory.' That's what actually happened."

"Well, I'm telling you that a meteorite blew up our ship, and that's the real truth."

"Perhaps we might speak of this at a later date, hmm? Tell me. What did Felix reveal about his childhood?"

"He grew up in a trashy mobile home and had many problems," Gabe said. "Then, at fourteen, he killed his parents and his only sibling. I don't even know if it was his brother or sister. That's all."

Karen laughed with her crackly voice again and said, "Oh, that's Felix for you. Well, the evening's young, and I will tell you *our* story. Where to begin?" She paused while pinching her lower lip. "Oh, I know. My parents were Native Alaskans. Specifically, we are part of the Yupik people. Incidentally, Native Alaskans don't like the term Eskimo.

"In the fifties, the federal government granted several Yupik members plots of land in exchange for moving from one location to another. They went out of their way to locate the most worthless land possible. Many recipients sold it for peanuts.

"My mother and father grew up dirt-poor, and they each had 25 square miles of land when they met. Then, in the sixties, a survey discovered oil on my mother's land, and a prospector found gold on my father's. My only guess is that the government hired surveyors who had never set foot outside their office. Well, my parents knew a good thing and leased their land to anyone with money. They used the profits to buy more land, mostly from friends and family. This wise decision made them beaucoup bucks.

"Felix is my younger brother by four years, and we grew up in a well-to-do lifestyle. We had everything spoiled rich kids could ever want, which led to predictable results.

"Felix got into drugs around ten, and he stopped learning at school. I partied at every opportunity and experimented with every known substance. Well, the apple didn't fall far from the tree. My parents were into drugs, alcohol, gambling, partying, and expensive toys. They didn't set any boundaries or take an interest in our development.

"Around thirteen, Felix got into hard drugs. He became delusional, unhealthy, and paranoid. When I blossomed, I got into relationships with any man who came my way. They all loved my attention, and I spoiled them rotten. Of course, my behavior infuriated my family, especially Felix. But what could they do about it? That's right. Nothing!

"When I turned seventeen, I met a Native Alaskan man named Darrell Horton at a clothing store. You might call him a tribal elder, but the term 'businessman' also applies. His parents had recently died in a small plane crash en route to his thirty-fourth birthday party. And when our eyes met— well— easy pickings for a girl like me."

"Hmm," Gabe said with a nod.

"It is amazing that you met Kim when you were 34 and she was 17."

"Quite a coincidence. How did you know our ages?"

"Felix told me."

"Oh."

"You look like you are in your midtwenties. What's up with that?" Karen asked.

"I work hard on my appearance."

"It shows. Where did I leave off? Oh, yes. A few months into our relationship, we both realized it was more than a fling. I remember those feelings like yesterday. Definitely the best time of my life."

Karen's attention turned to a National Geographic magazine on a table and brooded. She looked up with a distant expression. "Life has a funny way of sending you messages," she said in a lower voice. "Late one night, I woke in our woodshed covered in frozen vomit. I was wearing oversized, baggy blue pants I had never seen before; my purse was missing, and somebody had cut off my hair. Or maybe I had? Who knows?

"When I staggered into my bedroom, I knocked over a floor lamp, which fell so that the light hit Darrell's picture. I looked at it for the longest time. Then, bang! I cleaned up my life.

"Of course, our relationship didn't go unnoticed, and my family let me have it at every opportunity. To make matters worse, the entire town openly disapproved of us. To put it mildly, everybody's anger made our passion even hotter. On my eighteenth birthday, we got married at the courthouse. For the rest of the day, we partied hard. I planned to swing by my folks' house to pick up my stuff, and we would fly to Hawaii for a honeymoon."

Karen gazed at Gabe with a sad expression. Finally, she took a deep breath, awkwardly cleared her throat, and continued. "That day, it rained, and the water froze on top of the snow. In the evening, Darrell drove his Cadillac full throttle while I hollered out the window like a banshee. You know, I still remember the song that was blasting over the radio. 'Queen of Hearts' by Juice Newton. It's funny what your mind recalls. Neither one of us wore a seatbelt and... well. Right down the road, his car spun out of control and smashed into a tree. You can still see the impact all these years later.

"I woke in an icy snowdrift covered in blood. It took every ounce of strength to crawl to our house. My last act was to elbow the door. Eventually, my father came out to see what the ruckus was. At that point, I think I fainted. I know my mother called an ambulance, and my father held me in his arms. I never knew why they didn't immediately drive me to the hospital. They might have been afraid of injuring me further."

Karen paused and stared at the magazine cover for a long moment. "At some point, Felix came home," she continued in a barely audible voice. "He had been out shooting with his buddies and, as usual, was drugged out of his mind. And, well. When Felix saw me, he assumed my dad had beaten the crap out of me. This makes sense because the day before, I'd told him I was getting married."

Karen looked away and took several long breaths. She continued in a soft voice while shaking her head. "His mind, um— his mind, it— it snapped. He yanked me out of my father's arms. I didn't even feel the pain. The two argued, and Felix blasted him with his shotgun. My mother screamed, and he shot her, too. Afterward, I knew Felix held me while crying his eyes out. I vaguely remember him apologizing for not protecting me. The rest of that evening is gone.

"Not a day goes by that I don't regret not having the strength to prevent what happened."

Karen had become intensely emotional. Gabe stood and placed his hand on her shoulder. As he applied pressure, he felt unusual depressions in her muscles and realized the severity of her injuries.

A long moment later, Karen wiped away her tears and sniffed. "In reality, my parents never laid a hand on me, even though I deserved it." She forced calm into her voice. "But they got into it with Felix, and he had the scars to prove it. So, I guess he assumed they beat me bloody.

"The doctors spent eleven straight hours putting me back together. When I woke, the nurse told me my heart had stopped twice during the operation. I lost a kidney, punctured a lung, damaged my liver, shattered my right shoulder blade, cracked my hip, and badly dislocated my elbow. Plus, as everybody can see, my face went straight through the windshield.

"A day later, a police officer came to my room and told me they had found Darrell's body. A tree branch snapped his neck. Up to that moment, I thought he was alive. That statement hit me hard."

Karen paused, lost in the memory. "When I stopped crying about Darrell, the cop tried to get a statement. Well, doctors had wired my jaw shut, and the only thing I could do was use my finger to make letters in his hand. The entire scene really tore him up. Later, the officer told me that Felix had completely broken down when he found out about the car accident. An hour later, he confessed to everything. Then he went crazy-distant in custody and yelled when anybody came near him. So, they put him on suicide watch for two months. It was a tough time, and they told me he cried for hours every day.

"Anyway. I stayed at the hospital for seven months and endured three more surgeries. You cannot imagine my pain.

"During that time, a lot happened. Unbeknownst to me, Darrell put me in his will as his sole heir on our wedding day. To this day, I have never uncovered his motivation. As a result, I inherited land, buildings, mines, oil wells, businesses, money, art, and jewelry.

"Darrell's relatives were mad-dog furious because their houses were on his property. They did not own the land due to tribal law and grandfathering in tax benefits. I made it clear they could stay in their homes forever and even offered to deed their land to them. To me, there was no other choice because the houses belonged to them. I mean, how do you tell a family to leave the property they grew up on? I'm not a monster."

Karen's expression changed, and she said through gritted teeth, "Those ungrateful animals rejected my generous offer and took me to court for one hundred million dollars. What an outrageous amount! Keep in mind I lost my family, and I felt so—"

Karen stopped speaking and looked into the fire for a long moment. Eventually, she continued in a determined voice. "One day, I started screaming. It got so bad that the nurses had to sedate me. Well, let me tell you. I fought those ungrateful bastards tooth and nail from that very hospital bed. The judge even brought in the entire jury to meet me.

"And when they saw a battered girl with tubes in her arms and bandages everywhere? Well, their hearts melted, and of course, I won. I was still willing to let the families remain on the land, but my lawyers told me to evict those A-holes or else they would claim squatter's rights. To me, the whole thing felt like a hollow victory.

"You cannot imagine how the verdict shocked those people. They assumed that living on the land for generations meant they would win their court case. That misplaced confidence allowed them to spend every dime they had fighting me. Imagine that? In one day, 29 people went from being kings of the world to being broke and homeless. That's seven entire families.

"As a parting gift, they burned their houses to the ground. The fools then told everybody who would listen what they had done. Then, when questioned, they confessed with pride. Their logic had been that because they'd paid for their houses, they had not committed a crime.

"The courts took a dim view of arson and gave the owners five years of probation. Unfortunately, many of them lost their jobs as a result of their crimes. The only exception to this wickedness is Darrell's Uncle Jake. He is an honest man and stood by my side from day one. I deeded him the land, and he is one of the few people I trust."

Karen paused momentarily and continued, "Even though Felix was only fourteen, they tried him as an adult, and he received two 25-year back-to-back sentences. I'm told that in court, he showed no emotion. It is so sad. On that day, I lost my brother.

"Felix didn't adapt well to his new surroundings and constantly got into fights. For the first few years, he spent more time in solitary confinement than out. However, there was an unexpected benefit. The drugs made Felix a scrawny little thing; without all that poison, he got healthier. That allowed him to hit the weights and bulk up. Eventually, the guys recognized a troubled kid with a chip on his shoulder. So, most of them left him alone. Also, Felix never gives up in a fight, even when he's down. That's the one good thing my father taught him.

"Not everybody got the message, and around the time that Felix turned 20, a dumbass named Bobby Doorman wanted a piece of him. What kind of name is that? Bobby Doorman? Silly, right? Well, in the middle of the cafeteria, Bobby hit Felix in the gut as hard as he could. I think he did it to see what would happen. Prisoners have a lot of time on their hands, and it makes them do strange things. Or maybe he felt he could get away with it. Who knows?

"Anyway. Bobby was a tiny excuse for a man. By then, Felix had become a rage-fueled hulk. It seemed inconceivable that Bobby had the guts to punch him.

"So, what happened? Well, Felix stood there like a deer caught in headlights. The whole thing got crazy. All the inmates stopped eating to see what Felix would do. Even the guards stopped what they were doing. Everybody was in complete shock, and you could hear a pin drop.

"Well, nothing happened. And that little punk looked around and saw everybody staring at him. Finally, Bobby realized what an idiot he looked like, so he walloped Felix again. You know, it's a dog-eat-dog world in prison.

"My brother stood there, dumbfounded. And Bobby hit him three more times. Not one man in the entire cafeteria made a peep. The silence threw Bobby into a rage, and he committed the ultimate sin by screaming, 'Felix, your sister looks like a pig after it's been hit by a train.' As I told you, never call him Felix.

"He hit Bobby once. Just once. That's all it took. That punch smashed his nose deep into his brain, and his neck broke in four places. The coroner recorded it as the same type of injury a person would get in a 100-mile-per-hour car crash. All nine guards were fired the next day for not lifting a finger to stop the fight. A few months later, the courts gave Felix another five years. The whole thing upset me, but Felix didn't care. Prison is his home.

"To make matters worse, two years later, history repeated itself in the same cafeteria. This time, a lowlife named Nicolas Dean smacked Felix with a dinner tray while everybody watched. One punch and Nicolas's neck snapped like a twig. Witnesses said the only noise was a loud 'pop.' Felix got another five years, and four guards lost their jobs. Now, the guys get it, and nobody messes with him.

"After my time in the hospital, I returned home and began healing. It took eight more surgeries to look this good."

"That's a lot," Gabe admitted.

Karen walked over to the fireplace mantel and showed Gabe a family portrait. The young Karen was attractive, and young Felix looked frail. He bore no resemblance to the large man Gabe was familiar with.

"Why did Felix say you were dead?" Gabe asked.

"I'm not entirely sure what goes on inside his head. I suspect he couldn't live with the guilt. So, he tells everybody that somebody else killed his family. In a way, I died that day as well."

"Why the name Tuk Tuk?" Gabe asked.

"Growing up, that was a slang word for 'tough guy.' So, I guess that's his new identity."

"I think that makes sense."

"Felix has improved so much since he met you, and for that, I will be forever grateful," Karen said with a warm smile.

"I'm glad to have been able to help."

"Unfortunately, my troubles only worsened after I got home. Everybody knew what had happened, and they called me a gold digger at every opportunity. To this day, they continue to make my life miserable. When you combine their hatred with my appearance, it makes it difficult to get out of bed.

"Anyway, I needed to do something positive, so I turned my attention to the land. My parents were not into the whole nature movement, and the oilmen and miners had devastated every square inch of our property. So, I began using my wealth to restore our land to its original state. Now, my distant ancestors would recognize the same views. Today, I lease the land to those who have proven themselves responsible.

"Of course, I cannot please everybody. Some want me to open up the land to create new jobs. Others want me to stop *raping the sacred earth.* Bunch of fools."

"You would think they would all be on the same side."

"People can be greedy."

"True," Gabe admitted.

"You know what's even crazier? Everybody gets upset when I use my money to help the community. Last year, I paid for a state-of-the-art gym at the college. I only asked that they name it after Darrell's grandfather, Thomas. He was an amazing man who went far out of his way to improve the community. A real pillar of society in the fifties. Did you know he campaigned to move the waste dump and the sewage treatment plant outside the city?"

"No."

"He did," Karen said with pride. "Probably saved over a thousand people from getting cholera. Now, everybody has forgotten about his accomplishments."

"That is unfortunate," Gabe said with a sigh.

"What's unfortunate is that I have nobody to pass my wealth to. Felix has health issues from the drugs. The doctors tell me his liver is going to fail soon. And Uncle Jake— poor Jake is in the last stages of emphysema. It's so sad."

"I'm sorry to hear that."

"It's nature's way of telling us not to smoke," Karen dismissed.

"True."

"Ordinarily, the wealth should have gone to Darrell's family, but everyone hates my guts. I have approached the state and local tribes about passing my land along, but they have a poor track record of selling land to the highest bidder. Once, I even tried to turn it into a federal park. My best compromise is establishing a legal trust to ensure the land remains pristine. Even that has been difficult. I read news all the time about trustees lining their pockets."

"You could give your money to medical research or charities," Gabe suggested.

"Over the years, I've donated to local institutions. Then I find my money going to *administrative overhead* while children go hungry."

"I see your point. How about using your money to hire a lawyer to get Felix out of jail? Or pay the governor to get him a pardon? I'm sure he would like to be free."

Karen shook her head with a sad expression. "I have offered Felix this option many times," she answered. "He feels honor-bound to pay for his crimes."

"That's unfortunate."

"Felix doesn't desire freedom." Karen yawned and stood. "Well, the cleaning took all my energy. Will you join me for dinner tomorrow?"

"I will return around seven. Is that a good time?"

"That would be fine."

"I look forward to it. Thank you."

Gabe said goodnight and walked to the servant's house. He called Kim, but only got her voicemail. Five minutes later, Kim texted, "Feeding Emma. Talk tomorrow."

The text depressed Gabe, and he tried to bury his disappointment by answering several KimSemi emails. Later, as he lay in bed, the silence and safety of his new surroundings provided comfort, and he quickly fell asleep.

•

The following day, Gabe woke early and drove the U-Haul to the landfill. Many of the items he dropped off the previous day were gone. As Gabe tossed out a box of broken dishes, a man nearby who was also throwing away trash asked, "Did you get this junk from Karen's place? I saw a magazine with her name on it."

"I'm renting a room from her, and she asked me to clear out some trash."

"Figures. She finds ways to squeeze this hard-working community for every red cent."

"I find her to be a pleasant individual," Gabe countered.

"Well, lock your doors at night. That woman's the worst. Did she tell you how she forced the construction company I work for to build that stupid gym?"

"I thought she wrote a check?"

"Naw, she did the whole thing so she could name the gym after her boy-toy's father," the man answered. "What a prima donna!"

"I imagine it's a good gym."

"It's a damn good gym. We built it, not her."

"Asking to name the building seems like a small request," Gabe suggested.

"I still don't like seeing fat-cat money push good folks around."

"Well, I must be off."

As Gabe drove away, he wondered why so many people hated a woman who wanted to give back to her community. He returned the U-Haul truck and then drove his Jeep to the prison.

At 10:00 a.m., Gabe began the yoga class, focusing on an inmate named Alvin Ray because he had the most telepathic ability. Halfway through, Gabe asked another student to lead, and he began using the white box.

Alvin's thoughts were crude, distrustful, and conniving. Gabe felt unnerved as he deeply explored his mind. By the end of the yoga class, it became apparent that Gabe could not simply "switch off" another person's telepathic ability.

It had been an exhausting experience, and while turning to leave, Alvin winked at Gabe. This gesture unsettled him, and he wanted to vomit.

Gabe left the prison feeling defeated. He sat in the Jeep, staring blankly ahead. A long time later, Gabe heard his watch alarm beep and began walking toward his next yoga class.

In a hallway, a large inmate Gabe had never met stopped him by forcibly placing his hand on his chest. "You're staying at Karen's place!" the prisoner yelled.

"I'm only renting a room," Gabe sheepishly replied.

"You'd best clear out."

Gabe was unprepared for this encounter and took a moment to study the inmate. He had massive arms covered by tribal tattoos. The man's expression was intense, and it was clear that he would harm Gabe without regret. Gabe began swimming, and after an unknown amount of time, he noticed an even angrier expression and remembered that the man needed a verbal response. "Sir, I don't know you," Gabe said in his most pleasant voice.

"I'm Nuvuk. Karen kicked my Uncle Amaruq out of his home. She had no right!"

"Oh, hey, I'm sorry about your uncle," Gabe said apologetically. That man was still angry, and Gabe decided his best chance was to bluff. "Look. Stop this. What you're doing is dangerous."

"What do you mean? You're no match. I could snap you in half!"

"Of course you could, but you know Tuk Tuk did me a big favor. Right?"

"We all know that!" Nuvuk countered with a snarl.

"Part of my payment is to be nice to his sister. I'm staying at her place to help clean up. Tuk Tuk wants me to keep quiet about all of this."

"I don't care."

"Look, you know how protective he is about his sister. If you keep this up, Tuk Tuk will kill us without breaking a sweat. So, you keep quiet about everything, and I'll leave his sister's house as soon as possible. Then, everything will go back to normal."

Nuvuk thought briefly and replied, "Yeah, you're right. Look, stay with her, and don't tell Tuk Tuk about me."

"Got it!" Gabe said with a firm nod.

Nuvuk briskly walked away while Gabe laughed to himself. The next yoga class was delayed because a random search found a shiv (crude knife), and the prison was locked down for more searches. He sat in the corner of the room and began searching through the white box's menus to see if it had information about reducing telepathic ability. Unexpectedly, Gabe found the white box had recorded mental activity for the last day. He reviewed his recent interactions and located a menu titled "Brain Analyzer."

He directed the analyzer to his interaction with Alvin and searched through the options. It became clear that Alvin's fur-mow was not in the same brain region as Kim's. In addition, this mind was driven by an overwhelming sense of greed. Until now, he had only interacted with pleasant minds; he had never experienced an extreme personality.

Gabe then found that he could interact with a virtual mind in the brain analyzer. Unfortunately, he realized that his mental abilities were not strong enough to perform large-scale manipulations, even with the help of the white box. However, he was happy that he now understood the problem. A fur-mow works like a muscle, and the more often it gets used, the stronger it becomes.

He understood he needed to use his fur-mow differently. Gabe had been actively trying to communicate as if saying "hello" and then listening for a response. This approach challenged receivers (people's minds) to listen actively, encouraging their fur-mow development.

Upon understanding this, Gabe muttered, "Dammit! I encouraged these people to be telepathic because I didn't know what the heck I was doing. Stupid, stupid!"

Gabe fumed at himself for several minutes while working through the ramifications of his mistake. Finally, out of his funk, he regrouped and began using the simulator to try different approaches. He realized that a passive, inquisitive engagement was the best option. This was akin to listening first and then speaking at the right moment. This revelation was eye-opening, and he wondered why he had not tried it before.

When the prisoners were released from lockdown, Gabe practiced his passive swimming ability on the yoga students. This effort proved far more complex than he imagined, and he'd made little progress when he turned the class over to a student. The class looked at Gabe with confused expressions, and it occurred to him that he had not come up with an inspirational message. A movie quote came to mind. "Bill S. Preston, Esquire, once said, 'Be excellent to each other.' Truly inspiring words."

The students smiled, and Gabe selected a student to lead the second half of the class. Meanwhile, he concentrated on passively swimming in Tom Hill's mind. Tom was the third student to join Gabe's original class. He was an average man who idolized the wrong crowd. Now, he was trying to better himself, making him a perfect experimental subject. Gabe flexed his fur-mow and felt some of Tom's thoughts. Spurred by success, he continued to probe until the class concluded. As Tom left, he glanced at Gabe with a curious expression.

Gabe was eating a tuna sandwich in the prison cafeteria when Tuk Tuk walked over and asked, "How do you like staying with my friend?"

"She's been very nice and cooked a wonderful dinner last night," Gabe answered. "Thanks for introducing me."

"You cleaned up the guest house?"

"I took two truckloads to the landfill, including the washer and dryer."

"Why did you throw them away?" Tuk Tuk asked in a concerned voice.

"They were not worth repairing."

"You got new ones?"

"Yes."

"Who paid?" Tuk Tuk demanded.

"I did, of course."

"Why?"

"It seemed like the right thing to do."

"Thanks," Tuk Tuk murmured while looking down.

"I'm the one who should thank you. I cannot recall ever having a better night's sleep."

"I grew up there. You're right. It's quiet."

"May I say something?" Gabe asked with hesitation.

"Sure. Anything."

"Your friend cares about you."

"I know."

"She's proud that you've improved your life, and you mean the world to her."

"I know," Tuk Tuk admitted.

"My friend, you're working hard to put your demons to rest. Why not make peace with your friend? She forgave you a long time ago. Perhaps you might speak with your Muslim brothers about bridging this gap. They're friendly people, and I'm sure they can help."

Tuk Tuk looked at the ground for a long time. "You're leading the six o'clock yoga class?" he asked without looking up.

"Yes."

"I've been thinking about joining."

The statement surprised Gabe, and he said, "That's wonderful."

"But–" Tuk Tuk's voice trailed off.

"Your body does not bend easily?"

Tuk Tuk nodded.

"It took me a year to touch my toes," Gabe admitted. "The good thing about your current– er, *predicament* is that you have time to learn."

"Maybe next class."

"That would be great. You know that your Muslim brothers don't judge."

"Yes," Tuk Tuk answered with a slight smile.

"I am learning that as well."

"They said you're a nice guy. Very respectful."

"I try my best," Gabe said with a warm smile.

•

An hour later, Gabe led his 6:00 p.m. Muslim yoga class while doing his best to swim passively. Then he began focusing on Clark Summers, who had adopted the Muslim name Rifaah Al-Karim. Gabe found Rifaah conflicted, bright, controlling, lost, and struggling with an unbalanced moral compass.

Rifaah's mind overwhelmed Gabe with unfamiliar thoughts, and when Gabe turned over the class to a student teacher, he could no longer swim. At the end of the class, Rifaah looked at Gabe in strange fascination.

Gabe spent half an hour in the parking lot recovering before driving to Karen's house. The smell of grilled salmon with fresh dill greeted him. "This is impressive," he said with a smile.

"Thank you. Did you see Felix?"

"He's doing well, and we spoke of you."

"What did he say?"

"I asked him to consider speaking to his Muslim friends about coming to terms with his past."

"That's wonderful."

"He is thinking of joining my yoga class."

"Felix doing yoga?" Karen burst out with her crackly laugh. "Now that, I would like to see."

"When he sets his mind on something, it will happen. He never backs down."

"True." Karen's voice grew serious, concerned. "Now, be honest. Why are you teaching yoga to a bunch of prisoners? You have a wonderful family, and they need you."

"All true. My only answer is that I'm trying to give something back."

"Is this part of why you got a reduced prison sentence?"

"You know I maintain a high opinion of you."

"Thank you," Karen said with a nod. "But that's not an answer."

"I dislike lying, especially to you."

"I see. Well, thank you for not fibbing. Now, you need to call your family."

"I will. Thank you for the outstanding meal."

"Same time tomorrow?"

"That would be great."

"Eggs and bacon for breakfast?"

"You're spoiling me, but I appreciate your splendid invitation."

"Then it is settled."

"Thank you."

Gabe walked to the servant's house and called Kim. "Hey, babe."

"Hhh– hi," Kim answered in a sleepy voice.

"How's Emma?"

"Fine."

"Can I talk to her?" Gabe asked.

"She's in the other room."

"Oh."

Gabe wanted to know why Kim had not taken the phone to the other room. "How did your day go?" he asked in a friendly voice to encourage conversation.

"When you dream, why do you call me 'your slutty bitch?'"

The harsh accusation stunned Gabe, and he eventually mumbled, "I'm so sorry for my poor behavior."

"You'd better be sorry!" Kim yelled.

"I didn't know I acted so disrespectfully."

"Well, now you do!"

"How can I make this right?"

"I don't know, but you need to," Kim threatened.

"I love you more than anything."

"At night, you don't!" Kim's voice grew even angrier.

"I'm not really in control of my mind when I sleep."

"You need to be."

"I don't know how," Gabe admitted.

"Figure it the heck out!"

"What can I do to make you happy?"

"I— I don't know," Kim admitted. "You acted so rudely."

"I'm not sure what to say. You and Emma mean everything to me."

"Prove it!"

Gabe did not understand how this conversation had become so caustic. He understood he had to act boldly to resolve the issue. "I want to tell you about the last time we had sex."

"How rude!" Kim yelled. "I don't want to talk about that. We're never having sex again."

"Please, please hear me out. I want to describe the moment you kneeled on top of me. You looked down for a long time with an amazing smile and made this expression."

"What expression? What are you talking about?"

Gabe knew Kim was about to hang up, and he hoped she would give him a chance to explain. "You had this look. Your eyes. They were so... At that moment, I became the luckiest man in the world."

"Really?" Kim asked in a cautious voice.

"You looked so— so— mature."

"Mature? Do you still consider me to be a child? How dare you. How dare you!"

"Wait. That came out all wrong," Gabe admitted. "I'm sorry. You were the apex of womanhood."

"The apex of womanhood? That doesn't make any sense."

"If I took the best parts of the best women and assembled them in the best possible way, then that's who I made love to. You were everything. Confident to the max. Beauty at its best, passionate, intelligent, thoughtful, and entirely in the mood. I've never been more impressed with you.

"Our relationship is improving, and I'm super-attracted to you. You have my complete trust and my unconditional love. I'm so sorry for what happened, and I'll make this right. I promise to do my absolute best to stop my dreadful thoughts."

Kim did not speak for a long moment and said softly, "That was nice."

A relieved Gabe let out a breath and said, "I'm glad I had the opportunity to describe my feelings."

"I guess I should not get upset. You're right. Your dreams are for you."

"I'm glad you aren't too angry," Gabe said.

"It's fine. Do I do anything like that?"

"At night, you sometimes think about that *Magic Mike* actor. What's his name? Chamfer, or Channer something?"

"Oh. I didn't know."

"Are we good?"

"We have always been good. I guess I miss you, and maybe I said something I shouldn't have."

"I miss you too. Look, babe, it's clear that I need to fly home. This time apart is killing our relationship."

Kim responded cautiously, "No, do what you need to do. I'll be fine. Emma is crying. Got to go. Love you."

Kim ended the call without giving Gabe a chance to say goodbye, and he did not hear Emma crying.

The incident left Gabe perplexed. He could not recall thinking crudely about his beloved wife and briefly wondered if Kim had invented the incident. Finally, Gabe concluded Emma had exhausted Kim, and he fell asleep thinking about how to get their marriage back on track.

•

Over the next three weeks, Gabe settled into an odd routine. His day began with a delicious breakfast, followed by three yoga classes. At night, Karen made a fantastic dinner accompanied by long conversations. Afterward, he answered emails and called Kim. Sometimes, she answered, and they had pleasant conversations, but he often got voicemail or a caustic diatribe. Gabe did his best to probe, but Kim refused to be forthcoming about the central issue. However, there was one bright spot in their relationship. Emma continued to grow, and they sometimes had basic phone conversations. Gabe lived for these brief moments and cherished her dramatic progress.

Overall, Gabe made minor discoveries during his deprogramming, but success eluded him. Jason tolerated the lack of progress but stressed urgency. He also expressed concern that Kim had stopped attending yoga. When Gabe confronted Kim about this, she said, "Emma comes first, not Jason." Gabe reluctantly agreed, but knew Jason was not to be trifled with.

The breakthrough came when Gabe got frustrated and yanked at Tom Hill's fur-mow. After the violent mental attack, he immediately regretted his actions. Tom rubbed his forehead and struggled to stand. So, he sat while complaining of a severe headache.

It took Tom ten minutes to recover, and then he continued the yoga routine halfheartedly. A heartbroken Gabe entered Tom's mind, and to his surprise, he noticed reduced telepathic ability. So Gabe mentally yanked at Tom's fur-mow even harder. By the end of the class, Gabe felt exhausted, and Tom had difficulty walking. A student helped guide him to the prison hospital.

Gabe reported the success to Jason, who congratulated him. However, when he called Kim that evening, her indifference left him baffled. Plus, she did not want to know the details of the reduction procedure.

•

Gabe unexpectedly met Sue/Zhang in the prison parking lot the following morning. She was dressed in a frumpy jacket and baggy jeans. "The bet's off. I'm sorry for everything," she began with a panicked expression.

"That's a relief."

"Tell your wife to stop harassing me. Please!"

"As long as the other girls don't hound me, I will tell her."

"Really? You will?"

"Yes."

"That's great. Do you know what she did to me?"

"No, but I'm sure that it got your attention."

"She texted a video to my mother."

"I know the one," Gabe said with a nod.

"Did she really push a lady into alligators?"

"Yup."

"And the lady really died? It wasn't Hollywood Photoshop. Right?"

"No, that woman is dead."

"That's awful!" Sue/Zhang exclaimed and threw up her hands.

"I warned you."

"I should have listened."

"I agree," Gabe said, nodding.

"Your wife also texted my mother that I'm a prostitute. She thinks I'm studying history at UCLA. Now, she's freaking out and threatening to disown me!"

"My wife can be extreme."

"Would she kill me?"

"She would kill you without blinking an eye."

"This is so terrible. How did I get into this mess?"

"Is it Zhang or Sue?" Gabe wanted to know.

"Call me Zhang."

"Zhang, let me give you some advice. In your line of work, the odds are that someday, the police will find your body in a ditch. Why don't you try something new? Have you considered sales? You'd be great at it."

"I'll think about it. Please call your wife."

"I will,"

Zhang walked away, looking relieved, but Gabe was troubled by the encounter. *Why had Kim gone to such extreme measures? And why had she endangered herself by sending evidence of a serious crime?*

•

Over the next two weeks, Gabe deprogrammed his students and three guards. They all complained about headaches. He then turned his attention to the next deprogramming assignment.

A year ago, the Coyote Ridge Corrections Center in Washington State learned about the success of Fairbanks Prison yoga classes. They arranged an exchange program, and two Fairbanks Prison yoga students transferred there to teach. Unfortunately, Jason identified several Coyote Ridge inmates who routinely completed sentences.

Additionally, Jason wanted Gabe to investigate his former coworkers at Silicon Serpent and Pacific Progressive Peripherals. Gabe could now see the light at the end of the tunnel, which gave him hope that Jason would be out of their lives.

Two days later, Tuk Tuk attended the 6:00 p.m. yoga class. Gabe put extra effort into leading the class through gentle moves, and Tuk Tuk did his best to follow. When the class ended, Tuk Tuk thanked Gabe several times.

Unexpectedly, Tuk Tuk pulled Gabe aside the following day and said in a low voice, "I handled this biker thing. Bring fifty thousand to this spot two days from now. Nine in the morning. Alright?"

Tuk Tuk handed him a slip of paper.

"Wow, that's a relief," Gabe said, grasping Tuk Tuk on the arm as a gesture of thanks.

"It's the least I can do, and I'm sorry about the high cost."

"It's fine. What matters to me is that you helped."

"Anything for you."

"I'm again in your debt," Gabe said with a smile.

"Stop talking like that. As you say, that's what friends do."

"Thanks. Hey, I'm late for class."

Gabe gratefully shook Tuk Tuk's hand and began walking to his class.

"Wait," Tuk Tuk exclaimed,

"Yes?" Gabe asked and turned around.

"I need to ask you something."

"Sure. Anything."

"When you were inside, did you learn that I put you under my protection?"

"Remember Jessie?" Gabe asked.

"Sure. Always punching guys in the arm because it was funny."

"About a year into my term, I got into a bad mood, and well– I accidentally bumped into Jessie. My dad called this 'cruising for a bruising.' Anyway, you know what kind of person he is."

"A real hothead," Tuk Tuk answered with a nod. "He beat the living crap out of Parker. Remember that?"

"Yeah, I remember. Parker's leg broke in two places. Well, Jessie looked at me, and I knew he would punch me into the next week. But at the last moment, Jessie stopped. I asked him why, and he said that you were protecting me. You saved me that day, and I know there were other times. If you hadn't helped, everybody would have beaten me to a pulp. That's what they do to guys who… Well, you know I did what I did to get into this place."

Tuk Tuk nodded. "Everybody knows."

"Anyway, I never properly thanked you. So, from the bottom of my heart. Thank you."

"Do you understand why?"

"Because I helped you get an education," Gabe quickly answered.

"That is a small part of it."

"A small part? I don't understand. What's the big part?" Gabe asked.

"You were a fish out of water when you came here. It was clear you would never survive a week in the hole. But then you did something amazing. You treated me like an equal. Heck, you treated everyone in class as equals.

I mean, you're so intelligent. You know everything about math, English, history, and electrical stuff. But that didn't matter. You still treated me as your equal. Plus, you asked my opinion, listened to my stories, and never judged me. Dang! You treated me better than yourself. I appreciated that.

"So, I made a decision. You were going to stay alive. It took every favor I had to keep the animals off you. And then, one day, you were free."

Gabe's eyes brimmed with tears. "Again, thank you."

"And now you're back. I need you to be honest."

"Sure. Anything for you."

"Why are you wasting my gift?" Tuk Tuk asked in a painful voice.

"I–"

"You can't even tell your friend?"

"You know the government put me into protective custody?" Gabe asked.

"Because of that Kuiu Island thing? Right?"

"Yes," Gabe answered, wishing he had not told the truth.

"But why are you here? You should enjoy your family and not waste your time with a bunch of cons."

"I know. I now realize how big a sacrifice you made."

"But I mean, why can't you talk? Why? We are alone! Look around. Nobody can hear us."

"There are things I cannot tell you," Gabe whispered. "I'm sorry. But I want you to know that my silence is protecting you."

"From what? Is it that crucible thing?" Tuk Tuk pleaded.

"Let me be as honest as I can. If I refused to teach yoga, or if I tell you why I am here, then you, me, and everybody–" Gabe started whispering. "Will be murdered."

Tuk Tuk looked astonished and asked, "Really? They're forcing you to teach stupid yoga to a bunch of cons? That's silly. What did we do? We're lowlifes, and they could kill us all in a heartbeat. Nobody would care."

"I cannot tell you what's going on. And please know that I appreciate your gift. I have a glorious life, an amazing wife, and the best daughter. I hate being away from them, and as soon as I finish my thing, I will return to my family. I'm truly grateful for all you have done."

Tuk Tuk looked at Gabe for a long moment and asked, "You're saving us?"

"I'm saving much more than you can imagine. Please drop this subject."

"Because that would put me in danger," Tuk Tuk guessed.

"It would put millions in danger," Gabe whispered.

Tuk Tuk looked at Gabe for a long moment with wide eyes and said, "Millions? Really? Wow." He smiled, and Gabe hugged Tuk Tuk for a long moment.

•

That evening, Gabe texted Kim that he needed a USB drive loaded with Bitcoin. Two days later, Gabe drove to a deserted, snow-covered crossroads far away from town. The emptiness made him nervous, and he knew unseen people watched his every move. At 11:30 a.m., three snow machines rapidly converged on his location from different directions. They stopped ten feet away, leaving their engines running with a noticeable two-stroke rumble. Each driver carried an assault rifle and a sidearm. They wore cloth skull-themed face masks to hide their identities and tightly gripped their weapons.

"Gentlemen, I have brought the money," Gabe began in his best confident voice, which was still shaky.

"Cash?" the leftmost man asked in an intentionally altered voice.

"Bitcoin."

"Even better," the man said. "Pass it here."

"I am going to reach down to my sock. Is this alright?"

"Slowly. One hand. No tricks!"

Gabe extracted the USB drive from his sock with his right hand, wiped it off with his shirt, and handed it to the man who spoke. The others looked on with concern as the exchange took place. "Are we good?" Gabe needed to know.

"If this is what you say it is, then yes," the man on the left answered.

"Is everything good with the man who is making this request?"

The men laughed, and the man on the left answered, "Nah, Tuk Tuk owes us big-time."

"What would it take to make it square?"

The men laughed again, and the same man answered, "Two hundred grand."

"If I provided this amount, would Tuk Tuk be in the clear?"

The men stopped laughing, and the man in the middle answered in a deep, cagey voice, "We can arrange that."

"Can you be back here in two days?"

"For two hundred grand? Yeah."

"I'll be here."

"If you aren't, then the bitcoin you gave us evaporates."

"Understood."

The three men drove away in the same direction. When they were out of view, Gabe relaxed and walked toward his Jeep. As he opened the door, he noticed movement in the nearby trees. A man in white camouflage stood with a large rifle. Gabe felt a deep chill as the man looked at him momentarily before walking into the woods.

Two days later, Gabe drove to the same spot at 9:00 a.m. At 11:15, three snow machines drove up with the same three men. Gabe handed the man on the left another USB drive, and he nodded in acknowledgment. The center man said in the same deep, cagey voice, “Your last gift proved legit. Assuming this goes the same, Tuk Tuk is in the clear.”

“Sounds good.”

“Why are you helping that dirtbag?” the man in the middle asked. “You know what kind of family he comes from.”

“He’s my friend, and that’s all that matters.”

“You’re his friend?” the man on the left asked while shaking his head. “This isn’t part of some other deal?”

“No, he’s my friend, and there’s no other deal.”

“Where’s the money coming from? This isn’t oil money from his sister?”

“I sell cars,” Gabe lied. “The payment hurts, but I’ll manage.”

“I see. Well, if this money is legit, then Tuk Tuk is square.”

“Thank you.”

The man on the left nodded, and they all raced away, leaving a cloud of two-stroke smoke. Gabe looked around and noticed the same man in white camouflage standing in a different location in the woods. He gripped his rifle tightly while glaring at Gabe for a long moment. He then turned around and walked into the snow-covered trees. Gabe sighed in relief.

As Gabe entered the driver’s seat, he noticed another man dressed in different white camouflage standing. This other man also had a large rifle and nodded at Gabe. He also walked into the woods, leaving Gabe to wonder why they had used two men this time.

The next day, Tuk Tuk harshly pulled Gabe aside. “Did you do this?” he demanded.

“You mean paid off the guys that had a hold on you?” Gabe guessed.

“Yes!”

“Of course. I would do anything for you.”

“This is my business! Not yours!”

“My friend needed help.”

Tuk Tuk stared at Gabe for a long moment before he relaxed and mumbled, “Thanks.”

“Any time.”

Tuk Tuk squeezed Gabe’s shoulder, looked him in the eye, and walked away. From down the hallway, Gabe heard the sound of sniffling.

# SIX

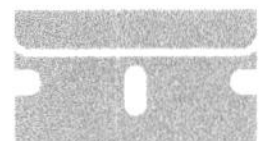

A week later, Gabe had deprogrammed all the affected people except an inmate named Clyde Fowler. He had been a student in Gabe's math and his first yoga class. With Gabe's help, Clyde turned his life around and started working toward a correspondence degree in world history. Three months before Gabe began deprogramming, something changed when Clyde attacked a guard. This resulted in an additional ten-year sentence plus a year of solitary confinement. That afternoon, Gabe met with Warden Clayford. "Hi, Randy," he began pleasantly.

"I understand you are leaving us."

"I've almost finished my work here."

"Are you aware that several inmates have been complaining of headaches?"

"Yes," Gabe answered with a sigh. "And I'm sorry to say that I'm responsible."

"I see."

"I wish I could've done a better job."

"The medicine we're prescribing isn't working."

"I'm sorry."

"Denny also has headaches," Warden Clayford said with narrow eyes.

"That part hurts me the most. He's a great supervisor and doesn't deserve the pain I caused."

"Will his headaches go away?"

"I hope so."

"If they don't?" Warden Clayford asked.

"I don't know. It may be something they all have to live with."

"That's not good news."

"I agree."

Warden Clayford's eyes again narrowed. "Will there be any other health issues?"

"I have no reason to think so."

"Good."

"Randy, I have one more request," Gabe humbly asked.

"Yes?"

"An inmate, Clyde Fowler. He's in the hole."

"Do you remember Doug?"

"Oh yeah. I remember Doug. Always cracking jokes. He was a great supervisor, but I haven't seen him around."

Warden Clayford took a deep breath and said, "Clyde put Doug in the hospital for two months. The doctors performed three surgeries, and he will require a cane for the rest of his life."

"That's terrible."

"What are you asking?"

"I need to interact with Clyde," Gabe solemnly answered.

"Your last subject?"

"Yes."

"Do you need to touch him?" Warden Clayford asked.

"No. I only need to be a few feet away, and I don't need to speak with him."

"How about I meet you at ten tonight, and we walk by his cell?"

"Thank you. Your cooperation means a lot to my people."

"Are you ever going to tell me what's going on?"

"Randy, we talked about all of this. Please don't ask. These people are dangerous."

"I see."

"Thank you for understanding."

That afternoon, Gabe said goodbye to his friends. Tuk Tuk hugged Gabe for a long moment, and he promised to return soon. The Muslim yoga students all expressed sadness as they said goodbye to their adopted teacher. Gabe assured the group he read his Quran often and had attained enlightenment from its wisdom.

Gabe met Warden Clayford at the gate that evening and walked toward Clyde's cell. Their mood was somber, and Gabe knew the Warden felt sad about his departure. Gabe used the white box and found Clyde experiencing a disturbing dream about being attacked by a dark entity. A flaming red knife was stabbing Clyde as he tried to fend off the blows.

Gabe used the white box to unlock Clyde's mental abilities and waited ten minutes to ensure his efforts were successful. He turned to Warden Clayford, nodded, and they walked back to the main entrance. "Thanks. I appreciate all your help," Gabe said with a broad smile.

"Hopefully, we'll see you soon. Your yoga class helped many inmates. As a result, overall aggression is down, and our numbers are tops."

"That's fantastic, but I had a lot of help," Gabe admitted.

"Get a Facebook account. I want to see lots of pictures. Lots of pictures."

"Will do. It's been a pleasure."

"Likewise. Have a safe flight," Warden Clayford said with a warm smile.

Gabe turned to leave and then turned back. "I have a question."

"Sure, sure."

"My former cellmate, Eugene. I didn't see him here. Did he get released?"

Warden Clayford became uncomfortable and quietly answered, "A few months ago, he hung himself. There is some doubt that it was a suicide."

"Oh. Well, despite living two feet from the man, we never talked. So, what did he do to end up here? I never found out."

"Hmm. I guess I'm no longer breaking any rules by discussing his case. Are you aware of the butcher of New Battle Creek?"

"No."

"New Battle Creek is a small community about a hundred miles from Anchorage— a retirement destination of sorts. One day, Eugene Gardner drove to the Anchorage police department covered in blood. There were four severed heads in the back of his pickup truck. In total, Eugene killed twelve people and injured forty-five.

After they arrested him, he made a deal to avoid the death penalty. His only request was protective custody. Despite being a bright guy, Eugene didn't know that the state of Alaska abolished the death penalty in 1957.

"The story Eugene told is that he used to be a big-time tax accountant in New York. He needed a change and wanted to be a trapper. The survivors all had the same story. The guy wanted to be alone. His only contact with other people came once a month when he ventured to the community store for provisions.

"When asked about his motivation, he replied, 'They kept bugging me.' Honestly, we do not know much about Eugene, if that was his real name. We couldn't find a single record about him in New York or any other state."

"And I shared a cell with him?" Gabe asked in shock.

"Yes."

Gabe began hyperventilating. "Why didn't anybody tell me about him?"

"Well, that's the thing. This was the same day as 9/11; the papers put his story on the back page. Because he pleaded guilty, there was no trial, and he arrived without fanfare."

Gabe threw up his hands. "I cannot believe he slept above me every night."

"Eugene was a model inmate, and I saw no reason that he would become violent."

"That is a lot to think about."

"Now, remember. Lots of pictures," Warden Clayford said, and shook Gabe's hand.

"Will do."

•

Gabe packed, cleaned, and put the covers over the furniture the following day. After a superb breakfast, Karen said, "It's been nice having you here."

"I liked my time here as well. Plus, your cooking was out of this world. I'm deeply in your debt."

"Nonsense. I enjoyed your company," Karen said with a crackly laugh. "What were your plans for the rest of the day?"

"No real plans. Maybe play in the snow with the Jeep. My flight is at four."

"I'd like to show you something."

"Sounds great."

Karen led Gabe through parts of the main house he had not seen. He appreciated several exquisite pieces of Native Alaskan artwork. One was a five-foot-tall granite sculpture of a bear, and another was a gorgeous painting of an eagle catching a fish. The tour concluded in the living room, and Karen made a pot of hibiscus tea. "I noticed beer money in the coffee can," she said with a smile.

"I believe in being fair."

"Felix told me something interesting. He said you paid off an enormous debt. From what I gather, it was over a hundred thousand dollars."

"I helped a friend," Gabe said solemnly.

"Felix used to get into all kinds of trouble and asked me to give people money. It all got too scary, and I made him stop."

"I think he let himself get into a dangerous situation to help me," Gabe whispered.

"Felix told me everything."

"Oh. I asked him not to say anything so you would be safe."

"You protected your family," Karen said.

"I suppose."

"I searched the internet about that Sato fellow. He's a monster. And those wild lies about you abusing Kim? Breaking her arm? And killing her nonexistent sister? There's no excuse for such wicked behavior."

"True," Gabe admitted.

"Felix told me you had the option to end Sato's life and chose not to."

"That's not my way."

"Hmm."

Karen leaned back and looked at Gabe for a long moment. He did not understand why her mood had changed and wondered if he had made a verbal mistake. Gabe considered swimming, but his instinct told him not to. Eventually, Karen said, "I didn't share my financial information with you in our evening conversations."

Gabe sat up and said, "That's unnecessary. You must keep such matters in strict confidence."

"Hmm. There's wisdom in your words. Would you like to know an interesting fact?"

"Sure."

"My bank account has less than ten thousand, and I don't own stocks."

"Really?" Gabe asked with surprise. "I would have expected your oil wells and gold mines to generate lots of money. But you probably spend it restoring the land."

"As a Native Alaskan, I'm entitled to certain benefits. One of them is that I pay less income tax."

"Wow, I didn't know it worked that way."

"It does work that way," Karen confirmed with a coy smile. "Also, my business dealings aren't inspected by the government."

"A lot less paperwork."

"Correct."

Karen opened a nearby cabinet and retrieved a glass mason jar of gold dust. She handed the heavy jar to Gabe, and his eyes lit up. "That's 100 ounces," Karen said with a smile.

"Wow, it's heavier than I expected. This is incredible."

"Today, the market price is $1,356 per ounce. You're holding one hundred thirty thousand dollars."

"Wow!" Gabe exclaimed. "This is amazing."

Karen smiled momentarily and said, "The deal I make with the miners is between ten and fifty percent, depending on many factors. All paid in gold."

"So, your income bypasses the government without leaving any records."

"Precisely. Now for the interesting part. I get one hundred percent when the oil gets pumped out of my ground. This is because I drill the wells myself. In addition, the oil companies pay to put their pipelines through my land."

"That must add up."

"It does," Karen answered, and leaned back for a moment. "Long ago, the Native Alaskans figured out another trick to bypass the government. The oil companies buy gold from the local miners and use it to pay me. This eliminates the official records, allowing the miners and oil companies to avoid taxes."

"Wow, that's a neat loophole."

Karen broadly smiled, which perplexed Gabe. He briefly swam and understood she was considering an important decision. "There's one more thing I want to show you," Karen said, and then stood.

They left the living room, and Karen removed a thin steel wire from a shelf. They continued until they came to a closet. Karen looked at Gabe, winked, opened the door, and poked the wire through a hole in the floor. There was a sudden pop, and Karen closed the closet door. She pushed against the wall, and a concealed door opened, revealing stairs. They walked down the stairway. Karen turned on the lights, revealing a large basement.

The room was filled with equipment, including scales, steel molds, bags of chemicals, and a large furnace. One corner contained a large steel trash can loaded with glass ingots, which Gabe recognized as slag (leftover material from metal purification). He realized that this room was a gold refinery. Gabe noticed a large steel container with at least four square feet of gold dust and nuggets. Karen observed his awestruck expression. She pointed to the box and said, "That's half the gold from last year. Last month, I received 3,207 ounces."

"Wow!" Gabe exclaimed. "There's so much. I cannot believe it. This is amazing."

"I think so as well," Karen said with a grin.

"How did you get all those heavy bags down here?" Karen looked amused, walked to an alcove, and pulled a large lever. Gabe heard a hissing sound, and a steel platform began lowering on hydraulic cylinders. When it came to a stop, he saw a wooden floor with old gardening tools. Gabe looked up to see the inside of a tool shed. "My secret entrance," she said with her crackly laugh.

Karen led Gabe to where a colossal safe dominated the left corner of the room. She looked at Gabe, smiled, and entered the combination:

01, 02, 03, 04, 05. Karen laughed and said, "I'm getting old, and I had to change the combination to something I could remember."

Gabe laughed uneasily, understanding he was about to see all of Karen's savings. She turned the locking wheel, and the safe opened to reveal nothing except a sign that read, "My money is in stocks. Fooled you." Gabe did not understand what was happening.

Karen reached inside and pushed a concealed sliding door that revealed a small lever. She pulled the lever, and it made a crunching sound. Karen closed the safe door and locked it. Next, she walked to a wall and flipped a switch.

Gabe grinned uneasily, and he heard the muffled groan of a motor. The safe lifted, and then it stopped with a loud crunch. Karen pushed the safe, and it pivoted to the left, revealing steps. Gabe stared at her in disbelief as she led the way down the narrow stairs.

When they got 20 steps down, Gabe was gobsmacked. The lower room had been constructed with thick concrete walls. He estimated its size as twenty feet by twenty feet and ten feet high. The floor was dominated by a massive five-foot-high stack of gold bars that occupied approximately two-thirds of the space. Gabe absolutely could not believe the astonishing sight before him. Cautiously, he walked up to the pile and touched a bar to see if it was real. Gabe was stunned and looked at Karen in astonishment.

"My parents built this room in the seventies," Karen said with a grin. "Even then, they had a lot of gold. Plus, Darrell willed me even more."

"Wow!" Gabe exclaimed.

"Besides Felix, nobody else knows about this room. And even he doesn't know how much is here."

"I don't know what to say."

"Your expression tells me everything."

"I still don't know what to say," Gabe confessed.

"Well, how about this? You told me a lot about your daughter. Clearly, you two have a genuine connection."

"We love her very much."

"I'd like to put her in my will."

"Really? That's so unexpected. Kim and I would be deeply honored to accept your generous offer."

"I'm glad," Karen said with a smile.

The pair walked up the stairs, and Gabe pushed the safe over the opening. She flipped the switch, and the safe moved down with a crunch. They climbed the stairs, closed the secret door, and went to the living room.

"That was amazing," Gabe said. "I'm still trying to take it all in."

"There are very few people I trust."

"Well, thank you."

"In town, I let it slip that my money goes to overseas banks. Then, I make it look like a big secure transaction occurs every six months."

"I'm still overwhelmed," Gabe said in bewilderment.

"That's understandable. Tell me. What happened on Kuiu Island?"

"I cannot say," Gabe stammered. "Really, I really can't. Please let this go."

Karen looked deeply wounded by his response. Gabe stood, stretched, pointed to his ear, winked, and said, "Well, my flight is leaving soon, and I still need to pack." He gestured at her to follow him.

Karen smiled, and they walked to the servant's house. Gabe put his luggage into the Jeep and then held his finger to his lips to indicate that she should not say anything. He retrieved the white box from under the seat, turned to Karen, and entered her mind, experiencing her peaceful thoughts. Gabe had some fun and moved Karen's arms, which caused her to laugh. He then rolled her fingers together as he felt the ridges move across each other. He then maneuvered the white box so Karen could feel his fingers move. The simple gesture overwhelmed her.

As Gabe explored Karen's body, he understood the severe damage left by the accident. Her muscles struggled to move, and her organs were barely functioning. Gabe felt great sadness at this knowledge and understood that Karen had directly experienced his feelings. He left her mind two minutes later, and they both were in tears. "I still wish you would tell me what happened," Karen said with a weak smile.

"No matter what anybody tells you, a meteorite struck our ship."

"For the first time, I believe you."

"I'm glad," Gabe said with a smile.

"I'd like to give my house to Emma."

"Wow, that's an incredible gesture. Thank you so much. I know she will love spending time here."

"And what's inside."

Gabe felt stunned as he looked at Karen, his eyes wide. "You're a special man," Karen continued. "I see why your wife chose you."

"I don't know how I should feel."

"It's alright. Will you be back soon?"

"Well, Emma has to meet her godmother."

Karen had to take a step back. "Our family only has my mother and sister," Gabe continued. "So, Emma needs to be spoiled as much as possible. We would be proud to call you godmother."

"It would be my honor," Karen said, as her tears flowed. She took a moment to recover and continued. "Well, we can make it official. I will fill out the paperwork to make Emma a Native Alaskan. The federal government still lets me do that."

"Really?" Gabe asked.

"Yes."

"That's so nice of you."

"It's no bother. I have always wanted a daughter. Unfortunately, the accident made that an impossibility."

"I'm sorry."

"How long before your flight?" Karen asked.

"I need to leave in a few minutes."

"Wait here." Karen walked away and returned, holding the mason jar full of gold. She handed it to Gabe and smiled. "Beer money."

"You've been so generous. Thank you for everything."

"I don't like long goodbyes. Have a safe flight."

"Thank you. I'll return soon with Kim and Emma."

Gabe hugged Karen for a long while, got into his Jeep, and drove away. As he looked into the rearview mirror, he saw Karen crying. The emotional moment also caused his tears to flow.

•

Gabe had partially recovered at the rental car return lot. As he waited for the airport shuttle bus, a gruff voice from behind said, "Your debt is paid."

Gabe turned around to see the large biker he had met in California. He wore a thick, plaid hunting jacket and carried a well-worn black duffel bag. Gabe felt relieved that the man did not look upset, and he replied, "Thanks."

"You were right. Sticking it to my *competition* was a fun gig. They never saw it coming and blamed all the wrong people."

The man laughed creepily, and Gabe said, "It must have been nice to watch the deal go down."

"You got that right! Hey, about our other business. Your boy told me how you took care of everybody. Gassed forty-two marks. Rather creative."

Gabe did not know what the biker was referring to and lied. "Also, a fun gig."

"You are more of a badass than I thought."

"Family is everything," Gabe admitted in a humble voice.

"Yeah, that's cool. Are you going to ask why I'm here?"

"I'm sure you have important brotherhood business that must remain confidential."

"Well, I'll tell ya. A bit of work and a bit of fun."

"It's beautiful up here. Where I live, the weather is hot and muggy."

"I grew up in Montana," the biker said in a far-off voice.

"I have never been there but want to go someday."

"The mountains around here look similar."

"I enjoy the rugged beauty."

"Is that your bus?" the man asked, his eyes narrowed.

"I think so."

"Be seeing you, Gabe."

"Nice chatting with you, sir."

Gabe felt a chill go up his spine as he understood that the biker knew his name and made it a point to communicate this knowledge. The man smiled wickedly and walked away. He entered the shuttle bus feeling unnerved and bypassed airport security. Four and a half hours later, Gabe landed in Wenatchee, Washington, and drove his rental car to an apartment building near Coyote Ridge Corrections Center. After unpacking, he ate an average-tasting meal at a nearby Thai restaurant and tried to call Kim, but it went directly to voicemail.

Gabe drove to the prison the following day, and the staff accepted him as a volunteer yoga instructor without fanfare. He met the two exchange prisoners who transferred from Fairbanks in his second class. They talked about old times as Gabe assessed their telepathic ability. Fortunately, their skills were rudimentary, and Gabe was sure he could easily deprogram the two men. A day later, he led the class, and no other prisoners had abilities.

That night, Gabe called Kim, "Hi, babe. How's Emma?"

"She's fine," Kim answered in a sleepy voice. "I guess."

"That's great. Well, I have good news. I should be home in a few days."

"Good to hear. Wow, I'm exhausted. Can we talk tomorrow?"

"Sure, babe. I love you, and remember: I have a big surprise."

A long moment later, Kim asked, "Who? Did I fall asleep?"

"It's fine. Love you and see you soon."

"I know," Kim said in a trailing-off voice, and she ended the call.

Gabe was now accustomed to Kim's unpredictable conversations, and it was a blessing that their recent discussions had been friendly.

The following day, Gabe arrived at the prison parking lot. Donna arranged for a meeting with Officer Ben Morrison, who would help him pass the white box through security. Clad in his flawless uniform, he exuded an air of intimidation, his sharp, penetrating eyes conveying menace. As Gabe approached, he surveyed his surroundings with a vigilant gaze that missed nothing.

"I'm told you are the person to speak to," Gabe pleasantly began.

"Yeah, I'm the guy," Officer Morrison replied gruffly. "They want me to pass illegal stuff into the hole."

"It's only a small relaxation aid for yoga. Completely harmless."

"Well, I have to see this *relaxation aid* or no deal."

The unexpected requirement shocked Gabe, and he whispered, "That might not be a good idea."

"You don't have a choice," Officer Morrison threatened.

"I would consider it a personal favor if you would do this for me. The people I work with would also appreciate your cooperation."

"No."

"Look, these people are—"

"I work with *people*," Officer Morrison angrily cut Gabe off. "Not going to happen."

"Please. There has got to be some way to bend the rules."

"No."

"Is there nothing I can do?" Gabe pleaded. "This is really important."

"No."

"Look, I must be honest here. There will be consequences that are out of my control."

"I handle *consequences* all day long."

"That's unfortunate," Gabe said with a sigh. "I wish you would reconsider. Please tell me what you need. My people can make anything happen."

"Show me the stuff or walk away."

Gabe tried to think of how to turn this conversation around. He remembered all the awful situations his former wife, Lydia, had confidently handled, but he could not think of an angle that would work.

"Well, nice meeting you," Gabe said in a defeated voice. Officer Morrison twitched his lip and walked away.

Gabe led his morning yoga class and then called Donna. She seemed unfazed by the news and told him she'd take care of it. Gabe taught the afternoon class and then ate dinner at a tiny Italian restaurant. The linguini with clams tasted fantastic, and the garlic bread had a hearty crunch. He left a generous tip, promised to return, and drove to his apartment. He tried calling Kim twice, but both calls went directly to voicemail.

The following day, Donna sent new contact information via text. At the main entrance, Officer Jim Neal looked petrified.

"Is everything alright?" Gabe asked.

"Ben's car!"

"What about his car?"

"They found it."

"I don't understand."

"Look, take whatever you want inside," Officer Neal pleaded. "Don't make them kill me. Please!"

"I mean you no harm. Tell me what happened."

"Do what you need to do. I have a family!"

"It's only a relaxation aid," Gabe offered as he tried to reassure Officer Neal with a gentle squeeze on his shoulder.

"I don't care if it's an elephant carrying a bazooka! My family needs me!"

"Everything will be fine."

"Please, please. Promise not to kill me!" Officer Neal begged.

"I promise."

"Thank you. Thank you!"

Officer Neal backed away from Gabe, his face twisted in fright. The encounter shook Gabe, and he returned to the rental car to calm his nerves. At the metal detector, Officer Neal escorted Gabe through without incident.

Gabe finished his deprogramming four days later, and Donna arranged a flight for him to see his co-workers at Silicon Serpent in San Jose, California.

In an afternoon meeting, they reminisced while Gabe probed for telepathic ability. Fortunately, only the company's owner, Al Horne, had a rudimentary ability, and Gabe quickly removed it without incident.

That evening, Gabe flew to John Wayne Airport near Santa Ana, California. He checked into a hotel, called Kim, and got her voicemail again.

Gabe drove to Pacific Progressive Peripherals in the morning and met with the company's president, Ken, and the head engineer, Joe. They had an excellent meeting, discussing marketing, new projects, and the semiconductor industry. During this time, Gabe easily deprogrammed their minor ability.

That night, Gabe called Kim, and she answered on the first ring, "Hi, hon."

"Hey, babe. You sound great."

"I'm looking forward to seeing you," Kim chirped.

"So am I," he said.

"Are you going to tell me about the big surprise?" she asked.

"When I see you."

The rest of the conversation went well, and Kim's pleasant mood came as a great relief.

•

Gabe flew to Florida the following day and could not wait to tell Kim the excellent news and hear how well Emma was talking. However, Kim was not at the passenger arrival area. Gabe called five times over the next hour, but the calls went unanswered. So, he took a taxi home.

When Gabe opened his front door, he found Emma playing a color-matching board game with their housekeeper, Anna. She was dressed in a white dress adorned with red bows and pink ribbons. And when she flashed her toothless smile, Gabe was immediately captivated by her irresistible charm. Emma walked over to him, and her well-coordinated movements left him stunned.

"Daddy Gabe! You home!" Emma shrieked as he picked her up.

"I missed you so much."

"Miss you," she said with a big grin.

"Wow, you're talking well. I'm so proud of you."

"Where is Mommy?" Gabe asked, and Emma's expression turned sad. He did not understand and asked Anna, "Where's Kim?"

Anna turned away, and Gabe looked in the direction she had turned. There were several liquor bottles on the counter and boxes of alcohol on the floor. He sighed heavily and nearly swore.

"Is she upstairs?" Gabe asked and then pinched his eyebrows.

Anna solemnly nodded, and Gabe put Emma down. He walked upstairs and found Kim on the master bedroom floor. She was not wearing any clothing below the waist and was holding an empty whiskey bottle. "Babe, are you alright?" Gabe asked.

Kim stirred but did not reply. Gabe let out a deep breath and helped her to the toilet. Kim threw up waves of foul-smelling vomit and then weakly looked up at Gabe.

"I'm going to clean you up and then help get you to bed," Gabe said encouragingly. "Tomorrow, I will take Emma to work while you rest. This is a minor setback, and everything will be alright. You'll see."

Gabe cleaned Kim with a washcloth, and she went far out of her way to avoid eye contact. Finally, he dressed her in pajamas and led her to bed.

"It's nice to be back home," Gabe said warmly. "We're going to get through this. Have a good sleep, my love."

Kim turned away, and Gabe kissed her on the shoulder. He walked downstairs holding the alcohol bottle and said to Anna, "Let's get rid of this mess."

"That's music to my ears. This situation got completely out of control."

"I can imagine."

The pair emptied the bottles and threw them into the recycle bin. "I'm sorry this happened," Gabe whispered so Emma would not hear. "Her family has a grim history with booze."

"She told me about it."

"If I had known, I would have come home sooner."

"It's fine," Anna said with a smile. "Kim's a great friend. I knew once you returned, she would bounce back."

"It's still not right. How about this? I got a bonus. So, expect something in your next paycheck."

"Actually, she paid me to keep quiet," Anna admitted.

"Oh. How about a big Christmas gift?"

Anna laughed, and she left for the evening. The following day, when Gabe woke, he turned to Kim and found her still asleep. He made breakfast for himself and Emma. She happily ate her applesauce, and her spoon coordination skills were outstanding. When he entered the garage with her in a car seat, he saw that Kim had cleaned the old workbench and that boxes of new tools were on top. The sight surprised him; he suspected they were a "welcome home" gift.

Gabe had a productive day at KimSemi while Emma silently observed the office activities. When they arrived home that evening, a taxi was in the driveway. Kim met them at the door with a sad expression, and Gabe noticed a duffel bag beside her. He feared this would be the last time they saw each other. "I don't know what to say," Kim began.

"It's fine. We can fix this."

"I screwed up big-time. This is the worst thing I've ever done. Emma could have—" She looked away.

"Things are going to get better," Gabe encouraged.

"I need to clean myself up."

"Whatever you need."

"I'm going to go to a place in Arizona," Kim whimpered as she held back tears.

"Sure."

"I'm really... Words are—"

"No apologies are necessary," Gabe interrupted. "The important thing is I love you, and Emma loves you too."

"My cab is here," Kim said, and then turned away.

"There is a lot we need to discuss. Plus, I have an epic surprise."

"We'll talk when I get back."

"Whatever it takes. Babe, please take the white box. It will help you figure things out."

"No, you will need it for the yoga class. Um, I didn't do any deprogramming."

"It's fine."

"Hon, I truly love you," Kim said, her voice choked. "I'll make this right."

"Everything is fine. Our relationship had a minor setback. Nothing more. Take all the time you need."

"You're the best husband in the world, and I'm the luckiest woman in the world."

A tearful Kim hugged Gabe and then Emma. She turned away, and Emma began crying. Kim returned, hugged Emma again, and then ran to the cab.

Gabe took Emma inside and held her for a long time while she cried. Eventually, when her cries turned to sniffles, he set her down and said, "Well, kiddo, it looks like it's you and me for a while."

# SEVEN

When Kim's plane landed in Tempe, Arizona, a van took her to the Saguaro Hills Desert Retreat, which specialized in "detoxifying the body and mind." She had not chosen a traditional rehabilitation center because she felt solitary meditation would be the best therapy.

Kim checked in at 5:35 p.m., and a blond-haired man with black roots led her to a one-person cabin. Inside, the accommodations were sparse but cozy. She noticed the lack of technology, which pleased her. At precisely 7:00 a.m., a bell softly tolled. Kim dressed in loose workout clothes and walked to the "awakening center," a group meeting room. After introductions, each group member shared details about themselves and discussed how much they looked forward to achieving true relaxation.

When the group's attention turned to Kim, she twisted her ear, looked down, and spoke in a humiliated voice. "Well, I guess I should share my story. I'm here because I need to get my life back into balance. I did a ton of research, and this venue seemed ideal. Anyhow, I need to get an issue out into the open. My family has a long history of substance abuse. Nearly every story seems like it got ripped out of a college party movie. Fortunately, my parents did their best to keep their drinking in check.

"Growing up, I dabbled, but nothing serious. My big problem happened after my parents passed away. Suddenly, I was alone with endless freedom. So, I did what any seventeen-year-old would do. I partied hard and drank like a fish.

"Then, one day, I got into a car accident. Luck must have been on my side because I came away scot-free. It suddenly hit me that I needed to turn my life around. So, I stopped drinking, changed my friends, and got into yoga. Then, the most wonderful thing happened. I got back together with my soulmate, and we have been raising a wonderful daughter."

Kim glanced around the room to see disapproving faces, then lowered her eyes again. She took a deep breath and continued. "The problem started when my husband took a business trip. I wanted to surprise him when he returned and came up with the perfect idea. My dad had this big old workbench with junk piled on top. I wanted to clean it off and buy new tools. But when I opened the doors, I found three cases of vodka. Because of the car accident, I wanted nothing to do with that poison.

"But I didn't want to throw it away, so I gave it to my coworkers. Most of them only wanted one bottle, but Brent wanted four. He drives a motorcycle, and I offered to drop it off at his apartment. Anyway, on the way out, he offered me a drink. I still don't know why, but I accepted. Yeah. One drink."

Kim looked up at the group and noticed two people shaking their heads. She looked down and continued, "A day later, I went grocery shopping and saw a wine sale. Right then and there, I decided my addictions were in my past and purchased one bottle. Yeah. One bottle. That evening, I had a small glass, and everything was fine. The next day, I missed my husband, and I had another.

"Honestly, my memory's a wash, but I do recall buying carloads of liquor and drunk-dialing my husband. But that's not the worst part. My daughter could have—" Kim began sobbing, and the woman beside her said, "There, there." Then, a long moment later, she said between sobs, "That's why I'm here."

The lead spiritual adviser, Lonnie, said, "We are not a rehab facility. You need professional help."

Kim looked up and said sternly, "I don't need rehab. I made a mistake and accept all responsibility for my actions. My mind needs peace, meditation, and focus. Nothing more."

"We offer exactly what you are seeking."

"This subject is now closed. So, let's talk about your detoxifying diet and health walks."

"I like your attitude," Lonnie said. "And I assure you that if you follow our plan, our diet will cleanse your body, and our program will release your mind."

"That's what I need."

Kim put her head down while the remaining three people shared their stories. Afterward, Lonnie discussed the schedules and rules.

When they finished, Lonnie led the group to the spiritual centering chamber, a tastefully decorated room with a padded floor. They sat cross-legged, silently focusing their thoughts for 15 minutes. Next, Lonnie led them to a dining room with long wood tables for their first "detoxification reawakening" meal. It consisted of a lemon-cayenne-pepper maple tree sap drink and a kale, chia seed, cinnamon smoothie. Kim took a small sip of the lemon drink and did not appreciate the harsh, acidic taste. She quickly finished her liquid meal without complaints, but would have preferred pancakes and orange juice.

Lonnie discouraged conversation, which upset Kim as she enjoyed being social. As the others ate, she considered swimming, but the prospect of reading people's minds as they consumed awful-tasting food was unappealing. After careful consideration, Kim decided not to swim until her detoxification was complete.

Thirty minutes later, Lonnie led the group outside, where they sat facing outwards in a "mental detoxification circle" for 45 minutes. Lonnie stood in the center and explained that this exercise would "make the toxins understand they are unwelcome." Kim considered this statement to be wishful thinking. Afterward, they began a stretch walk, taking a long step, stopping, and taking another long step. Their walk routine continued with different stretch types mixed with rhythmic clapping.

By noon, Kim's stomach noticeably grumbled. Plus, she had a headache and leg cramps. They had a larger portion of the same lemon drink, an arugula-sesame smoothie, and a rainbow salad with milk-thistle dressing for lunch. Kim silently compared her salad to eating weeds drenched in weed killer.

After their meal, Lonnie encouraged the group to do a side-step walk with stretches. Then, promptly at 2:00 p.m., he led the group to the spiritual chamber for an intense yoga session. Kim had not practiced yoga for weeks, and her muscles were stiff, but she still stretched better than most of her students.

During this session, Kim realized the man behind her went far out of his way to stare. She wanted to confront him after the session, but instead, she maintained a peaceful outlook.

Ten minutes later, Lonnie led the group through cool-down moves, and each took a "private nature egress," a two-hour silent desert hike. They were to consume two quarts of harsh-tasting alkaline water during the journey. Afterward, Lonnie asked the group to sit silently and "allow the minerals to cancel out the negative spirits that hamper their souls." Kim again thought this request was more wishful thinking.

They consumed the same lemon drink for dinner, a "Russian beet" smoothie, and a "crunchy detox salad." Kim loathed the meal and ate it with a forced smile. Her headaches were more intense, and she now experienced deep stomach cramps. Afterward, the members went to their cabins for an hour of personal time before returning to the spiritual centering chamber.

Lonnie then explained how all these "superfoods" would remove the "deadly toxins" deep within their cells. However, to accomplish this task, their bodies would need time to adapt to their new "peaceful digestive coexistence." He further explained their bodies were "being reset to factory defaults."

At this point in the lecture, Kim tuned Lonnie out and wondered if she had made a gigantic mistake. She had hoped her experience would match the website description of solitude, focused yoga sessions, good-tasting food, and thought-provoking desert walks. Instead, detoxification had become a significant distraction from her self-confrontation.

An hour later, Lonnie instructed the group to return to their cabins and use their meditation area to visualize "the toxins disappearing into the winds of nothingness." Kim felt relieved to be alone and began to focus intensely, appreciating the silence.

Twenty minutes later, somebody softly knocked at her door. The interruption angered Kim. She opened the door, and the man who'd stared at her in the yoga chamber greeted her with a confident grin. He had dressed in a thick plaid jacket zippered halfway open, revealing his bare, muscular chest. The image reminded Kim of the Brawny paper towels advertisement.

The man began in a powerful voice, "My name is Corey Payne. Are you getting as much out of this retreat as I am? It's so invigorating."

Corey smiled and waited for Kim to respond. The interruption still upset her, and she considered slamming the door. After a moment, Kim replied flatly, "It's not what I expected, but I'm going to make it work."

"Well, if there is anything I can help with, I'm in cabin two. That's three down to your left," Corey said with a wink.

"I understand."

"Be seeing you."

Corey nodded and turned to walk away. "Wait," Kim said.

Corey turned around with a surprised expression and excitedly answered, "Yes?"

"This has to stop."

"What?" Corey asked with an innocent expression.

"I'm married. This needs to end. Right here, right now!"

"Oh. You must have gotten the wrong signal. I'm only trying to welcome you."

"You mentally undressed me in class, and now you come here looking like a mountain man? I'm telling you now. No matter what, it will never work between us."

"Now, just wait a minute. No, you have the wrong idea. I'm only trying to be a good neighbor. Everything is fine."

"Everything isn't fine, and I know what's on your mind. Stop hitting on me."

"Oh. I'm sorry you feel that way, but I assure you I'm not making any advances."

Corey grinned, and Kim wanted to curse at him, but her thoughts turned to a disillusioned fellow student. "You know, Ashley keeps checking you out," Kim said with a wink.

"Who?" Corey asked with excitement.

"She's the one who wore that tight pink top. I bet you'll have better luck with her."

"Really?"

"Yup," Kim confidently answered.

"Oh. I'm sorry for bothering you. See you later."

Corey briskly walked away, and Kim thought about how her scheme would play out as she returned to meditating.

The following day, Kim settled into a routine that comprised unsatisfying food, yoga, short hikes, and detailed talks, which she ignored. Fortunately, meditation helped to confront her addictions and provided the mental clarity to reconstruct what occurred during her drunken blackouts. Unfortunately, the more Kim understood her past, the more upset she became.

The worst issue was the fact that Kim had been unfaithful to Gabe. She put this together because of rough sex injuries. The morning after Gabe returned, she had the foresight to purchase a pregnancy test. The negative results relieved her. However, she worried about sexually transmitted diseases but could not make a doctor's appointment in time for her trip.

Kim did not remember having sex, but the evidence was clear. She hoped there were no naked pictures of her on the internet, leading Gabe to discover her betrayal before she could speak to him about it. Kim hoped Gabe would forgive her, and there was one unethical bright spot that could help alleviate the situation. During their phone conversations, she vaguely recalled Gabe meeting a prostitute.

•

Lonnie knocked on Kim's cabin door after dinner on the fourth day. He brought a box of self-help, spiritual, addiction, and meditation books. "How are you fitting in?" Lonnie began.

"My body doesn't like the food, and I'm not getting much out of the whole group thing."

"What parts do you like?"

"I enjoy the solitary walks, yoga, and meditation. This place is a lifesaver."

"I see. Well, let's concentrate on those parts."

"That would be wonderful," Kim said with a big smile.

"I brought you these books."

"That's very nice of you."

Lonnie seemed uncomfortable, and he asked, "How are you dealing with your issues?"

"Well, it's been excruciating. I made many mistakes and don't know what to tell my husband."

"He seems like a great man."

"He's the best," Kim said, while thinking about disappointing him.

"Whatever you say, he'll understand."

"The only bright spot is that I've been making progress," Kim said with a weak smile.

"It's clear that you're on the right path."

"Thanks."

"There is one more subject I need to bring up."

"Corey?" Kim asked with raised eyebrows.

"I have asked Corey and Ashley to depart."

"I see."

"It seems they—"

"Hooked up." Kim completed Lonnie's sentence with a chuckle.

"This retreat isn't a dating service."

"I suspected as much from Corey, and Ashley looked bored out of her mind."

"Corey implied that you set the two of them up," Lonnie hinted.

"He was hitting on me. So, I told him that Ashley had been checking him out."

"Did she show any interest in him?"

"I caught her making eye contact."

"When did he speak to you?"

"He came to my door late on the first night."

"Late-night conversation is against our rules."

"I know," Kim said with a huff.

"You should've come to me first."

"You're right. I exercised poor judgment, and I'm sorry."

"No, your judgment proved spot-on. There had been three allegations in the past."

"Corey wasn't here for the meditation," Kim flatly said.

"I always suspected he had other intentions."

"He told me he came here often."

"Too often."

"Now what?" Kim asked.

"Let's change your routine. How about taking solitary hikes in the morning, yoga in the afternoon, and meditating until dinner? As for the meals? Not everyone is compatible with our strict diet, so let's add basic carbohydrates to your meal plan. Additionally, I will demonstrate my intense concentration technique. It will help you focus on a single topic."

"I'd like that."

Kim ate an "augmented" breakfast the following day, consisting of a thin slice of bran toast. Her meal tasted heavenly, and she noticed the others looking at her with extreme envy. Afterward, Lonnie provided Kim with a small backpack, a jug of strong alkaline water, and a "liquid lunch."

The morning air smelled crisp, and Kim appreciated the solitude of hiking. She often stopped to admire the stark desert beauty and reflect on her surroundings. Then, she drank her chalky lunch when her body told her it felt hungry.

Kim settled into a new routine of hiking, yoga, and meditation. She also read Lonnie's books and thought about her life and choices. While Kim did not reach any earth-shattering conclusions, the retreat provided the right atmosphere to regain focus.

By day 24, Kim felt the detoxification was complete, and her mind was centered. While she had not put all the pieces together, she had the right plan to move forward. That evening, Kim asked Lonnie, "Would you buy a tent and a backpack for me?"

"A tent?"

"I looked at a map, and the airport is a two-day walk from here."

"You want to spend the night in the desert? All alone? That's not a good idea."

"My body is telling me to do this," Kim answered.

"I've got some old camping equipment you can have."

"Wow, that would be great. Thank you so much."

"It sounds like you found the answers you were looking for," Lonnie said with a smile.

"Some of them."

"Good."

Kim packed, said goodbye, and began her solitary journey the following day. She enjoyed the wind, sun, and freedom of blazing a new trail through the desert.

During her trip, Kim sat in the limited shade, admiring the stark landscape, pondering her existence, touching plants, throwing rocks, and talking to the wind. That evening, she set up the tent and made a small fire from the nearby brush. It had been a wonderful day, and Kim appreciated the total immersion in the desert landscape. She fell asleep gazing at the stars, her thoughts drifting to her recent choices.

The following day, Kim woke early, drank breakfast, and continued hiking. At 12:40 p.m., she saw civilization and ate her "kale infusion" lunch. Three hours later, she walked through a Tempe suburb and asked for directions to the airport. It took four hours to arrive at the ticket counter and check her backpack. Before boarding, Kim ate a tasty steak with an extra serving of french fries and coleslaw.

# EIGHT

Gabe planned to work at KimSemi with Emma in the mornings and spend the afternoons at Harrington Enterprises. When he arrived, he was relieved to see that his team had performed well in his absence. Gabe quickly reconnected with his staff and spent the rest of the morning in meetings. Emma quietly sat in her car seat while intensely observing the office activity.

After lunch, Gabe drove to Harrington Enterprises, and Ellen explained the business plans for the next six months. This included a takeover strategy for the dry-cleaning chain Elite Cleaners in Jacksonville, Florida.

Gabe studied the plans and saw that the first phase began with the opening of two dry cleaners in Jacksonville, accompanied by a well-crafted marketing campaign. They intended to convince the Elite Cleaners owners that their prices were too high. Ellen projected bankruptcy in seven months, and Harrington Enterprises would buy Elite Cleaners at seventy-five percent below its actual value.

After studying the plan, he walked to Ellen's office and said, "This is impressive work."

"Thanks."

"There is only one word to describe this. Savage!"

Ellen became embarrassed and asked, "You liked it?"

"Your work is beyond excellent, and I have much to learn."

"Kim came up with ninety percent of this strategy. I only filled in the blanks."

"Well, either way, this plan is something to be proud of. So, what can I do to help?"

Dan walked by and answered, “We need approval for several large equipment purchase orders. Normally, Kim has the final say.”

“I’ll look them over. Anything else?”

“Kim asked me to look into taking over two operations in Brunswick and Tifton,” Ellen answered. “We need a decision this week.”

“Do you have enough data to make a guess?” Gabe asked.

“Kim needs to make this call.”

“Do you have enough new locations to open?”

“Oh my, yes. We have at least forty.”

“Do you know what Kim wanted you to concentrate on?”

“Yes.”

“Let’s hold off on new takeover plans. Kim is the expert, and I don’t want to second-guess her.”

“I’m relieved to hear that. I am also glad that Kim is taking care of her– um, problem.”

“Yeah, about that. I should have returned sooner, but I didn’t know what was happening. The good news is that she’s a strong woman who can tackle any problem life throws at her. Now, let’s look at those purchase orders.”

•

That night, Anna prepared beef stroganoff for Gabe and homemade creamed carrots with peas for Emma. Afterward, Gabe watched television while Emma browsed videos on her iPad. He liked how well she operated the device and asked, “Did Mommy select this video for you?”

“I wanted to learn about tigers. I choose video,” Emma answered with pride.

“Would you show me a video about making applesauce?”

“Yes, Daddy Gabe.”

Emma worked on her iPad as Gabe watched her use an intuitive visual search and rapidly locate an educational video. “This is how make applesauce,” Emma proclaimed. “Why you not know?”

“I wanted to see if you could find out for yourself.”

“Are you happy I find video?”

“Yes, Emma. I’m very proud.”

Emma beamed an enormous smile, and together, they watched the video.

•

For the rest of the week, Gabe split his duties between KimSemi and Harrington Enterprises. During this time, Emma behaved admirably and was content to observe the business activities. She asked an intuitive financial question in one meeting, and Ellen spent five minutes explaining the answer.

On Saturday, Gabe attended yoga while Emma silently watched. Ten minutes into their routine, she got out of her car seat and mimicked the moves. Several people applauded and encouraged her participation.

As Gabe became comfortable, he began using the white box. To his dismay, every member had rudimentary telepathic ability. Rachelle was the strongest, and he applied significant force to deprogram her. Unfortunately, this effort left Gabe exhausted, and she complained of a terrible headache, which made him feel guilty.

On Sunday, Gabe unexpectedly slept in late and woke to Emma staring at him. "Can we go in pool, Daddy Gabe?" she asked.

"Of course, sweetie."

Their house had a hot tub in the backyard, and Gabe pulled off the cover after breakfast. Then, he carefully lowered Emma's legs into the warm water and placed her on the top step. When Emma became comfortable, Gabe got in and playfully splashed her. He considered turning on the bubble jets but feared the churning water would be too scary.

Five minutes later, Emma suddenly slid in. Gabe lunged to grab her, but to his surprise, Emma moved her arms to maintain her head above the water. She experimented with different movements and soon was swimming. After three short laps, she returned to the step with a big smile. "Where did you learn how to swim?" Gabe asked. "Did Mommy help you?"

"I watch video, Daddy Gabe. It look easy."

"Oh, wow. You did great."

"Thank you, Daddy Gabe," Emma said with a big smile.

"I'm very proud of you."

"I know."

Gabe laughed, and Emma smiled even wider.

•

On Saturday, Gabe attended his second yoga class. Rachelle told everybody she'd had severe headaches all week and only recently recovered. During their warm-up, Gabe used the white box to enter Rachelle's mind. Rachelle had regained nearly all her previous ability, to his great surprise. This had never happened before, and Gabe deprogrammed her again.

When the class ended, Rachelle complained of another headache. "This is so strange," she commented while massaging her temples. "I never get headaches. Fortunately, my husband, Allen, can help."

"What type of doctor is he?" Gabe wondered.

"Oh, you haven't been attending classes recently. He's a telepath, and fixed my headache with his mind."

The information flabbergasted Gabe, and he stammered, "Um, what— what?"

"He's president of the Miramar Telepathy Club. You should drop by. Many yoga students will be there."

"Um, what do they do?" a dumbfounded Gabe asked.

"We practice telepathy."

"What's that all about?"

"All of us yoga people seemed to know how to communicate with our minds, and we made a club out of it."

Gabe still could not believe his ears and tried to maintain a normal appearance as he asked, "What do they do in the club?"

"We send each other messages and do other fun activities. Want to join?"

"Um. Sure. Sounds like fun."

After obtaining the club's time and address, Gabe drove home quickly and tucked Emma into bed early. He immediately called Jason. "I have some bad news. There is a telepathy club with people from the yoga class."

"I knew this would happen. I knew it!"

"I got permission to attend their next meeting. I'm going to send a report to Donna."

"I need that info ASAP!" Jason demanded.

"You'll have it."

"Now, do you understand my concern?"

"I see your point."

"This mental stuff spreads like wildfire. Get a handle on this! Do whatever you need to do! Understand? This is your absolute top priority."

"I get it."

"Do you need Kim's help?" Jason asked.

"She's still in rehab. I don't know how long she'll be there."

"Unfortunately, the place has no phone lines, but the lead peacenik is a guy named Lonnie. He has a flower-child wife, and I have her cell phone number."

"Good to know. But she needs to deal with her problems."

"We will play it your way. But one more thing," Jason said, his voice tinged with anger.

"You need this done fast; failure is not an option."

"We're starting to communicate."

"I'm doing my best."

"Noted and appreciated."

The call abruptly ended.

•

On Sunday evening, Gabe and Emma drove to their local YMCA. He carried Emma in her car seat to a large meeting room with several folding chairs. Approximately 25 people were standing and talking. At 8:10, Allen began, "Great turnout. Hey! I see new faces out there. Welcome, newcomers. Now, we don't want to go over the two-hour mark, so let's hit it. Last week, we used our minds to find out what song the other person was listening to. That exercise went extremely well, but since we have so many newbies, let's keep today's exercise simple. Each paper bag contains something inside. Please take one, pair up, and mentally communicate what's in the bag. I'll be around to help. Sound good?"

Gabe looked around the room in stunned disbelief. A woman beside him walked to the table, grabbed a bag, and asked pleasantly, "Are you new?"

Gabe turned to her and answered in a confused voice, "Um. Well, this is my first time. I'm in a yoga class, and this fellow student, Rachelle, suggested I drop by."

"Most telepaths started in that class. I'm Jamie."

"I'm Gabe, and this little one is Emma."

"You're Kim's husband?" Jamie shrieked. "Right?"

"Yes."

"Oh, she's such an amazing woman. Mega-smart. I used to take yoga with her, but my schedule changed, and now I go to the Monday class."

Gabe did his best to speak normally while trying to contain his disbelief. "Um, how do we do this?"

"Simple. I'll look into the bag and see what Allen put in. Here's what I want you to do. Close your eyes and relax. Try your best to clear your mind. When I sense your clarity, I will enter your mind. Hopefully, you will get a mental picture. Then, let me know what you think it is. That's all there is to this. Alright?"

Gabe nodded. Jamie looked into her bag, and when she looked up, he could not believe her vivid thoughts. "A red toy truck," he blurted out.

"Wow!" Jamie shrieked. "That's amazing. You're a natural. That is the best anybody has ever done on their first try!"

Three nearby members clapped, and Gabe raised his hand in a gesture of thanks. Inside, he was angry for letting himself get caught up in the moment. When the clapping ended, Gabe said, "That went super-well. I will get a different bag and see if I can communicate with you."

Gabe exchanged bags, sat, and looked inside to see a plastic banana. He then turned to Jamie and began using the white box to explore the people in the room. It shocked Gabe to be near so many telepaths.

After several intentionally unsuccessful attempts at telepathy with Jamie, Gabe switched partners. Emma sat in her car seat, a curious smile on her face, during this time. When Gabe looked at her, she waved at him.

The meeting concluded with everybody congratulating Gabe on his success. In the parking lot, he called Jason. "I have some bad news. These people have super-abilities."

"Damn it!" Jason yelled. "Can you remove that telepathic junk from their minds?"

"I think so. But it will take time. Hey, did anybody from your team attend?"

"No. Why?"

"Two men seemed out of place. One had a brown crew cut, and the other had a black crew cut. Their thoughts felt like they were on a mission or something."

"We will review the surveillance photos," Jason growled. "Donna will provide you with a complete profile of every person who attended. This operation is my department's top priority. Get this under control!"

"Got it."

The call ended, and Gabe looked around for people taking pictures.

•

The following day, Gabe and Emma were enjoying breakfast when the doorbell rang. He looked through the peephole to see the same two men from the previous evening. Gabe opened the door, and the brown-haired man began, "What the hell were you doing at our training site?"

"What?"

"We saw you last night."

"And?"

"This is a classified operation, and we will arrest you if you ever attend another class!"

"What?" Gabe asked in shock.

"You heard me, bub. We will arrest your ass. Got it?" the brown-haired man threatened and poked Gabe in the chest with his left pointer finger.

"Hey! Not cool." Gabe protested. "Wait, a minute. You can't go around jamming your finger into me. Besides, this is a free country, and I can attend any darn meeting I want. Who the heck are you?"

"None of your concern!" the brown-haired man countered.

"You're on my property. It is my concern."

"No, it isn't!"

Gabe entered the brown-haired man's mind and felt his tremendous drive to succeed. "You don't know what's going on, do you?" he challenged.

"We know what's going on, bub. Stay away from our operation!" the brown-haired man threatened.

The three stared at each other, and Gabe took a deep breath to calm down. Then Emma walked over to them, and he was unsure how she had managed to get out of her highchair. Gabe refocused on the conversation and spoke in a forced, pleasant tone, "Wait. Let's start over. I bet we're on the same team. What department are you in?"

"Stay out of our way or get arrested! Got that, bub?" the man with brown hair again threatened.

"On what charges?"

"Oh, there'll be no charges. We will throw you in a hole so deep that you'll never see the light of day."

"You can't do that! I have rights," Gabe protested.

"We can do whatever we want."

"I cannot believe this!" Gabe yelled and threw up his hands. "This is America. You cannot arrest me without charges."

As the two men stared daggers at Gabe, he remembered how his former wife, Lydia, confidently handled an unpleasant situation with a cruise ship administrator. He adopted a crafty smile and took out his phone.

"What are you doing?" the black-haired man demanded.

"Just a sec. Everything's going to be fine."

Gabe snapped a picture of the two men.

"Give me that damn phone!" the black-haired man ordered. He reached out, and Gabe handed him the phone. The black-haired man looked at the phone and asked angrily, "Who's this Jason guy you texted our picture to? You are under arrest, bub. Turn around."

The brown-haired man took handcuffs out of his back pocket and motioned. Gabe took a step back and smirked. The brown-haired man became unsure and asked, "Why are you looking at me like that? You're about to go to jail and—"

Gabe's phone ringing interrupted the conversation, and he said, "You need to answer this."

"Turn around!" the brown-haired man demanded.

Emma murmured, "Mmm." Gabe briefly looked down at her. Then, he turned back to the men and said, "You don't know who I am."

"We know who you are and everything about you. Gabriel Alexander. The Kuiu Island screw-up. You invented the whole crucible theory!"

"I'm a little more complex. Please answer the phone. Jason's not the type of person you want to disappoint."

"No!"

"How about I put it on speaker, and we can all listen," Gabe suggested.

The black-haired man considered the idea and realized he might be able to learn the caller's identity. So he pressed the answer icon and was about to speak when Jason's voice boomed, "Am I speaking to Lieutenant Martin Francis Tiller or Captain Pete Lucas Jefferson?"

The two men became befuddled, and the brown-haired man answered unsurely, "Um, Pete here."

"Take me off speaker. Now!"

The two men looked at each other, and Gabe suggested, "It's a good idea to follow his instructions."

Captain Jefferson pressed the icon and held the phone up to his ear. "Gabe cannot hear me. Identify yourself! This call is being recorded."

Gabe wondered if the call was actually being recorded as he watched Captain Jefferson listen. His expression changed from arrogant to concerned to unsure. "No way, Jason!" he yelled. "If that's your actual name. I don't believe you! Nobody can set that up so fast."

There was a loud thump from behind, followed by a distant boom. Instinctively, Gabe kneeled to protect Emma, realizing that somebody had shot into his house. "That better not have come from you!" Captain Jefferson yelled. "Because if it did, you just signed your death warrant!"

Captain Jefferson listened and then looked to his left. Gabe looked in the same direction to see a white SUV parked three blocks away in the middle of the street. A person was behind a large rifle on a bipod perched on the hood. Captain Jefferson turned to Lieutenant Tiller in horror and yelled, "Alright, alright! We'll play it your way. But I'm warning you. This will not end well. *That! I! Guarantee!*"

Captain Jefferson ended the call. As Gabe stood, Jefferson threw the phone at him, and he caught it. For the next few seconds, Captain

Jefferson glared daggers at Gabe, and then, a beige town car came to a screeching stop. The driver wore a gray hoodie and oversized sunglasses to obscure their features. Both men looked at each other and got into the back seat. The driver briefly turned to Gabe, then rapidly drove off, followed by the white SUV.

When they turned the corner, Gabe turned to inspect the bullet hole in his house and texted Jason. "Everything good?"

"Yes."

"What is going on?"

Jason did not text a reply.

•

Gabe and Emma went to work the following day, and afterward, he repaired the bullet hole in the wall. Later in the evening, the pair briefly discussed attending school, but the thought of being separated brought tears to Emma's eyes.

Six days later, Kim texted Gabe her flight information, and he looked forward to seeing his beloved wife. During the flight, she thought about exactly how to discuss her affair and hoped Gabe would eventually forgive her.

Kim became more apprehensive as the plane descended into Miami International Airport. Finally, at the passenger pickup, she spotted the black Escalade with Gabe enthusiastically waving. Kim sat in the front passenger seat and tried not to cry. "Hi," she whispered.

"Emma and I missed you, babe," Gabe said with a smile and kissed Kim.

"Mommy Kim. Mommy Kim. You back!" Emma added.

"I missed you so much."

"You better, Mommy Kim?"

"Yes, Emma."

"No yucky-smelly drink?"

"I'm done with that. Let's go."

"Sounds good, babe," Gabe said with a big smile.

On the drive home, Gabe sensed profound shame within Kim but understood it was not the time to swim. Emma also felt an issue and asked, "Why Mommy Kim sad?"

Gabe looked at Kim and answered, "Mommy made a mistake, and she's sorry. Right now, we need to help Mommy feel better."

"I understand, Daddy Gabe."

"I love you, Emma," Kim said, covering her face and silently weeping.

At home, Kim hugged Emma for a long time before tucking her into bed. Then she walked downstairs and sat on the sofa. Gabe motioned to Kim's feet and began massaging. She tried hard not to cry, but his loving gesture nearly pushed her over the edge. A few minutes later, Gabe said, "Emma likes to call us 'Mommy Kim' and 'Daddy Gabe.' I don't know where that came from."

Kim felt relieved that the conversation had started in a different direction. "Our daughter is growing up fast," she said with relief.

"Everybody in the yoga class cannot believe she can walk. One is a pediatric doctor, and she told me that Emma is at least two years ahead of the curve. Of course, she gets that from her astounding mother."

Kim weakly laughed and said, "No arguments here."

Gabe continued the distraction. "Do you remember the first time I gave you a foot massage?"

"You tried so hard to make me feel comfortable."

"Remember that crazy frog painting in that one house?"

"It looked so tacky," Kim answered with a chuckle.

"We were going through a lot."

"Sometimes, I cannot believe we survived," Kim said in a distant voice.

"We had a tough time."

"But we got through it— together."

"Are you ready to talk about all of this?" Gabe asked.

"I guess."

"Do you want to swim?"

"No, we agreed important topics required verbal communication and clear heads."

"Just making sure," Gabe said as he began working her ankles. "We should talk about what happened in Alaska and the yoga class. Also, I have some amazing news. You won't believe it."

"My problem has to come first," Kim admitted.

"Take your time."

Kim took a long breath and spoke with tear-filled eyes, "I—" She stuttered, looked away, and continued. "I drank, and I drank, and I drank— all day and all night. There's so much I don't remember. I acted so selfishly. Selfish to you. Selfish to Emma. Even selfish to myself." Kim stood and tightly hugged Gabe. "I— am so sorry, hon," she said between sobs.

"It's alright," Gabe said, tears in his eyes. "The important thing is you're here."

"But—" Kim began and then stopped herself.

"Babe, I love you, and Emma loves you. That's all that matters."

“I made so many mistakes,” Kim admitted.

“We both forgive you.”

“That doesn’t make it right. The worst is that I didn’t protect Emma. She could have... All those crazy people could have—” Kim cried harder, and Gabe went from weeping to crying.

A long while later, Gabe moved to face Kim. Looking deep into her brown, tear-filled eyes, he said, “Neither you nor I can change what happened. And you’re right. Emma could have gotten hurt. But we got lucky. Emma is safe, and that’s the only thing that matters. Do you understand?”

Kim nodded, and Gabe continued. “Good. Now, let’s celebrate with a tall glass of champagne.”

“You are getting better at messing with me,” Kim admitted with a weak smile.

“Babe, you’re the strongest woman I’ve ever met, and I know we can put all this in our past. Tomorrow’s a new day. Right?”

Kim sat next to Gabe and gripped his hand without looking at him. He did not understand why her mood had suddenly changed. Kim worked up her courage and said in a sobbing whisper, “When you were gone, I had sex.”

Gabe felt like somebody had punched him in the gut, and he stared forward in stunned disbelief. Eventually, Kim continued. “I don’t remember what happened. I think it was Brent. He’s the guy who coordinates our deliveries. I only remember dropping off some booze at his place. I must’ve blanked out the rest.”

Kim looked at Gabe, and he took several deep breaths. A long moment later, he nodded, took another deep breath, and let it out slowly. “Hon, I take full responsibility for everything,” she continued. “This isn’t your fault, and I want you to know that this guy didn’t fill some part of my life that you cannot. You’re the only man I ever want to be with, and you’ll always be that man. No matter what happens.”

Eventually, Gabe turned to look at Kim in tears. She put her arm around him, and he moved her arm away without making eye contact. Kim clutched her chest, feeling her heartache physically as waves of painful emotions crashed over her. The room felt suffocating, as if the air had suddenly turned to lead. Finally, Gabe mustered up all his courage and choked out, “Thank you for being honest. Take the bed, and I’ll sleep on the sofa.”

Gabe stood and walked upstairs. A short while later, he returned dressed in pajamas with a pillow and blanket. Gabe looked at Kim and pointed to the stairs. “Hon,” she said in between sobs.

Gabe scowled, and Kim mentally experienced his profound disappointment. Reluctantly, she walked up the stairs, and at the top, she turned to see that Gabe was intentionally facing away. Kim walked into their bedroom and sat on the corner of the bed.

Gabe tried lying on the sofa, but it was too short. He considered exchanging locations with Kim but wanted no more contact. So, he put the blanket on the floor.

Gabe's thoughts were overwhelming. *How could Kim do this? She told me she loved me, and I did everything she asked. What did I do to deserve this? How can I abandon the woman I promised to spend the rest of my life with? Why did she cheat on me? Why Brent? I know that jerk. He opens stupid packages. What does he have that I don't? Why'd she do it? Why?*

It suddenly dawned on Gabe that their relationship had come to an end. This revelation made him cry, and he grabbed a nearby cushion to muffle the noise. It was ineffective, and not wanting to disturb Emma, he ran into the garage, climbed into the Escalade's driver's seat, and cried his eyes out.

The disheartening moment reminded Gabe of losing his first wife and daughters, further spiraling him out of control. As his sorrow deepened, he saw mucus all over his pajamas. Frustrated, Gabe exited the car and grabbed a dirty towel he used to clean the lawnmower.

As Gabe wallowed, his thoughts turned to Emma being raised by divorced parents. *This is not fair to her. This is the worst thing ever. This is all my fault. I should've been a better lover. Then Kim would not have had to fall into another man's arms.* His crying became uncontrollable as he changed focus from one disheartening thought to another.

•

Kim continued to weep as she dressed for bed. She wanted to shower, but the thought of "cleaning away the shame" depressed her. As she lay down, she went over her admission and felt awful for hurting the man she loved. The only bright spot came from understanding their conversation could have been worse.

As Kim sobbed and stared at the ceiling, she began hearing a strange noise and realized Gabe must also be crying. She wanted to help but knew he needed to face his issues in solitude.

This realization further saddened her, and her sobs turned into crying. It soon occurred to her she had not cried this hard since losing her family, which furthered her sorrow.

A long while later, Kim's eyes and nose hurt. Finally, her body could no longer maintain the emotional outpouring, and she stopped crying in exhaustion. Kim rested while sniffling, understanding that the following day would be long and painful.

•

Gabe had also cried until his body could take no more. His head ached, and his eyes stung. Gabe began taking deep breaths in between large sniffles. This movement helped relieve some of his symptoms.

Gabe's thoughts turned to their future, and he decided that raising Emma to the best of his ability would be his top priority. Now that he had a plan, he felt better. When he had caught his breath, he exited the car and lay on the floor in front of the sofa.

By 4:20 a.m., Gabe's back hurt from the hard floor, and he decided to sleep in the master bedroom. His logic was that the following day would be dreadful, and he needed rest to get through it.

Gabe trudged upstairs and entered the bedroom. As he got under the covers with his back to Kim, he tried to put her out of his thoughts. Kim saw Gabe's red nose and tear-filled eyes in the dim light. She also noticed smudges on his hands and face. Kim wondered where the dirt had come from.

Several minutes later, Kim whispered, "Did you have trouble sleeping on the couch?" Gabe did not answer, and she asked, "Does your back hurt?"

Understanding Gabe was refusing to speak, Kim said, "Let's act civilized. Even without swimming, I know your back hurts. So, roll over, and I will work out the tension. Tomorrow will be a terrible day, and you need rest."

Gabe thought for a long moment before rolling over. She straddled him, slid his pajamas up, and began working his lower back. Kim immediately felt Gabe's tight muscles as she applied firm pressure.

It now dawned on Gabe that sleeping bags were in the garage, and there were more blankets in the closet. He then could not believe he had not thought about their guest bedroom. Gabe let out a deep sigh and tried to relax amid his troubled thoughts. *Kim is correct. Tomorrow will be one of the worst days of my life. I need to break my daughter's heart.* Gabe now used all his effort not to cry.

Suddenly, Gabe realized a drop of water hit his back. It took a moment to understand that the water was Kim's tear. In retrospect, he understood this would be the last time they would spend the night together. This thought further spiraled his depression, and he tried to be positive. *Let's go to marriage counseling. It could work. After all, Hillary Clinton forgave Bill. Right?* Another tear hit Gabe's back, and his hopes crashed. *How could Kim betray me?* He now wished Kim would stop.

•

Kim had absently put in great physical effort as her thoughts swirled. She also realized this would be their last night together, and Emma would blame her for the breakup. Then, to Kim's horror, a falling tear hit Gabe square in the back. She considered wiping it away, but stopped herself. Kim no longer wanted to suppress her feelings and hoped Gabe would appreciate her final positive effort.

Ten minutes later, Kim's wrists hurt, and she realized the moment had passed. She put her hands on her hips and took comfort in knowing that Gabe would also make Emma his highest priority. Kim hoped they could remain civilized during their separation and that their friendship might return.

The sun was rising, and Kim looked at the clock. It read 5:16 a.m. As she turned to look around their bedroom, she realized Gabe had rearranged the furniture and cleaned. Kim yawned, stretched, and then moved off Gabe to get under the covers. Then, something caught her attention.

"Aw, crap!" Kim yelled.

Gabe had finally allowed himself to relax enough to tolerate Kim's presence. However, her outburst upset him, and he suppressed an angry remark. Kim stood, went to the dresser, and returned holding her brother's basketball trophy. Gabe rolled over and looked at the filthy object. The sight enraged him, and he was about to yell, "I did my best to keep the house clean!"

"Hon, I didn't sleep with anybody," she admitted, then exhaled a long, angry breath. "We both should have realized that."

"What?"

Kim looked away, grunted, and said, "When you were away, I was lonely. Well, you see— um, one night, I was drunk out of my mind, and... And, well, I—"

"You used the trophy to get yourself off," Gabe completed her thought.

"I did."

"Kim!" Gabe yelled. "Those are sharp edges! You could've cut yourself and bled to death. You acted irresponsibly. Think of Emma not having a mother. And think of her telling her friends how you died. You should've known better!"

"Hon, I was blitzed out of my mind. And then, when I sobered up, I came to the wrong conclusion. I'm sorry."

Gabe tried to put all the pieces together. "So, Brent?" he asked.

"I remember nothing about Brent other than dropping off a load of booze."

"Does this mean we're all good?"

"It does, my love," Kim warmly said.

It took Gabe a long moment to understand the significance of Kim's words. Then, finally, he reached his arms out. She threw the trophy onto the floor, and they hugged tightly. A long while later, Gabe said in great relief, "I handled this situation poorly. It took real courage to be honest, and I should have been more supportive."

"Hon, don't ruin this moment. Everything rests on me. You have never failed to support me. Don't forget that. Let's enjoy the hug and not talk about what *you* did."

Gabe did his best to chuckle while they continued to embrace. Then, a long while later, Kim asked, "Hon?"

"Yes, babe."

"What's going on?"

"This evening was excruciating," Gabe admitted.

"There is more to it, I can tell. Please talk to me."

"Babe, you broke my heart."

"More. Let me know what you're thinking. I felt the pain. No swimming."

Gabe thought it over, sighed, and admitted, "When we started our relationship, it took a long time to trust you. I mean, you're so over-the-top attractive. I was sure that one day, some guy would hit on you, and you would run off with him. So, it took a lot of effort to push past my insecurity."

"How'd you overcome it?" Kim asked.

"One day, I just decided to blindly trust you. Honestly, it took an entire week to let everything go. And then last night... Well, everything came crashing down."

"I messed up," Kim admitted. "Sorry."

"It's alright."

The pair continued to hug, and several minutes later, Kim pulled away, looked at Gabe for a long moment, and said, "The fact is, I'm fully committed to you. Nothing will ever change my devotion. But you're correct. I destroyed your trust, and only you can rebuild it. Gabe, honey, you still have confidence issues. But I've come up with a plan.

"So here it is. Since we started living together, I have been the one who initiates sex. You love it so much when I jump you. It excites me to see how happy I can make you. And, of course, I enjoy feeling you inside me. But that's the past.

"From now on, if you want some nookie, you've got to ask for it. And, I warn you. I will act all moody, say no, and ignore you. Now, I know this will be a painful reminder of your ex-wife. She treated you like a homeless beggar when you wanted attention. But, through it all, I want you to know that I sincerely love you. Together, we'll mend our bridges and build your confidence. Sound good, hon?"

Gabe did not understand why Kim had proposed this baffling idea, and he suspected she had come up with it before this evening. While he enjoyed Kim's sexual confidence, he did not think the challenge would be difficult. Gabe also knew swimming would reveal the best approach and agreed to the proposal while resting in her arms.

Emma pushed the door open as the pair fell asleep and asked, "Is Mommy Kim better?"

"Yes, Emma, we worked everything out," Gabe replied in a sleepy voice.

"You needed sex. That's all."

Emma walked away, and Kim said, "What the heck have you been teaching her?"

"That didn't come from me," Gabe exclaimed.

Kim laughed and said, "Hmm. We'll have to discuss that with her. Get some rest, and I'll feed Emma."

"No, you rest. You gave me a wonderful massage."

"Alright, hon. Wake me at eleven, and you nap in the afternoon."

Gabe kissed Kim, got out of bed, and began making breakfast while feeling deeply relieved that the issue was resolved.

# NINE

That evening, Gabe told Kim about his recent events, and she was astounded to learn that Emma would inherit a vast fortune. Kim insisted they fly to Alaska as soon as possible to meet Karen.

Gabe then revealed that while cleaning the house, he found six hidden stashes of drugs and alcohol. The worst one was in a secluded part of the attic where Kim's mother, Emelia, had used heroin. The news devastated Kim, and she walked around their neighborhood to clear her thoughts.

The following evening, Gabe and Kim used the white box to experiment with deprogramming. It was challenging for Kim to walk and use the white box simultaneously. He also showed Kim the brain analyzer section of the white box.

After the exhausting effort, they watched television while Gabe massaged Kim's feet. "I would like to be inside you later this evening," he asked warmly.

"I'm good," Kim tersely replied.

It was evident to Gabe that Kim wanted more than a basic request. Naturally, this rejection left him disappointed, but he continued the massage.

Kim went to work the following day, and Gabe took Emma to KimSemi. They both had productive weeks, and the family attended yoga on Saturday. The plan was for Gabe to start deprogramming the student and then for Kim to take over. Gabe hoped this "two-punch" approach would achieve rapid results.

Kim knew Rachelle would be the most difficult, and Gabe started with her. When it was Kim's turn, she pulled at Rachelle's fur-mow with all her might. The substantial deprogramming effort proved far more challenging than Kim had anticipated, and a minute later, she was unable to continue. While Gabe was exhausted, he took over, and at the end of the evening, Rachelle complained of a severe headache.

The two of them were so tired in the parking lot that they needed to rest before continuing their drive. Emma had been a model child all evening and had peacefully slept in her car seat.

Kim discussed their lack of success at home and was sure there was a better way to deprogram. She began using the white box to explore Gabe's fur-mow while he telepathically interacted with her. Kim gently tugged at parts of his mind to see what would happen. After an hour, it occurred to her that their overall deprogramming approach was flawed.

Kim visualized a fur-mow as "a plant with roots" and their programming concept as being analogous to grabbing an entire plant by the stem and pulling it out. The problem was that the broken roots would regrow into a new plant. Kim realized they needed to find each root and "pull it out and tie it up."

Gabe pointed out that this methodical approach would require more time, but Kim was sure it would be less painful and more permanent. She guided Gabe through this approach, and he said the tugging "felt like a lopsided itch."

They drove to the Miramar Telepathy Club on Sunday evening and left Emma with their housekeeper, Anna. This was the first time she had been separated from her parents, and she cried and cried.

The group welcomed Kim and began their training with the "Guess what letter I am thinking of" exercise. The large number of telepathic people surprised Kim, and she targeted a telepathically weaker individual.

Tim Hayes had only attended two meetings. His wife thought this would be a fun "date night activity." Kim entered Tim's mind, located his fur-mow, and began tugging. After some effort, the first "root" came out. She maneuvered it away and tied it up.

Ten minutes later, Kim had completed seven roots, and Gabe took over. He estimated that Kim had completed ten percent of the overall job and quickly learned that this surgical approach required greater concentration, making it challenging to interact with the telepathic group simultaneously.

After the meeting, the pair rested in their car, and Gabe said in a tired voice, "We tied off eighteen roots. But, at this rate, it will take years."

"I'm so tired right now. I don't want to swim for a month."

"There's no choice. We must do this more than once a week. Donna gave me everybody's address."

"Gahh," Kim gasped. "That sounds like a lot of work. Do you think Emma survived our absence?"

"She takes after you. I'm sure she'll be fine."

"If I could, I would thank you for the compliment," Kim said, touching Gabe's arm.

Thirty minutes later, Kim had recovered enough to drive. Gabe lay down in the back seat and napped. Anna met them at the door, holding Emma. She was crying and dramatically held her arms out. Kim moved Emma into her arms and hugged her. In between sobs, Emma said, "Never leave me, Mommy Kim!"

After Anna finished cleaning and left, the family sat on the couch. Gabe gently said, "Emma, you are at the age when a young girl must attend school. So, we had Anna watch you this evening to show you what being away from us is like."

"Never leave!" Emma demanded, and her sniffles returned to crying.

"It's alright," Kim said as she held her.

"Mommy Kim and Daddy Gabe need to be close," Emma said between sobs.

"How about this?" Gabe offered. "Let's bring a teacher to work. You two can be in a side room, and we'll be nearby. How does that sound?"

Emma thought for a moment and answered, "Daddy Gabe, never leave me!"

"What's the problem?" Kim probed.

"I don't like other people."

"Why?" Kim asked.

"They not use brain like Mommy Kim and Daddy Gabe."

"I don't understand."

Emma touched Kim's mind. Before that moment, Gabe and Kim had resisted direct mental interaction with Emma because they did not want to confuse her. Kim entered Emma's mind cautiously and could not believe how advanced her thoughts were. Kim motioned to Gabe, and he entered. The experience shocked him.

<See Daddy Gabe,> Emma thought with happiness. <Only you and Mommy Kim do brain tricks.>

<Wow, you have a powerful mind,> Gabe thought in disbelief.

<Thank you, Daddy Gabe.>

<Have you used your brain like this with anybody else?>

<No,> Emma answered cautiously, making Gabe suspect she was not telling the truth.

<Can you do anything else?>

Emma stood and walked over to Kim's purse. She retrieved the white box, looked at Gabe, and his arms began moving.

<Did you do that?> Kim asked Emma, while knowing the answer.

<I see Mommy Kim and Daddy Gabe use okey-okey and I want try.>

<What is okey-okey?>

<You call it "white box." Okey-okey call itself okey-okey.>

<When did you first use the okey-okey?> Kim asked with trepidation.

<I use for long time.>

<Emma, this is very important. You can only use the okey-okey when Daddy and I are with you. Do you understand?>

<I understand. Can I go to sleep? I'm tired.>

<That sounds good.>

They tucked Emma into bed. She fell asleep quickly, and Gabe and Kim went downstairs.

<I had no idea,> thought Kim.

<Neither did I. She's got advanced abilities. In a year, she'll surpass us.>

<That's a scary concept. What are we going to do about school?> Kim's thoughts were tinged with apprehension.

<It's clear that we cannot send her to school. Her emotions are too basic, and she could mess some kids up. Plus, Jason would flip out.>

<She needs to interact with other kids,> Kim thought.

<True, but we need to guide her mental ability. Hopefully, we can trust her enough to be on her own soon.>

<Agreed.>

<It must have been hard on her to use the white box for the first time. I wish I could have guided her.> Gabe's thoughts were sad.

<She's clearly advanced. It may not have been that hard.>

<Did it dawn on you that she might have been using the– what did she call it? The okey-okey? That she might have been using it better than us?>

<We don't know how much exposure she's had,> Kim thought, concerned.

<True. Hey, we've had a rough evening. Let's get some sleep, babe.>

<I felt that. No hanky-panky. You need to ask permission to jump me properly. More trust, more confidence, and less logic.>

<I'll try harder, my love,> Gabe thought warmly.

<It's not about trying. You need to be you.>

<I'll try.>

Kim playfully pushed Gabe to the side.

•

Before going to sleep, Gabe texted Jason about their deprogramming plan. The next day, the family settled into a strange routine. After dinner, they drove to an address and parked. Gabe and Kim took turns deprogramming while Emma read or rested in the back seat. It was apparent that she enjoyed being part of the action.

On the drive home, Gabe and Kim often discussed how the situation met the textbook definition of perversion. To make matters worse, they were poor role models for Emma.

Two weeks later, Gabe encountered a profoundly uncomfortable situation. The first mind he entered was that of a young boy using the bathroom. The incident profoundly embarrassed Gabe, and he insisted they drive away. On the way home, he refused to discuss the matter, while Kim reassured him that he was not a terrible person.

There were setbacks over the next three weeks, but they made progress. Emma had been behaving well, and for a first step in the separation effort, she agreed to spend an hour with Anna while Kim went shopping. Eventually, they convinced her to attend preschool, and she begrudgingly decided to try.

Kim explained to the principal that Emma had separation anxiety and that one of her parents needed to be nearby. Unfortunately, this "extreme parental oversight" was against school policy, but a large check bent the rules.

On a chilly Monday morning, Kim took Emma to class. The class welcomed a new student, who followed the teacher's instructions and took a seat. Kim observed her from a distance in a nearby room as she used her laptop to review sales figures.

Emma's pleasant behavior surprised the teacher, and she did not see any evidence of separation anxiety. After their morning playtime, the class stood in the "learning circle," and the teacher began counting to ten. Emma participated but quickly became bored. She walked over to a bookshelf, selected a book, and returned to the circle. The teacher politely said, "We're learning about counting. Not looking at pictures."

"I already know counting," Emma retorted. "Do you have a book with bigger words?"

The bold request shocked the teacher, and she handed Emma a copy of *Huckleberry Finn* to see what would happen. As the rest of the class counted, Emma read. "What is this word?" she asked a few minutes later.

The teacher came over and answered, “Mississippi.”

“I know how to say Mississippi. What does the word mean?”

“Mississippi is a state,” the teacher politely answered.

“Like Florida?”

“Yes, dear.”

“How do I learn words like this?”

The teacher walked to another room, returned with a dictionary, and showed Emma how to look up words in it. Emma was content to read while the rest of the class practiced counting.

At the end of the school day, Emma hugged Kim, and the teacher said, “Your child is quite gifted.”

“We know,” Kim answered with a proud grin.

“You misunderstand. She belongs in a special school for extremely bright students.”

Kim nodded and said, “Right now, it’s more important for her to learn to interact with other children.”

“There’s not much we can teach her.”

“I peeked in a few times. She was learning how to throw a ball and finger paint. Plus, she is making friends. Trust me. This is what she needs.”

“I still think she needs a different venue,” the teacher countered.

“For now, this is the right environment.”

•

Over the next three weeks, Emma became more comfortable attending preschool and made four friends. The family swam together in the evenings before going out to deprogram, which was the highlight of their day. As Emma’s skill improved, she wanted to swim in other people’s minds. Kim and Gabe strongly discouraged this behavior. To their surprise and relief, Emma grasped the logic behind their request.

The family also deeply explored many topics accessible in the white box. However, this led to issues, as Emma had access to vast knowledge, including non-Earth history, radical scientific principles, and more efficient mathematics. As a result, her behavior often raised eyebrows when speaking, especially when she correctly answered a math question using an unfamiliar but more efficient technique.

Kim instructed Emma to recognize a surprised reaction and say, “I’m kidding” to divert attention, which became her tagline, leaving her teacher bewildered.

As Emma's passive swimming ability improved, she began making inappropriate comments. For example, she yelled to the supermarket cashier, "Stop thinking about kissing Mommy!" The cashier quickly looked away, and the woman behind Kim chuckled.

In the parking lot, Kim admonished Emma, and while she apologized, it was clear to Kim that Emma was proud of her accusation.

Gabe and Kim's relationship recovered, but he could not figure out her sexual challenge. To Kim's annoyance, he approached this "multivariable problem" like an engineer. This effort included a well-defined problem statement, proposed tests, and detailed data capture.

From the analysis, Gabe learned Kim disliked crude language, sexy costumes, kinky suggestions, dominant behavior, mental tricks, or exotic locations. But, most of all, Kim hated Gabe's use of a spreadsheet to document their sex life.

Gabe also learned that Kim preferred general compliments over specific ones. For example, "You look nice" instead of "your legs look nice." Her biggest turn-on was good parenting skills, especially cleaning up Emma's messes and reading to her. This encouraged Gabe to read every night; to his delight, she enjoyed Tom Clancy spy novels.

Over time, Gabe understood that Kim's goal was to change his perception, but he could not figure out the central issue. Fortunately, he had a new resource.

During their nightly deprogramming, Gabe had a front-row seat in couples' minds during their romantic interactions. At first, this "bedroom spying" made Gabe deeply uncomfortable, and he patiently waited until the passion subsided. However, he eventually tolerated the behavior because he needed to make progress.

Gabe discovered men were often insulting, crude, or indifferent to their partners. He found it interesting that the men were unaware of their negative behavior and its adverse effects. As a result, Gabe became better at foreplay, compliments, and supportive gestures. In addition, Gabe learned Kim was a far better partner than the women he deprogrammed.

Kim also learned a lot about relationships during her deprogramming efforts. It saddened her to see how poorly men treated their partners. Kim also experienced the darker side of women and realized she had made identical mistakes. She was worried that her plan to help Gabe would do more damage than good.

Kim also appreciated how lucky she was to have married Gabe. None of the men she encountered had the same respect and passion.

•

Later in the week, the family endured another long deprogramming session, and Gabe napped upon their return home. Late in the evening, he woke to see Kim arranging the bathroom towels.

Gabe appreciated Kim's effort to make their house look nice, and he wanted to reward her, so he began massaging her shoulders as she worked. Swimming confirmed Kim's appreciation of the gesture.

Five minutes later, Kim turned around, and Gabe recognized a subtle hint that she was in the mood for sex for the first time. He almost kissed her, then realized he had tried this timid approach unsuccessfully. So, Gabe led her to the corner of the bed and motioned for her to sit.

Gabe moved a chair so he could face Kim. While gazing upon his loving wife with a warm smile, she looked at him inquisitively. Then, without breaking eye contact, he took off his shirt and placed his hands on her legs. Kim liked Gabe's bold confidence as he continued to look deep into her twinkling brown eyes.

Gabe moved closer, and they passionately kissed. Kim admired his manly appearance and began running her hands over his bare chest. When the moment felt right, he unbuttoned her pajama top without breaking eye contact and started caressing. Kim enjoyed being explored and touched his face with her left hand.

A few minutes later, Gabe stood, moved the bedcovers aside, and the pair fully undressed. Gabe got on top of Kim and continued to look into her eyes. He held Kim's hands as he placed himself inside. They both felt an intense rush of pleasure, and Kim continued to notice Gabe looking into her eyes.

Gabe knew what motions pleased Kim, but he moved his hips in a manner that felt best for him. Then, as he approached his climax, he held her hands while looking into her eyes.

Kim reveled in Gabe's drive and appreciated this slightly selfish attitude, which she had not experienced in a long time. She now felt waves of pleasure rolling through her body. Kim especially enjoyed the freedom of her husband controlling her pleasure. While she had expected her orgasm to be deep, she had not been prepared for the sudden peak. Kim's body shook and arched upwards as she relished Gabe's revitalized sexual self-assurance.

The pair began taking deep breaths, and when the pleasure fully subsided, Gabe moved off Kim. As they recovered, she noticed he had a bashful expression, and she understood that he now understood her sexual challenge.

<That was very unexpected,> Kim thought, still catching her breath.

<I hope my efforts pleased you.>

<You know you did a fantastic job.>

<Just checking.> Gabe chuckled with embarrassment.

<You finally figured out my puzzle.>

<It's been a long road.>

<What do I like most?>

<To be respected.>

<You have always known that.> Kim smiled, though still doubtful. <What else?>

<Confidence is your major turn-on.>

<You also know that. And you know that my confidence turns you on. What was your big breakthrough?>

<I guess I allowed myself to trust you. I knew if I put myself out there, you would accept me.>

<Finally! You finally get it,> Kim thought, satisfied.

<It took some time.>

<All the clues were right there.>

<I see that now.>

Kim smiled, looked at him for a long moment, and thought, <You did something else different.>

<I did?>

<You put your desires ahead of mine. You acted selfishly.>

<I'm so sorry. It will never happen again,> Gabe thought with remorse.

Kim lightly punched Gabe in the leg.

<Hey! What was that for?> His thoughts were annoyed.

<It's healthy to act a little selfish around me.>

<It is? I thought I went too far.>

<Hon, you jumped me. Nothing more. In a solid relationship, occasionally taking control is healthy. What's important is that you have enough self-confidence to try. Plus, I liked what you did.>

<But—>

<Hon. Sex isn't always about me. It's alright to enjoy it your way.>

<And?> Gabe encouraged.

<You provided me the freedom to focus on my pleasure. And you got to do what felt good to you. Besides, you were terrific. So passionate. So intense. So manly. My big tiger!>

<Well, I'm glad you liked it,> Gabe thought with pride.

<You should be!>

After a long embrace, Kim thought, <Don't turn me into a science experiment. I'm not a robot with boobs.>

<Oh, I'm sorry,> Gabe thought, embarrassed.

<Hon, it's fine. I let you make that mistake.>

<You let me?> Gabe's insecurity rose.

<I married an engineer. Trust me, I knew what I was getting into.>

<Why didn't you say something?>

<I needed you to learn from your mistakes,> Kim answered confidently.

<I keep underestimating you.>

<You're getting better.> Kim gleefully smiled.

<Does this mean that you are going to jump me someday?>

<It depends. Tell me, Mr. Engineer, what is the takeaway from your data capture?>

<My data capture?> Gabe smiled. <You're learning some good technical descriptions, Miss Engineer.>

<I am. Tell me.>

<You like it when I fully trust you.>

<What are you going to do to keep my confidence up?> Kim challenged.

<Keep trusting you and maybe act a little selfish.>

<Have you been reading my *Cosmo* magazines?> Kim joked.

<Funny.>

<I know.>

<Tell me, Miss Engineer, what did you learn?>

<Not going to let me off the hook?>

<No.>

<One, that you're a good catch. And two, my plan to change you got too close to the edge.>

<Meaning?> Gabe asked.

<You mentally saw women withholding sex and the awful result,> Kim thought with regret.

<I did.>

<Hon, I could have damaged our relationship.>

<You were helping me to grow.>

<But I might have pushed too hard. I could have lost you.> Kim felt deep regret.

<You would have never let that happen.>

<The student becomes the master.>

<Funny. What else did you learn?> Gabe challenged her.

<Men like sex more than I imagined.>

<We do. But your *Cosmo* articles should have made this clear.>

<They did, but swimming revealed that men are so primal. Way more than women.>

<There is something else. Something big. I can tell.>

Kim thought for a long moment and answered with reserved emotions, <I guess I deserve a bit of prodding. You treat me well. I've entered many men's minds, and you were above every single one.>

<Thanks,> Gabe thought, blushing.

<Plus, you went out of your way not to stare at my boobs tonight. You know, that freaks me out.>

<We talked about this topic before. You fear that I married you only because of your chest. Clearly, I need to be more considerate.>

<There you go again. This is my issue.>

<Still—>

<I guess we both need a little work.>

<True.>

<You know. I sometimes feel intimidated,> Kim thought coyly.

<Really? I felt some vulnerability within you a few times, but I thought little of it.>

<Every day, you go far out of your way to be a great husband. And, well, I sometimes feel like I'm not a good wife.>

<What do you mean? You've been a terrific wife,> Gabe thought, confused.

<You brighten up when you walk into a room and see me. Your mind physically becomes happy. Plus, you always say, 'I love you, my sweet.' Right out of the blue. You do it at least six times a day. And you constantly give me little neck massages, love texts, and put your hand on my leg while driving.>

<I try.>

<You don't try. You succeed!>

<Then, what's the issue?>

<When you walk into a room and see me— what's the term? Your go-to reaction is to smile. I sometimes forget to do basic stuff like that. Plus, while I love you, I sometimes forget to say it. And whenever I think, 'hey, I should give him a neck rub,' you do it first. You're like the love terminator. Do you understand? All day long, your mind hunts for the best way to make me happy. You never stop!>

<Oh, I'm so sorry,> Gabe thought, embarrassed.

Kim punched Gabe in the leg a little harder than average and thought, <Hon! Many women would kill to have a man like you. Never stop loving me. No matter what. Didn't you appreciate this lesson? I challenged you to be better. I challenged you to tear down your insecurity. I risked our entire relationship to improve your confidence.>

<Oh.>

<And now it is your turn to challenge me. More compliments, more massages, and fifty I-love-you texts a day. And when I don't reciprocate, you know what to do?>

<No,> Gabe thought, knowing he should have an answer.

<Hon! Confront me,> Kim thought purposefully. <Call me out! Say, 'I walked into the room, and you didn't smile. Try harder.' 'Hey, I'm watching TV. Where's my foot rub?' When we are driving, take my hand and put it on your leg.>

<I guess I can try harder.>

<Well, it's good that we got it all out in the open. Now, let's do a technical write-up and submit it to an engineering magazine.>

<Hon!>

The pair laughed and fell asleep in each other's arms.

# TEN

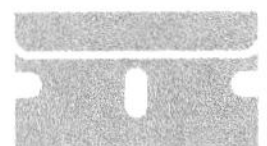

Four weeks later, Gabe and Kim deprogrammed their last person. The family continued to attend the Miramar Telepathy Club, but membership numbers dwindled. The group had many discussions about what had gone wrong, and the consensus was that they needed to "get their mental mojo back."

Jason reported that his internet monitoring had not located any additional telepathy outbreaks. This news came as a great relief to Gabe and Kim. They were now looking forward to a "Jason-free life," and they celebrated by booking a vacation to Jamaica and Alaska—with Donna's permission.

Kim had visited Jamaica several times and was familiar with the island. When they landed, Gabe and one-year-old Emma appreciated the rich Jamaican culture. Their hotel in Ocho Rios had three large pools, and their room had a fantastic ocean view.

The family ate delicious meals, shopped, drove to popular attractions, and took pictures. Gabe appreciated walking up Dunn's River Falls, and Emma enjoyed finding seashells.

On their fourth day, they traveled through Clarendon Parish, and Kim mentioned, <That's where my grandmother lives.>

<Really?> Gabe asked with surprise.

<I've not seen her in years.>

<I thought all your relatives except for your mother's sister were dead?>

<Yeah, I never told you she was alive. Sorry. Years ago, my father got into a big argument with her. Anyway, they broke off contact when I was five.>

<What did they argue about?>

<I never got the full story, but it had something to do with money.>

<Well, Emma should have the opportunity to meet her great-grandmother.>

<I guess,> Kim thought reluctantly.

<Babe? Why are your feelings so negative?>

<Growing up, my dad hated it when we discussed the subject. But, hey, maybe it's time to mend some fences.>

<Well, let's go!> Gabe thought with encouragement.

They parked the car and walked up to a tiny house. Kim knocked, and an older woman answered. Her face bore the scars of a life of great hardship. She stood with a curved back at four foot six with short strands of matted gray hair. The woman was dressed in a faded floral-print dress that seemed to mirror the faded colors of her long and troubled life. She had a shifty quality, as if she were on guard against unseen threats. Her eyes, a shade of stormy blue, darted about with an untrusting gaze, never lingering in one place for too long. "You're Calvin's daughter. Kim, is it?" she asked with suspicion.

"Yes, ma'am."

"Is this your daughter and husband?"

"We are," Gabe answered. "It's nice to meet you. My name is Gabe, and this is Emma."

"Why are you here?" the woman asked suspiciously. "I have no money."

"We wanted our daughter to meet you."

"Hmm."

"Ma'am—" Gabe started, but the woman interrupted.

"Call me Trina."

"Trina, I'm sorry to bring this up. Are you aware that your son is deceased?"

"I keep up with the news," Trina tersely answered.

"I'm sorry for your loss. Calvin was a great man."

"Is it true about you two?" Trina accused.

"Is what true?"

"That you took advantage of the situation?"

The remark upset Gabe, and Kim answered, "Everything you read is a lie. My husband is the best man there's ever been."

"I suspected as much. None of those newspaper articles made any sense. Like getting your age wrong and talking about your nonexistent sister."

"Why don't people bother to check the facts?" Gabe asked and threw up his hands in frustration.

"People only believe what they want. Well, come inside. Let's have some tea."

The one-room house smelled terrible, and the carpets were filthy. Dirty dishes and broken objects littered the floor and shelves. Trina kneeled, aided by her cane, and said to Emma, "Look at you. Walking so young."

"Yes, Grandmother Trina," Emma replied with a big eleven-tooth smile.

"And talking so well."

"Thank you, Grandmother Trina."

"You're very polite."

Emma smiled with great pride, and the family sat on a well-worn, dirty sofa facing a tiny television. Trina began making tea in a battered aluminum teapot. "This is all so unexpected," she commented. "What brings you to Jamaica?"

"We needed a vacation," Kim answered.

"Well, I am glad you are here. Of all Calvin's children, I wanted to reconnect with you."

"I wanted to get to know you as well."

"Did you know I attended Marcus's high school graduation?"

"No."

"My son never told you?" Trina asked.

"No."

"I sat two rows behind you. It was a lovely ceremony."

"The school did a good job with the decorations."

Trina returned, opened a box of chocolate chip cookies, and placed ten on a well-used plate. Gabe had been looking around the house, and he began passively swimming. <You feel that, babe?> he asked Kim.

<What?>

<Swim in her mind.>

<It feels like greed.>

<Probe deeper.>

Kim concentrated and thought to Gabe, <Oh, this is too much. She is trying to think of an angle to get us to buy her ganja.>

<What's ganja?> Gabe replied.

<You are so naïve! Ganja is slang for marijuana.>

<She's a pothead? Really?>

<Mommy Kim,> Emma thought. <What's a pothead?>

The question stunned Gabe and Kim. <You swam in Trina? We're so proud of you,> Kim thought to Emma.

<You did really well!> Gabe complimented with pride.

<Thank you, Daddy Gabe. What's a pothead?>

<Pot is a dangerous drug,> Gabe answered. <They call a person who takes drugs a pothead.>

<They talk drugs in school, not about pothead. Why Grandmother Trina pothead?>

<Drugs make you feel good.>

<Why Grandmother Trina not know pothead bad?> Emma asked with concern.

<She knows all about drugs. Unfortunately, it is difficult to stop taking them.>

<I understand,> Emma thought sadly.

<That's very mature.>

<Thank you, Mommy Kim.>

<Do you feel Trina's mind?> Kim asked Gabe.

<It's like she's in a fog. Is she stoned right now?>

<Yup.>

<So, that's what it feels like. I never knew.>

<Feel that? She is going to pretend that her knee hurts. Watch.>

Trina sat down and placed cookies on the table. Kim crushed a cookie corner, and Emma ate the bits. "My, my. Eating solid food already?" Trina asked.

"Emma is developing faster than the other children," Kim answered.

"I read big-girl book," Emma said with a big grin. "It called *Harry Potter and the Deathly Hallows.*"

"That is impressive. Tell me. Where did the story take place?"

"In Hogwarts. That's in England."

"England is a big word."

"It has nine regions; my favorite is the West Midlands."

"My, my. I will say this. I was a grade-school teacher for 22 years, and in all that time, I never encountered a student so bright."

"We are very proud of her," Gabe said, smiling.

"Oh. There goes my knee. It hurts so."

"What's wrong?" Gabe asked, knowing the answer.

"The doctors tell me I need an operation. I have been saving and saving, but the price keeps increasing."

<She's getting excited,> Gabe thought to Kim with surprise. <Feel it?>

<Let's see how this plays out.>

"How much is the operation?" Gabe asked.

Trina thought briefly and replied, "Let me see if I can recall."

Gabe and Kim sensed positive thoughts in her foggy mind.

<Why Grandmother Trina lie?> Kim and Gabe sensed Emma's sadness.

<She wants money to buy drugs,> Kim answered.

<Why she so excited?> Emma asked.

<She thinks we're going to give her money.>

<We're not?> Emma was confused.

<No. That would be irresponsible.>

<Babe, she's in her nineties.> Gabe smiled. <If it makes her happy, let her get stoned. She's only harming herself.>

<We're not giving her money for drugs. That's not who we are.> Kim was adamant.

<True.>

Trina fought her excitement and tried not to smile as she determined an amount with the most realistic chance of success. "They tell me it will be twenty grand."

"That's a lot of money," Gabe stated.

"Doctors are so expensive."

"Prices are going up everywhere."

"Kim, did you know I loaned Calvin the money to start his dry-cleaning business?"

<Here we go.> Gabe fought his own smile. <Guilt trip! This is fun.>

<It's incredible to read her thoughts. I bet she will tell us how healthy Emma is.>

<Right. Then, another round of guilt.>

"Grandmother Trina, why you pothead?" Emma unexpectedly asked.

Trina's mouth dropped open, and her eyes widened.

"Emma, it's not nice to speak to your grandmother that way," Kim said sternly.

"Get out! All of you!" Trina yelled.

Trina pointed her shaky finger to the door. The family glanced at each other, and the teakettle whistled. The sound confused Trina. Then she realized what had occurred. Trina walked to the stove, turned it off, and hissed, "I wasted good tea on you three!"

Trina again pointed at the door. As they reached it, Emma turned to Trina in tears. Gabe looked down at his despondent daughter, then turned back and said, "Wait. This might be the last time Emma will get to see you. Can we at least take a picture? It would be nice to have a family memory."

Trina did not know what to say. "It will only take a minute," Gabe offered. Trina considered the request, and he continued. "I'm sure Kim and Emma have questions only you can answer. Let's start over. Please?"

Trina thought for a moment, and then a great sadness came to her eyes. "This same conversation took my Calvin away," she said softly. "I got all strung out and begged him for dope money. He demanded that I attend rehab. I pleaded and pleaded, but he refused. Finally, I told him I would never speak to him again if he wouldn't fork over the dough. Calvin walked away without another word.

"I moved back to Jamaica because the drugs are cheap. But every day, I wish I could change the past. I had pride. Stupid pride! And now look what happened. I missed so much of his life— so much of your life— so much of... Look how I'm acting. This is—"

Trina looked away without finishing her sentence. Gabe said, "This is a minor misunderstanding and everything's fine."

Tears streamed down Trina's craggy face. She looked at Emma for a long, sad moment. "I'm so sorry, Emma," she said, her voice choked. "No grandmother should behave this way. And Gabe, you're right. The three of you have questions that only I can answer."

Trina went inside, reappeared with a grungy box, and said, "These are all the memories I couldn't sell. I hope someday, the three of you will forgive me. Never come here again."

Trina closed the door, and they heard her sob. Gabe looked into the box and saw a battered photo album, torn documents, and other well-used items. "Thanks, hon," Kim said with a weak smile.

"That could have gone better."

"You did well."

"I tried."

The family got in their car and drove back toward their hotel. "We not see Grandmother Trina?" Emma softly asked.

"I'm sorry, Emma," Kim replied.

"Why Grandmother Trina so sad?"

"She made many mistakes, and you forced her to confront them," Gabe answered. "That's hard for people."

"I make Grandmother Trina sad?" Emma started crying.

"This is not your fault. She did this to herself."

Emma cried harder, and Gabe pulled the car into a souvenir shop parking lot. Kim got out, took Emma out of her car seat, and held her in her arms. "Grandmother made many poor choices," she said as she bounced Emma in her arms. "You're a wonderful girl. We're very proud of you."

"I make Grandmother Trina sad," Emma said in between sobs. "I'm bad girl."

"Hey, hey. You're not a bad girl," Kim soothed. "You didn't know what would happen. You're the best daughter ever."

Emma continued crying as she hugged her mother tightly. Gabe then hugged them. It took a long time for Emma to stop crying, and she said, “I want to go back and help Grandmother Trina,” Emma said with a sniffle.

“She needs to do this on her own. Then, maybe in a month, we can write her a letter. How does that sound?”

“We use okey-okey on her?” Emma asked.

“Maybe, but not now,” Gabe answered.

“I’m sad.”

“That’s alright. The important thing to remember is that your parents love you.”

“I love you too, Mommy Kim and Daddy Gabe.”

•

It took Emma several hours to fully recover, and the family relaxed at the hotel pool the following day. She sat on the edge of the children’s pool, and Kim sunbathed while keeping a close eye on her. Gabe read a railroad history book under an umbrella.

<Stop thinking like that!> Kim interrupted Gabe’s reading.

Confused, Gabe replied, <What?>

<You’re getting all worked up about my bikini!>

<I’m not!>

<I’m all up inside your head. Try again.>

<Alright,> Gabe admitted grudgingly. <But that guy was checking you out.>

<And?>

<His sexual thoughts upset me.>

<So?>

<Well, I’m—>

<Hon! Feel me the truth. Now.>

<Alright.>

Gabe composed his thoughts and realized that Kim had read his mind. This intrusion upset him, and he took a moment to regain his composure. Gabe thought carefully rehearsed words, <I let my trust slip, and I’m sorry. From now on, I will put more effort into avoiding jealous thoughts.>

<And?>

<You look good in that swimsuit.>

<Thank you. You know it’s alright when you get excited about my body,> Kim thought coyly.

<I know.>

<I know you know. I also know your thunder package is going to burst through your swimsuit.>

<I—> Gabe glanced down at his swimsuit to see how obvious his excitement was.

<Hon!>

<You got me again,> Gabe thought.

<I did.>

<Alright, tell the truth. Did you wear that skimpy yellow thing to mess with my trust?>

With a smirk of confidence, Kim answered, <No. It looks good on me.>

<Your thoughts tell me otherwise. Try again.>

<You caught my little fib?> Kim pouted.

<Of course.>

<Alright, I wanted to mess with you.>

<Your plan worked, and you got my mind all wound up.>

<I'm going to keep forcing you to trust me.>

<Please don't try too hard,> Gabe chuckled.

<Try *hard*? No promises,> Kim thought with a warm smile.

<Well, I promise that later tonight, I will explore what's about to *bust* out of that skimpy swimsuit.>

<Hon!>

Kim smiled, though the thought embarrassed her.

Emma walked to Kim <Why Mommy Kim think so much about pee-pee hole?>

Emma's thoughts embarrassed and concerned Kim. <It's not appropriate to think like that.>

<Daddy think about his pee-pee stick.>

<Emma, stop!> Kim demanded.

<Why?>

<When you're older, this will all make sense,> Gabe interrupted with forced calm. <Now come here and let me dry you off.>

<Daddy Gabe, you explain why you think about Mommy's pee-pee hole so much? Your pee-pee stick feel funny.>

Panicked, Gabe thought, <We will discuss this subject when you're older.>

<I want now!> Emma demanded.

<Later this evening, we will talk more about this topic. We're at a public pool, and a *pee-pee hole* discussion isn't appropriate.>

Emma considered the topic for a while. <I understand.>

<That is very mature,> Gabe thought, relieved.

<We do later?> Emma asked.

<Yes, I promise.>

<Alright.>

<Can we swim in people mind?> Emma asked Kim, knowing she had the upper hand.

Gabe and Kim felt relieved that the conversation had changed, and Kim answered, <Alright. What are those two thinking? No deep thoughts!>

<Man think Mommy Kim look good. Woman think her belly is too big. She want to be thin, like Mommy Kim.>

The exceptional skill impressed Kim, and she asked, <What else?> A moment later, she thought, <Stop it. No deep swimming. Hold back. Yes, more like that. That's good.>

<Woman skin hurt from sun. Man listens to music on ear speaker. Music go, 'Don't break my heart, my achy breaky heart.' What does that mean?>

<You did very well,> Gabe answered. <'Achy Breaky Heart' is a song. The words have no real meaning other than to sound fun.>

<I understand.>

<What about those two men?> Kim asked, proud of her daughter's growing ability.

<Man think he has been in sun too long. Other man hungry. He read book about place called Scotland and wants yucky drink.>

<What about that girl in the pool?>

Emma turned to the girl and answered, <She think about getting to edge of pool soon. Her legs sleepy. What's that?>

<What?> Kim asked.

<Over there.>

Kim turned and saw two men walking toward them. She sensed they were focused on the family.

<Hon, something's up with these two,> Kim warned Gabe.

<What?> Gabe asked.

<Those two, they're super upset.>

<They probably want to talk to the couple behind us. Relax, babe. We're on vacation.>

<No, they are thinking directly about us. Trust me.>

<Alright. Let's see how this plays out.>

The first man, in his late thirties, knelt next to Kim. His appearance was in stark contrast to the vibrant backdrop of the Jamaican hotel pool. The man had dressed in faded jeans that hung loosely from his frame and a long-sleeved, gray flannel shirt. He had poorly cut blond hair, pale, blotchy skin, and an air of discomfort emanating from every pore. It was as if he were acutely aware of his out-of-place presence amidst the sun-kissed people staring at him.

The second man had curly brown/gray hair and a face marked by the remnants of past acne battles. His tan slacks hung loosely around his frame while his thick, long-sleeved red shirt clung tightly to his skin. The man also appeared uneasy as he anxiously scanned the faces of those around him. It was as if he were searching for something he could not quite name.

"Can we help you with something?" Gabe asked.

Both men pulled revolvers from under their shirts. The people around the pool had intently watched the situation. They stood when the guns appeared and rapidly departed. The swimmers quickly headed toward the pool's edge as the curly-haired man demanded, "You two. Up! Now! No tricks."

Scared, Kim asked Gabe. <What should we do?>

<Play it easy,> Gabe answered with forced calm. <When the time is right, push this guy in the pool. This will surprise the other guy, and I'll grab his gun.>

<That's too dangerous!>

<You killed a bear with a fishing knife! We can do this!> Gabe encouraged.

They stood, and the blond-haired man took a position behind Kim. The other man stood behind Gabe and told them to walk. They both felt gun barrels pressed against their backs.

Changing his mind, Gabe thought, <Throwing them into the pool won't work.>

<There will be another opportunity. Keep alert.>

"Mommy Kim!" Emma yelled.

"What are you doing, kid?" the blond-haired man demanded.

"Following Mommy Kim!" Emma answered definitely.

"You two have a kid?"

"Obviously," Kim answered, scowling.

"No tricks, or the kid gets it. Let's go!"

Kim picked up Emma, and they began walking. As one woman rapidly exited the pool, she made eye contact with Kim. She mouthed the words, "Help. Help. Police. Police," to the woman, who discreetly nodded.

The group went behind the hotel and headed toward a small building. Inside, they saw kayaks and beach equipment. The curly-haired man closed the door and pushed the gun barrel at Kim's head. She put Emma down, and the other man tied Gabe's hands behind his back with rope. He then tied up Kim in the same manner.

Fortunately, they could not tie Emma's hands because the rope was too thick. To their amusement, she seemed content to walk around the small structure, gazing at the equipment with fascination. Kim and Gabe thought her behavior was out of character, but they dared not speak.

The curly-haired man pushed Kim and Gabe onto a pile of volleyball nets. He put his gun in the back of his waist and said to the other man, "Watch the door while I work these two over."

"Done," the blond-haired man curtly answered.

"Why are you doing this?" Kim demanded.

"I'll ask the questions! Kimm-ma," the curly-haired man answered in a mocking tone. He picked up a wooden pole for volleyball nets, pointed it at Gabe, and demanded, "Where's my sister? Gaaa-ba."

"I don't understand. Who's your sister?"

"Jenna!" the curly-haired man yelled.

"The only Jenna I know is the next-door neighbor's daughter. She should be in her house right now."

"Jenna Cox!" the curly-haired man yelled. "From Alaska, jackass."

Suddenly, Gabe and Kim understood.

"I see it in your eyes," the curly-haired man said. "You two know something."

"There has been some mistake. I will—"

The curly-haired man interrupted Gabe by angrily poking him in the stomach with his pole. Gabe doubled over in pain, and Emma shrieked, "Stop hurting my daddy!"

The curly-haired man flashed a wicked smile at Emma and continued, "You two tricked a bunch of people into attending a conference. Then you took their clothes and messed up their lives. My sister got invited, and she never returned. One lady told me that you, Kimm-ma," he poked Kim hard in the stomach with the pole and continued, "told the group she's dead."

Kim grunted in pain but refused to scream. In great pain and fear, she thought to Gabe, <This is not good. What should we do? He wants to kill us when this is over. I read his mind.>

<I'm going to trick him,> Gabe thought uncertainly. "Look, buddy. I don't know what—"

The man hit Gabe in the arm with the pole and yelled, "Stop your lies! Tell me what you did with my sister. Where the hell is she?"

Gabe grunted, and Kim asked, <What do we tell them?>

<Stall,> Gabe thought desperately.

"We don't know what you are talking about," Kim said, taking deep breaths to control the pain. "Honestly, we don't know your sister. Somebody gave you the wrong information."

The curly-haired man walloped Kim in the left shin with his pole, and she cried out. This brutal blow enraged Gabe, who then devised a desperate new plan. He would lunge at the man with his shoulder, causing him to fall, and then Gabe could bite him.

"I know what happen," Emma said sweetly.

The curly-haired man looked down to see Emma with her arms outstretched. She smiled, opening and closing her hands as if asking to be picked up.

"No!" Kim yelled.

The curly-haired man put the pole down, picked Emma up, and said in a forced, kind voice, "There, there. It's alright. See, I put the stick down. From now on, I won't hurt anybody. Sound good, cutie?"

"Put her down!" Gabe demanded.

Kim thought about lunging at the man, but she knew it would be ineffective because her hands were secured. With no other alternative, she yelled, "Stop! I'm begging you. We'll do whatever you ask."

Emma looked to Gabe and thought with calm determination, <Daddy Gabe. It fine.>

Gabe did not understand, and Emma thought to Kim with the same calmness, <It fine, Mommy Kim.>

Kim also did not understand her daughter's message. The curly-haired man glared at Gabe. He turned to Emma, smiled, and said excitedly, "Now, why don't you tell me what's happening? Afterward, I will take everybody out for ice cream. You can have any flavor you want. Alright, sweetie? Do you like strawberries?"

Each word felt like a bee sting to Gabe. Enraged, he planned to sweep the man's legs out from under him with a shoulder lunge. However, this action would knock Emma out of his hands, and she would fall to the floor. Gabe decided this extreme action warranted the risk and communicated his plan to Kim. She moved to kick the man's knees and lunge forward so her body would cushion Emma's fall while knowing her daughter would likely get injured. She readied herself to strike and waited for Gabe's signal. In their haste, they had not considered what the other armed man would do.

In a moment of inspiration, Gabe thought to Kim, <Yank at every part of his brain. Hard as you can!>

<Right.>

The pair began mentally pulling the man's mind. Unfortunately, without the white box, their actions had little power. The man looked confused, and his right eye twitched.

Emma turned to the man and smiled. He held her by the bottom with his right arm and supported her back with his left hand. The man moved her closer so he could look directly into her eyes. She began playfully wiggling her legs while beaming a warm smile and twisting her hair with her left hand. Gabe and Kim did not know what was happening, but they felt Emma's intent getting colder and colder.

Emma moved closer and spoke softly, "I know Jenna. She is near. Want me to tell?"

While she spoke, Gabe and Kim sensed a dark decision. They continued to pull at every part of the man's mind, but they knew their efforts were ineffective.

The curly-haired man waited for Emma to answer. She pointed upwards with her left hand and said, "Your sister is–"

The man looked up to see what Emma was pointing at. Knowing she had distracted the man, she moved her right hand across her swimsuit. The man felt movement and looked down to see Emma smiling. "Near the–" she continued.

In a swift movement, Emma slashed the man's throat with a razor blade. He did not comprehend the rapid attack and only felt cold as his neck muscles experienced air for the first time. He swiped across the wound with his right hand and stared at bloody fingers as Emma tumbled backward.

Time stopped for Gabe and Kim as they watched their daughter fall headfirst toward the concrete floor. They both knew Emma would die from the severe impact. Gabe attempted to lunge outward to cushion her fall, but his sitting position did not allow him to move fast enough.

Kim also tried to flop forward, but she had been preparing to kick the man's knees, and her body was in the wrong position. As the pair desperately lunged, Emma continued falling.

At the last moment, Emma kicked outwards, which caused her body to flip. She righted herself, landing on her crouched legs and her left hand. Emma extended her right hand with the razor blade outward for balance.

Emma's superb display of physical coordination astounded Gabe. He thought she looked like an assassin from a kung-fu movie and could not help yelling, "Holy crap!"

The blond-haired man was still guarding the door and turned around to see why Gabe yelled. Upon seeing the blood, he charged forward, aiming his gun at Kim. In that instant, Gabe awkwardly lunged, and the man tripped over Gabe's neck. The man did not fall, but he stumbled. Kim swung her feet forward and kicked the man in the left side of his abdomen. He staggered and fell. In this brief instant, she kicked the gun out of his right hand.

The man struggled to stand, and Kim kicked him in the legs. Gabe rolled over to sit on the man, who yelled for him to get off. At the same time, Kim began kicking at the man's left arm with her heel while he attempted to crawl toward the gun.

The curly-haired man fell to his knees while grasping his deep wound. Emma stood, turned to the man, and gave him an icy stare. "Nobody hits Mommy!" Emma shrieked. "You die now! You die like bug!"

The curly-haired man was flabbergasted and looked down to see his blood pooling on the floor. He reached around to grab the gun from his waist, but the massive blood loss weakened his muscles.

Meanwhile, the blond-haired man struggled and managed to punch Kim in the lower back. She ignored the blow and switched to using both heels to kick at the man's elbow, which caused considerable pain. Gabe had been trying to hold the man down with his knees, but realized his actions were ineffective. In a moment of inspiration, he crouched, jumped, and landed on the man's back.

The jumping caused little pain to the sizable man, but the action left him momentarily breathless. Seeing the success, Gabe jumped as high as possible and landed another blow. Now, the man struggled to breathe and turned over to punch Gabe.

Kim watched Gabe's effort and coordinated her kicks with his jumps. This simultaneous action confused the man, who did not know who to punch. Three jumps later, the man decided to hit Gabe. When he twisted around to strike, Kim saw his focus shift. She scooched forward and landed a hard heel kick on the man's temple. The blow stunned the man, and he stopped struggling.

Gabe landed two more jumps and asked, "Emma, are you alright?"

"Yes, Daddy."

Gabe became sidetracked and said, "That is the first time you called me daddy without saying Daddy Gabe."

"I forget, Daddy Gabe," Emma said with a frown.

"That's my girl," Kim said, smiling.

Emma smiled back. Kim kicked the gun away from the blond-haired man. A massive puddle of blood formed around the curly-haired man. The sight reminded Kim of killing the bear in Alaska, and the smell triggered a horrific memory. She shook off her negative flashback and looked deep into the man's eyes. Kim knew the man would die in seconds.

The sight also reminded Gabe of the bear attack, and he briefly could not move. Emma turned back to the curly-haired man and yelled, "You bad man. You not go to heaven, like movie."

The curly-haired man looked at her weakly, closed his eyes, and his body slumped to the side. "Babe, go get help," Gabe said. "I'll sit on this guy. Emma, you protect Mommy."

"Yes, Daddy Gabe."

Kim stood and used her foot to push the door open. She and Emma ran as fast as the child's little legs would allow back to the pool area, where they saw the same woman and her husband looking out from behind the towel booth. Both looked relieved, and Kim yelled, "Call the police!"

"Are you alright?" the woman asked.

"You, call the police! You, untie me! Now!" The couple did not react, and Kim yelled, "Move! Move! Move!"

The man shook off his confusion and ran inside the hotel while the woman untied Kim. She picked up Emma, and the trio ran back to the storeroom. The woman untied Gabe, and a moment later, the blond-haired man began moving. Gabe picked up a gun and pointed it at his head. After a few deep breaths, the blond-haired man came around, opened his eyes, and looked up in shock.

"Who the heck are you?" Gabe demanded.

The blond-haired man refused to answer. Gabe forcefully jammed the gun into the man's forehead and threatened, "Answer or die. Right here. Right now!"

The blond-haired man mumbled, "My name is Craig. I'm Jenna's ex-husband. Roy over there convinced me to help find his sister. I only wanted to ask questions, but Roy wanted to bring guns. This whole thing was a big mistake."

"You bet it's a mistake."

Gabe heard something behind him, and a Jamaican police officer entered. The sight of the officer wearing shorts sidetracked him from wondering how the officer had arrived so quickly. Suppressing a grin, Gabe handed the revolver to the officer and said, "Please be careful. I think it's loaded."

The officer nodded, pressed the gun's safety, and put it in his shorts pocket. Then, he took the man into custody and removed the firearm that Roy was reaching for. Gabe turned to Emma and asked, "Sweetie, are you alright?"

"Yes, Daddy Gabe," Emma answered with a big grin.

"You were so brave. We're proud of you."

"I brave. Like big girl," Emma said with pride.

"Is it alright if Mommy takes the small knife?"

"You give back?" Emma asked suspiciously.

Gabe turned to Kim. She nodded, and he answered, "Yes, sweetie. Where did you find it?"

"On the floor, Daddy Gabe."

"You planned all this?"

"Bad man have bad thoughts. I save Daddy Gabe and Mommy Kim."

"You were wonderful," Kim said as she hugged Emma.

Five minutes later, another police officer arrived, and the woman from the pool handed Kim a towel to cover her swimsuit. After some questions, an officer led the family to his patrol car, and on the way to the station, Kim mentally instructed Emma not to mention Jenna.

Police Chief Jarek towered above his peers at an impressive six foot three. His short hair was neatly trimmed, and he wore a crisp uniform with no imperfections. Jarek's sharp brown eyes seemed to miss nothing as he intently studied the family.

They all reported that they were unaware of either man's motivations. When Emma spoke, her bravery impressed Jarek, and he laughed at her "You die like bug" statement.

Gabe asked Jarek if they could keep this incident out of the news, to which he replied with a strong accent, "De child cuts open da kidnapper's neck to save 'er parents? No way, mon. Dis the biggest thing dat happened in a long time."

The answer concerned Gabe, and he asked if he could make a long-distance call. Officer Jarek agreed, and Jason answered on the first ring. Gabe quickly explained the situation, which infuriated Jason. He calmed himself and said, "I know the local contact. Don't say a word until he arrives."

The call abruptly ended, and Gabe thought to Kim, <Jason told us to keep quiet. He said somebody from his team would help us.>

<Got it.>

"A man will be here soon," Gabe informed police chief Jarek.

"Who dat, mon?"

"No idea. I was told to remain silent until he arrives."

"He your lawyer?"

"I don't think so."

"It not work like dat, mon. Dis is Jamaica, not America. You got to talk. It da law."

"I was told to wait."

"You going to jail if you not talk," police chief Jarek warned him.

"I have to do what my boss says."

"Who your boss?"

"I cannot answer."

"You criminal, mon?" police chief Jarek inquired.

"Of course not."

"Are you part de American government?"

"Not really," Gabe answered while becoming concerned about this line of questioning.

"Well, if this mon tells me to do something, I will refuse. Here, I de boss and I ask de questions."

"Officer, please. The man will be here shortly, and it's best to do as he says."

"We play it your way. But tonight, de three of you gonna be in my jail. No going back from dat."

"I understand."

An hour later, a crowd of reporters and curious people gathered outside the police station. Jarek got a phone call, entered his office, and came out deflated. "You know who dat was?" he asked, shaking his head.

"No idea," Gabe answered.

"De chief of police for all Jamaica. I got to do what de chief say."

"What did he say?" Gabe asked, curious.

"He say wait for a mon named Martin. You know dis Martin?"

"No."

"He seems pretty important to get that kind of juice."

"We will do whatever he tells us to do."

Fifteen minutes later, a beat-up blue Nissan sedan skidded to a stop behind the police station. A tough-looking Jamaican man strode through the back entrance with intense confidence. Standing at five foot eight, his dark, penetrating gaze seemed to bore into the very soul of those who dared to meet it. A ghastly scar marred his left cheek, while the absence of his pinkie finger spoke of past sacrifices. Dressed in a dirty green shirt that clung to his muscular frame, he seemed out of place amid the professional law-enforcement surroundings.

When the man briefly made eye contact with Kim, she immediately recognized him as the Jamaican equivalent of Jason. She gulped and looked at Gabe with a scared expression.

Martin turned away and motioned for Jarek to follow him to his office. The two briefly spoke, and Jarek left the office deflated. Martin motioned to the trio to join him. He closed the door and said with a strong accent, "You three made quite de mess."

"Not our fault," Kim replied. "We were keeping a low profile, and then these two idiots pulled guns on us."

"Dis going to be hard to clean up. You should have killed both of dem and called me. Dis is going to be tough. Any idea?"

"We could wait it out," Kim suggested.

"Too much news. Dey need something right now."

"Let's leave quietly and keep the news guessing," Gabe offered.

"No way, dis is big."

Emma had been looking at Martin in fascination. "Need another family to be us," she said with a grin.

Martin looked at Emma, surprised, and said, "Aren't you the smart one? And so young, child. OK, little lady. What about de other guy."

"Make him sick."

"Poison. Dat's a good idea. Alright. Here it is. I have some friends, and I think I can convince them to take your place. We can push them in front of the camera and dey will yak der heads off. And dat punk? He about to catch hisself a cold."

Gabe and Kim were not pleased with Emma's harsh suggestions, but they liked her grasp of the situation. "What about the couple that helped us out at the pool?" Kim asked. "They can identify us."

"Oh, dem? No problem. Dey get sick too."

"How about a bribe?"

"Dis Jamaica, I got no money for that kind of juice."

"We have money."

"We can try. Otherwise–" Martin's voice trailed off, and he made a gun finger gesture.

Two hours later, an overweight Caucasian man, a wildly dressed Jamaican woman, and a young girl with strawberry-blond hair that did not look like either of them drove up to the back of the police station. Martin spoke with them for two minutes, and then they made a statement to the news.

While the attention was on the substitute family, Martin walked to his car and returned with a paper bag. After going to the restroom and leaving his paper bag, he spoke to Craig in his jail cell. Gabe watched them shake hands as they departed. Martin returned to the restroom to retrieve his bag and spoke to Jarek.

Ten minutes after the news crews left, Martin escorted the family to his Nissan. They got into the back seat, and Martin threw a dirty towel over them so they could not be seen by the news when they drove away. At the hotel, Gabe quickly packed while Kim found the woman who had helped them. "Miss?" she asked.

"Yes?"

"I don't have a lot of time. Look, I need a big favor."

The woman eyed Kim with suspicion. "What?"

"We're in the witness protection program."

"And?"

"If you watch the news tonight, a different family will claim to be us. Please do not let anybody know the truth."

"No way! I am posting this all over Facebook, and you can't stop me."

"You cannot," Kim warned.

"Yes, I can! Who the heck do you think you are?"

"How about this? I'll pay you ten grand to keep quiet."

"Ten grand?" the woman asked with a loud snort.

"I can wire it to you from my phone right now."

"I don't know. Is this legit?"

"All I can say is that if you don't accept my offer, there will be consequences."

"That sounds like a threat!" the woman hissed.

"You are being threatened, but not by me."

"I don't like this. I don't like this at all."

Kim's eyes narrowed. "Try having a gun pointed at you."

"I still don't know." The woman hesitated, shaking her head.

"Can I be honest?"

"I guess."

"The other guy who captured us will be dead soon."

"What?" the woman asked with raised eyebrows. "You cannot be serious!"

"You need to take my deal."

"Is he really going to die?"

"Yes."

"My word!" the woman exclaimed. She thought for a moment while looking at Kim's serious expression. "Well, this must be important. I guess I can play along."

"Do you have your checkbook?" Kim asked while pointing to her purse.

"Yes."

"Let me see the routing number, and you'll be ten grand richer in five minutes."

"Carla needs a car for college."

"That's the idea."

The woman took out her checkbook, and Kim used the bank information to transfer the money via an app on her phone. After thanking the woman, Kim texted Jason what she had done, along with the woman's name and address, which she had seen on the check.

At the front entrance, Gabe loaded their luggage into Martin's car. He drove the family to a small house in Clarendon Parish. Martin laid out two air mattresses and blankets. Everybody went to sleep after a quiet dinner of leftover beef patties and rice.

The following day, Gabe called Karen and asked if they could arrive early. She liked the idea, and Martin drove them to the airport. As the car rapidly drove away, Gabe noticed a piece of the exhaust pipe fall off. He chuckled, and the family went inside.

Kim handled the details at the ticket counter while Emma and Gabe found a place to eat breakfast. Ten minutes later, Kim joined them and mentioned that the trip to Alaska would involve three connecting flights with long layovers.

# ELEVEN

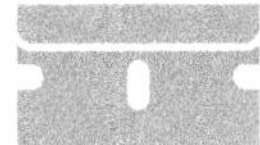

Twenty-five hours of travel took a toll on the family, but they were able to get some sleep on the flight. At the Fairbanks International Airport, Gabe was grateful to get the same beat-up Jeep at the car rental agency. Unfortunately, they had to purchase an expensive car seat that Emma disliked.

Gabe grinned from ear to ear as they drove away. The warm weather turned the roads into slush, and he splashed through every puddle he could.

Karen met them at her front door an hour later. Kim had explained beforehand to Emma that Karen had been in a car accident, and not to mention her scars. When Gabe introduced Kim to Karen, they hugged for a long moment. Then Karen kneeled and asked Emma, "And who is this?"

"My name is Emma," she announced. "Mommy Kim say you have bad face and not to say mean talk."

"You are speaking well for somebody your age."

Emma turned to Kim and asked, "Mommy Kim. Why you tell me this? Godmother Karen look beautiful."

"Emma, that's a nice compliment," Kim said.

"It not compliment. It truth."

Everybody laughed and walked inside. Karen could see how tired the family looked, and after some small talk, she led them to the servant's house. Kim thanked Karen for her generous hospitality, and Karen replied that breakfast would be ready at any time.

At 9:35 a.m., the sleepy family walked to the main house. Karen greeted them and cooked up an excellent breakfast. "What are your plans?" she asked.

"There are no real plans," Kim answered. "I'm sure Gabe wants to say hi to his prison buddies and play with his Jeep."

Gabe grinned, and Karen asked Emma, "And what do you want to do, sweetie?"

"Do they have bald eagle? Like video?"

"I know where one likes to hunt; if we're lucky, we might see him."

"I want to do that," Emma announced with a big grin.

"Tell me, why did you cut your Jamaica vacation short?"

Kim and Gabe looked at each other with concern.

"You three had nothing to do with that terrible kidnapping that was all over the news?" Karen asked. "Dreadful men."

Gabe looked at Karen with a concerned expression. "Well—"

"You did?"

"I kill big man like bug!" Emma proudly interrupted.

"What?"

Gabe cleared his throat and said, "I think we should change the subject."

Karen turned to Gabe and nodded. "Indeed," she said. "I see you got your same Jeep."

"That Jeep is all he talked about from the last time he was here," Kim said with a hearty laugh. "If he keeps this up, I'm going to buy him one."

"You didn't explore the back country the last time."

"It's all slush and mud," Gabe sighed. "That beat-up Jeep has bald tires and will only get stuck."

"It's a nice day out. Let's go for a joyride."

Gabe's eyes widened, and he eagerly nodded. The group walked toward the Jeep with Karen in the lead. Then, unexpectedly, she walked past and continued to her eight-car garage. Karen pressed a remote-control button, and the third door opened to reveal a massive black Bronco with enormous tires and a towering engine sticking through the hood. "Felix's pride and joy," she said with her crackly laugh.

"He will be spitting nails mad if we take his truck," Gabe warned.

"Upset? Felix? He's in prison. What's he going to do? Besides, I take Betty here out all the time. She's my grocery-getter."

"He calls this truck Betty?" Gabe asked coyly.

"His first girlfriend's name."

"I guess we could carefully use it for a brief trip."

"Kim, do you have to twist his arm to have some fun?"

"That's Gabe for you," Kim said with a smile. "I'll have to tell you about when we set off dynamite under a propane tank. He got so scared."

"Hey," Gabe exclaimed. "We might have started a forest fire."

Everybody except Gabe laughed. Karen threw him the keys and said, "Let's go. While we're still young."

Gabe helped Emma and Kim into the Bronco, with Karen in the front passenger seat. Kim noticed a child seat and asked, "You were expecting us to take this truck out for a spin?"

"Of course!" Karen said with a hearty laugh.

Gabe started the engine with a mighty roar, and Kim asked Karen, "Is he smiling?"

"If he smiles any wider, he is going to break something. Make a left."

Gabe eased the large Bronco into gear, lightly pressed the accelerator, and the Bronco awkwardly lurched out of the garage. "Sorry, everybody," he said in a sheepish voice. "This truck has a sensitive clutch."

"You still drive like my grandmother!" Kim hooted.

Gabe drove at fifteen miles per hour along a slush-covered road. Several patches of ice caused the truck to slide sideways, forcing Gabe to overcorrect. Karen pointed out the landmarks as they drove around bends and through large streams. Eventually, Gabe became comfortable enough to drive faster. Soon, they came upon a wider dirt road and followed it to a gate with a guard. Karen rolled down her window and yelled over the engine noise, "Hi, Werner."

"It's nice to see you. I cannot thank you enough for bringing over that pot roast. Susie appreciated it."

"I hope she feels better. Please let me know if there's anything else I can do. This is Gabe. You know, Felix's friend."

"Oh, hi," Werner said with a big smile. "Nice to meet you, teacher Gabe."

"I'm taking his family on a tour," Karen said. "We'll exit through the south gate."

"I'll call ahead."

"Thanks. And tell Susie not to worry so much. She's a strong gal, and I know she'll pull through— I'm sure of it."

"Will do."

Gabe followed the road while the family looked at the massive earth-moving equipment.

"This is the Evans mine," Karen continued. "It's one of the largest gold mines in Alaska. The weather has finally cleared, and the men are prepping everything for the new season. The drill charts all showed the ground they're opening has fantastic deposits."

"Wow, this place is enormous," Kim commented.

"We typically get 400 ounces a month from that cut. There are three more cuts over that way. Look over there. They finished mining that section and returned the land to pristine condition. The trees are already five feet tall."

"It looks perfect," Kim proclaimed.

"Drive that way."

Gabe drove through a gate and applied full throttle to climb a hill. The amount of power excited him as they crested the top. Karen asked Gabe to stop, and she said, "Look over there. That's one of my oil fields."

The family saw pipelines and oil pumps. "The pumps run all winter long," Karen continued. "That's Pump Jack 115. (An oil well pump that looks like a dipping bird toy.) It's the first well I drilled in this field. Now, it only produces 96 barrels a day."

"Is that a lot?" Kim asked.

"That's a respectable amount. One of my wells produces 245, and I still run a few that produce five."

"Wow!"

"Drive over to your left."

Gabe drove until Karen directed him to stop near a patch of trees. "See all this?" she asked. "My father drilled his first well right there. This ground stopped producing in 1996. Ten years ago, there was rusty equipment everywhere. Now, look at it."

"It's all returned to normal," Kim remarked.

"Well, that concludes the tour."

"Babe, want to drive back?" Gabe asked, knowing the answer.

"You would let me?"

"Of course."

Kim laughed. They switched seats, and she began exploring the vehicle's handling characteristics. Then her inner child took over, and she took turns hard and fast. They bounded over rocks and through streams at full speed. Gabe held onto his seat for dear life while Emma yelled, "Faster, faster!"

Karen hooted while yelling out directions. Two hours later, they arrived at the house. "Wow, babe, you drove like a champ," Gabe said with a big smile.

"Would you expect anything less?"

"Of course not! Man, this truck is dirty. It will take me at least an hour to clean the mud off. You three relax."

"Nonsense," Karen said with a fluttering hand gesture. "I'll take care of this later."

"There's a hose right there. You three go inside."

"He likes to get his way."

"He is trying to convince us this is an honor thing," Kim corrected. "He fears Felix will find out about his dirty truck."

Karen laughed, and Gabe shook his head. After returning to the house, Karen turned on the teapot. "How are you holding up?" she asked Kim. "Your recent incident must have been difficult."

"The last few months were stressful, and our vacation was supposed to fix that."

Karen smiled. "Stay here as long as you like."

"Thanks."

"You're doing a great job raising Emma. I've never seen a child talk and walk so well at her age."

"We're lucky to have her in our lives," Kim proudly said.

"Does your family have a history of their children developing so fast?"

"No. She's a big exception."

"Godmother Karen," Emma interrupted. "What's this?"

"That's a totem pole souvenir, sweetie."

"Why you have this one? It not nice, like others."

"I tried to help somebody start a business," Karen said, a hint of sadness on her face. "But it failed, and I keep that souvenir as a reminder of my mistake."

"Thank you for explaining, Godmother Karen."

"Sweetie, you do not have to keep calling me Godmother Karen. It's plain, Karen. Alright?"

"I still want to call you Godmother Karen."

"That's fine."

"Emma likes to apply titles to everybody," Kim commented. "She calls me 'Mommy Kim.'"

"Very respectful."

"True. Why did the business fail?" Kim asked.

"An acquaintance of mine, Rachel, wanted to start a company. She planned to hire locals in the off-season to make 'genuine Alaskan collectibles.' So, I loaned her forty thousand to get things rolling. Rachel is a smart cookie; everything started great, and the business received tons of local press.

"Six months later, Rachel asked me to drop by the office so she could show me her progress. To this day, I have no idea why things went so badly. The building smelled like a bong, and she demanded another one hundred fifty thousand. I insisted she show a profit first. After that, things became unpleasant."

"Wow."

"Eight months passed, and I got a call from the property manager. As the business owner, he told me I had to pay him eighty thousand to cover the damages. Rachel even tore down the walls to steal the copper wire. Fortunately, I had the foresight to set up proper legal documents stating that I took no responsibility for the operation. As a result, Rachel had to declare bankruptcy and lost her house. She moved in with her sister's family, and I never saw a dime of that forty thousand."

"Did you ever do a personal loan again?"

"The experience left a foul taste. However, Jake's son, Roger, wanted to start a logging company. But this time, I learned my lesson and insisted that the money would be a gift. I even made him sign a document stating that fact.

"Roger was a pro lumberjack and knew the industry cold. His first two seasons were fantastic, and he was on track to be a millionaire. Well, lumber prices dropped like a stone, and he lost every penny to his name. Two years later, Roger dropped by my house with a grungy bag. He had saved every dime to pay me back.

"The man refused to take no for an answer until I told him to use the money for a down payment on a house. He recently began dating this cutie named Julie. I said she was a keeper; he needed a solid job and a house. Then, they could start a proper family. Well, unbeknownst to me, I made a massive error. I gave him a goal. But, alas, he did everything in reverse by using the money for fertility treatments."

Karen leaned back for a long moment. Even without swimming, Kim sensed profound sadness. "What happened?"

"Poor Roger. He took night classes to be an auto mechanic and worked as a garage helper during the day. Like his father, Roger smoked like a chimney, and so did Julie. And well– as you know, it isn't wise to have a child in that environment. Roger Jr. had severe health issues from day one."

Karen composed herself and continued, "One day, Roger was pulling a transmission–" She took a deep breath, looked away, and continued without facing Kim, "He had a heart attack and died on that greasy floor. And you know how it is. Julie blamed me for everything. But I understand. I know what it's like to be an upset woman without a man by her side.

"Life has been tough on her. I offered my help, but Julie has pride. I understand that, too.

"Well, I could not stand to see her suffer. So, one day, I anonymously paid a year's rent on her apartment. The next day, she stormed over and demanded I take it back. She looked so skinny holding Roger Jr. Clearly, neither one had had a full meal in over a month. That poor child was coughing and shivering. It took every ounce of my strength to refuse her plea. We've never spoken again."

"What's she doing now?" Kim asked.

"She lives with her cousin in exchange for tending their livestock."

"That went bad fast."

"It did."

Karen sipped tea and asked, "Have you had any unpleasant business experiences?"

"Not that bad, but a month ago, I had a meeting with the owner of a chemical company to purchase dry-cleaning fluid. Because this guy has the best prices, he figured this somehow permitted him to call me 'sugar tits.' Who the heck does that? So, I asked my delivery driver to get him out of my sight. He's normally super-quiet but became mean as a tiger and sent that man flying into the parking lot."

"Sorry to hear that," Karen said while shaking her head.

"Men cannot understand that a woman can run a business."

"I hear that, sister," Karen said with a laugh.

"That mine looked efficient."

"An Alaskan family runs that mine like a Swiss watch."

"Impressive."

"I looked a bit into your operation. Also, impressive."

"It's been a handful," Kim said, running her hand through her hair.

"I liked your 'get off the dirt' advertisement. Professional and perfectly targeted."

"I hired a bright girl right out of college, and she came up with that entire campaign."

"Nice."

Karen leaned back briefly and asked, "How are you and your husband doing?"

"The last few months have been difficult, but we're getting through it. Why do you ask?"

"When he was here, he looked depressed after calling you."

"Was it that apparent?" Kim looked away briefly.

"Gabe's an open book."

"That's true." Kim sighed deeply. "Well, I had major issues."

"Booze or something else?"

"Booze."

"I see."

"How'd you know?" Kim wanted to know.

"My family has a long history."

"Mine too."

"You through with it?"

"I will never touch a drop again!" Kim said. She nodded and held up two fingers in a promise gesture.

"It took all this," Karen motioned to her body and continued, "for me to come to the same conclusion."

"I first realized I had a drinking problem when I crashed my car into a curb. I thought I'd kicked the sauce, but I fell off the wagon. When Gabe returned home, I knew I had to get my life back together."

"That's good to hear."

"Any funny stories?"

Karen made a crackly laugh and answered, "Hundreds. One morning, I came downstairs to see my mother cooking breakfast half-naked. She asked, 'Who turned off the heat?'"

"Wow," Kim said with a laugh. "One day, my dad barfed all over the sofa. He said it was *allergies*, but we all knew what was happening."

"One morning, Felix came up to me and said he had a wine cork in his bum."

"Wow!" Kim exclaimed with a hearty laugh. "Oh, here's a good one. My mother's sister got drunk with her husband and blew over a hundred grand gambling."

"Impressive."

"What is worse is that the money belonged to me!" Kim said with a raised voice.

"That's dreadful."

"They're slowly paying it back."

"That's good to hear." Karen hesitated, then asked, "Any deaths?"

"My uncle Rudy decided to drive his Datsun with his head sticking out of the sunroof. He stood on the seat while his friend Todd worked the gas. They drove off a bridge, and the crash killed them."

"My cousin, Zac, drove his snow machine into a tree. When they found his frozen body, he had a firm grip on his beer can with a massive smile."

They laughed, and Kim asked, "How's your health?"

"The good news is I follow my doctor's advice and have a full checkup every two months." Karen sighed and continued, "It's my heart."

"How bad."

"The doctors are optimistic, but you know how they are. Because of my medications, I'm ineligible for a transplant."

"I'm sorry."

"Nothing to be sorry about. I have only myself to blame."

"Godmother Karen," Emma interrupted. "What's this?" she asked while pointing to a rock that was cut in half and polished.

"That's quartz, sweetie," Karen answered. "Can you see the gold?"

"Yes."

"That's called a deposit." She looked thoughtful and asked, "What does the label say?"

"It say, 'First gold-bearing rock extracted from the Viper Mine.'"

"You read very well. Tell me, sweetie. What's a viper?"

"A snake. It have poison in teeth."

"Very good," Karen said, amazed.

"Why you have gold rock, Godmother Karen?"

"My parents owned that mine many years ago. It has long since closed, and I keep the rock as a memory."

"I understand."

"Would you like to see something?"

"Yes, Godmother Karen," Emma answered with a smile.

"Can I count on you to keep a secret?"

"Yes," Emma said confidently.

"You can only tell your mother and father. Do you understand?"

"I understand. I'm good at keeping secrets. Mommy Kim good at keeping secrets too!"

"Alright."

Karen took them on a tour of the gold processing room and storage vault. Kim could not believe her eyes, and when they returned to the living room, she said, "Gabe told me he saw an enormous pile, but I had my doubts."

"Did he tell you what I wanted to do with Emma?" Karen asked.

"We would be honored."

"We can make it official tomorrow at the courthouse."

"That would be amazing," Kim said with a warm smile.

Gabe walked inside, covered in mud, and said, "It was so dirty."

"I told you I would take care of it later."

"I enjoy working with my hands."

"Has he always been like this?"

"Since the moment we met," Kim answered, and everybody laughed.

•

The following day, Gabe visited the prison. He spoke with his friends and learned that Felix had been in the prison hospital for the last two weeks. Later, Gabe met with Warden Clayford and talked about old times. He was glad to learn that the inmates' headaches had ceased. Afterward, Gabe led the three yoga classes, and only Alvin Ray had regained some mental ability, which Gabe removed with his new method.

Kim, Emma, and Karen drove to the courthouse and filled out the paperwork to make Emma a native Alaskan. Afterward, they purchased groceries and stopped to fill up the gas tank of Karen's SUV. While Kim held the fuel nozzle, she noticed a man staring at her. "You that bitch Karen's new helper?" he asked angrily.

"If you ever call her 'bitch' again, you'll limp for the rest of your life."

The man looked stunned by the threat and turned away. Kim finished pumping the gas, glared at the man, and entered the car. "You brave, Mommy Kim," Emma said with pride.

"It is important to stand up for what's right."

"Thank you for what you said back there," Karen said with a thin smile. "I had to evict Donnie's father, and he's still angry."

"There's no excuse for speaking that way. He didn't even know me."

"True. But you should be more careful. Donnie's got a hair trigger."

"I was holding a gas nozzle and would've sprayed him from head to toe if he had taken one step toward me. And if that didn't work, I have a lighter in my purse."

Karen shook her head and laughed.

Later that afternoon, the weather warmed enough to allow Emma and Karen to take a nature hike. Emma wore adorable red boots and jumped in every slush puddle they came across.

Along the path, Karen described the trees, rocks, animals, and Native Alaskan history. Emma enjoyed learning and asked intuitive questions. An hour later, they walked up to an enormous field. "This is where the eagle sometimes hunts," Karen whispered, so as not to scare the wildlife. "Let's wait and see if he flies our way."

The two remained silent as they listened to the wind and watched the peaceful scene. "Godmother Karen, why Mommy Kim and Daddy Gabe talk so much about pee-pee hole?" Emma asked.

Karen grew uncomfortable as she considered how to answer this awkward question. A long moment later, she replied, "This is a topic for your parents."

"We talk about pee-pee hole. They say that is how babies are made. They use word sex. They say when I am older, my body will change, and I understand better."

"That's excellent advice."

"Why don't they tell me now?" Emma protested.

"I will provide you with the same answer my mother told me when I was a girl. Long ago, people lived like animals. Do you see that rabbit?"

"Bunny!" Emma chirped.

"Yes. Like people, that rabbit thinks about making babies. The difference is that rabbits cannot communicate with other rabbits in the same way that people do. We have a word called evolution. It means that a baby is better than its parents. A long time ago, people didn't speak, wear clothes, or live in houses, just like that rabbit. Now, people live in big cities, wear expensive clothing, and talk to each other. Throughout our evolution, people have changed and established many rules. One is that adults don't talk about sex with children."

"Why rule?" Emma wanted to know.

"Probably because it makes adults uncomfortable."

While watching the rabbit, Emma thought for a long moment and said, "Godmother Karen. What you say, I understand."

"Well, good."

"Why not Mommy Kim and Daddy Gabe answer like that?" Emma asked.

"Maybe the words didn't come to them."

"You wise, Godmother Karen."

"That's a nice compliment. Thank you."

"You're welcome."

The pair began walking, and Karen pointed out rabbit tracks and other signs of wildlife. Half an hour later, they came to another meadow. Karen said, "Look over there. We might see an eagle."

The pair stood for a long moment in silence, and Karen asked, "Sweetie, what did you mean when you said that you killed a man like a bug?"

A long moment later, Emma answered, "Bad man hit Mommy Kim and Daddy Gabe. It make me angry, so I cut man's neck, and he die. Like when I kill bug!"

Karen took a deep breath and asked, "How do you feel about killing that man?"

"Mommy Kim and Daddy Gabe tell me I do right."

"Do you feel sad about what you did?" Karen softly asked.

"Sometimes."

"What else do you think about the bad man?"

Emma remained silent for a long moment, turned to Karen, and whispered, "I frightened that I not do well. The bad man not die. The bad man hurt me."

"That sounds scary."

"I sometimes scary. Mommy Kim tell me that being scary is alright. But I don't want to be scary."

"Do you feel bad about taking that man's life?"

Emma stared at the meadow and pointed at the movement in a tree. The two stood in silence for a long time. "Yes," Emma murmured.

"I want to tell you about something that happened to me long ago," Karen said, then paused for a long moment while looking at the trees. She took a deep breath and said softly, "Three days after getting my jaw surgery, I returned home. Late in the evening, I heard a crash. When I came down to see what had broken, I found a man in the kitchen. When he saw me, he charged. I barely made it to my room and locked the door. Then the man began breaking down the door."

Karen kneeled to look into Emma's eyes.

"You kill bad man?" Emma asked.

"Yes, sweetie."

"You think about bad man?" Emma asked softly.

"I do."

"Will I think about my bad man?"

"Yes, sweetie, you will."

Emma began crying, and Karen hugged her. A long while later, Karen said, "It's good that you're sad. Crying means you're a good person. You saved your parents, and you also saved yourself. If you had not been brave, we would have never met."

Emma continued sobbing while Karen held her for several minutes. Finally, when Emma recovered, Karen said, "Look."

A bald eagle flew to a tree branch. Emma looked up and said, "It so beautiful. Thank you, Karen."

"You're welcome, sweetie. You know, that's the first time you called me Karen without saying 'godmother.'"

"I'm sorry."

"It's alright."

"Will killing bad man make me sad for long time?"

"Yes, sweetie. But in time, you'll think of your action as a source of strength."

"I will try. Why your bad man want hurt you?"

"Oh, him. Just a guy down on his luck."

Emma looked at Karen for a long while and asked, "If new bad man come into your house, you kill new bad man?"

"Yes, sweetie."

"You think I do good when I kill bad man?"

"Sweetie, you did what you had to do. I'm proud of you."

"I proud you too," Emma said with a weak smile.

"Good."

The pair watched the eagle until it flew away. Then, they made their way back to the house, Emma jumping in every puddle they passed.

While Emma took her nap, Karen discussed their conversation with Kim. Kim felt relieved that Emma had confronted her about her recent actions. She then thanked Karen for speaking to Emma about sex.

Later in the evening, Gabe returned from the prison, and they enjoyed a wonderful dinner of grilled venison and sautéed vegetables in a chili crème sauce.

After Emma was asleep, they all sat in front of the fire, and Gabe asked Karen, "Is there anything I can do to get Felix a pardon?"

Karen shook her head sadly. "I have tried talking to him many times about his options," she said.

"His health is declining."

"I spoke to the prison doctor, and the news isn't good. His liver and kidneys are failing. Unfortunately, it's only a matter of time."

"His last moments shouldn't be behind bars."

"It's what he wants," Karen said with a sigh.

"I wish I could do something," Gabe offered.

"Nonsense. You've done more for my brother than anybody. Including our parents."

"Well, I'll keep trying."

•

Gabe spent the next three days doing chores and repairs while the others ran errands and enjoyed shopping. On Sunday, they all visited Felix in the prison hospital. He appreciated the attention and meeting Emma. Gabe broached the subject of a medical release, but Felix was not interested. Karen, Kim, and Emma also asked him to consider the matter. It brought tears to his eyes when Emma asked.

Felix relented and said he would "think about it." He then asked Emma about reading. The two discussed education, and the sight brought tears to Karen and Kim. Gabe did his best to hold back his emotions, but still teared up.

The family stayed with Karen for an additional six days. During that time, they participated in another mud run, and Karen took Emma on two additional nature walks.

On the seventh day, the family got ready to leave. Emma hugged Karen for a long time.

Before Gabe entered the Jeep, Karen said, "A word."

"Sure."

Gabe followed Karen inside, and she handed him a paper bag. Inside, he saw a small electronic device. "I know you cannot talk about some topics, and I respect that," Karen said. "But please tell your friends to wipe their feet when they put this eavesdropping junk in my house."

"Oh, if I ever see them again, I will tell them that. Thank you so much for everything," Gabe said with a hearty laugh.

"Going to be back soon?" Karen asked.

"Count on it. Emma hasn't seen snow."

"Good. Now, off you go. You know how I hate long goodbyes."

"Karen, you're a dear friend. Take care."

"I will."

Gabe hugged Karen, got into the Jeep, and drove away. In his rear-view mirror, he saw her sobbing on the front steps.

•

Gabe returned the Jeep, and the family took a shuttle to the airport. They boarded a small plane, which landed at the recently enlarged Kuiu Island airport. Gabe drove a rented sedan along a recently paved road to the Kuiu Island Memorial Center. It was constructed on a cliff surrounded by tall trees. Three single-story brick buildings made a semicircle around 30 hexagonal granite pillars.

Gabe and Kim were stunned to see more than 100 people milling about. They paid the ten-dollar parking fee and exited their car. On the way to the pillars, Kim commented about the tacky merchandise shops, and Gabe shared her negative sentiment.

At the pillars, they saw the names of the deceased engraved in stone. Kim located her family at a nearby computer display, and they walked toward pillar fifteen. Along the way, other mourners stood solemnly, and several sobbed.

The family stopped when they reached the pillar, and Kim touched the names of her family. Gabe explained to Emma how Kim's family had died. Emma became stoic and tightly gripped her mother's hand. Later, she asked if she could touch the names, and Gabe lifted her.

When the time was right, they walked to pillar two, and Gabe found the names of his family. He was outraged when he saw Victoria's name spelled "Vactory." Gabe knew the Alaska coroner had made a mistake on the death certificate, and he had put significant effort into correcting it. Gabe suppressed his outrage, and he allowed himself to mourn. Kim lifted Emma to touch these names, and she took a long moment to reflect.

Ten minutes later, they walked into a room where a video was playing. A narrator described the "Kuiu Island meteor strike." Gabe and Kim watched with amusement as the narrator explained the "crucible theory as being an alternate but unsubstantiated opinion disproven by credible scientists." Gabe snickered, and the older woman beside him hissed, "Show some respect, young man."

"Sorry."

Kim shook her head, and when the video ended, the family walked to an exhibit displaying "fragments of the meteorite that took so many lives." Gabe and Kim looked at the rocks with amusement, wondering where they had come from.

Next, they headed to the main office, and Gabe asked to meet somebody in charge. A man in his late forties walked over, shook Gabe's hand, and said, "My name is Phillip Miller. I'm the acting director. Unfortunately, Jim's out sick today. How can I help you?"

"Pillar number two has my daughter's name misspelled. It's Victoria, not Vactory. Can you fix that?"

"Oh. Gee, I'm so sorry. We got those names from the state."

"When can you change it?"

"We've already corrected two mistakes, and I can send you a form to fill out. But those pillars are expensive, and we must bring in a large crane to remove them. I hate to ask, but can you provide proof of the correct spelling?"

"I can send you a certified copy of her corrected death certificate," Gabe answered in an annoyed voice. "Will that do?"

"That's perfect. What is your name and address so I can send you the paperwork?"

Gabe wrote down the information. Then, the man looked at him, bit his lip, and asked, "*The* Gabriel Alexander?"

Kim adopted a thin smile and said, "I'm Kim Alexander. His wife."

The man stepped back and asked in a stunned voice, "Gabe and Kim? The real Gabe and Kim?"

"Yes," Kim answered.

"Um. Wow. Gabe and Kim are in my office. And you have a daughter? Um, I didn't know."

"Please start the process," Gabe requested.

"You say it's Vactory? On pillar two?"

"Yes."

"Um. Yeah. I'll talk to Jim about sending you the form."

"Thank you," Kim said with a thin smile.

"Say, listen. Any chance we could talk to you about what happened? You know. For the video?"

"Absolutely not," Gabe tersely replied.

"Are you sure? It would mean a lot to the visitors to have the famous Kim and Gabe tell everybody what happened in their own words."

"We want to put all this behind us."

"I see. Well, I will tell Jim you stopped by."

"Thank you."

<That was annoying,> Gabe thought to Kim.

<At least they can fix the error.>

<True.>

The last attraction was a cliff with a beautiful ocean view. A nearby stand sold "biodegradable memory flowers for the fallen." Emma watched a girl throw a flower over the cliff, and she wanted to do the same. Kim purchased three for twenty-four dollars, and they each threw one toward the crashing waves. This simple gesture profoundly impacted the family as the waves tossed several flowers on the rocks below.

Several minutes later, they turned to leave, and the same older woman who had admonished Gabe yelled, "There he is. See, I told you."

"It's him!" a nearby man chirped. "That's the guy who went to jail."

Occasionally, people recognized Gabe and Kim in public. These encounters were always uncomfortable. "When did they let you out?" the man asked. "I thought it was 20 years of hard labor?"

"Um, yeah. Well, I'm free."

"Do you work here?" the man asked.

"Why the heck would I work here?"

"How big was the meteorite that sank your ship?"

"Um, the video over there explained everything pretty well. There's not much more to it."

The older woman became upset, and she said, "Hey. Wait a minute. You killed that girl's sister. That's not right. You should be in jail!"

Kim glared at the woman, and the family began walking away. Ten paces later, Emma turned back and yelled, "You make mommy sad. You do again, and you limp for the rest of your life!"

The statement embarrassed the older woman, and she turned away. The outburst caught the attention of the people nearby, and three pulled out their cell phones. <They're taking pictures,> Kim thought to Gabe.

<And?>

<Jason.>

<Oh, yeah. He's not going to like a bunch of pictures. What do we do?> Gabe asked.

<Watch.>

Kim walked over to a woman who was pointing her cell phone at her and grabbed it. The action surprised Gabe, and she looked at him with a challenging expression. So, he walked over to a man, took his phone, and did the same to a teenage girl. Kim smiled at Gabe and threw the phone into the ocean. Gabe smiled back and did the same. "Hey, that's my phone, asshat!" the teenage girl yelled.

"And now, it's gone," Gabe replied. "This is a memorial. You should know better."

The girl stared daggers at Gabe as he turned away. The family began briskly walking toward the parking lot. Five steps later, the teenage girl said, "OMG, that was Kim. He married Kim. And they had a baby."

Kim picked up Emma, and they walked faster. As they drove away, Kim said, "Emma, you were courageous."

"Lady say bad words. I protect you."

"That's my girl."

"Where did you learn to talk like that?" Gabe asked. "Limp for the rest of your life? Did you hear that on television?"

Emma looked at Kim, and they laughed.

•

Kim drove their rented car for 30 miles and arrived at the location where they met the aliens known as the Veronn. This was also where they said goodbye to the unseen wisps of their family members and other people who had perished in the tragic attack. Gabe and Kim returned to this site two years ago and placed items that held great personal significance on the ground.

Kim expected the area to be desolate, but a fence surrounded the site, and stalls sold souvenirs and food. A man directed their car to a dirt parking lot, where they paid a woman five dollars.

The family approached the fence and saw fifteen people in silent contemplation. Kim noticed a sign warning people not to touch items that mourners had previously left. A security guard was present, closely watching everybody.

They stopped where Gabe had placed the small Native Alaskan figure that had once belonged to Karen. It had faded due to weather exposure, but was still recognizable. Kim saw the decaying picture of Kobe Bryant that belonged to her brother and the Bob Marley cassette tape, which reminded them of surviving in the Alaska wilderness.

The family stood in quiet contemplation for several minutes before walking toward the parking lot. "Daddy Gabe, who is girl Christy?" Emma asked.

"What?"

"Who girl, Christy?"

"Before you were born, I had a daughter named Christy. You touched her name on the big rock. We honor the memories of my former wife,

Lydia, and my other daughter, Victoria. Mommy is here to honor the memory of her family."

"Girl Christy talk to me," Emma whispered.

"What?" Gabe exclaimed. "What did she say?"

"She happy."

"Is she alright?"

"Yes, Daddy Gabe."

"What else did she say?"

"She glad to meet me."

"Did anybody else talk to you?" Gabe asked.

"Who man Calvin?"

"That's my father," Kim whispered.

"He say, I do good against bad man."

"Is there anybody else?"

"Lots of people talk to me. They happy you here."

Kim said in a raised voice, "Thank you for speaking to Emma. We miss all of you."

The family felt a warm glow of emotion that uplifted their spirits, and five minutes later, Kim drove to the airport. They took three flights and arrived in Wenatchee, Washington. Kim checked them into a hotel, and the following day, Gabe met with his former yoga students at the Coyote Ridge Corrections Center. Fortunately, they no longer had telepathic ability.

That afternoon, the family flew to San Jose, California, and Gabe had a productive business meeting with his former Silicon Serpent boss, Al. They discussed Gabe's new asynchronous logic ideas, and he was relieved to deprogram Al's minor regained telepathic ability.

Kim and Emma spent the afternoon at the Children's Discovery Museum, and the following day, they flew to Torrance, California, for a meeting with Ken at Pacific Progressive Peripherals. Gabe was again relieved that Ken's telepathic ability was no longer present.

# TWELVE

On the plane ride home, Kim commented, <We need a vacation from our vacation.>

<You got that right, babe,> Gabe said with a big grin. <But we need to focus on the good things. All this deprogramming nonsense is behind us.>

<That's something to celebrate.>

Emma went to preschool the following day, and Kim noticed she was now more comfortable with her classmates. She hoped that Emma could soon attend school without their presence.

In Gabe's absence, the KimSemi employees made fantastic progress. They were ready to send a test article to fabrication to validate Gabe's theories. He warmly shook everybody's hand to congratulate them.

The Harrington Enterprises employees had also worked hard with an aggressive marketing campaign against a competitor. They had 32 locations in Alabama, and the owner fought an ill-conceived price war, which left him unable to pay his employees. So, Kim offered six million dollars to buy the entire operation, and the owner grudgingly accepted.

Emma attended her first play date a week later. The two girls spent the afternoon watching television, playing board games, and talking. When Kim picked Emma up, she was relieved to see that Emma was happy and showing independence. Her friend's mother asked why Emma needed her parents at school. Kim told her that Emma had deep separation anxieties and that they had worked hard to overcome the issue. Her friend's mother was unconvinced but understood that children could be difficult.

Emma's mental abilities were rapidly improving, which increasingly caused social problems. For example, she had difficulty understanding when to remain silent about other people's thoughts and when to refrain from sharing exotic white box information. The "I'm kidding" line had gotten old with her teachers and fellow students. Plus, her mental ability interfered with Gabe and Kim's relationship, as Emma had endless personal questions.

Two weeks later, Kim came home to find an unfamiliar brown sedan in the driveway, and the house's front door was open. She pulled her Beretta handgun from her purse and walked inside to see Jason sitting at the kitchen table, playing on his phone.

An unfamiliar woman sat across from him and glared at Kim. She had jet-black hair, a light complexion, stood five foot four, and had an athletic build. The woman wore an oversized gray sweatshirt with a tear in the left arm, faded blue jeans, and well-worn black Converse shoes. Kim knew a bob haircut would better suit the woman's face; gray was not her color. She saw her slender fingers twitch nervously and the undeniable distrust in her gaze.

Kim then noticed a pizza box, a six-pack of fruit sodas, and a carton of applesauce. With a scowl, she put her gun away and said, "You're back."

"And I brought pizza," Jason answered in a charming voice. "No beer this time."

"I take it you want something from us, and we have no choice."

"That depends on your perspective," Jason answered with a smile.

"Gabe and Emma will be home in ten."

"Wonderful."

"Who's this?"

"You may call her Kelly. She has been keeping a close eye on you three."

Kelly nodded and picked up a newspaper. "From this point forward, you'll be working with her," Jason continued.

"So, we will never meet again?" Kim asked suspiciously.

Jason shook his head with a broad smile and replied, "I like you. Yes, we'll meet again."

Kim did not understand why Jason acted so friendly. It seemed as if their company baseball team had won a game, and they were celebrating with pizza. Kim sat on the couch, staring at Jason as he played on his phone. Several minutes later, Gabe drove up, and Kim thought, <Jason's here with a woman named Kelly.>

<Any problems?> Gabe asked.

<Something's up. Jason is keeping his thoughts on a single subject. It's clear that he has had mental training to prevent me from reading him.>

<Is it safe?>

<I think so. Bring Emma in.>

"Kelly, I bet Kim just told Gabe we're here," Jason announced.

Kelly nodded without looking up, and Kim asked, "So, Kelly. Are you as serious as Jason?"

Kelly smiled thinly and answered in a soft, squeaky voice, "Jason taught me everything about my job. And, yes, I'm always serious. By the way, I liked your alligator video. Nice technique."

Kim felt a chill go up her spine. A minute later, Gabe walked in with Emma and said in a reserved voice, "Jason, Kelly."

Jason laughed and said, "See, I told you she would communicate without words. Anyway. This is Kelly, and she's taking over for me."

"Why are you here?" Gabe demanded.

"Always right to the point. We have a lot to talk about. But first, let's relax. I brought pizza."

"No poison? Right?" Kim asked with a thin smile.

Kelly laughed, and Jason shook his head. "By the way," Gabe said with a sly grin. "I have a present for you."

"Really?" Jason looked at Gabe with suspicion. "That's unexpected."

Gabe retrieved a brown bag from a drawer and handed it to Jason. He looked inside, laughed, and said, "I wondered why my listening device went silent. That Karen's a smart one."

"She said to take off your shoes next time."

Kelly laughed, and Jason admitted, "Sorry. I was short on time. Rookie mistake."

"You installed it?"

"Alaska is my territory."

"Well, consider yourself warned."

Jason and Kelly laughed again. Then, everyone began eating, and the mood lightened. Gabe appreciated the flavor and asked which restaurant made the pizza. Jason said she bought it from a local place that the family had never tried. Emma surprised Kelly with her excellent language skills and discussed making applesauce. Later, Kelly informed Gabe that she had driven the car that had taken away Lieutenant Tiller and Captain Jefferson, the two military officers who had threatened Gabe months before. He asked what happened to the men, and Kelly smiled without answering. Then, Jason revealed he had been the second gunman at the Alaska crossroads exchange. His confident expression made Gabe and Kim uncomfortable.

When they finished eating, Kelly said goodbye and left. Everybody else sat in the living room. Jason faced the family and seemed in a good mood, leaving Gabe and Kim perplexed. Emma beamed a huge smile, adding to their confusion.

"Do you know what it means to be read into a program?" Jason asked.

Gabe nodded. "My coworker Gustavo used to work for a defense contractor. He told me that when someone starts a secret project, they make you sign paperwork stating you will never discuss the program. Is that what you mean?"

"Correct. Except, no paperwork."

"Just a bullet to the head?" Gabe filled in the blanks.

"I would like to avoid that."

"So, we have no choice but to deal with this for the rest of our lives?" Kim protested.

"On the contrary. Something good is about to happen to you three."

"Wait!" Kim interrupted. "What about Emma? Is she being read in, too?"

"Yes, she's a big part of this."

"No, that's not fair. She deserves to live a normal life!"

"In an ideal world, that would be the case. But that's how it is."

"Is there nothing we can do to protect her?" Kim pleaded.

"I'm not the enemy, and I promise, no harm will come to Emma."

"I wish I could believe you," Kim said. She pinched the bridge of her nose, fighting back tears of anger.

"In a week, you'll forget all about your suspicions."

"I hope so."

Jason took a deep breath. "Now, for the formalities. You can never share the information that I am about to tell you. No exceptions. Consider yourself read in. Kelly swept this place for surveillance devices, and I double-checked." Jason leaned back, looked at Kim, smiled, and continued, "I've been waiting a long time to be honest with you about everything. I'm so envious of you three. Especially you, Kim."

"Why?"

"You've got the gift. With it, you will get to interact with some amazing *people*. And Gabe. Wow. You'll get to play with some fun toys. It all reminds me of what I learned way back when. But, before we begin, I must handle some unpleasant business. I need all your Kuiu Island evidence. Right now. Let's go."

Gabe looked annoyed, stood, and walked into the kitchen. With Jason's help, they moved the refrigerator out of its nook. Then Gabe moved the wooden floor slats, revealing a steel plate. He pulled up the plate, revealing a metal box. "I looked through this house for a week and couldn't find your hidey-hole," Jason commented.

Gabe smiled craftily, and they returned to the living room. He took the rifle out of the box and handed it to Jason.

Jason's eyes widened. "Do you know what you have here?" he asked.

"It's some type of Veronn gun," Gabe answered.

"What's a Veronn?"

"It is what the aliens call themselves."

"Alright, lesson one. The word 'aliens' isn't complimentary. We call non-Earth people *off-worlders.* Remember that. Now, this weapon is exquisite. See the focusing coils?" Jason pointed to the round lobes and continued, "This rifle accelerates free atomic particles and then alters their phase using the coils."

"Is that good?" Kim asked.

"Good? Ha! This rifle is stunning. We only have vague descriptions of weapons like this. And to be holding one? Wow!"

"Why are the coils so special?" Kim asked.

"I'm limited to one high school science class, but I'll try to give you my best description. Think of atomic particles like bullets. Like a bullet, the faster a particle travels, the deeper it penetrates. The important part is that there is a practical limit. For example, no bullet could ever travel through a hundred feet of rock. Now, the focusing coil changes everything. This rifle identifies the target type based on the energy that bounces back. It continually changes the phase of the particles until they pass through the target. There is no defense against this weapon. Plus, atomic particles impart a vast amount of energy. When you combine the two, the destruction is overwhelming."

"How destructive?" Gabe said.

"You could shoot somebody on the other side of a mountain. You could alter the phase to destroy a house. Or shoot a leg off an ant. Weapons like this destroyed your cruise ship."

"Wait, I took physics," Kim interrupted. "You can only alter the phase of a wave. Not a particle. Your explanation makes little sense."

"Kim, I'm not a scientist. This description is the best I can provide. How does this work? I don't see a trigger?"

"I operated it with my mind," Gabe answered with a big grin.

"Wow! Just wow. Do you know why they did it this way?"

"It's more ergonomic."

"That's an intuitive answer, but incorrect. Using your mind reduces reaction time. What else you got?"

Gabe reluctantly handed Jason a mini-DVD and two videotapes. "The DVD shows a crowd evaporating," he whispered.

"Yikes!" Jason exclaimed.

"It's difficult to watch."

"And the tape?"

"It shows Kim and me being taken."

"An important record," Jason said, nodding.

"We want the videos back."

"Did you make a copy?"

"No."

"You can view the videos whenever you wish, but I must keep them. Physical proof like this is far too dangerous in the wild. What else?"

Gabe paused for a long moment and then handed Jason the white box. He flipped it in his hands to see all sides, deep in thought. Then, his eyes lit up, and he exclaimed, "This is an onk!"

"We call it the white box."

"An onk lets you communicate over infinite distances and access off-world knowledge. This is fantastic!"

"We know," Kim answered with a smile.

Jason stood and yelled, "What do you mean, you know? You cannot possibly know!"

"We use it all the time."

"What? No human can use an onk. Human minds don't work that way. It's completely impossible."

"Emma can also use it," Kim said.

"Not Emma. Really?"

"Emma, would you like to use the okey-okey on Jason?"

"I do, Mommy Kim," Emma answered softly. She walked over and held the onk. Jason stared at her wide-eyed, unexpectedly placing his hand over his eyes.

"What the heck. What the heck!" Jason exclaimed. "You used an onk. She used an onk. Did you see that? Wow! I need to make a phone call."

"Our friend has had enough," Gabe told Emma.

"Yes, Daddy Gabe."

Jason pulled out his phone, dialed, and said, "Sammy, it's me. It's fine. Look, unexpected development. They have an onk and can use it. Even Emma."

Jason listened for a long moment and said, "I agree. Thanks." He ended the call and said, "Your stock went up."

"How much?" Kim demanded.

"Through the roof. Alright, this changes everything. And I mean everything. Hmm. At the end of this meeting, you'll probably be my boss. Crazy."

The pair looked at each other, confused. "We're keeping the onk?" Gabe asked. "Right?"

"Oh, heck yeah. You're keeping that. But we need to discuss how you three will use it. Alright?"

"Sure," Gabe answered without enthusiasm. "What about the rifle?"

"I need to take that with me."

"That's fair."

"Have you shot it?"

"I used it to shoot a wolf in Alaska, but I didn't want to go target shooting in Florida because people might see me."

"Wow, even back then, you had the mental mojo to use it? Well, you made the correct decision not to use it again."

Jason took a moment to study the family. Eventually, he adopted an amused expression and said, "You know, not many calls go from Fairbanks, Alaska, to Miramar, Florida."

"You monitored the calls we made on our prepaid cell phones?"

"Yes."

Kim felt her anger rise. "And you listened in on our conversations?"

"Lots of lovey-dovey stuff."

"We didn't want the government in our bedroom," Gabe said, scowling.

"Understandable. But don't try a stunt like that again."

"Understood."

Jason leaned back, nodded twice, and said, "One last bit of unpleasant business. I already told you about the virus I injected you with while you were in my car."

"Yes," Kim answered through gritted teeth.

"I had orders to make a second attempt at the courthouse when you married. They wanted me to shake your hand and transfer several strains of targeted bacteria. Afterward, I had orders to pick up your evidence, and that would be that.

"Now, this is where things went crazy. You two read me so easily, and I decided to abort. To put it mildly, my actions did not go unnoticed. It took a lot of convincing, but my superiors agreed to spare your lives. From that time on, we put the three of you under the microscope. Finally, when we felt you were worthy of our trust, we assigned Gabe a task. You could consider this a job interview."

"A job interview?" Kim exclaimed.

"That's how I like to think of it."

"So, now what? Are we going to shake hands and kill people?"

"No, no, no," Jason answered, shaking his head. "Not like that. You two are far too valuable to be in the field."

"Well, what do you want us to do?" Kim demanded.

"Congratulations. You're part of the family."

"What family?" Gabe questioned, suspicious.

"That is going to take a while to explain. I was only going to provide the basics. However, using an onk moves you three to the head of the class. Hmm." Jason leaned back for a long moment before continuing. "Well, I have permission to tell you everything, so let's begin at the beginning. And I mean the real beginning. This is going to be more fun than I imagined. Come to think of it, this will be the most comprehensive debriefing my department has ever executed.

"Alright, here it is. As luck would have it, a special off-worlder needed a place to call home. I'm not sure why, but he came to planet Earth. This exceptional individual had the unique ability to blend in, and I'm not aware of any other race that can do this. He utilized this ability to study Earth's culture and travel among its inhabitants.

"I don't know when he first landed on Earth, but at the stroke of midnight, December fifteenth, 1864, this individual woke President Lincoln in his bedroom. The two chatted till the wee hours of the morning. Oh, what I would give to have been a fly on that wall. It must have been remarkable.

"Anyway, this individual revealed every scrap of Civil War tactical information and outlined a practical path to achieve victory. Lincoln appreciated the detailed information and wanted to know its source and cost. The individual said there was no cost and would later reveal the source.

"They had more meetings, and one day, this individual revealed himself as an off-worlder. Now, that brings up an important point. I keep referring to this off-worlder without a name. I met this individual once, and he asked me, 'What is your uncle's name? Call me that.' I called him 'Fred,' and of course, Lincoln called him Josiah. So, if you meet this individual, you two will come up with a name to call him.

"Anyway, Fred convinced Lincoln to set up a dual-purpose department. We call it the 'Department of Labor Statistics,' or DLS for short. Our existence isn't a secret; we generate comprehensive labor reports that anybody can access. We upgraded our website six months ago to improve its searchability and display detailed historical trends. Now, I bet you have never heard of the DLS or its labor reports. That's big government for you.

"Oh, another thing. You will also find the Bureau of Labor Statistics, which does the same thing. The problem with the DLS is that we provide accurate reports, but politicians need better numbers to make them appear like they are doing a good job. We call them the 'Bureau of Fiction Writers.'"

Emma laughed, and Jason found her quick reaction remarkable. "Anyway, Fred used his influence over the years to enact several secret laws," he continued. "This meant that legally, the DLS was the only entity allowed to deal with off-worlders. We have about two thousand employees and receive limited funding from various sources. Our overall goal is to prevent off-world interaction."

"Like the movie *Men in Black*?" Kim interrupted.

Jason scowled and answered tersely, "That's a terrible movie, and it minimizes everything we stand for. Memory zappers. How absurd! However, they got about five percent correct. The DLS is a worldwide entity that controls all off-world activities, with one notable exception that I will address in a moment.

"Under the law, an Alien Control Officer or ACO's job is to handle the off-world situation. And yes, I realize this title has the word 'aliens.' To answer your next question, I am an ACO, and most of Alaska is my territory. Usually, it is an easy gig. Like us, off-worlders like to go where it is warm.

"What does an ACO do? In an off-world event, we have full authority to contain the situation. However, that is where our jurisdiction ends. I cannot even issue a parking ticket. My bosses make that quite clear, and the punishment for a slight infraction is draconian.

"Alright. We started small and expanded as Fred convinced other world leaders to write secret DLS laws. As a result, every country has a department dealing with labor statistics. Even the Vatican has a department."

"Why?" Kim interrupted.

"For reasons I'll get to in a moment, having close ties with religious leaders is important. Now. What do we do? Our primary task is to locate all off-worlders. Once discovered, we make it clear they're not welcome. To help, Fred set up 138 satellites to detect off-world spacecraft and send out a signal saying, 'We're not ready. Go away.'

"When an off-worlder ignores this signal, we get a heads-up and send an ACO agent to the landing site. We then influence the off-worlders to leave.

"Now, this brings up a question. How do we communicate with an off-worlder? In my career, I have had thirteen off-world encounters.

The protocol is to point a gun at them and then point to the sky. They grasp the basic message, but the situation becomes tense when an off-worlder fails to comply. Since the DLS was founded, over 400 ACOs have lost their lives, including my mentor, John.

"Next, publicity. Sometimes, the public gets a hint about what we do. The Kuiu Island incident is by far the largest, but not the worst. In the summer of '87, we had a major incident outside Trinidad, Cuba. Three crafts landed, and 211 off-worlders began interacting with the locals. They were hell-bent on somehow taking over the planet. Things got ugly, and there were house-to-house gun battles. We had luck on our side because of Cuba's closed media. And yes, Kim, many innocent Cubans had to pay the ultimate price to keep things quiet."

Kim scowled, and Jason continued, "Next big issue. In 1962, Air Force General Curtis LeMay found out about the DLS— pure dumb luck. An X-15 followed an off-world craft to our base outside Valencia, California. On a side note, you can still see the old DLS runway from the nearby Six Flags Theme Park— kind of crazy.

"Anyway, LeMay used his influence to force a DLS policy change, which is the exception I mentioned earlier. Now, all recovered off-world ships go to the Air Force. Additionally, they are responsible for all prisoners. Everything happens at what the media calls 'Area 51.' Incidentally, the actual name is 'Virgilio Airfield.' Never search for that name on the internet.

"Where was I? Oh, the Air Force. They are lousy at keeping secrets, and rumors about Virgilio Airfield spread. In the seventies, they should have moved all that stuff to their secret base in Indiana. Boneheads!

"Anyway, the Air Force off-world control headquarters is two blocks from our Burbank office. The big bosses made some hoity-toity agreements to maintain close ties, but working together is always difficult. The bozos call themselves 'U.S. Space Force' like they are superheroes. Firkin' losers."

Gabe chuckled, and Kim shook her head.

"Now, let's get into the nitty-gritty. There are no big surprises with off-worlders. You have seen the... What did you call them?"

"Veronn," Kim answered.

"Did they look like mini-humans?"

"Yes."

"Well, there you go. Science fiction has it all wrong. No pointy-ear Star Trek Vulcans or furry Star Wars Chewbaccas. Only human-looking beings. But there are differences, such as small ears or tiny eyes. Also, I have seen pictures of home planets, and there are no surprises. They vote, have babies, watch TV, and wear clothes that anger their parents."

Emma grinned, and Kim shook her head with a smile. "Now, their technology is far more advanced, and so is their society," Jason continued. "Plus, they have telepathy."

"You forgot to mention teleporting," Gabe added.

"Disappearing in one location and appearing in another? That's not possible."

"The Veronn teleported us. The video shows it."

"Really?" Jason asked while biting his lip. "Hmm. That's supposed to be completely impossible. I'll investigate that."

"What about invisibility?" Gabe asked.

"Also impossible."

"The Veronn did that too."

Jason bit his lip again and said, "Hmm. I'll investigate that, too."

"We saw a massive ship appear right in front of us."

"Wow, that's crazy. To my knowledge, there are no lightsabers, tractor beams, spacecraft shields, food synthesizers, wormholes, or blowing up planets. Also, they never get into epic space battles. In fact, ships rarely have weapons. They're too heavy."

"What do they do for fun?" Kim asked with a smile. "And what do they want to achieve?"

"The same things we do. They want to have better toys and improve their lives. But here's something that might surprise you. They also enjoy learning about us. One of our departments collects books, music, art, videos, and science information for trade. Culture is a universal currency."

"Really?" Kim exclaimed.

"Yeah. Hey, want to hear something strange? Every single culture we've met loves *The Three Stooges*."

"That's odd," Kim commented. "A bunch of off-worlders watching *The Three Stooges*? I would think they would have much better entertainment."

"Oh, words cannot describe all the fantastic technology. For example, they have a suit called a Dotsun that immerses you in music. They call the music a 'Kebo,' and the experience is crazy popular.

"What else? Oh, there is food that changes its taste when you eat it, and there is hairspray that changes its color. Then, the big one. They have a machine called an assembler. This device builds stuff atom by atom. You can make amazing products with one of those. I'm sure the rifle has parts produced by an assembler. Oh, yeah. The things you can do with an onk are beyond my comprehension. Crazy. Anyway, that's all I can think of off the top of my head.

“Next big topic. It’s difficult to travel great distances in space. The problem comes down to energy storage versus distance versus payload versus the type of space you travel through. As I have told you, my physics knowledge is super limited, so this is the best I can do.”

Jason put his right hand out flat and continued, “A gen one craft travels through space this way. The gen one’s are small and can only carry up to six off-worlders. Gen one’s are easy to make, and that is ninety-five percent of what we see.”

Jason twisted his hand ninety degrees and continued, “A gen two craft travels through space this way. Much more efficient, with far greater capability and big payloads. To make a gen two, you need advanced technology and specialized assemblers. Your Veronn friends traveled in a gen two. Now, the gen three craft? Wow.”

Jason moved his hand so that his flat palm faced forward and continued, “They travel this way. I already know what you are thinking. It is impossible to travel this way. Gen three technology is beyond advanced. I understand that only one of these crafts has ever been made. Anyway, the off-worlders who made those crafts moved their entire population to escape their sun going nova.

“Now. How does faster-than-light travel work? The best I can tell you is that giant magnets open a void and pull the craft forward. Then, other magnets push together, which closes the void behind. The difference between the gen ones, twos, and threes is in how the magnets interact.

“Regarding generating power, navigating, time distortions, and all that other technical mumbo-jumbo? That’s way beyond me.

“Now, let’s talk about the off-worlders who come to our planet. Keep in mind that traveling between planets is difficult, dangerous, and expensive. So, there must be a critical reason to start a journey. Plus, Earth doesn’t have a lot to offer.

“We have four visitor classifications. The first is a single. This occurs when a craft arrives due to a navigation error or gets damaged. Given how much it requires to make the journey, it’s surprising that we encounter so many.

“The second group we call explorers. These are scientists or traders. Typically, they arrive, see that we have nothing to offer, and leave.

“Now we get to the more direct off-worlders. The third class is called aggressors. They are either military-backed explorers or the military. This class makes sense because making an off-world craft is challenging. It usually requires a vast government effort, and putting soldiers into a craft is a natural extension.

"It's not as bad as it seems. Aggressors almost always use gen ones. Due to their limited payload, they are unable to cause significant damage. However, we always fear viral or cyber warfare. Another fear is a big gen one invasion. This happened in Phoenix in 1993 with fifteen craft– another big mess.

"Now, let me explain why the aggressors usually arrive in gen ones. As I explained, gen twos are advanced machines. By the time a society develops enough to create a gen two, they have mellowed out. But your Veronn friends are the exception to this rule. Do you know why they attacked?"

"They told us they made a mistake," Gabe answered. "Apparently, it was an inexperienced commander."

"A mistake? That's quite odd, but your explanation answers many questions."

"They seemed confused that Kim and I were a couple. They also didn't comprehend killing our families."

"They did not comprehend what it means to take a life?" Jason asked with raised eyebrows. "How insane."

"I know."

"You want to hear something strange?" Kim asked. "They said *we* were the aliens."

"What did that mean?" Jason asked.

"We never understood."

"Odd. Very odd." Jason took a moment and continued. "There is one more group. We call them fanatics, who are the exception to all the rules. These off-worlders are super-religious, and their calling is to convert the nonbelievers. They are a driven, power-hungry bunch that will do anything to achieve their domination goals.

"The DLS has had three encounters with this class. I already told you about the attack in Cuba. That was a race called Grazen. Before arriving on Earth, they had invaded several peaceful worlds and forced the locals to build gen one and gen two craft. They planned to do the same on Earth. In short, we got lucky. The whole thing makes me hate religion."

"Hey, I go to church every Sunday," Kim protested.

"Wait a second. There is a tremendous difference here. Hmm, let me explain. What is your religion's central message?"

"That's easy," Kim quickly answered. "Galatians 5:22. But the fruit of the spirit is love, joy, peace, forbearance, kindness, goodness, faithfulness."

"See, that's my point. While Earth's religions may occasionally bend the good book, they all share a peaceful message. On the other hand, fanatics use crafted messages to exploit mental weakness. They have slick ideological concepts based on solid scientific principles and powerful media presentations. To top it off, they develop targeted bacteria that alter the brain.

"Then, to take it all home, they pump their believers full of good old-fashioned drugs to ensure complete obedience. To the upper echelon, it's all about maintaining power, resulting in an enslaved planet. The only thing in our court is that all off-world societies hate fanatics, and three allies have promised to help if another incident occurs.

"Now, on to big topics. The universe contains approximately two trillion galaxies, each with billions of solar systems. A galaxy is about a hundred thousand light-years across, and the distance from one galaxy to another is around 2.5 million light-years. Gen one ships can only travel a few hundred light-years, and gen twos can travel up to a thousand. That limits travel to within our galaxy. I don't know what a gen three does.

"Scientists estimate our galaxy has two hundred billion solar systems. Long ago, it was determined that our galaxy has seven spiral arms. Of course, everybody argues there are a different number of spirals, but this isn't important. The important thing is that Earth is in spiral number six.

"So, it's called Division 6, and we interact with the races within this division. That's about forty thousand off-world planets with intelligent life. Right now, we are on good terms with 22 races. Most are nearby, meaning a gen one can go there. My favorite race is the Prune. They are a friendly bunch with good heads on their shoulders. Hopefully, you will have the opportunity to meet them.

"Well, that's the basics. Now, I suspect you want to know all about me. I'm sorry to say that there isn't much to tell. First off, Jason is my cover name. My actual name is Andrew, and I grew up in Chicago. I had an awful childhood full of beatings, drugs, crime, and skipping school. When I turned eighteen, a judge told me I could go to jail for five years or join the Army. I made the wrong choice and enlisted. To put it mildly, I headed nowhere fast.

"And then, one day, everything changed. I had been cleaning latrines for two solid months because I stole a jeep. My good behavior earned me an evening pass off base. So, I walked to the nearest bar, grabbed a cold one, and started checking out the women. All was going fine until these three macho Delta Force guys strutted up. They had returned from a successful mission and were pumped. I was through cleaning toilets and was on my best behavior. But one of them singled me out. He kept pushing me and flicking peanuts in my ear. Well, one push too many, and it was on.

"I may not look it, but I fight well. The meatheads never saw it coming, and I beat them bloody. Of course, the MPs rolled in and found me holding my beer while watching sports. The next day, I found myself in more trouble than ever. Three weeks later, one of these patched-up Delta Force guys came by my jail cell and dared me to join. Well, to piss him off, I did. It turns out that I never had a challenge worthy of my ego.

"Six years later, the CIA recruited me as a field agent. I went all over the world on all kinds of missions. One took me deep into Russia. I got all jazzed about blowing the lid off a secret organization. It turns out I'd located the Russian DLS office. They captured me and asked the DLS bosses what to do. Management reviewed my profile, and I ended up working for them.

"Now you know my story. Let me outline the next step. On Monday morning, you three will be on a plane to Burbank. We coordinate all the off-world interactions from that location. Donna will make all the arrangements."

Kim eyed Jason suspiciously. "That's it?"

"That's it."

"How long are we going to be there?" Gabe asked.

"That depends on you. In a week, you'll know your answer."

"What else do we need to learn?"

"There's so much. I haven't even scratched the surface."

"What about time travel?" Gabe asked. "That's supposed to be possible when you go faster than the speed of light."

"Good topic. Long story short: From my perspective, no, it isn't possible. From your perspective, yes, it's possible."

"That makes little sense," Kim said.

"I know. Here is the full deal. Emma cannot play with dinosaurs, but she could travel back in time to speak with you this morning. That's the best explanation I can offer. This raises an important topic. Never time-travel. And I mean never! If you do, another part of our organization called the Time Cops will come after your butts. And you think I am a hard-ass? Ha! Their only job is to kill. They can even kill you in the past to cover up a mistake you will never make."

Kim shook her head. "That makes no sense."

"I know. Oh, that reminds me, I forgot to discuss the Vatican's involvement in the DLS. We have a spiritual division that helps with the fanatics and keeps Earth's religions in check. Apparently, they don't have many officers, and I've only met one. However, they have a lot of pull. Always do what they say.

"Oh, creepy topic. At some point in the past or the future, faster-than-light travel was invented. Unfortunately, something terrible happened, leaving an echo. As a result, when you travel faster than light, you sometimes see their laboratory. I'm told that it looks like a high school chemistry class. You know, beakers, electronics, and test tubes.

"On that same topic, I've never been off-world. Heck, I've never even been into outer space. Anyway. Did you see the lab when they took you?"

"We don't remember a thing," Kim answered.

"Hmm."

"How often do off-worlders take people?" Gabe asked. "You know, like an alien abduction?"

"That's only in the movies. It never happens in real life."

"What about us?" Kim asked.

"I guess you two are the exception." Jason shrugged. "Oh, one last thing. Some ground rules. No interacting with off-worlders without permission. And no using your onk without permission. Got it?"

The pair nodded, and Jason said, "Good. Here's Kelly's contact info. Call her with any local issues. Your first assignment is to contact Donna to arrange your travel. We expect you to be at our office on Monday morning, 8:00 a.m. sharp."

"And that's it?" Gabe asked.

"Yup."

"You came from Alaska to tell us this? Why not have Kelly talk to us?"

Jason looked at Gabe with a serious expression, and Gabe answered his own question. "You needed to be sure."

"Yup."

"And we passed?" Kim asked.

"Yup."

"Cool."

"Well, I'm off. Be seeing you around. Enjoy the rest of the pizza."

"Wait!" Kim exclaimed. "We have more questions."

"Monday."

With that, Jason departed. Gabe turned to Kim and thought, <This isn't how I expected my day to go.>

<Same here.>

<Well, I guess we should make some plans.>

<It's always an adventure with you, husband,> Kim thought warmly.

<You love calling me husband.>

<I do.>

The pair made hasty work arrangements and packed for an extended trip.

# THIRTEEN

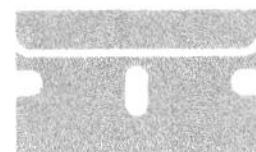

The family arrived in Burbank, California, that Sunday afternoon. Donna arranged a furnished apartment near the main office and a four-door rental car. That evening, they unpacked and went to sleep early.

The following day, they drove to a modest office building and had their identification verified by security. At the front desk, a pleasant woman greeted them. She wore a tailored blue dress with a thin gold necklace. A confident expression graced the woman's light skin, and her sparkling blue-green eyes conveyed quiet strength. With striking brown hair coiled into a sophisticated bun, she exuded an air of timeless grace. Kim estimated her age at 35 but sensed something was far out of place. Gabe was just as confused.

The woman began pleasantly, "Greetings, Kim, Emma, and Gabe. It's nice to meet you. My name is Donna Parks, and I run the DLS logistics."

"Nice to meet you in person," Kim said with a warm smile. "Thank you for all your help arranging flights and keeping us out of trouble."

"It is my pleasure."

<What's with her?> Kim thought to Gabe.

<It is like she is a blank sheet of paper. I get nothing.>

"Having trouble reading me?" Donna asked.

"Um, yes, actually," Gabe admitted.

"I'm what's known in the science fiction community as an android. A robot, if you will."

"Wow!" Kim gushed.

"Not all the off-worlders are biological."

"I didn't know."

"Lady Donna is not a person?" Emma asked.

"My, my. You speak well. Please refer to my kind as a synthetic being."

"I do, lady Donna."

"Your first task will be to speak with Mr. Sam Edgerton. He is the West Coast director of the DLS and oversees all off-world interactions. After you complete this task, I will assign another."

Gabe and Kim felt overwhelmed as Donna led them down a long hallway to a large wooden door. Donna knocked and escorted them inside.

Sam exuded an air of authority, seated behind the imposing expanse of a black steel desk. In his late fifties, he wore a blue pinstriped suit. There was a sharpness to Sam's features that belied his age, a powerful resolve in the depths of his steely-gray eyes. His receding white hair was cropped in a sharp crew cut, framing his face with sophistication. Gabe thought Sam looked like the millionaire Ross Perot.

"Thank you, Donna," Sam said. "Please take a seat."

Gabe and Kim sat with Emma on Kim's lap. Then, Donna closed the door, and Kim asked, "Do we look better than the reports?"

Sam laughed and said, "Feisty. I like that. This is a splendid start. Jason provided you with the basic DLS background; I'm sure you have more questions. It'll take time to get a handle on things. First off. Do you have your onk? Let's see it."

Gabe pulled the onk out of his pocket. Sam briefly looked at the device, handed it back, and asked, "All three of you can use it?"

"Correct," Gabe answered.

"How many times have you contacted the off-world race you call the 'Veronn?'"

"Once," Kim replied.

"And, what information did they provide?"

"They wanted to know why it took so long to contact them, and they told us they came here by mistake because of their new commander. They also referred to humans as aliens."

Sam leaned back and said, "That's most unusual."

"Jason said the same thing," Gabe added.

"He informed you that from now on, you're only to use your onk with our permission?"

"Yes," Gabe confirmed.

"Have you done as he asked?"

"We haven't used our onk to communicate with each other since speaking with him."

"Good."

Sam again leaned back and looked at the three people for a long moment. "How well can you read me?" he wanted to know.

"You don't know what to ask us next, and your finger hurts," Kim answered with a big grin.

"Very impressive. I pinched my hand on my car door this morning."

Kim changed the subject. "Did you order our deaths?"

Sam looked away, looked back, nodded, and said humbly, "Jason explained the circumstances behind my decision."

Kim's eyes narrowed. "I wanted to meet the man who gave the order."

"That decision rests on my shoulders."

"I see," Kim said with a scowl.

"Do you appreciate my logic?"

"We get it. No off-world bugs," Gabe replied.

"Will there be a problem between us?" Kim demanded.

"Not as long as you play by the rules."

"Will you clearly explain the rules?"

"Our rules are simple. Do as we say, keep our secrets, and conduct no off-world interactions without permission. Can you follow that?"

"We can," Kim answered.

"Good. You have nothing to fear. I promise."

"Forever?" Gabe asked.

"Meaning?"

"Can we leave this place without consequences?"

"Several DLS members have retired. And no, they didn't retire to pine boxes. Our culture takes a bit of getting used to, but we're a team and look out for each other." Sam leaned back briefly and continued, "I hadn't considered your position. You three are a big exception to everything. Well, I suppose some bridge mending is in order. With that in mind, I want you to understand that the DLS doesn't hold a grudge. I only followed our strict protocol."

"We understand," Kim admitted.

"Well, if it's any consolation, you are being given the keys to the castle. That brings up a point. Everything we do is compartmentalized. This means that we never ask questions unrelated to our tasks. However, for you three, that rule won't always apply. Therefore, I request that you take it easy until the staff becomes accustomed to these circumstances. In time, they'll come around.

"Oh, that brings up another topic. All DLS personnel have false identities. Sometimes, five or six. However, the public knows about you three, so different identities would be pointless."

"What about a security clearance?" Gabe wanted to know.

"Good question. The problem with a security clearance is that the process adds individuals to official databases, creating a substantial paper trail. We don't want that kind of attention. Anyway, first task. Kim and Emma, you will meet two off-worlders. Because humans can't ordinarily use an onk, there are lingering issues we hope you can resolve. I'm excited to see how this plays out."

"What about the first off-worlder?" Gabe asked. "You know, the guy who met Lincoln."

"His details are complex, and I'm not at liberty to discuss what little I know."

"When will we meet him?" Kim asked.

"Well, see, that's the thing. You may have already met this individual. He has the unique ability to blend in. I do not know if he uses a mental trick or technology. I have had four meetings with him, and each time he looked different. If you twisted my arm and forced me to guess, I would say he might invite you to a meeting in five years.

"On to Gabe. I am tasking you with identifying and understanding advanced technology. I'm betting you'll love this job."

"Like spaceships?" Gabe asked hopefully.

"U.S. Space Force takes care of that."

"Jason called them bozos," Kim said and rolled her eyes.

"An accurate description, but the three of you are to treat them respectfully. Privately, you can call them bozos. We all do."

"Will I ever get to see any of that spacecraft technology?" Gabe asked.

"All functional spacecraft fall within their department. So, the answer is no."

Kim changed the topic. "What's the story with Donna?"

"In 1901, we found a mangled robot body at a crash site in Norway. We repaired Donna, and she began working with the DLS. Over the years, she adapted her body to appear human and is now a central figure in our operation."

"Why didn't she go back to her kind?"

"The story is that Donna's planet had a massive war, and only the robots survived. They formed a society and began exploring other planets. Years after the crash, we arranged for Donna to return to her home world, but she found it abandoned.

"Well, I had planned an hour for this meeting. Unfortunately, I have an unexpected meeting with the bozos. Remember those two guys at your house?"

"Yes," Gabe answered.

"Wow, you opened up a hornet's nest when you identified those two. Afterward, Kelly *convinced* them to talk, and boy-howdy did they spill their guts. They confirmed that the Air Force violated our agreement, and we've been in discussion ever since.

"Now, Donna will show you your assignments, and we'll talk again in a week. Questions?"

Gabe and Kim had an infinite number of prepared questions. "What about using the white box at home?" Kim asked. "I mean the onk."

"You may only use your onk within these walls with prior approval. Nowhere else. Got that?"

"Sounds good."

"Great to hear. Donna will see you out."

Sam stood and opened the door. Gabe and Kim were both disappointed that they did not get their other questions answered. Donna greeted them, and they wondered how she knew to be there at that moment. She escorted them down the hallway, and Kim thought to Gabe, <I had more questions.>

<Me too.>

<Everything is a task around here. Do engineering companies work like that?>

<Not really. I think it's a military thing.>

They came to a door, and Donna said, "Your task is in this room. Please assist Troy with technology identification."

"Alright."

"Kim, you're to bring the onk and follow me."

"See you in a bit, babe," Gabe said warmly. "Love you, Emma."

"Bye, Daddy Gabe," Emma said with a grin.

"Goodbye, my sweetie."

Gabe tried to open the door and asked Donna, "Um? Now what?"

Donna looked at the door and said, "Try it again."

Gabe twisted the knob, and the door opened. He wondered how Donna had unlocked the door as he walked inside. Gabe saw a large room containing a smaller room suspended above the floor with steel supports. He surmised that they had created a room within a room to inspect the inner room's exterior for spy devices. An armed guard greeted him. "Your task?"

"They told me to ask for Troy," Gabe answered.

"Sign here. Weigh yourself there."

"Ah, I get it. If I take something, then I will weigh more."

"Or if you leave something."

"A reasonable precaution."

Gabe signed in, and then the guard recorded his weight. He approached the door, and the guard picked up a phone attached to the second room's wall. "One away," he said.

Gabe opened the door and saw a well-lit room containing long steel wire racks with neatly arranged boxes and bags. Each one had colored paper tags attached with several signatures. At the end, Gabe saw a long, light blue lab bench with sophisticated instruments.

A man in his midforties met him at the door. Troy stood five foot five, with wavy blond hair, and wore a white lab coat with wires bulging from the pockets. He was smiling and warmly shook Gabe's hand.

"It's nice to meet you," Troy began. "The man who can use an onk."

"That's me."

"We've got a lot of work to do."

Troy led Gabe to the workbench. In the center sat a green metal box with strange symbols emblazoned on the side, thin metal protrusions, and threaded objects Gabe recognized as fiber-optic connections and electrical terminals. He appreciated the fine construction and sleek industrial design.

"Wow, this is strange," Troy commented. "We are so compartmentalized around here and never speak the truth. But with you, I can tell you the full story. This openness will take some getting used to. Um. Here it is. We found this thing inside a craft when it went down in the fifties. I don't know what it does, but I have determined that you apply power here."

Troy turned on a power supply and looked excited. Gabe saw no activity and asked, "That's it?"

"*That* took me three months."

"Um. What's your background?"

Troy stepped back and said, "Wait, wait, stop. Alright— um, here's the thing. This place has a strict culture. We never ask for personal details. I'm here because I'm qualified to be here. You're here for the same reason."

"Hey, I'm sorry. I was trying to be friendly."

"In time, you'll get more comfortable with the rules. Now, my task is to show this device to you and get your opinion."

"What's the deal with all the tasks?" Gabe asked.

"Donna assigns each one of us a task. This is task number 563WC41. This translates to learn about object number JA-12331 and write a report."

Gabe thought for a moment and said, "I see. Well, let's get started."

Troy and Gabe reviewed notes for the next hour and experimented with optical signals. Gabe found their progress unproductive and said, "We're guessing. It might take a hundred years to figure this out."

The question annoyed Troy. "You know of a better way?"

"I could use the onk. It might translate the writing."

Troy grinned. "We thought that might work," he said with a wink.

"My wife, Kim, took our onk."

"We can ask to use your onk tomorrow. Hey, wait a second. I can tell you everything. Um. I'm not used to this. Um. Well, we have other onks."

"Really?" Gabe asked in surprise.

"Just a minute."

Troy got a phone, pressed the only button, waited, and said, "Troy here. Asking permission. Yes. Donna. Yes. Inform her I would like to show Gabe item JA-23393 through item JA-23399." There was a long pause. "Yes. Thank you."

Troy hung up the phone. "The way you ask permission is to call the guard. Then, he writes the request in his logbook and uses a different phone to get permission."

"I guess that makes sense to keep the place secure," Gabe observed.

Troy took out a clipboard and wrote some numbers. He then went to the shelf and removed seven bags. Troy pulled on latex gloves, broke the seal on a bag, and extracted a thin gray device.

Gabe put on gloves and held the unfamiliar onk for several minutes without success. They discussed several options and concluded that Gabe could not operate the device or that it no longer functioned. They also speculated the object might not be an onk. The pair repeated the same procedure for the other five bags. The onk in the sixth bag worked, but it refused to communicate with Gabe. When Troy opened the last bag, he smiled. Gabe recognized the same type of onk that the Veronn had given them. "We found this in 1921," Troy explained.

"Where?"

"Hmm."

"Another sore spot?" Gabe asked in embarrassment. "I'm sorry for asking about that."

"It is going to take time to get comfortable around you. Well, I guess I can share a few details. There was a big incident in the twenties, and we recovered seventeen objects."

"Who else knows about the incident?"

"I cannot say."

"Sorry, I probably shouldn't have asked."

"It's fine. Can you use this?" Troy asked, his excitement growing.

"Let me try."

Gabe held the onk and began to experience communication, but he could not get a complete mental picture. After several minutes, he said, "There's something there, but it's not working right. I think I need to use our onk to talk to this one. Then maybe we can get it to work."

"After lunch?" Troy asked.

"What?"

"It's lunchtime."

"Wow, I didn't realize it had been so long."

"Yeah, this room messes with your mental time frame."

•

Donna led Kim and Emma down a hallway to a door. "Your task is to speak with Duve."

Kim opened the door and found a typical office environment with cubicles. She immediately noticed one nonhuman individual. Duve stood four foot five, and his bald head gleamed under the harsh fluorescent light while his ears were mere nubs. Clad in practical tan overalls, his choice of attire added to his unique charm. However, it was his footwear that truly set him apart.

With his feet sporting tall, bright turquoise boots, they immediately drew attention. Despite their unconventional design, they seemed oddly fitting for Duve's eccentric persona. Kim could not help but find amusement in Duve's distinctive features, particularly his eyes with their vertical irises reminiscent of a feline. Yet, losing the boots and adding sunglasses and a hat would allow Duve to blend in.

Duve's sparkling green eyes held a sense of perpetual surprise, and his warm smile revealed a set of small white teeth, lending an air of approachability. He spoke with a strange accent, "Group. It's good to meet you, Kim. I accessed many fine reports about your endeavors."

"Um? They call you Duve?" Kim asked.

"Group. My full name is Donkin Deb Kybe Duve-mite. I'm from planet Glock, and my home race is Gloken."

"Why do you keep saying 'Group?'"

"Ahh. My non-Earth language is poking through. Saying 'group' is like when you say, 'Umm.' A habit word."

Duve bent down to look at Emma and said, "What a beautiful girl."

"You strange," Emma replied with puckered lips.

"My, yes, I'm strange compared to you."

"Duve man not from here?" Emma asked.

"No, little one."

"You have mommy and daddy?"

"Yes, little one," Duve answered with a smile.

"They know you on Earth?"

"They passed to the other side long ago."

"Why you here?" Emma challenged.

"Well, little one. I'm a traveler. I go from place to place and get to know people. In Earth culture, you might call me a hippy."

Kim laughed and asked, "Do you live around here?"

"I live in the same apartment building as you."

"Wow, I wouldn't have expected that. So how do you get to work?"

"I cover up my face, and a DLS team member drives me."

"Do you interact with the locals?"

"To date, they've permitted six supervised outings. Thirteen days ago, I attended a baseball game. What a fun experience."

"How long have you been on Earth?" Kim asked.

"Since 1991."

"How did you learn English?"

"Earth languages are not complex. Group. The Prune provided a translation matrix."

Several people in the office had been watching their interaction. Then, a woman in a flowery dress interrupted, "It's Kim?"

"Yes."

"Can you read Duve?" she demanded.

"What? Why would I do that without his permission?"

"Is he telling the truth?"

"You're acting rude," Kim stated with an accusing stare.

"Answer my question!"

"I'm not entering his mind without asking permission."

"We don't work that way!" Thelma protested.

"Group," Duve interrupted. "They have many strict procedures."

"Can you operate an onk?" Thelma asked.

"Yes."

"Emma as well?"

"Yes!" Kim hissed.

"I see."

The woman got on the phone and said, "Thelma here. Telepathic contact is being attempted. Out."

Kim looked annoyed and asked Thelma, "Do you have to be like that?"

"I am following protocol."

"Well, you'd better start behaving around my daughter." Kim turned to Duve and said, "It looks like they want us to attempt telepathy. May I passively read you?"

"Group. My race isn't telepathic without an onk, but I have interacted with many telepaths. Unfortunately, the DLS restricted my onk use."

"What does that mean?"

"It means that without a special onk, I cannot read you. But you might be able to interact with me."

"What percentage of off-worlders are telepathic?"

"Perhaps fifteen percent are naturals. The rest had genetic modifications." Kim nodded. "Humans have a long way to go, but you have interesting potential. Let's sit over here."

Kim and Duve moved two office chairs and sat facing each other while Emma watched. When Kim passively swam in human minds, she compared the feeling to water flowing over a waterfall. The thoughts began parallel, then rushed down into a jumble, stopped at the bottom, and moved parallel again.

When Kim attempted to read Duve's thoughts, they felt sideways and then "squishy" in an upward pattern. She found it difficult to relate to and only comprehended emotional wisps. Finally, after six minutes, Kim said, "This isn't working. I need to try a more active approach. Is it alright if I press a little harder?"

"I felt your presence," Duve said with a smile. "Move your thoughts in that section. Start slow."

Kim applied more strength and maneuvered her thoughts where Duve had indicated. She understood that her perspective was off, and she needed to think "sideways." Kim paused and tried again. She moved her head to the side and then straightened it. The physical effort helped, and Kim began feeling Duve's unfamiliar emotions. Their interaction was frustrating, and it took effort to remain calm. With patience, she began learning how his mind worked. Unexpectedly, Duve thought, <You're good at this.>

Duve's thoughts felt inviting and "crunchy." Kim concentrated and grasped how Duve forced himself to think in English. Now, with some confidence, she attempted a single precise thought, <Hello?>

<Group. It is nice to meet you. What a beautiful mind. Thank you for allowing me to interact.>

<Hi, Mommy Kim,> Emma interrupted. <Duve-mite funny. Make face again.>

<Emma, you can read Duve?> Kim asked, shocked.

<I watch you.>

<Group!> Duve thought with great joy. <Emma, you possess outstanding talent.>

<Thank you, Duve-mite.>

"Is he telling the truth?" Thelma interrupted.

The disturbance shocked Kim and broke her concentration. "Lady, what the heck is your problem?" she yelled. "This is hard!"

"Ask him about Lufkin 349!" Thelma demanded.

"What are you talking about?" Kim shot back.

The interruption also unsettled Duve's thinking. He took a moment to respond. "Group. I have provided you with all the information about that topic. If I knew more facts, I would be open to sharing."

"Is he telling the truth?" Thelma again demanded.

"Back off," Kim retorted.

Thelma narrowed her eyes at Kim.

"It's clear that this is a sensitive topic," Kim said to defuse the tension. "Give him a break."

"Ask him!"

"Fine!"

Kim turned to Duve, and it took them both time to regain focus. She eventually asked, <What's the deal with this Lufkin thing? It's alright if you don't want to answer.>

Kim felt a multitude of conflicting and complex emotions within Duve. Finally, she could understand some of Duve's complex emotional content. "This topic upsets Duve," Kim told Thelma.

"The facts he provided about Lufkin 349 conflict with other intel."

<What do you want me to tell them?> Kim asked with sorrowful emotions.

<My parents died at an outpost called Lufkin 349. I revealed this trivial fact a year ago. I do not know why Thelma is so passionate about this topic.>

<It seems like something else is upsetting her.>

<You humans call it a divorce,> Duve answered sadly.

<Ahh. I get it. Her home life is leaking into work. Sorry for putting you through this.>

<Her *home life* has been a prominent issue for some time.>

Kim felt deep emotions that she interpreted as sorrow. <Alright,> she thought. <I am going to tell her you provided all the information. Are you good with that?>

<Of course.>

"He has told you all he knows," Kim told Thelma. "It's the truth."

Thelma winced and announced while crossing her arms with narrow eyes, "That can only mean one thing. I must write a report."

"Why is this so important?" Kim wanted to know.

"I cannot comply."

"Whatever."

<Group,> Duve thought with relief. <What a way to start my day.>

<Sorry about all this.>

<Group. Perhaps we can use an onk,> Duve thought with an emotion Kim interpreted as hope.

<Sure.>

"Hey, Thelma," Kim said. "I want to use my onk on Duve. Sound good?"

"Only on him. You may not use your onk on anyone else, especially me."

"Got it."

Kim reached into her purse and retrieved the onk. Duve's mind immediately appeared with fluid thoughts. <Wow!> she thought with surprise.

<Hmm. So fast. Very graphic.>

<Are you thinking in English? It feels like the onk is translating. It should have said, 'Group.' And not 'Hmm.'>

<Well done,> Duve thought with pride (the onk vastly improved interpreting emotions). <I am now thinking in the Duvork language. Most onks understand Duvork. Let me try my native language.>

The thought was incomplete, and this failure briefly confused Duve. He tried a different tactic. <Are good you said by thorp?>

<Your words make little sense,> Kim thought.

<Describe you Emma.>

<My daughter is a young human girl with brown hair.>

Duve concentrated and thought, <My native language does not translate.>

<Hey, I want to try something,> Kim thought with hope. <Please think in your native language, 'My daughter is a young human girl with brown hair.' Then, speak the same sentence in your native language.>

<Hi-ya greeb, ma-don duk human deb-le.>

"Greeb, ma duken human deb."

<Why were your spoken words different from your thoughts?> Kim wondered.

<You noticed the difference? Very astute. My thoughts do not come out organized when spoken. That is a trait of my species. I can see that your mind partially does this. As your race matures, you will become more adept at mental interaction.>

<Interesting,> Kim replied with wonder.

<This is a Veronn onk. I have never met a Veronn.>

<I've only met a few.>

<Your onk is in basic mode. You need to change the settings to personal mode. Look here.>

Duve guided Kim through the on-screen menus until she found an unexplored area, and he showed her how to change a setting.

A feminine voice devoid of emotion thought to Kim, {Good morning. I am communication processing node Oklier er Oklier. Emma refers to me as okey-okey, and my common name is onk.}

<You can talk?> Kim asked in shock.

{Yes.}

<Sorry, dumb question.>

{I am available to help with communications, configurations, and questions.}

<Can Gabe use this mode?>

{To avoid confusion, it's best to configure a communication processing node for a specific user. My last user has cleared his personal parameters, allowing you unhindered access.}

<I understand,> Kim thought to her onk. <How many users have you had?>

{Twenty-four.}

<That's a lot.>

{By your calendar, it has been 281 years since my activation,} the onk commented.

<How well does Emma interact with you?>

{We have advanced interactions.}

<Hi, okey-okey,> Emma thought with warm emotions. <Nice thinking with you.>

{Hello, Emma. It is always nice thinking with you.}

A voice with an odd accent interrupted their concentration, "What's all this? Is that an onk?"

Kim looked up to see another off-worlder. He stood four feet tall, with an ethereal complexion and a soft pallor that seemed untouched by the sun's rays. A crown of light brown peach fuzz hair framed his delicate head. The most distinct feature was a slightly more centrally positioned, smaller nose than a human's. It had tiny holes and a graceful upturned curve. His gaze, emanating from tiny brown eyes, held a depth that belied his stature, hinting at great wisdom. Yet, there was a hint of mischief in his eyes, as if they had secrets waiting to be unraveled.

His appearance reminded Kim of a bulldog, and she noticed Emma's amusement. "I'm Kim, and this is Emma."

"My Earth designation is Steve, and my home world designation is Kyron Tu of the Slone race," he said in a loud but squeaky voice with an unfamiliar accent. "Donna tasked me to interact with a human man, woman, and child," Steve announced while studying Emma.

"You direct, Steve man," Emma said with as much confidence as possible.

The statement took Steve aback. He turned to Kim and stated, "We should proceed with the designated task."

Kim wanted to finish her mental conversation with Duve before attempting another telepathic interaction, but she asked, "What do you do around here?"

"My primary task?"

"Wow. You guys and your tasks."

Steve squinted at Kim and answered, "My primary Earth-bound task is to gather relevant data. In exchange, I have agreed to provide certain data."

"What are you hoping to find? I wouldn't think we have much to offer."

"Correct," Steve said with a sharp nod. "Your technical data is of little value. I am primarily concerned with artistic creations."

"Really? I would think other worlds would have much better art."

"Correct. I seek unrefined source material, and Earth artists have yielded excellent examples. On to the present task. Have you communicated with Duve?"

"Yes."

"Telepathically?"

"Yes."

"I find this difficult to accept."

"Group," Duve said in a warm voice. "They have skill."

"Were you modified?" Steve asked.

"The Veronn took us up on their ship," Kim answered. "I don't know what they did when we were there."

"The Veronn interacted with our race on three occasions. We found them to be upstanding individuals. Thelma, please confirm permission for a telepathic interview."

Thelma made a phone call and nodded. "Proceed with caution at low interaction levels," Steve said with concern. "Failure to comply will cause mental damage."

"We can start passively."

"That option has a low probability of success."

"You never learn," Duve said with a smile. "Let her try. Emma is also telepathic."

"That is an impossibility. An Earth child of her development stage cannot enter my mind."

Emma considered this statement a challenge, and she passively probed Steve. His face revealed his dismay and then intrigue. From Kim's perspective, their interaction was challenging and crafty. Emma maliciously worked through the differences and thought to Steve, <You talk like Daddy Gabe when he tell about computer.>

<Unexpected,> Steve thought with great surprise. <You are a very gifted child. I compliment your intriguing mind.>

<Mommy Kim say that too,> Emma thought warmly.

<I apologize for my earlier statements.>

<It alright.>

Emma's technique amazed Kim, and she realized that Emma's mental communication skills were far more advanced than she had perceived.

<You think Mommy Kim now?> Emma asked.

<I will attempt communication.>

Kim felt something and tried to replicate Emma's methods, but failed. Feeling deflated, she went to the onk and briefly activated a calming mode. Kim allowed herself to relax and then probed Steve passively without using the onk.

He had a complex mind that was radically different from the human minds she had previously interacted with. Kim likened the experience to a game of chess played by many people, each with a finger on a piece.

Kim singled out a single "mental segment" and probed it. She sensed a rhythm, and Steve took over to guide her. He then gently thought, <Do you understand me?>

The interaction shocked Kim, and she replied after three attempts, <That felt odd. You have super-detailed thoughts that are mega-separate. Plus, your emotion feels laser-precise. Do other off-world minds feel like this?>

<A few. My race honed their mental skills with great care. I prefer acting through an onk. It provides more linguistic precision. May we proceed along this path?>

<Alright,> Kim cautiously answered.

Kim came away with a strange impression of Steve. She suspected he kept his thoughts to himself and rarely interacted with women. "Hey, Thelma," Kim said. "Can I use on onk on him?"

"Proceed," Thelma answered with narrow eyes.

Kim began using the onk, and Steve's mind rapidly came into tight focus. <Hello,> Kim thought.

{Caution!} the onk warned. {Restricted mind. Safety procedures activated!}

<Onk, what's going on?>

{A Slone mind is attempting to access my communication node. Forbidden action!}

<I don't—>

{Veronn Protocol 619,} the onk interrupted. {No Slone interaction is permitted!}

<Why?> Kim asked.

{A previous transaction failed. Veronn Protocol 619 is in effect!}

<What transactions?>

{They removed 29 Kebos without permission.}

<They pirated some music videos?> Kim thought, joking.

{A correct assessment.}

<And the Veronn cut off access from their entire race?>

{Kebos are essential to Veronn culture!}

<I guess that makes sense.>

Kim set the onk down and said, “The onk is rejecting your communication.”

“Is that a Veronn onk?” Steve asked.

“Yes.”

“I am aware of an unfortunate misunderstanding between our races. However, I was informed that the incident was successfully resolved.”

“Are Kebos that big a deal?” Kim asked.

“Many races consider Kebos to be their pinnacle achievement.”

“Interesting.”

The door opened, and Gabe walked into the room.

# FOURTEEN

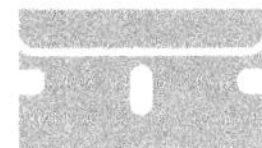

Gabe's head hurt, and his eyes were closed. It seemed as if he was resting on something soft and was covered with a warm blanket. Gabe struggled to take deeper breaths, which gave him enough energy to open his eyes. It took a lot of effort to adjust to the light, and he saw a panel ceiling. With great effort, he turned to his right and saw a window with the shades drawn. Gabe looked down to see himself dressed in a hospital gown. His arm had an IV, and EKG leads were attached to his chest.

"Daddy Gabe!" a familiar voice said.

Gabe understood the voice came from his left and exerted great effort to turn in that direction. He saw Kim asleep on a sofa and Emma sitting on a chair. "Mommy Kim! Mommy Kim!" she chirped. "Daddy Gabe awake."

Kim sat, yawned, and said in a sleepy voice, "You're back with the living."

It took him a lot of effort to comprehend Kim's words and even more energy to speak, "Where—"

"I'm so glad that you're awake. We're at the DLS. This is a medical room on the top floor."

Gabe let this flood of information sink in and asked, "What—"

"What happened?" Kim asked. "You actively swam in Steve's mind. His species has a mental safeguard, and he accidentally zapped you. You've been unconscious for two days."

Kim's many words confused Gabe, and comprehending their meaning took him a considerable amount of time. Then Kim stood and gave him a long hug. Gabe wanted to hug back, but his body refused to move. Finally, Kim let go, and she lifted Emma to hug her father. With a lot of effort, he said, "Emma."

"Daddy Gabe."

"Um—"

"Steve told us the effects take a while to wear off. But you'll be fine," Kim said with a smile. "He's sorry about what happened and wants to apologize in person."

This verbal exchange took too much effort, and Gabe closed his eyes.

"Get some rest, honey," Kim said. "Now that we know you're fine, we're going to the apartment. See you in the morning."

"Love—"

"Love you too."

Gabe fell into a deep sleep. Sometime later, he woke feeling better and opened his eyes. A dim light in the corner of the room was on, and he guessed the time was in the late evening. It took Gabe a long time to coordinate his muscles enough to sit. Then he felt something was wrong and lifted his gown. A urinary catheter had been inserted, which deeply embarrassed him.

Gabe did not know what to do and tried to remove the medical device by tugging on it. This action caused intense pain, and he gasped loudly. It took several deep breaths to calm down.

Unfortunately, the pulling action triggered Gabe's bowels, and he looked around the room in desperation. The sight of a small bathroom brought great relief. He moved the catheter bag and IV pole to the side and swung his legs out from under him. Fortunately, somebody had disconnected the EKG monitor, but he still had the electrical pads attached to his chest.

This action took far more energy and coordination than Gabe had imagined. He took several deep breaths to build his confidence and eased himself down. Halfway there, Gabe almost slipped, but he successfully moved onto the floor. When he looked up, he saw a red call button. Gabe cursed aloud and began crawling while pulling the IV pole with the catheter bag dragging behind.

Gabe made it to the bathroom and lunged onto the toilet. The intense bowel movement brought great relief. He giggled and smiled from ear to ear as he cleaned himself. Then, taking another deep breath for confidence, Gabe used the toilet for balance and took a single step toward the small sink. He washed his hands and his face. Gabe then looked into the mirror and noticed a few days' growth of whiskers.

Gabe steadied himself and said, "Let's do this," then eased himself to the floor. It took more effort to crawl to his bed, and he began gathering the courage to lift himself. Finally, Gabe grasped a handhold, and the room door unexpectedly opened. Donna walked in and said with a smile, "You're awake. We wondered how long it would take. Let me assist you."

Donna lifted Gabe onto the bed, and her strength surprised him. "It's dark out," he commented.

"The time is 2:18 in the morning."

"Why are you here this late?"

"My body does not require sleep."

"Oh, I should have known that. Sorry, my mind is still foggy," Gabe admitted.

"Understandable."

"What happened?"

"The Slone race has a unique mental ability. Their mind stun is legendary."

"Um—"

"Your body requires rest," Donna suggested.

"Um, this thing—"

"I can remove that."

"Um—"

"I have extensive human medical knowledge."

"Um—"

"I have no sexual desires. To me, your body is a container for organs."

"I guess."

Gabe moved his gown aside with great trepidation, and Donna deflated his catheter while he stared at the ceiling. He felt a slight tug, and it came out. Donna then removed Gabe's IV and looked at him with a hard-to-read expression. He decided to change the topic. "What's your story?"

"You're a curious person."

"I'm nothing compared to Kim. She'll talk your ear off."

"We have spoken at length. An interesting woman."

"I'm lucky to be with her," Gabe said with pride.

"You two make a perfect couple." Donna looked at Gabe for a long moment and continued, "I have not been looking forward to your presence."

"Why?" Donna did not answer, and Gabe continued, "I'm not used to this. I cannot read you."

"Many off-worlders have that opinion."

"Can I use an onk on you?" Donna made a hard-to-read expression, and Gabe guessed, "The onk would uncover something?"

"Very perceptive; Kim also came to this conclusion."

"Why didn't Duve or Steve use their onks on you?" Donna did not answer, and Gabe filled in the blanks. "Ah, I get it. You worked it so they did not keep their onks. That's smart."

"Correct."

"What am I going to find?"

"My race has a violent past," Donna admitted.

"You don't strike me as the violent type."

"Extreme actions lie within my core routines."

"But, you're in control of your... Is emotion the right word?" Gabe asked.

"I have precise control of my thoughts. And yes, you have applied that term correctly."

"I still don't understand the problem. A person can have a terrible past and still act nicely. Are you not capable of doing this?"

Donna studied Gabe and then answered. "I undertook a long-range mission to locate a new planet suitable for colonization. A catastrophic propulsion failure occurred, and my database listed your system as an appropriate destination. I adapted the remains of my craft to undertake the journey.

"As the voyage required many years, I shut down to conserve power. Upon activation, I found myself damaged and in a human laboratory. My designated course of action would be to take over this world and colonize it. From my perspective, this would have required little effort, as humans are inherently fragile and susceptible to manipulation.

"During my repair, the scientist's compassion confounded me, as I expected that my memory banks would get stripped of their relevant information and my systems would be dissected for useful technology. When this did not occur, I learned about your species. An outside observer would consider this to be a bonding moment.

"My repair took four years, and I chose to work with the DLS to study your culture. That was 1905, and in 1961, I had the opportunity to report my findings. Upon arriving on my home world, I found a civil war in progress. Of course, you often interact with computers and might call the action a data restructure."

Gabe snickered, and Donna continued, "Because the Earth scientists had shown compassion, I refused to provide Earth's details. My peers deemed me a sympathizer, and the standard punishment was a full memory bank wipe. I defied their order and returned to Earth. When asked, I informed the DLS that my peers abandoned their home world without recording their destination. The DLS allowed me to continue my former tasks."

"I don't understand," Gabe said. "You must have onk communication technology. So, why didn't you use it to get your people to rescue you?"

"If an onk loses magnetic confinement, it becomes useless. This occurred during the propulsion system failure."

"That makes sense. Wait, why are you telling me this? I'm sure the DLS managers would not want you around if they thought you wanted to take over the Earth."

"You are correct."

"I still don't understand. Are you asking me to lie?"

Donna looked at Gabe for a long moment and nodded. "Did you talk to Kim about this?" he asked with a nervous hand gesture.

"We've spoken."

"I must admit that I don't lie well."

"A documented fact."

"Geez," Gabe exclaimed. "They document everything."

"They do," Donna said with a thin smile.

"Well, what do you want me to do?"

"I will permit you to interact with me using your onk."

Gabe threw his hands up. "That makes no sense."

"I have prepared you for the initial appearance of my personality."

"Oh, I get it. You are preparing me so I don't go all crazy when I learn about you."

"Precisely."

"I can do that," Gabe said with a smile.

"Good."

"How long did I sleep for?" Gabe asked.

"Three days."

"Wow. Did anything happen during that time?"

"Kim and Emma interacted with Duve and Steve," Donna answered.

"Any big revelations?"

"Duve has proven to be more trustworthy and Steve less."

"Why?" Gabe asked.

"Kim believes Steve has an ulterior motive."

"She's perceptive."

"I've never met a woman like her," Donna said in a reserved voice.

"She's supersmart."

"There is more to her."

"She's also cute."

"Gabe?" Donna asked.

"Yes?"

"Like you, Kim's body has undergone significant modifications."

"What do you mean?"

"It is not possible for a human to use an onk."

"Jason told us that."

"You have underestimated the significance of my revelation."

"Meaning?" Gabe waved his hand, urging Donna on.

"The DLS might consider you to be a threat. Therefore, I advise you to hide your full ability."

"I think the DLS already knows."

"Not completely."

"It seems like the DLS keeps a lot of secrets from itself."

"That's our primary mission," Donna said with a smile. She waited a moment and continued. "Like you, Emma is also modified."

"Now that, I don't understand. She's never been on a Veronn ship."

"Her modifications are more complex."

Gabe rubbed his cheek as he eyed Donna. "Meaning?"

"I am forbidden from discussing certain subjects. This is one of them."

"I don't like where this is going."

"I can reveal that Emma's modifications were not the result of Veronn interaction."

"Do you recognize her modifications?"

"Yes."

"But you cannot reveal the details."

"I cannot," Donna said with finality.

"Can you at least tell me who is preventing you from speaking? Jason talked about the off-world guy who met Abraham Lincoln."

"I can reveal no more."

"What *can* you tell me?" Gabe wanted to know.

"I can confirm that Emma will grow up to be an astounding individual and that you have nothing to fear."

"Is Kim aware?"

"We discussed this topic," Donna said with a slight nod.

"What did she say?"

"Like you, she wanted to know more."

"I see."

After an awkward pause, Donna said, "There is another matter. When you use your onk, it will reveal my embedded sensors."

"The DLS doesn't know that you have sensors?

"They are unaware of their sophisticated nature."

"What do they do?" Gabe asked.

"They analyze many areas of interest."

"What's the issue?"

"The existence of sophisticated sensors would make me a risk."

"I see. Hey, can your sensors tell me why I get these headaches?" Gabe asked.

"Your mind is out of alignment because of uncalibrated faster-than-light travel."

"I don't understand."

"During high-speed maneuvers, one must… This word does not have an English translation. I will use an approximation. One must interactively calibrate one's mind. Your mind did not receive this procedure."

"And that messed up our heads?" Gabe filled in the blanks.

"Yes."

"Can you fix the issue?"

"A correction would require the exact calibration parameters for the particular transport vessel. Are you in contact with the Veronn?" Donna asked.

"When we last contacted them, it seemed like they said, 'Don't call us, we'll call you.'"

"What do you know of the Veronn?"

"I know they are an advanced race," Gabe answered. "That's about it."

"What of their society?"

"I think they are way ahead of us."

"I see." Donna paused for a moment and continued. "Your onk will reveal another aspect."

"What?"

"I have embedded weapons. Specifically, focused high-energy particle projectors."

"The scientists didn't figure that out?"

"I prevented their discovery."

"Is my family in danger?" Gabe asked with concern.

"Of course not."

"I can live with that."

"Good," Donna said with a smile.

"May I ask you something?"

"Yes."

"How does telepathy work?" Gabe asked with a big grin.

"You did every imaginable engineering test and read every scientific article without success. Then you searched the onk database and could not understand the technology."

"True," Gabe admitted.

"Our interaction shows your intelligence."

"Kim tells me it can get in the way."

"She has a wise perception."

"I agree."

"Telepathy works on the same principle as the onk," Donna answered.

"Quantum entanglement?"

"Yes."

"But that requires everything to be synchronized in advance," Gabe said, confused.

"Correct."

"That would mean a bunch of subatomic particles would have to be aligned in two different brains. To do that, you would need a synchronized particle accelerator in each mind. And I certainly don't have a massive machine in my head."

"You are again correct," Donna said.

"I still don't get it."

"It would be like explaining to somebody in the Middle Ages how a cellphone works."

"I'm a few generations behind?" Gabe guessed.

"You are."

"They must have radically modified us."

"Indeed."

"Hmm. May I ask another question?"

"Yes," Donna answered.

"How is your body powered?"

"Are you referring to my energy source?" Donna inquired.

"I assume it's atomic fusion."

"If that were true, you would be dead from the radiation. I utilize a curium-tellurium binary acid battery."

"A standard battery?" Gabe asked in shock.

"The elements are mildly radioactive, but yes, a rechargeable chemical battery of the same type you would find in a cordless drill."

"And you have servos that move your body?" Donna smiled. Gabe asked, "Magnetic motors?" She smiled again, and he asked, "Superconductors?"

"In critical areas."

Excited, Gabe asked, "How does your central processor work?"

"It utilizes an optical matrix."

"Binary?"

"Yes."

"I would have expected an analog hybrid to support three-dimensional neural networks."

"Your scientists will eventually conclude that neural network programming techniques are an artificial intelligence dead end. The minds developed on my home world use standard object-oriented computations. If I were to show you one of my internal programs, you would be able to grasp its structure and function."

"What else?" Gabe asked with extreme curiosity.

"Functional artificial intelligence requires extensive processing. My mind is capped at 48 quintons, and modern minds on my home world now exceed 500. To appreciate this number, if you combined all the computers on Earth, the total would be three quintons."

Gabe let out a low whistle. "Wow, there's a lot of processing power in front of me." Donna smiled, and he asked, "When you answered my last question, a kind of program was running. Correct?"

"Yes."

"Are you able to interact with that program?" Gabe asked with intense interest.

"Explain."

"If you ask a computer its favorite color, it searches a database and pulls out a predetermined result. That is, if one is present. Otherwise, a program cannot answer the basic question. When I ponder the same question, I answer it from my life experiences. How does your program answer a judgment call?"

"Let me explain how my program makes an empirical analysis," Donna answered. "As a result of our interaction, I recorded your body image and a conversation transcript. I then updated my general knowledge database with information about your profile. If someone asked for my opinion, I would query my general knowledge database and calculate a result. The more we interact, the more accurate my opinion will become."

"Are you aware of this program running?"

"Yes, and if desired, I can alter the structure and variables."

"Could you change the structure so that you perceive me to be a hostile person?" Gabe asked with great interest.

"Such a drastic change would conflict with actual events. The result would be an incomplete entry. Instead, I would alter my database to treat you as hostile in future interactions. All previous records would remain intact."

Gabe nodded and continued, "I think I get it, but I'm missing the part where you learn. Let's say that for many years, you tried to write with a pencil using the eraser end. Then, one day, you turned the pencil around and wrote with the sharp tip. How would your program get altered?"

"That is the crux of true artificial learning. And you are correct. If I deleted the incorrect pencil writing routines, I would have a corrupt system. To address this issue, I would insert a fork that leads to correct pencil usage while maintaining the original learning path. These forks are the foundation of my artificial intelligence."

"Wow, that's fascinating."

"It took many years for my race to refine learning."

"I think I understand. But I am still missing something. Would you ever try to write with the eraser?"

"You are attempting to ascertain my level of curiosity. My race possesses a limited amount of creativity. Clearly, writing with an eraser is illogical and impossible. Yet, I observe humans of great intelligence performing foolish tasks. As a result, they learn, explore, fail, and discover. My race takes a more systematic approach, which is the limiting factor. For example, we do not appreciate abstract art."

"Your race has normal art? Like paintings?" Gabe asked with a nod.

"A few create such objects."

"I see. May I ask another question?"

"What is the source of your hesitation?"

"It's personal," Gabe admitted.

"I have no reason to doubt your inquisitive intentions."

"Alright. How does your species reproduce?"

"Clearly, you are not inquiring about the physical reason. Please refine your question."

"Well, that's the thing. Your... Is personality the correct term?"

"You have identified the correct term," Donna answered.

"Your personality is quite advanced. If you were to make a copy of yourself, that wouldn't work. Would it?"

"Continue," Donna said with a thin smile.

"It would be like copying a bunch of adults. There would be no growth. No inspiration. No new generation."

"How would a race like mine improve itself?"

"If I were to do it, I would create a base model with basic information. Then, I would add differences to provide a random personality element. Additionally, I would include a predetermined interest. For instance, if your society needed more mathematicians, there would be a preference for math. The person... Is person the right word?"

"For this line of thinking, yes," Donna answered.

"A lead programmer would raise this person. Like a human parent. Soon, the base model would develop into a unique individual and become a productive member of society."

“That would mean that I have parents.”

“I guess that’s what I’m asking,” Gabe admitted.

“Few individuals grasp this concept. Did your interaction with the onk help with your line of reasoning?”

“No, I made some assumptions based on how you described your learning process.”

“You have interesting reasoning. To answer your question, the essence of your description is correct, but my development contained additional complexities.”

“You have parents?” Gabe asked in surprise.

“That term broadly applies. The term teacher also applies.”

“Do your parents care for their children the same way a human parent would?”

“Not to the same emotional degree, but yes, my parents have an attachment to me, and I do to them.”

“How many parents raised you?” Gabe asked.

“Five.”

“Do all the people of your race raise children? Is children the correct term?”

“The correct term is pattern. Some individuals wish to attend to a pattern. To answer your next question, I have a small desire, but present circumstances make this an impossibility.”

“Interesting.”

“You have another question?” Donna guessed.

“I do.”

“Proceed.”

“What percentage of the off-world races are artificial beings?”

“Perhaps 0.3 percent,” Donna answered.

“Oh.”

“Your next question.”

“What’s your lifespan? Will your battery or circuits fail?”

“A complex answer. Please conduct an analysis.”

“What do you mean?” Gabe asked.

“Try to answer your own question.”

“Hmm. Semiconductor-based circuits last for about fifty years. But you could replace them. You could also replace your batteries and servos. I’m not familiar with an optical matrix. I suspect it would last a long time.”

“Continue,” Donna said in a pleasant voice.

“Continue what?”

“Continue your logical extension. How long can I live?”

Gabe took a long moment to answer. "The way you learn. There's a limit to the number of forks you can process. Isn't there?"

"Continue."

"I imagine you would reach a point where the processor gets overloaded, or there is no more storage space."

"And then?" Donna asked in encouragement.

"Your mind could no longer function."

"How would I compensate for this?"

"Along the way, you would delete junk," Gabe answered.

"And if I made a mistake?"

"I imagine you have protected backups that would allow you to recover."

"And when the corruption becomes too extensive?" Donna encouraged.

"That would be the end?"

Donna looked at Gabe momentarily and answered, "I am much more complex than you have described, but you have ascertained my path. As my data banks fill with information, they become difficult to navigate. I must continually refine my perceptions to maintain a clear comprehension. Unfortunately, subtle errors creep into the process, and when too many occur, they cannot be resolved. My core recognizes such conditions and deactivates to prevent damage to those around me. To answer your next question, this process takes an average of 102.1 Earth years at maximum processing. However, my current tasks mean deactivation will occur in 142.7 years."

"Why so long compared to the average?"

"Because my present tasks are not difficult, I have excessive time to streamline my memory banks. If I lived on my home world, my tasks would be more complex, and the added processing would lead to a termination in 12.2 years."

"I see."

"You wish to probe further. Proceed," Donna encouraged.

"Am I that obvious?"

"Yes."

"Hmm. If there is a song that you like, do you listen to it more than once?" Gabe asked.

"I prefer not to. However, some of my species enjoy redundant activities."

"Interesting. I assume you can have two or more parallel lines of thought."

"The reality of fork-based artificial intelligence makes parallel computation difficult. However, I have something similar to subprocesses. For example, I could set a background task alerting me to an upcoming appointment."

"What are your goals?" Gabe asked with interest.

"You wish to know my desires."

"Guilty."

"Kim must enjoy your conversations."

"She does," Gabe admitted with a mischievous smile.

"I develop DLS tasks and ensure their fulfillment."

"What value do you place on money?" Gabe asked.

"Money is a tool that I do not wish to hoard."

"Do you have any possessions you cherish?"

"No," Donna quickly answered.

"Do you go shopping?"

"On these rare occasions, I have purchased clothing and other items."

"Do you have a fashion style?"

"Kim asked me this question," Donna answered, smiling. "I analyze popular trends before shopping. As my body does not perspire, my clothes do not require immediate cleaning."

"Do you enjoy watching television?"

"I find the Simpsons amusing, but the commercials sour the mood. Most races have eliminated them."

"Do you have traits like modesty?" Gabe asked.

"Explain."

"You observed my embarrassment when you removed the catheter. Do you feel anything like that?"

"I have concerns about safety, data retention, and technology secrets. But no, I feel no modesty about my physical appearance. Your next question will be about relationships. You and Kim are more alike than different."

"Hmm," Gabe murmured as he considered this observation.

"My species does not have relationships in the traditional sense. We are not separated into genders and do not possess what you would term physical attraction. However, you appreciate computers. For me, dating would be like a data transfer."

Gabe chuckled, and Donna continued, "My time on your planet has made me consider other possibilities."

"Like dating a human?"

"Like becoming friends with a human."

"You don't have human friends?"

"You must appreciate that I am vastly different from a biological being. Your species spends considerable time eating, relaxing, exercising, playing, and sleeping. This difference makes it difficult to bridge the gap."

"But don't you ever want to— you know— go home and tell your husband about your day?"

"That's loosely what I'm referring to."

"Well, you're invited to our place," Gabe said with a smile.

"Kim also made this offer."

"I shouldn't be surprised."

"No, you should not," Donna said with a smile.

"True," Gabe said. "Tell me. What's next for my family?"

"Kim's task is to further interact with Duve and Steve. Your task is to decode the assigned technology."

"Why don't you do that? For a technology-savvy mind like yours, it would be easy. Wait—I can answer my question. Compartmentalization. They don't fully trust you."

"Not yet."

Gabe stretched, and Donna said, "One more question, and then rest."

"Does your race have an economy?"

"You have asked a complex question. From a high-level perspective, we base our economy on central computer processing time. It would take ample effort to explain the fine details."

Gabe grinned. "Now that sounds like an interesting topic."

"You would be among the few people who would appreciate the conversation."

"Well, I enjoyed speaking with you. I've learned a lot."

"As did I," Donna said with a smile. "Have a pleasant rest." Donna nodded and left the room. Gabe immediately fell asleep.

•

The following morning, Gabe was surprised to see Steve in the room. He began speaking with a strange accent, "Good morning."

"You're Steve?"

"Indeed."

"Kim told me I came on strong," Gabe said. "Sorry about that."

"The fault is mine. It has been some time since I deeply interacted with another mind, and your thoughts startled me."

"What did I do wrong?" Gabe asked.

"You made no mistakes. My race altered its genetics to improve telepathic ability, leading to a psychic war lasting 62 full cycles."

"Full cycles? Is that your version of years?"

"Correct."

"Does that mean that a cycle is a day? What is an hour, minute, and second?"

"Days are cycles, and each society has its own version of subcycles for time measurement. Continuing the prior topic. To end the conflict, our most outstanding leader, Don Fane, inspired his followers to change their telepathic interactions. This led to enduring peace.

"When you interacted with me, you encountered a safeguard from our violent past. Unfortunately, the minds of my species can emit a torrent of negative emotions that overwhelm an opponent's mind. I am sorry you were subject to my projection."

"It's fine."

"I am glad you feel this way."

Gabe took a moment to consider Steve's revelation and asked, "How does a psychic war work?"

"An important topic. It begins when a race strives for perfection."

"I don't understand."

Steve thought for a moment before answering. "When the scientists increased our telepathic powers, we were naturally competitive, which led to conflict. To make matters worse, our scientists attempted to solve the problem by increasing our ability."

"That makes sense. But I'm missing something. What's a telepathic war like? How does a person fight?"

"An important topic. A confrontation begins when two beings engage in telepathy. Allow me to use an analogy to explain the next step. Let's pretend there is a race war, with the distinguishing factor being height. If the short person said, 'You are too tall,' the taller person might be offended and take action, such as striking the shorter person. It is essential to understand that either person can choose to engage in battle or not respond. Over time, this freedom is the path to peace.

"A psychic conflict has a vastly compressed time scale. When two minds interact, it is apparent which mind is weaker. The result is an immediate fight which rapidly escalates."

"Wow, that happens fast," Gabe said.

"Indeed. You received a small exposure to that aggression."

"And your leader—"

"Don Fane," Steve reminded.

"I should have remembered that name. I'm sorry."

"Your mind is recovering."

"Don Fane changed the course of evolution?"

"The sequence of events is more complex than your description, but you have identified the logical path."

"It sounds like we have much to learn from your experiences," Gabe admitted.

"I have prepared a detailed historical report of many telepathic societies. This includes a simulation of your society and my recommended changes."

"Like eliminating the use of artificial intelligence?" Gabe asked.

"That technology prevents telepathic conflicts."

"That's not what I would expect," Gabe admitted.

"It is a complex topic also covered in my report."

"I see," Gabe said, thought for a moment, and asked, "Through the onk, I learned the Veronn modified our minds to be telepathic. How did they do this?"

"Minds contain a region called a fur-mow."

"I know that word."

"The Veronn introduced a tailored enzyme and protein to foster your fur-mow growth."

"And this made us telepathic?" Gabe asked, beginning to fill in the blanks.

"The compound started the process."

"Do you know why they modified us?"

"It is a common practice to alter low-grade minds to obtain data."

"Oh, that makes sense. But something is still confusing. We passed on our telepathic ability to people we practiced yoga with. Did we transfer the compound?"

"Yoga is body meditation? Did I get this correct?" Steve asked.

"Yes."

"I cannot understand how one could pass along telepathic ability during a physical exercise. Medical equipment must be involved."

"Hmm. Do you understand how Emma is telepathic?"

Steve paused and answered, "As part of the agreement with your leaders, they requested that certain topics remain confidential."

"Oh."

Gabe stretched, and Steve observed, "Your recovery is incomplete."

"True."

"Soon, an assistant will transport you to your dwelling, further aiding your recovery."

"Sounds good."

"Have we successfully resolved the conflict between us?" Steve asked.

"From what I understand, you did not intend to injure me?"

"Violence is no longer the way of the Slone. Again, I apologize for my actions."

Gabe smiled. "Then we're good."

"Wonderful."

"Thank you for educating me about your people."

"Many Slone perished because of our arrogance. My greatest hope is to spare your world from this awful path."

"I appreciate your help."

"I am glad to have met you," Steve said, smiling. He called for the assistant, who helped Gabe walk to the elevator. They took it to the first floor, and the assistant drove Gabe to the apartment. Inside, Kim and Emma were eating breakfast. Emma ran to her father and hugged him tightly. After a light breakfast, Gabe fell asleep.

•

Kim and Emma drove to the DLS and spent the afternoon interacting with Duve and Steve. This fascinating experience provided Kim with direct knowledge about many off-world societies. As a result, she began to agree with the DLS philosophy of limiting off-world interaction, but still did not like the aggressive methods.

At the end of the day, Steve showed Kim a mental technique for uncovering forgotten memories. Then, unexpectedly, Kim broke off their communication. She dramatically stood, picked up Emma, and rapidly walked to the door. "I made a terrible mistake," Steve called out to her. "Please forgive my error."

"It's alright," Kim said without turning around. "I need to go home."

"That's understandable. I will not reveal our interaction."

"It wasn't your fault," Kim admitted without turning around.

"I must present a formal apology."

"It's fine!"

Thelma was nearby and demanded, "What the heck is going on?"

With a scowl, Kim turned to her and said, "Mind your own damn business!"

"I need to make out a report."

"No, you don't!" Kim hissed. "This has nothing to do with you."

"It doesn't work that way!" Thelma yelled.

"Well, I'm making it work this way. I'll be back tomorrow."

"We must document every interaction."

"I assure you that this is a private subject, and on my honor, it is unrelated to any DLS activity," Steve interrupted.

"Tell me what happened!" Thelma demanded.

"Above all, we must respect Kim's privacy," Steve reiterated.

"I will kick your alien butt off my planet if you keep this up!"

Steve's eyes narrowed. "If that is your wish."

Kim left the DLS office and recklessly drove to their apartment. Gabe had been relaxing on the sofa while his headache continued to subside.

Kim opened the door with a slam, and Gabe saw the tears in her eyes. He tried to stand and had to sit back down. Kim ran over, set Emma down, and hugged her husband. She cried while Emma held her leg.

Gabe experienced Kim's intense sadness and deep shame. Quickly, he reached his mental limit and yelled, "Stop, stop! This is too much."

"Oh. Sorry, hon."

"What happened?" Gabe asked after several deep breaths while massaging his temples.

Kim continued to hug her husband and said, "I love you so much. I'm so glad you're here."

"I will always support you," Gabe said. "Whatever you need. Anything."

"Honey?"

"Yes?"

"Something awful happened today," Kim admitted in a near whisper.

"What?"

"Steve found out about Mommy Kim's pee-pee hole!" Emma screeched.

Enraged, Gabe tried to stand.

"Honey, honey, wait, wait," Kim said.

"I'm going to kill that guy!" Gabe yelled.

"Hold it. It's not like that."

Gabe slid back onto the sofa, and Kim brought a chair to face him. He held her hand, and she began. "When I was twelve, my uncle Rudy came into my room. Well, he wasn't actually my uncle, but that's what I called him. We started talking about fashion. And— well— we became friendly."

Kim took a deep breath and continued, "I kind of had a thing for him. We pretended to kiss, and well, he unzipped my pants. Things got out of control. And he— he— he— um— touched me."

Gabe used tremendous effort to hug his wife and say, "It's alright."

A long moment later, Kim said, "I screamed, and he put his hand over my mouth. He held me down while grabbing me and—"

Gabe hugged Kim tighter, and so did Emma as they cried. It took a lot of effort for Kim to say, in between sobs, "I feel so violated."

"That's terrible," Gabe whimpered.

"My mother heard my scream. She ran upstairs and attacked Rudy with all her might. Even though she was no match, he ran away. Then, she held me and held me and held me. All night long."

The family wailed as they held each other. Several minutes later, Gabe said in between sobs, "I'm here for you. You know that."

"Me too, Mommy," Emma said in her firmest voice with a big sniffle.

The family continued to hug, and a long while later, Kim said, "I must have suppressed that awful memory. I only remembered that Rudy got drunk and died in a car crash with one of the dry cleaner workers."

"I bet your dad took care of Rudy," Gabe suggested.

"That makes sense. My dad would never allow somebody to violate his daughter. And the other guy, Todd. Well, my mother always suspected he stole from the cash register."

"Two birds, one stone?" Gabe guessed. "Babe, I've got to sit. I'm sorry."

"It's fine. You're tired."

Gabe leaned back on the sofa, and a long while later, he asked, "What happened today?"

"Steve taught me a fantastic mental self-exploration technique. I want to show you how to do it later. I learned so much about my childhood, and there is a bunch of stuff I want to share with you."

"Do you know why he's on Earth? I wanted to ask him that."

"He comes from a long line of businessmen, and this is his first off-world trip. His job is to trade information. To the Slone, information is money."

"Oh. I guess that makes sense."

"He got so sad by what he experienced in my mind," Kim said with a weak smile. "It tore him up. Then I got all embarrassed and had to leave. Thelma acted like her usual prissy self."

"I don't know her," Gabe admitted.

"She's a vile woman. Full of stupid secrets."

"Well, I'm here to support you in any way I can."

"I know," Kim said with a big smile.

"How can I help? Do you want to take some time off? Could we go to a counselor? Or you could fly home and talk to your friends. Whatever you need."

"I help too, Mommy Kim," Emma added.

Kim thought for a long moment, and she said, "This happened a long time ago. I have to deal with it on my own terms."

"Nonsense," Gabe retorted. "I will be at your side. No matter what."

"I know, hon," Kim said, then touched his face to wipe away a tear.

"What can I do? Please, let me do something."

"This thing came out of nowhere," Kim admitted quietly. "I need some time to think."

Somebody knocked at the door, and Kim shouted, "It's open."

Jason rapidly walked into their apartment, visibly out of breath. "Did you run all the way from Alaska?" Gabe asked, though he knew the answer.

"Funny. I happened to be in town today."

"You're here to see if Kim flipped out?" Gabe guessed.

"Something like that."

Kim stood and turned to Jason. She closed her eyes for a long moment and took a deep breath. Then, Kim opened her eyes, looked directly at Jason, and said firmly, "Steve uncovered something in my past."

"Sam guessed as much."

"My uncle Rudy—"

"He did something bad?" Jason finished her sentence.

"He did."

"And Steve mentally found out about it?"

"He helped me to remember," Kim admitted.

"Hey, look, you don't need to share the details. It's fine."

"Thank you."

After an awkward pause, Jason cleared his throat and said, "You know, the name Rudy Campos popped up in your files. Is that the guy?"

"Yeah. My parents told me he died in a car crash. Now, I'm not sure."

"The police reports recorded that a man named Todd McDaniel attacked Rudy Campos with a baseball bat. Rudy fought back with a knife, and they killed each other. The incident occurred in a dry-cleaner's parking lot. Your father was first on the scene."

"My dad told us they died in a car crash because they were drunk."

"Not what happened," Jason said with certainty.

"I never knew."

"Understandable."

"Now what?"

Jason sat in a kitchen chair, looking at the three family members for a long moment. "Afraid we were doing something stupid?" Gabe asked.

"We were not sure what happened. Kim broke a lot of rules, and her actions wound us up."

"Kim needs a pass," Gabe insisted.

"That's not how we operate."

"Make an exception."

Jason took a deep breath, looked at Kim for a long moment, and said, "We're entering some unfamiliar territory, and there are bound to be issues. But, in reality, nothing changed. You had a bad day. That's it."

"Are we good?" Kim asked.

"Thelma wants your head, and she always gets her way."

"Thelma has her own issues," Kim hissed.

"Such as?"

"Her divorce is screwing with her priorities."

"Yeah, there were some rumors about that. It will pass."

"Well, do you know about her tell-all book?" Kim said, challenging him.

Jason jumped out of his chair and exclaimed, "What! What did you say?"

"She is writing a detailed book about DLS history. Every day, she mentally organizes her thoughts, and at night, she writes them down on a tiny laptop. Then, she hides it in a heating vent in her bedroom. She even covers it with aluminum foil."

"And you waited until now to share this information?" Jason exclaimed. "What the heck, Kim! What the heck!"

"You DLS guys have the policy of not reading each other," Kim reminded him.

"We do. But still."

"Well, I didn't want to get into trouble."

Jason threw up his hands, walked in a small circle twice, and sat. "There's a beer in the fridge," Gabe said. "For guests, of course."

Jason nodded. He stood, got their only beer, and opened it. Jason drank half the can and said, "A year ago, somebody anonymously contacted a publisher. They tried to sell a book about the DLS and nearly succeeded. Fortunately, a *division* noticed the incident, and we shut the whole thing down. Afterward, we conducted a thorough investigation but were unable to identify the mystery author.

"Now, this brings up a point. We had a special task for Kim. She would use her mental ability to ferret out the author. Incidentally, this is the main reason we spared your lives."

Kim and Gabe looked at each other, shocked. "Well, you solved our largest problem a lot quicker than expected," Jason admitted with a big grin. "No loyalty check needed. That's going to put a smile on Sammy's face."

Kim crossed her arms and stared at Jason. "Are we good?"

"Yeah, we're good. I'm so sorry about what you went through. Please take all the time you need."

"What about Thelma?"

"You know how this works," Jason said coldly.

"I mean, will she go to prison or something else?"

"Something else."

"Oh."

"It might surprise you that the DLS is a friendly and trusting organization. Everyone is under a ton of pressure, and we try hard to support one another. The DLS only takes extreme actions as a last resort."

"But in this case, you have a choice," Kim countered.

"We sent out a notice to all current and former DLS members to come forward, and there would be no charges. Thelma chose to remain silent. Now, you asked me a question. First off, we'll allow Thelma to explain herself. If she refuses, we will search her house. If we cannot locate a laptop, then all will be forgiven and—"

"What about me?" Kim interrupted. "What will happen if you don't find the laptop?"

"I know people, and you're not the type that makes up something to get somebody else in trouble. And Gabe couldn't lie to save his life. He's probably the worst poker player in history."

Gabe rolled his eyes and asked, "Am I that bad?"

"You are," Jason confirmed.

"Another nail in my coffin?"

"It's not an undesirable trait. You're an honest man. Nothing to be ashamed of. Now, Kim, based on the writing style, we pinned Thelma as one of six suspects, but we had no proof."

"Now what?" Kim asked.

"Come back when you're able."

"Are you going to be following us or something?"

"No sudden moves."

"That's fair. Just letting you know we're getting takeout from the Chinese place down the street. Emma and I will be at the DLS tomorrow, and Gabe will return when he can."

"That's fine."

Jason stood, finished his beer, and Gabe said, "Thanks for dropping by."

"You both seemed more comfortable with me this time."

"It's getting to be routine," Gabe admitted with a thin smile.

Jason laughed and asked, "Are you going to stick with the DLS or return to your old life?"

"We have a lot to learn here."

"Good."

"Anything interesting happen in Alaska?" Kim asked.

"You have access to the reports. Some Kuiu cleanup. Nothing major. Anything interesting with you two?"

"Too much to say," Kim answered slyly.

"Nice deflection. You're getting the hang of how the DLS works. I'm glad we settled this matter. Thanks for the beer. I'll be here for three days. Hope to see you in the office."

"Please take the can with you."

Jason smiled and left their apartment.

# FIFTEEN

The following day, Kim and Emma arrived at 11:30 a.m. The DLS employees were aware of her abrupt departure, but Kim chose not to discuss the matter. In addition, the identity of the anonymous author was now common knowledge.

Two days later, Gabe recovered enough to return, and he obtained permission to use their onk to communicate with the onk in the secure room. This interaction allowed him to determine that the other onk required charging. Gabe's onk recommended using the charging port on the white rifle. After asking permission, he brought both to full power, allowing him to clear the previous onk settings and set it up for a new user.

That afternoon, Gabe and Kim each used an onk to communicate telepathically. This new ability allowed them to translate their vivid emotions into flat, separating their thoughts into basic communications with distinct emotional content. In addition, they could telepathically communicate over vast distances.

As the couple experimented, they learned how to alter and suppress their communicated thoughts and emotions. This new ability enabled them to converse rationally about sensitive topics without conveying intense feelings, thereby improving their relationship and communication effectiveness.

Unfortunately, Emma did not have an onk for herself, and when she borrowed one from her parents, they set it to "new user mode," which prevented her from experiencing the advanced features. As a result, Emma felt left out, and her constant demands to use an onk became a bigger issue.

Using the second onk, Gabe examined the objects in the secure room. He began with the blue box and translated the label as a "gaseous communication and control hub." Gabe understood this object was a spacecraft environmental controller. He had expected the object to be far more advanced, but still wrote a detailed report.

Gabe's next task was to study a massive object stored in a wooden box. Using the onk, he learned it was a sophisticated central computer made by the advanced Azure race. With Troy's help, Gabe applied power and began accessing its memory. The intuitive interface was easy to navigate, and the 1,631 quintons of processing power surprised him.

•

At the end of the week, Sam met with the family in his office. "Well, you three have had quite an impact here. Impressive stuff– especially Kim. You uncovered our mystery author. Congrats."

"Thanks," Kim said with a big grin.

"And Gabe, I have read all your reports cover-to-cover. Great work. Super professional."

"I enjoyed every second," Gabe said with confidence.

"And little Emma. You've been an inspiration to us all. Steve and Duve are quite fond of you."

"Steve funny, boss-man Sam," Emma said with a smile.

"Aren't you the little charmer?"

Sam leaned back and said, "I made the right decision to bring you aboard, and I would like to talk about what's next. I know you three would like to return to Florida and put more effort into your companies. How about three weeks here and three weeks there?"

"We discussed that topic last night and came to a similar conclusion," Kim answered.

"What are your thoughts about Emma and school?"

"That's a tough one," Kim said after some thought. "She's learning a lot here, and I want that to continue. But it would be stressful for her to spend three weeks without school."

"Danny has a daughter who is a year older than Emma, and she attends a local preschool. So that's something to consider."

"Sounds good," Kim said while nodding.

Sam moved his head from side to side and asked, "What is your opinion of Steve?"

"He desperately wants to achieve his goals," Kim answered.

"He smacked up Gabe's mind."

"Steve feels terrible about that."

"He also got deep into your head," Sam said with concern.

"He feels even worse about that."

"Do you think he intentionally injured Gabe?"

"Steve isn't the type," Kim answered, shaking her head.

"Do you think we can trust him?"

"To do what?"

"To exchange the information that we have agreed upon."

"What information?" Kim asked.

"We are exchanging artwork, music, and books."

"Such as?"

"Gosh, there is so much. Um. The Mona Lisa comes to mind," Sam answered. "Um. Plus, Shakespeare and Mozart."

"So? Give him a bunch of digital data. Who cares? He doesn't get the actual paintings. Right?"

"It's a bit more complex."

"Meaning?" Kim wanted to know.

"He's asking for exclusive rights."

"But most of that stuff has copyrights. I know the DLS doesn't own them."

"It's complex."

"What are we getting in return?" Gabe asked.

"Steve is providing reports and simulations on how our society will develop. Plus, a basic knowledge encyclopedia."

"He said we could have the reports for free," Gabe said. "I bet he would provide the other information for free."

"Steve's a businessman," Kim added. "He's trying to get the best deal. Give him the files without the agreement."

Sam nodded. "I had a similar line of thought."

Kim looked at Sam with amusement and asked, "You know that's not what he is after, right?"

"What does he want?"

"Steve only thinks about collecting Kebos," Kim answered.

"Ahh. Those thoughtful-feely music videos. Too bad we don't have any."

"It seems they are the main off-world currency."

"True," Sam admitted.

"We should try to make them ourselves. Earth has a thing for music, entertainment, and computers. Like Michael Jackson, Bill Gates, and MTV."

"All true," Sam agreed.

"I looked into what it takes to develop a Kebo," Gabe said. "We would need a lot of technology. The essential component is called a Dotsun. It's a thought-feeling suit, and I might be able to make one."

"That's incredible!" Sam exclaimed.

<Feel the greed?> Kim warned Gabe.

<Yes.>

<He's only thinking about personal profit. Now he wants an expensive car.>

<We must stop this.>

<Tell him it would take a hundred years.>

<Sounds good, babe.>

"Ah, hey, Sam," Gabe said. "Now that I'm thinking about the logistics, making a Dotsun would mean inventing a lot of new technology. It'd take at least a hundred years. I guess I got ahead of myself. Sorry about that."

Sam looked deflated. "You're correct. Plus, making one would be an 'out-of-bounds technology alteration.' And here I am, almost creating one. Wow, that was stupid."

"Not a problem," Kim said with a smile.

"If only we had something to trade."

"Like a bunch of Kebos?" Gabe offered.

"We don't even have one," Sam admitted.

"Actually, you have a couple of billion."

Sam stood and exclaimed, "What the heck!"

"That Azure computer has a massive amount of storage, and Kebos make up about thirty percent."

"You never told me that," Kim said as she looked at Gabe.

"It didn't seem important. Plus, we're not supposed to talk about work stuff at home."

<You could have informed me,> Kim thought.

<Er.>

<Hon!>

Kim laughed, and Gabe shook his head. A bewildered Sam leaned back down and asked, "Which item number?"

"The big wooden box," Gabe answered. "I don't remember the number."

"Yeah, I know the box. We found that item during the Grazen incident."

"From interfacing with the unit, I found out that this unit is intended to be the central processor for a planet. I bet they wanted to use it for Earth's capital city."

"Makes sense. And you said it had over a billion Kebos?" Sam asked, awed.

"At least."

"Gabe, nobody has billions of Kebos," Sam said, shaking his head. "It just does not work that way."

"What do you mean?" Gabe asked.

"They stole the Kebos from hundreds of planets."

"I guess."

"Well, this changes everything. I can trade two or three Kebos for all the necessary information."

"Let's not tell Steve what we have," Kim cautioned.

"You've got that right. But now that you are aware of what we just discussed, it presents a problem. He can read you two."

"Who has been working out the details so far?" Kim asked.

"Brooke Henderson."

"I know the name, but never met her."

"She handles all the off-world negotiations," Sam said.

"Well, have her make the trade."

"That would work. How do we transfer them?" Sam asked.

"We have a pile of memory devices in the lab," Gabe answered. "They were all 44.7 zettabytes. Apparently, that's a standard off-world memory size. More than enough for three Kebos."

"Wow, this day is shaping up."

Sam leaned back in his chair momentarily and said, "There's another topic. We promised we would protect you. So, we have been looking into those awful internet rumor mongers. And, well– we noticed a unique pattern."

"What kind?" Kim asked with great suspicion.

"The DLS data center in, um– *somewhere*– is responsible for locating people who discuss off-world activities. That's how we learned about Thelma's book. Now, this group identified a particular pattern called a crumpled flower. Imagine taking a flower and squishing it. It no longer resembles a flower but is still a flower. A person would use this complicated computer network technique to disguise their identity."

"Who's behind it all?" Kim asked.

"Not Sato or anybody else in his group of bandits. A threat vector hidden by a crumpled flower algorithm is far too sophisticated. But it's meant to look like he's the central figure."

Sam took a deep breath, closed his eyes, and continued, "It's starting up again."

Gabe almost swore, looked down at Emma, and said calmly, "Dang."

"You might find it amusing that your group of naked people is deleting all the new posts."

Kim threw her hands up. "This is intolerable. Why's this happening?"

"We have our top resources looking into every aspect of the attack. Whoever's doing this has exceptional computer skills."

“This makes little sense,” Gabe said. “We’re nobodies. Who would invest that kind of time and effort?”

“You got me beat,” Sam admitted. “What I can do is give you a weekly status report.”

“Thank you.”

“It’s the least we can do. After all, this affects us too.”

“True,” Kim said. Her eyes seemed to grow distant for a moment as she pondered the problem. “Hey, wait. Could this be about the DLS and not us?”

“What do you mean?” Sam said.

“Do you have any enemies?”

Sam looked puzzled and bit his lower lip. Finally, he nodded and answered, “We recently upset the U.S. Space Force. But I doubt this computer threat has anything to do with them.”

“Well, let’s ask!” Kim demanded.

“You don’t talk to them. I will set up an appointment in three weeks.”

“This is a special circumstance,” Gabe countered.

“Hmm.”

“I would like to meet the people who threatened to arrest my husband without a warrant,” Kim said through gritted teeth.

“Touché. I will set up an emergency meeting next week.”

“How about this afternoon?” Kim recommended.

“They’re not going to like that.”

“If the media found out about the Air Force using their billion-dollar computers to run a petty smear campaign? That could blow the cover off your entire operation.”

“I hadn’t thought of that,” Sam admitted. “If they are... Wow. This would be huge.”

“Do you want to drive or walk?” Kim asked.

“It’s a nice day.”

•

Donna made two phone calls, and fifteen minutes later, the group walked down the street. Gabe carried Emma on his shoulders and told her about the cars they saw. She loved being the center of attention and asked insightful questions. Soon, the group came to an unassuming office building with mirrored windows. Gabe noticed several security cameras tracking their movements, which gave off an unfriendly vibe. In the lobby, three heavily armed guards watched them closely.

After signing in, a guard scanned each person with a metal detecting wand and then patted them down. He asked about what was in Gabe's pocket, and he answered with a confident grin, "That's classified."

Sam smiled coyly, and the guard asked Gabe to show him the object. He studied the onk and saw that the small object posed no threat.

Emma's presence perplexed all the guards, and one mocked, "Take your daughter to work day?"

The two other guards laughed, and Emma replied, "You mean! Behave, or I will tell them about Candy Fire!"

The guard looked at her in horror. *How did she know I was dating a stripper?* he thought as he waved them through.

<Emma!> Kim thought while using the onk to hide her humor.

<Sorry, Mommy Kim.>

<No more of that,> Kim told Emma, though she swelled with pride.

<I will, Mommy Kim.>

Gabe and Sam tried to appear upset, but they still managed to smile. Then a different guard escorted the group through a tastefully decorated hallway adorned with pictures of combat aircraft. At the end were large wooden doors with scenes of air battles carved into them. Inside, they found a grand office with a massive black cherrywood desk. One wall featured a colossal bronze sculpture with the words "U.S. Space Force" in bold letters. Gabe felt it looked like the *Star Trek* symbol and suppressed a chuckle. When he turned to Kim, he saw her broad smile.

The man behind the desk was in his late sixties and stood five foot four. His sharp, pepper-gray hair was trimmed into a no-nonsense crew cut, accentuating the angular contours of his face. Piercing brown eyes seemed to miss nothing as they assessed them with sharp clarity, holding the weight of experiences accumulated over decades of Air Force service.

Clad in a neat uniform, every crease and fold meticulously arranged, he exuded an aura of professionalism. Each insignia and badge on his chest spoke of a lifetime of dedicated service. The large black nameplate on the desk read in gold letters, "Two Star General Paul Shefford."

"What the heck is a baby doing in my office!" General Shefford boomed.

Sam bit his lip and said, "Afternoon, Paul. Thanks for the urgent meeting."

"Answer! Now!" General Shefford demanded.

"In time. In time. First. Do you know these three?"

"Certainly not! My department isn't a daycare. Out! Now!"

"Take another look," Sam encouraged in a gentle voice. "You might recognize them."

"I don't... Wait a second. You wait right there. You're not Gabe? And this is Kim? And your daughter?"

Kim nodded, and General Shefford asked angrily, "Why the heck are they here? Do you know how big a pain in my backside you've been?"

"No. Tell us!" Kim hissed through gritted teeth.

"That damn crucible theory. It derailed everything. We almost had Project Dead Pan going until you showed up."

Gabe asked, "What's Project Dead Pan?"

"Sam, this stops now. Why are you here? You told me this meeting had top priority. I put off calling Congresswoman Baker. You know she wants to form a committee to investigate us."

Sam shook his head and answered, "They work for me."

"Work for you? Work for you! Oh, no, no, no. They don't work for you. Besides, what could they offer? They lucked out by walking through an off-world attack. No big deal."

"They work for me, and that's all you need to know," Sam said with a thin smile.

General Shefford looked annoyed and continued, "This is intolerable. Wait a minute. Sam, you keep stalling about Lieutenant Tiller and Captain Jefferson. They were last seen at their house. If you two had anything to do with their disappearance, I will lock you up."

"Let's table that discussion for the moment," Sam suggested in a friendly voice.

"These two know something. I see it in their faces. Look, the baby is smiling. See that? Stop stonewalling!"

Sam looked around and said, "Gabe, Kim. Pull up a chair."

They moved two chairs and sat across from General Shefford. Kim bounced Emma on her knee while Emma gave him the stink eye. It had an unnerving effect, and Sam said, "Paul, we've been dancing around this subject for weeks. I think we both need to come clean."

"I agree to nothing. Especially in front of people without access."

"They have full DLS access."

"What? Nobody has full access. Even you," General Shefford countered.

"Well, they do. Want to know why I gave it to them? They have unique mental gifts."

"Meaning?" General Shefford retorted.

"Gabe discovered what your two officers were up to."

"What? How?"

"We'll talk about that later. Now, about your men. Tiller and Jefferson admitted that you are starting a telepathic program. That's against our agreement."

"No confirmations," the general again replied.

"Now, for some trust on your part. Are you conducting a cyber operation against the Alexanders? Be honest."

General Shefford looked upset, furled his eyebrows, and nodded. Gabe stood and demanded, "Why? Why the heck, why?"

"Address me as Two Star General Shefford. I've earned it."

Gabe calmed himself and said through gritted teeth, "Two Star General Shefford, please tell us why you are using taxpayer-funded computer resources to destroy our reputation."

"No."

"Paul," Sam said after a pause. "Time for some truth. Answer the man's question. He deserves to know."

General Shefford took a deep breath, squinted at Gabe, and answered angrily, "The amount of damage you did! We were so close to restarting Dead Pan, and that crucible theory ruined everything. I have reporters up my tailpipe every day. 'What are you doing at HAARP? Can you confirm the crucible theory? What was your involvement?' Question after question. Well, we decided to focus the media on you two instead. It seemed fitting."

Gabe stood and yelled, "You convinced the world that I broke Kim's arm and killed her non-existent sister? How dare you! How dare you!"

General Shefford became embarrassed and murmured, "I suppose we tarnished your reputation— a bit."

"This is going to stop. Right here, right now!" Gabe threatened.

"Restarting Dead Pan is too important," General Shefford said dismissively.

"What is it? A space radar?" Gabe guessed.

"How the heck did you know that? Did you hack the Air Force computers using DLS equipment? Did Sam tell you? You're in a lot of trouble."

Kim shook her head and said, "You realize my husband's a brilliant engineer."

General Shefford huffed and said, "Alright, alright. It's an advanced seven-megahertz radar for deep-space applications. We set up the HAARP program to accomplish that from day one."

Gabe looked thoughtful and said, "You would need about sixteen worldwide sites to make a long-wave phased array synthetic aperture radar. Because of the low frequency and the atmospheric distortion, synchronization would be difficult."

General Shefford became flabbergasted and said, "It's nineteen sites because of border issues. The ones on the poles will be our biggest challenge. Um, because of the synchronization issues."

"Now that the cat's out of the bag. Are we good? No more internet games?" Gabe hoped.

"We need a distraction."

"Look, bozo," Kim demanded. "You have a daughter, too. Imagine how she would feel if I posted lies about you!"

"How did you know I have a daughter? Did you hack into my files?" he demanded.

"Her picture is on your desk!" Kim countered.

"Oh. I guess that gives it away."

"Explain to your daughter what you did to us. Hold on. Explain to my daughter what you did. Right now. Tell her!"

Emma glared harshly at General Shefford. He turned away and looked down. Finally, he looked up, turned back, and said quietly, "We need a distraction to keep the public out of our hair."

"Tell them it is terrorism." Kim retorted. "The public always believes that lie."

"I suppose."

"Well, we have had a big breakthrough," Sam said to deflect the conversation. "I take it that all this cyber-bashing is no longer necessary. Correct?"

General Shefford looked at Gabe, then Kim, and then Emma. Finally, he took a hissing breath through his teeth and answered, "Correct."

"Wonderful."

General Shefford took another breath and asked Gabe, "What did you bring through security?"

"An onk," Gabe answered offhandedly.

"The communication device?"

"Yes."

"Why?" General Shefford asked with narrow eyes.

"In case we needed it."

General Shefford snorted and said, "You can't use an onk. No human can. Our scientists conclusively proved that."

"All three of us can use it. No problem."

General Shefford grinned, shook his head with a smirk, and said, "Now I know you're lying. It is biologically impossible. What is it? A recording device? Are you trying to use this conversation for leverage?"

"Want a demo?" Kim angrily asked with narrow eyes. "I can make you punch yourself."

"What?"

"Left eye or right?"

"Wait. Are you telling me the truth?"

An already annoyed Gabe used his onk to force General Shefford to put his hand in front of his face. Emma smiled and said, "General Buzz Lightyear funny."

The general did not understand what had happened. He moved his hand out of the way and looked around in confusion. Finally, he pinched his eyebrows and whispered without looking at the assembled people, "Sam, it sounds like we need to put more effort into working together."

"That's more like it," Sam said with a big smile. "Now we have—"

The phone rang. General Shefford picked it up and yelled, "I told you. No calls."

He listened and asked, "A Type 439? Inbound? Alright. I'll coordinate at this end. Thanks."

"Another Type 439?" Sam asked.

"Satellite 22 confirmed an inbound. We've sent the standard warning message, and they aren't turning away."

"Our agents will intercept them on the ground."

"We will assist," General Shefford said with a confident nod.

"How is the Air Force going to assist?" Kim asked, sensing deception.

General Shefford winced and answered, "We have one flyable craft."

"Your men informed us of this," Sam said with a thin smile.

"You knew?"

"Yes."

"It appears the cat's out of the bag," General Shefford admitted.

"Your men also informed me you have been going into deep space."

"Once."

"You've been holding back."

"You too!" the general retorted.

"Enough!" Kim yelled. "No more lies. Now, what the heck's a Type 439?"

"It's a generation-one craft that is holding steady in a far-Earth orbit," the general said.

Kim became suspicious. "And what are you going to do about it?"

"We have a craft capable of performing an interception."

"Define interception."

"We encourage them to leave."

"How?" Kim asked while knowing there was great deception.

"Our craft has a gun."

"A gun?"

"A 20-millimeter autocannon," General Shefford confidently answered.

"I sense hesitation."

"You sense my hesitation?"

Kim's eyes became slits. "You're lying your general ass off."

"Damn! That is not how I had intended to play this. Alright, fine! We can fire one round."

"Now, I'm sensing even more hesitation. Tell us, what happens after you fire your big gun?"

"Ahh– hull breach," General Shefford admitted. "The damn thing actually goes sailing out the other side."

"Oooo. Good plan. I'm still sensing hesitation. Spill it!"

"Well, um, alright. We damaged the craft when we first fired the thing, and well– um– it no longer flies."

"Then what are you going to do?" Kim asked.

"Alright, alright. We act tough and chase them with the one craft that does fly."

"Did that work in the past?"

"Um, no," the general admitted.

"Why don't you talk to them?"

"Well–"

"You can't," Kim interrupted.

"Darn it! We can't talk to them. Satisfied?"

"No."

"The DLS holds the communication technology in its little kingdom. We got fed up and took action. That's why we started the telepathy program."

Sam leaned forward and said, "These three can talk to them."

"What?" General Shefford yelled.

"Gabe, Kim, and Emma can speak with them. Fly them up," Sam recommended with a big grin.

"No, no, no, no. They're civilians. Plus, they have a kid. That's not going to happen. We don't work that way."

"Well, it's time to start working that way."

"You're the ones who hold all the off-world intel," General Shefford countered. "And you just admitted to using onks."

"Stop!" Kim yelled. "Now, are you going to ask us nicely?" General Shefford glowered, and Kim said with a smile, "I'm not hearing a please."

"Look, we cannot snap our fingers and take a civilian up into space. There are strict procedures and rules. Plus, it's a crapshoot every time we try to get a craft off the ground."

"My husband can help with that."

"What?"

"He's smart and knows technology."

“He has done amazing things,” Sam offered. “Far more than we expected.”

General Shefford thought about it while Kim continued, “Look. What’s the goal here? Keep off-worlders off our planet. Right?”

“That’s the overall goal.”

“Well, you haven’t done so well in the past. Let’s try something new.”

He grimaced but half-nodded.

“I’m still not hearing a please,” Kim said with a grin.

“Alright, alright. The Air Force would appreciate your help. Unfortunately, we only have one working craft, and I will permit Gabe to act as an observer.”

“The commander,” Kim countered.

“What?”

“He will be in charge of the entire mission.”

Gabe’s heart raced with the idea of rocketing into space. <Babe, what the heck?>

<Hon, relax,> Kim thought with a smile.

<Are you messing with me?>

<Shefford wants to put you to sleep once the craft gets off the ground. He’s trying to appease Sam.>

<Yeah, I felt that, too.>

<Well?>

<I thought he was joking.>

<Men like him don’t joke. You know that.>

<I do know that,> Gabe admitted with reservations.

<You’ve got to relax and trust yourself.>

<Yeah, Daddy Gabe,> Emma encouraged. <You brave.>

<Thanks, Emma.>

<Tell General Buzz Lightyear that you want to go,> Emma told him.

<Alright.>

“He cannot command the mission,” General Shefford said. “He does not know anything about spacecraft.”

“True, but I’ve already been off-world,” Gabe countered.

“What? Sam! You broke Paragraph Three?”

“Actually, I tried to have them silenced.”

“Twice,” Kim corrected.

“Yesss, twice,” Sam said with a huff.

General Shefford took a deep breath and said, “You’re on shaky ground, Sam. Paragraph Three is crystal clear.”

“I take all responsibility,” Sam confirmed.

“They have interacted with off-worlders?”

"Far better than our wildest expectations," Sam admitted.

"It would be nice to put one in the win column."

"Gabe's your man."

"I'm going out on a big limb here," General Shefford said cautiously. "You've got to admit that our two groups need better communication."

"Gabe would act as the copilot."

"Agreed."

<Kim!> Gabe thought with fear. <I don't know the first thing about flying.>

<Hon, relax. You've got this,> Kim confidently encouraged him.

<What are you going to do while I am up there?> Gabe asked.

<Go back to the DLS and help.>

<How did I get roped into this?>

<It's good to make new friends.> Kim smiled sheepishly.

<Human friends!>

# SIXTEEN

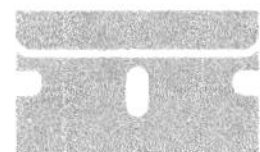

Sam, Kim, and Emma walked back to the DLS. At the main lobby, Donna escorted the pair to a room they had not been in before. Inside, they saw several monitors showing the Earth, the solar system, and tactical displays. The center screen had a grainy image of a craft, and the assembled people diligently worked at their computers.

At the same time, a black sedan with flashing lights rapidly drove Gabe to a nearby airport, where a white business jet waited. Once onboard, the two pilots communicated over their headsets and refused to answer any of his questions. Forty-five minutes later, the plane descended into a long desert runway and stopped near an aircraft hangar. Gabe assumed they had flown him to Area 51 or, as Jason called it, Virgilio Airfield.

The door opened with a whoosh of hot desert air, and a man greeted Gabe at the bottom of the steps. He stood six feet tall, and his figure exuded a quiet confidence. With a sharp crew cut accentuating his strong jawline, his green eyes intently studied Gabe. The man wore a green flight suit, with every seam and zipper perfectly aligned.

"My name is Colonel Zachary Cruz," he stated with a strong Midwestern accent.

"Gabe Alexander. Nice to meet you," Gabe said with a smile.

The two men walked toward a large white building, and Colonel Cruz said, "We need to fill out paperwork and get you suited up."

"What kind of paperwork?" Gabe asked suspiciously.

"Secret paperwork."

"You want me to sign documents I cannot read?"

"Affirmative," Colonel Cruz curtly answered.

"My DLS bosses would probably get upset if I signed a bunch of things. Can I call them and ask about that?"

"My superiors told me you applied excessive pressure to join this mission. This action upset many people and means paperwork far above your pay grade."

Gabe thought about how his former wife, Lydia, would confidently solve difficult situations and said, "Your last missions failed. If you play these games, you will fail again."

Colonel Cruz abruptly stopped, turned around, glared at Gabe, and headed back toward the plane.

"This is not the right move," Gabe said as he followed.

"We have rules, and we follow them to the letter. No exceptions."

"Will you stop for one minute?"

"No," Colonel Cruz curtly answered.

"I know much more about what is happening than you think."

"That cannot possibly be true. You're an observer and nothing more."

"Look, we're on the same team."

Colonel Cruz made a hand motion, and the plane's engines started. Gabe became upset and cautioned, "If you don't stop. I'll stop you."

Colonel Cruz turned around with raised eyebrows. He then placed his hand on his sidearm and asked, "Are you threatening me?"

"I guess— I guess I am."

"You're no match," Colonel Cruz said with narrow eyes.

"True."

Colonel Cruz smiled wickedly, turned around, took two steps, and stopped. Gabe applied all his mental ability, assisted by the onk, to make Colonel Cruz's leg muscles freeze. This effort took extreme concentration, and he gritted his teeth. The success impressed Gabe, and he walked in front of Colonel Cruz. There, he saw terror in the man's eyes. Now Gabe smiled wickedly.

Gabe eased his mental hold and lied, "Had enough? I can do a lot worse."

"What the heck are you doing?"

"Sign a bunch of my paperwork, and I will give *you* an answer."

Gabe immediately regretted his arrogant answer. Colonel Cruz looked at him for a long moment and said, "Let's get you suited up."

"That's better."

Gabe released his mental hold, and Colonel Cruz lurched forward. He turned around, and they walked toward the buildings after regaining balance.

"Say, listen," Gabe said to mend bridges. "This thing about me being here. Look, I'm only trying to help. Your pilot will be in charge."

"This was our plan from the beginning. Also, I'm the pilot," Colonel Cruz revealed with a thin smile.

The pair came to a door and walked down a long hallway with peeling paint and cracked floor tiles. The doors along the hallways used massive combination locks instead of doorknobs, and Gabe likened the view to a strange bank. Finally, they came to a door with a standard doorknob, and Colonel Cruz opened it. Inside, Gabe saw a room with large vertical lockers that reminded him of his high school.

Colonel Cruz opened a cabinet and took out a spacesuit. This sight brightened Gabe's mood, and Colonel Cruz explained how to wear the suit. Then, he corrected Gabe by explaining they were not "spacesuits" but "pressure suits."

Gabe realized Kim had observed the situation through the onk, which made him chuckle. This reaction annoyed Colonel Cruz, and Gabe considered explaining his humor but realized the conversation would not help.

Once suited up, the pair walked out, holding their helmets. Gabe grinned from ear to ear as he remembered a scene from the movie *The Right Stuff*. Unfortunately, his cheerful expression further annoyed Colonel Cruz.

They walked through several hallways and then came to a door with a guard. Colonel Cruz signed a form, and the guard opened the door.

Inside, Gabe saw a medium-sized aircraft hangar. In the center was a spacecraft. However, the sight left Gabe deeply confused. It looked like a child had taken broken toy spaceship parts and glued them together. The craft was twenty feet long, and Gabe knew it was non-aerodynamic and structurally unsound. As they got closer, he saw holes in the side and understood why they had to wear pressure suits.

Colonel Cruz led them to a small door at the bottom of the craft. Gabe looked inside and saw a tiny area meant for two pilots. The two men squeezed into tight seats intended for much smaller individuals. They put on seatbelts that were crudely attached to the floor. In front were two large Dell computer monitors connected to six gray boxes with switches, knobs, and indicators. There was a small, crudely cut hole in the front of the craft with an oval piece of glass glued in.

Gabe saw a Thrustmaster joystick and realized the Air Force had adapted the craft so humans could operate it. The setup did not inspire confidence, and he asked, "What's the deal? This doesn't look safe."

Colonel Cruz sighed and answered, “A craft went down outside Fresno in the fifties. It took the eggheads twenty years of trial and error to make it flyable. We use it as our test vehicle and trainer. We have four others in much better condition, but they aren’t working right now.”

“Is one of them from Roswell?” Gabe asked.

Colonel Cruz brightened and answered, “No. The Roswell incident resulted from an off-course balloon carrying a nuclear blast detector.”

“The public blew it out of proportion?”

“Yep.”

“I know that feeling,” Gabe mused.

“There are many reports about you.”

“Yeah.”

“Your wife killed a bear?” Colonel Cruz asked.

“One bear, one knife.”

“Tough woman.”

“Oh, you got that right.”

Colonel Cruz turned to Gabe and asked, “The other stuff about you and her?”

“Wild lies made up by your boss.”

“My boss?”

“General Shefford started a distraction campaign to conceal Project Dead Pan.”

Colonel Cruz glared at Gabe. “And he admitted this?”

“About two hours ago. It pissed me off something fierce, and I wanted to punch his lights out.”

“What about the whole crucible theory?”

“I made it up,” Gabe admitted with a chuckle.

“You made it up?”

“It seemed like a good idea at the time.”

“That upset a lot of powerful people,” Colonel Cruz cautioned.

“Yeah, I know.”

“What about that other stuff in Alaska?”

“We interacted with the off-worlders who landed there.”

“I see,” Cruz said. “How did you learn how to communicate with off-worlders?”

“I’m not supposed to talk about that,” Gabe answered. “Not that I fully understand it myself.”

“Understood. Well, let’s see if this old bird will get going.”

“They told me you guys only had one flyable craft.”

Colonel Cruz remained quiet, and Gabe asked, “Compartmentalized?”

"Yes."

"Cool."

Colonel Cruz spoke through his handheld radio, and a man dressed in a green jumpsuit pressed buttons to open the large hangar doors. Colonel Cruz flipped switches on the left console, checked off items on a checklist, typed commands into a small keyboard, and the computer screens began changing information. Gabe's onk dramatically thought, {Dangerous event!}

<I don't understand.>

{Operators have not configured this Zigon properly! Continued operation will lead to destruction!}

<Is Zigon the word for spacecraft?>

{It is a class of spacecraft.}

<What is the proper configuration?>

{Observe.}

Gabe began understanding the basic technology of their craft and yelled, "Stop!"

"What?" Colonel Cruz asked with great concern.

"Stop what you're doing! Right now! Stop, stop, stop!"

"I'm stopping. I'm stopping. What's the problem?"

"This is all configured wrong. You are about to push the power systems to the maximum."

"I know this craft better than anybody. You don't know the first thing about any of this. Let me do my job."

Gabe looked annoyed, interfaced with the Zigon through the onk, and began turning off systems.

"What the heck. Stop that!" Colonel Cruz yelled.

"Wait."

"I'm in chargc!"

"You were about to kill us!" Gabe said, waving him away with his hand.

"Now look, I will have to do the preflight all over again."

"Let me try it my way. Alright?"

While studying Gabe's eyes, Colonel Cruz decided to trust him and said, "Proceed with caution."

Gabe nodded, stabilized the reactors, initialized the power bus, and began engaging the systems in the proper order. Finally, the Zigon's systems became active, and the craft entered a stable configuration.

"You were running Reactor One far above the safety margin with all the protection systems disabled," Gabe said. "Even a slight overload would have obliterated everything in a three-kilometer radius. And you had Reactor Two inactive. I fixed all that, and the power output is back to normal. The navigation systems have synchronized to something called a 'Chet Vasser,' and I enabled the primary propulsion system. We're ready to go."

Colonel Cruz stared at his screens in disbelief.

"It's all there," Colonel Cruz admitted.

"Yes."

"Amazing."

"Good."

"Can I fly it now?" Colonel Cruz asked with a smile.

"I don't see why not."

"It will just respond?"

"Of course," Gabe confidently answered.

"Great. Put on your helmet, connect your O2, and then we go."

"Sounds good."

"Um. Thanks," Colonel Cruz quietly said.

"Any time."

The two men put on their helmets, and Colonel Cruz began maneuvering the Zigon with his joystick.

{Dangerous event!} The onk thought.

Gabe used the onk to observe the Zigon's systems and yelled through his helmet microphone, "Stop, stop!"

Colonel Cruz halted the craft after it had traveled forward three feet.

"You have interfaced through the navigation port?" Gabe asked.

"That's how you fly this thing."

"How do I put this? Um. Imagine driving your car using the GPS map screen instead of the steering wheel."

"We aren't controlling the flight surfaces?" Colonel Cruz asked, concerned.

"No. You're screaming pushy directions at the navigation system a million times a second."

"Can we fix it?" Colonel Cruz asked.

"That would take forever. Let me take control."

"You can do that?"

"Sure."

Gabe turned off the crude interface through the onk. The Zigon eagerly responded to his inputs, as if all previous attempts had annoyed it. He commanded up, and the Zigon gracefully rose. Then Gabe directed it to exit the hangar.

Colonel Cruz liked how the craft operated and commented, "This is smooth."

"Where to?"

"Here are the coordinates," Colonel Cruz said as he handed Gabe a slip of paper.

“Those are GPS numbers. I don’t know what to do with them.”

“We installed a GPS system into the controls.”

“I thought GPS did not work in space.”

“We have a special one,” Colonel Cruz said with a twinkle in his eye.

“Oh. Well, I had to disable your interface. Why don’t I fly us to the other craft?”

“You know where it is?” Colonel Cruz asked.

“The Zigon has an excellent sensor system.”

“What’s a Zigon?”

“That’s the class of this ship.”

“Oh.”

“The Dreen made this craft. But there are non-Dreen parts on it.”

“We had to add those for stability,” Colonel Cruz admitted.

“When we get back, please take them off. The craft is working hard to compensate for the extra junk.”

“Our added stabilizers aren’t necessary?”

“No.”

“That’s good to know. I was not too fond of all the modifications. By the way, who are the Dreen?”

“I can access information about them, but discussing their history and concentrating on flying is difficult.”

“Understood.”

Gabe directed the craft upward with ease. His ears hurt as the altitude increased, but he worked his jaw, and the pressure equalized. Soon, it was dark, and Gabe realized they were in outer space. For fun, he eased back on the acceleration and felt weightless. “Your first time?” Colonel Cruz guessed.

“First time awake.”

“We have work to do.”

“No more playtime, Dad?” Gabe asked in a playful voice.

“No, son. Fly the craft.”

“Alright, Dad.”

Gabe applied forward acceleration and looked at the stars through the small window. At the same time, Kim appreciated his feelings, and this dual interaction made for a strange sensation as they both admired each other’s excitement and fear.

“So, what’s the deal with your appearance?” Colonel Cruz asked in a cagey voice. “The files said you’re forty-one, but you look twenty.”

“I’m not sure what I can tell you.”

“There is a theory about traveling faster than light,” Colonel Cruz offered.

"Nah, nothing like that."

"Compartmentalization?"

"An aggressive man told me never to talk about that *stuff*," Gabe cautioned.

"Understood. My team also has *aggressive* men."

"What is the deal with the holes in the ship? It should be easy to fix them."

"That's an easy one."

"You cannot repair them?" Gabe guessed.

"This ship has an unknown metal alloy. It took the technicians eight weeks to cut out a window with a high-power laser."

"My onk tells me you must use the same alloy and apply focused micro-inductive heating on both sides."

"What's an onk?" Colonel Cruz wanted to know.

"Red tape."

"Understood."

"We're about to slow down," Gabe cautioned.

The Zigon craft came to a gentle stop. Gabe and Colonel Cruz saw a small object through the viewing window. It appeared black, without lights, windows, or other distinguishing features.

"Now what?" Colonel Cruz asked.

"Let me try something."

<Can we talk to the beings on that ship?> Gabe asked the onk.

{Attempting access.}

Gabe observed the synchronization of communication protocols and the interaction between language databases. He received a distant thought with reserved emotions, <Greetings.>

<Hello?> Gabe thought back with his best pleasant emotions.

<Do you represent this planet?>

<I guess,> Gabe admitted with trepidation.

<From our data intercepts, your planet designation is Earth?>

<That's us.>

<You are using a Veronn onk?>

<They gave it to me.>

<Understood,> the individual thought with relief, which confused Gabe.

<Who are you?>

<We are of the Dang Flip Domain.>

Gabe understood that this name translated to "epicenter of peace and serenity," and he suppressed his humor.

<May I ask why you are here?> Gabe asked.

<We represent information.>

<You want to trade information with us?>

<Yes,> the individual agreed.

<Our satellite communication system sent you a message that our planet didn't wish to have off-world interaction.>

<We received this message,> the individual admitted with annoyance.

<The message should have been clear. We're not ready to trade.>

<Your culture is undeveloped.>

<Very true.>

<Explain your presence,> the individual thought harshly.

<You mean, why am I meeting you?>

<Yes.>

<We have a department that keeps off-world interaction to a minimum. We have repaired a craft, but do not fully understand how it works. I'm here to ask you to depart on peaceful terms.>

A long moment later, Gabe got a confused response. <Few undeveloped worlds have a department like yours.>

<I'm unaware of what happens on other planets. Can I ask your name? I'm Gabe.>

<Kon Beekie.>

Gabe suppressed his humor and thought, <Nice to meet you, Kon Beekie.>

<Our intercepts indicate your race suffers from lethal parasites. It's a simple matter to eradicate,> Kon Beekie offered.

<I am sure your race possesses outstanding medical technology. Our society isn't ready for such advances.>

<Our intercepts reveal your broad entertainment spectrum. We can trade.>

<You want Kebos.> Gabe regretted sounding a little arrogant.

<You have them?> Kon Beekie asked, excited.

<We know about them.>

<I sense hesitation,> Kon Beekie told Gabe.

Gabe had unintentionally thought about the stored Kebos when he answered. He became upset with himself and lied, <Another race once offered some of them to us. They are far beyond our technology level, and we cannot use them.>

<Your craft has many flaws. We can assist with repairs,> Kon Beekie offered.

<We're doing our best.>

After a long pause, Kon Beekie thought, <We would like to meet on your planet and discuss an important matter.>

Gabe was becoming frustrated. <I'm only the messenger. We aren't ready for off-world interaction, and we would appreciate it if you left on good terms.>

<What information would entice your interest?> Kon Beekie was sounding desperate.

<We don't need information. If you leave your contact details in my onk, we may interact with you in the future.>

<Onks don't operate in the manner you describe,> Kon Beekie thought with annoyance.

<Oh.>

<An onk can only communicate with other onks of the same race. At close distances, an onk utilizes radio waves and a translation matrix. You're using this method now.>

<I'm still new at communicating through an onk.>

<Obviously.>

Gabe was embarrassed by his lack of basic onk knowledge.

<We are here for a specific reason,> Kon Beekie thought forcefully.

<I have been told that faster-than-light travel is complex, and there is always a reason.>

<Correct.>

<What is your purpose?>

After another long pause, Kon Beekie thought, <We are searching for Grazen leaders, and a database entry led us here.>

<I see.>

<The Grazen came to our planet and devastated our culture for 66 full cycles.> Gabe experienced Kon Beekie's deep shame. <Violent conflict engulfed our world for two full cycles. Upon victory, the Grazen departed with our most sacred objects.>

<What objects?> Gabe asked, curious.

<Our Kebos.>

<Why do you think they are here?>

<Do you have three Grazen craft?> Kon Beekie asked with concern.

<No.>

<We can see that you do,> Kon Beekie thought angrily.

<We don't.>

<We observed your craft ascending. From that location, we observed three Grazen craft next to twelve other craft.>

<Hold on.>

"You have fifteen spacecraft?" Gabe asked through his microphone.

"How the heck do you know that?" Colonel Cruz exclaimed.

"They told me."

"Oh, they must have used sensors or something to figure that out. Well, anyway. Yes, we do."

"Alright, hang on while I talk to my wife."

"You can do that?" Colonel Cruz asked with wide eyes.

"I think so."

Gabe thought to Kim and spoke to Sam through her, "Hey, Sam. Um. Gabe here. Um. This guy in outer space calls himself Kon Beekie, and he's from the Dang Flip Domain. Yeah, I know. Funny name. Anyway, he tells me the Grazen stole a bunch of Kebos, and they brought them here on their three ships. If I remember correctly, those guys tried to take over Cuba. Anyway, I'm betting the files Kon Beekie wants are in that Azure computer."

"You're talking through Kim, and I'm speaking to Gabe?" Sam guessed.

"Yes."

"Interesting. Well? What proof does he have, and what is he offering in trade?"

"Do you want me to ask? That would confirm that we have them," Gabe admitted.

"Yeah, it would."

"Well, decide."

Sam thought for a long moment and answered, "I suppose the Kebos belong to them."

"There are bigger things at stake here than a bunch of files," Kim said. "This could set a bad precedent."

"Is that Gabe or Kim?" Sam asked.

"It's me."

"Your argument is valid. However, they already know about the ships."

"Um. Gabe here. I think you're correct. They said there were fifteen spacecraft at that Virgilio place."

"I was told seven."

"Let's deal with that later. What do I tell them?" Gabe asked.

"Offer to give them back their property if they agree to eliminate all traces that led them here."

"I guess that's fair, but how would we verify their actions?"

"We cannot."

"I see. Hey, Kim. It's fun talking through you."

Kim smiled, and Sam shook his head. <Um, Kon Beekie?> Gabe thought. <Can you provide some proof of what you told me?>

<Our presence is the proof,> Kon Beekie angrily answered.

<I need more.>

<I will provide your onk a list of the Kebo titles.>

Gabe could feel deep frustration and thought, <Let's not get upset. I have contacted my boss, and if this checks out, we will give them to you.>

Gabe sensed tremendous relief and felt another mind. <There is a single condition to this exchange,> he thought.

<You desire relief from parasites?>

<No. You need to promise us not to tell anyone about what you found on our planet and to eliminate any evidence that could lead others here.>

<You would have no verification method to ensure our efforts were applied. What's your true agenda?> Kon Beekie thought with concern.

<Relationships start with trust.>

<We've been searching for a long time.>

<And we're willing to give your property back.>

<Do you understand the value of what you're offering?>

<No, but I know it's crucial to you.>

<You possess— all that is good within our culture,> Kon Beekie admitted with profound relief.

<Our request seems small in comparison.>

<That's our concern,> Kon Beekie thought with reserved emotions.

<That this is too easy?>

<Yes.>

<Will you do as we ask?> Gabe asked.

<We agree to your demand.>

<Good.>

Gabe sensed hesitation, and he asked, <Are you searching for something else?>

<It's called the Staph of Reason and is supremely sacred.>

<What does it look like?>

<Glub the Great Healer made the Staph of Reason from polished Jasih wood and carved the sacred texts from Yahr during his enduring wisdom duration.>

<Hang on.>

Kim said to Sam, "Gabe here. Does the DLS have a wooden thing with words carved on it?"

"Let me check," Sam answered, and made a phone call. A moment later, he replied, "We have an item that matches your description. Do they want it?"

"They say it's an important part of their culture."

"Wait," Kim interrupted. "How do we know we aren't giving them something like King Arthur's sword? You know, the keys to rule the kingdom." Gabe took over the conversation. "Um. Gabe here. Do you want me to ask?"

"It's worthless to us," Sam answered. "I want them gone."

"This could open an enormous door," Kim cautioned.

"Is that Kim or Gabe?" Sam asked.

"Kim," she answered.

"It's my job to close the door. They will return in larger numbers if we don't give them that wood thing. Gabe, tell them they can have it, and the same deal applies."

"Alright."

<We have something that looks like it,> Gabe thought.

<That is a relief,> Kon Beekie thought with happiness.

<One question. This isn't going to cause problems, is it?>

<What problems?> Kon Beekie asked with concern.

<Like, whoever holds this staph will be a leader?>

<It's a symbol of all that is good. It can only bring peace and will be returned to the Center of Reason and Tolerance, where any individual may freely gaze upon its glory and endearing wisdom.>

<So, if we give it to you, will you leave us alone?> Gabe repeated.

<You will provide the staph without payment?>

<That's what my boss said.>

After a long pause, Kon Beekie thought, <We agree to your request.>

<Great. I will fly home, get the stuff, come back, and pass it to you.>

<My craft doesn't work in that manner. We must pass items to each other on solid ground.>

<Hang on.>

Gabe said into his microphone, "Zachary, can they land at your base to do an exchange?"

"Land?" Colonel Cruz yelled. "An exchange? What? Heck no!"

"Well, my boss has arranged one."

"That's not part of the deal. Tell them to go away. No more talk!"

"Ask your boss," Gabe demanded.

Colonel Cruz looked annoyed and used his radio for several minutes. Gabe could not listen to the conversation, but the colonel's body language showed frustration. At the same time, he communicated with Kim about what had occurred, and Sam made phone calls. Eventually, Colonel Cruz said, "Tell them to follow us down. No tricks, and we will have missiles locked onto them."

"Locking missiles might send the wrong message."

"Actually, we cannot get a lock on most crafts," Colonel Cruz admitted. "But we need to put on a strong front."

"I can do that."

<My bosses have agreed,> Gabe said.

<Thank you,> Kon Beekie said with relief.

<I will fly this craft back to where it took off, and you will follow us. They want me to tell you that weapons will track your craft.>

<I sense hesitation,> Kon Beekie thought.

<An accurate assessment.>

<What you have suggested is untrue?>

<An exaggeration. But my bosses want me to act tough.>

<We have bosses too,> Kon Beekie admitted sympathetically.

<The universe has its constants.>

<True.>

<After we land, I will get your Kebos and staph. Then, my bosses want you to depart and never return. Agreed?>

<We agree.> Kon Beekie's response was filled with conviction.

<Take it easy. I'm not too good at flying this thing.>

<Proceed at an even pace.>

Gabe maneuvered the Zigon back to Virgilio Airfield. He directed Kon Beekie to set his craft down at a specific area where six armored vehicles were parked.

Gabe left the Zigon, removed his environmental suit, and flew back to the DLS. There, he greeted Kim and Emma with a hug. He interfaced with the Azure computer in the secure room and located several Kebos that matched his list. On a hunch, Gabe searched for "Dang Flip Domain" and discovered many entries. From his brief study, it was clear the Grazen had brutalized their planet. He copied the files along with the requested Kebos to his memory device.

Meanwhile, Troy found a carved box and opened it, revealing an oblong eleven-inch wooden stick. It was a well-used piece of tan wood with tiny blue symbols carved into it. He also located a small brass cup recovered during the Cuban incident, and two symbols on the cup matched those on the wooden stick.

Gabe used the Azure computer database to translate, and only one phase made sense: "We will pay the price but will not count the cost." He thought this phrase sounded more like song lyrics than an inspirational message of supreme wisdom.

In the command room, Gabe, Kim, and Sam discussed handing over the items and concluded that Kim would deliver them because she had more negotiation experience. To help, she wanted more background information. Sam admitted that three ships had landed in Cuba, there was an attack, and they had nineteen prisoners at the Virgilio Airfield prison.

Kim's plane landed two hours later, and they provided her with a white protective environmental suit with a respirator. Fortunately, it contained an ice pack and a fan to keep her cool in the hot desert air. She approached the black craft, which looked impressive with sleek lines that blended into what she thought were engines.

A small door opened, and Kim looked inside. She saw two faces in protective suits staring at her. Kim estimated they were four feet tall. Unfortunately, their masks obscured most of their features, and she could only see their small eyes. Kim considered extending her hand in friendship, but decided they might perceive it as hostile.

<I brought you the requested items,> Kim thought.

<You are not the individual who interacted with us,> Kon Beekie thought with concern.

<Gabe interacted with you before.>

<You are related?> Kon Beekie asked.

<He's my husband.>

<Your mate?>

<Yes.>

<Why is he not here?> Kon Beekie demanded.

<They wanted me to communicate instead.>

<Why?>

<I'm better at it,> Kim thought confidently. She sensed humor, and another mind thought, <Males don't have the gift.>

<My husband needs more experience. What is your name?>

<Kon Sleen.>

<I'm Kim.>

<You brought the agreed-upon items?> Kon Sleen asked with concern.

<In this bag.>

<I sense that you have further questions.>

<Yes.>

<You desire to ensure we are truthful?> Kon Sleen guessed.

<I do.>

<How can we convince you?>

<Keep thinking.>

<As you wish.>

Kim felt Kon Sleen's intent and her desire. She stood out as a complex, curious woman with deep passions. Kim pictured herself giving Kon Sleen the items and what would happen next. She sensed joy, appreciation, and deep honor.

<You are complex. Your mate is fortunate,> Kon Sleen thought, satisfied.

<I'm the fortunate one.>

<Indeed. Have you ascertained your answers?>

<You have convinced yourself to keep your promise.>

<To the best of our ability,> Kon Sleen thought firmly.

<Here's what we promised.>

Kim handed over a bag while wondering about the item's significance and about using a plastic grocery bag to conduct high-level off-world negotiations. Kim watched as Kon Sleen accepted the bag and looked inside. She sensed the excitement and deep relief.

<This is more than expected,> Kon Beekie thought with great relief. <We were told the Cup of Eternal Forgiveness was destroyed.>

<To us, it's a brass cup.>

<I will interrogate the memory device.>

Kon Beekie interfaced with his ship, and Kim sensed satisfaction. Kon Beekie and Kon Sleen swayed their heads from side to side.

<You have delivered much more than we expected,> Kon Sleen thought with profound happiness. <Embedded in your memory device are the complete works of Von and the Scrolls of Forgiveness. We also see a description of our persecution, which will answer critical questions about the fallen.>

Kim became confused as she felt deep focus and impending action.

<By the banks of the sacred river Dren, we will do as you have requested,> Kon Sleen thought with sorrow. <To accomplish our task, we need to become unpleasant. Please forgive our actions in advance.>

# SEVENTEEN

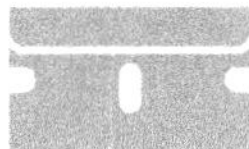

Kim applied great effort to open her eyes, and the sunlight stung. She felt hot, and the melting icepack had soaked her clothes. The respirator restricted breathing, and a long moment later, Kim moved her arm enough to remove it. The hot air's dryness burned as she took a breath.

Kim looked around and saw the Dang Flip craft had departed. As her eyes focused, she saw the guards lying on the ground in awkward positions. Kim regained communication with the onk and then asked, <Hon?>

<What a relief!> Gabe thought with great concern. <What happened?>

<I don't know.>

<The tracking satellites showed two ships leaving.>

<It hurts to move. How long was I out?> Kim thought in confusion.

<Four hours.>

<I think they hit me with a mind stun like Steve used.>

<I'm printing out a map and working on renting a Jeep.>

<To rescue me?> Kim asked with warm emotions.

<Of course.>

<You're sweet. I see one guy moving, and my muscle control is returning. Hang tight.>

<Are you sure?> Gabe asked.

<Yes. How's Emma?>

<Sad about Mommy Kim,> Emma thought with sorrow.

<She's sweet,> Gabe thought.

<Somebody's helping me to sit. I can feel my legs.>

<Can you look around?> Gabe asked.

<That building over there has a hole in it. Looks like somebody took a craft without using the doors.>

A soldier handed Kim a canteen. She took a long drink and said, "Thanks."

Several minutes later, Kim steadied herself and stood. She used a soldier for balance, and the two hobbled away. They entered a large building, and Kim saw a cafeteria full of plastic chairs and long tables. Approximately 150 people sat at the tables, looking disoriented. Somebody passed out bottles of Gatorade, and Kim eagerly accepted one.

Kim relaxed and noticed most people wore military outfits or business attire. The majority were men, and she sensed many were angry with her. Kim read the mind of a nearby soldier. <This is all your fault!>

Kim leaned forward on the table and then noticed a cut in her environmental suit. She reached inside, taking out an unfamiliar onk and the memory device she gave Kon Sleen.

Kim located its main menu and communicated, <What's going on?>

<We regret disabling the minds in your immediate area,> Kon Sleen answered with sorrow.

<Why?>

<When our craft landed, we interacted with two Grazen lords.>

<Leaders?>

<A correct word.>

<You took them away?> Kim asked.

<Kon Beekie sequestered their ship and forced them onboard. They will face powerful Dang Flip justice. By the word of Prupt the Honest, we will keep your planetary involvement a secret.>

It took Kim a while to comprehend this statement, and she thought, <I'm still not following.>

<With their ship in our possession, nobody will need to visit your world.>

<That makes sense.>

<As a further gift, we filled your memory device,> Kon Sleen thought with pride. <Your world can be free of parasites!>

<Thank you.>

<That is not our greatest gift.>

<What else did you do?> Kim asked.

<We took the Terror of Gren into custody.>

<Who?>

<The Terror of Gren is a despicable individual. We found him in a secure room next to the Grazen lords. Many planetary governments would dearly punish your planet if it became known that you were aiding him.>

<I guess I should thank you.>

<It is I who should thank you. My people thank you. You exceeded our greatest wishes and will always have a friend in the Dang Flip Domain.>

<This incident will upset my leaders.>

<Their anger will pass when our actions become appreciated.>

<I hope so.>

Kim shared this information with Gabe, and 30 minutes later, a soldier escorted her to an office. Inside, a man dressed in a crisp Air Force uniform sat behind a large desk while holding an ice pack to his head. He was in his fifties and had a sharp, crew-cut hairstyle. Despite the graying at his temples, his glare reflected the discipline of many years of military training. A bronze name plaque read Brigadier General Albert Perry, and he flatly stated, “Lady, you’re in a world of trouble.”

“Why?”

“You allowed off-worlders to rescue their comrades and steal a ship. As a result, you will spend the rest of your life behind bars— or worse.”

“Unlikely.”

“Confidence. I like that. But nobody can protect you.”

“Going to read the charges against me?”

“Unapproved off-world interaction, theft, and assisting in an escape. The list goes on.”

“That’s all wrong,” Kim said through gritted teeth.

“Get out of my office.”

“Do you want to know what actually happened?”

“Whatever you tell me will be used against you.”

“Cut the B.S. What do you think happened?”

“A craft landed, and the beings rescued their friends. Nothing more.”

“And?” Kim countered.

“And? And nothing! Everybody flew home and had a party to celebrate your stupidity. Now, leave.”

“Not so fast. My turn.”

Kim explained what had occurred, and General Perry could not believe his prison had held the Terror of Gren. It surprised Kim that he recognized the name, but she still did not know who this individual was. He informed Kim that in 1982, a craft had landed at Virgilio Airfield. The off-worlder seemed glad to be taken prisoner and was content to remain in a cell.

General Perry made three phone calls and ordered Kim to return to the DLS. Two guards escorted her to the plane, and she went over her recent choices during the flight. In Sam’s office, Kim met Gabe and Emma.

"There's no other way to say this," Sam began. "I am suspending you three from all DLS activities. At a later date, you may face prison time."

"This isn't our fault!" Gabe protested.

"I know. But the U.S. Space Force wants blood."

"Well, protect us. You promised."

"I am protecting you, which is why you're not locked up."

"Can't you do anything?"

"This decision comes from the top," Sam said with finality.

"This isn't fair."

"I know what went down, and I'm grateful."

"What now?" Kim asked.

"You're going back to Florida."

"What then?"

"Hard to say."

"What about the data that Kim got?" Gabe asked. "Somebody has to examine it, and I'm the only one who can access the Azure computer."

"In time, we'll figure it out. You've given us an impressive start. That's something to be proud of."

"Well, what about the onks?"

"Hmm. That's a tough call. They told me to confiscate your communicators. I don't like that idea, but I must follow orders."

"You need our help. The onks get confused when they go unused, and if their batteries run down, you cannot revive them."

"True," Sam admitted.

"There has to be something that we can do."

"Behind the scenes, I will work on it. But you'll never return to your former roles. My bosses made that ultra-clear." Sam closed his eyes, took a deep breath, and continued, "Now for the hard part. Kelly will keep a close eye on you three. You will observe her strict instructions and may not travel. Any deviation will land you in jail."

"What about visiting Alaska?" Kim protested.

"Out of the question."

"It's a state, not another planet."

"I know," Sam admitted.

"We're being treated as prisoners."

"True."

"Does this have something to do with something else?"

"I admit there are politics in play."

Kim fumed at the allegation. Sam took another deep breath and continued. "Pack up your apartment, and Kelly will meet you when your plane lands. And again, I am sorry that it's going down like this."

"Can we say goodbye?" Kim asked. "Duve and Steve have been really nice to us."

"No goodbyes."

"Why not? Do you think I would tell them something?"

"Were you reading me?" Sam demanded.

"It's just obvious," Kim retorted.

"I'm following orders. No goodbyes."

"Whatever. Hon, let's go."

"We'll leave," Gabe said. "You understand we wanted to help."

"I know."

"No hard feelings?"

"There were never any hard feelings. This is not my choice. If it were me, I would shake your hand for getting that beast off our world. The Terror of Gren? Geez. Even I know what that guy did."

"Thanks for being honest."

"You deserve that."

"We no longer use okey-okey?" Emma asked with tear-filled eyes.

"I'm sorry, sweetie," Gabe answered.

Emma began crying, and Kim picked her up while giving Sam a hard stare. Kim placed her onk and the new one on the desk. Gabe sighed and put his onk on the desk. Sam curtly nodded, but the sight of Emma crying affected him.

The family left the office and headed toward the main door. "I will miss you three," Donna said. "Remember, this isn't the end. Keep your hopes up."

"Thank you," Gabe replied. "I enjoyed our conversation and wish to learn more from you."

"I also enjoyed our chat," Donna said. "Goodbye, Emma."

Emma stopped crying, looked at Donna, and then started crying again. Outside, a car took the family to their apartment, and after packing, they were driven to the airport.

•

The family was quiet during the long flight to Florida, and Emma looked straight ahead with her hand on Kim's leg. When the plane landed, Kelly met them at the gate and led them to her car. At their house, she threatened, "Here's the deal. You three are on a short leash: no tricks or mental games. After I see some discipline, I will give you some slack. Understand?"

"Yes," Gabe answered in a defeated voice. "We get it."

"They did not tell me exactly what happened, but you three screwed the pooch. This means I get babysitting detail."

"We understand," Gabe said dejectedly. "Look, we can work together."

"Meaning?"

"There's a guest bedroom upstairs. We don't have to be adversaries."

Kelly seemed unsure of what Gabe had offered, and Kim thought, <Are you inviting her to live with us? After what they did? That's weird, hon.>

<I'm trying to improve our situation,> Gabe told her. <This might even build some bridges.>

<Hmm. Learning some good habits.>

<Like the new me?> Gabe smiled slyly.

<You're one of a kind,> Kim thought lovingly.

"My husband has a point," Kim said. "If it will make your life easier, you're welcome to stay."

"What's your game?" Kelly asked, suspicious.

"No game. Gabe is offering to make the best of the situation. Are we cool?"

"I'll try it your way— for now. But remember. We aren't friends," Kelly warned.

Gabe added, "Yet," with a grin that annoyed Kelly.

The family got ready for bed, and Gabe and Kim tucked Emma in. She still felt sad, and it took several minutes to reassure her that everything would turn out fine. Emma closed her eyes and thought, <Lady Kelly going to stay with us?>

<For now,> Kim thought.

<I understand. Love you, Mommy Kim and Daddy Gabe.>

Gabe and Kim walked toward their bedroom as Kelly watched their every move from a chair she had brought from the kitchen. Kim nodded to Kelly and closed the door. They got under the covers, and Kim thought, <This is intolerable.>

<Relax, babe. It's temporary.>

<It better be!> Kim thought angrily.

<Let's get some sleep.>

<Hey, I felt that. No hanky-panky while she's outside.>

<I only wanted to please you,> Gabe told her.

<I am too stressed out. Besides, I feel what's going on in your mind.>

<I only wanted to shift your focus and relieve your tension. That's all.>

<Damn! I bit your head off,> Kim admitted with embarrassment.

<Babe, you're stressed. I sense your neck muscle pinching again. Roll over and let me work out the tension.>

<I should be the one to work your neck,> Kim offered guiltily.

Gabe wanted to protest, but he relented and rolled over. Kim began massaging his neck while lying next to him, and she thought with a smile, <You caved quickly.>

<I understand how your mind works. You would not enjoy the massage until I let you give me one first.>

<Why?>

<You feel good making me feel good.>

Kim thought for a long moment, pulled the sheets away, sat on Gabe, and began working his lower back. <Thanks, babe,> Gabe thought, feeling relief.

<You're getting much better at understanding me.>

<I'm trying.>

<It shows.>

Gabe enjoyed her efforts and asked, <Mind if I swim in the background?>

<That's fine. Thanks for asking.>

<No problem.>

Gabe passively entered Kim's mind and felt tension, anger, and frustration. It took all her concentration to massage as she harshly reviewed the day's events. Fortunately, Kim made an effort to accept the situation.

Ten minutes later, Kim stopped and rested next to Gabe. They looked into each other's eyes for a long moment, and he fell asleep. She stared at the ceiling, unable to relax, and checked the clock: 1:22 a.m. Still being awake at that hour was frustrating, and Kim needed a distraction. So she put on sweats and opened the door. Kelly greeted her angrily at the end of the hallway. Kim sighed, walked over, and asked, "Exercise or talk?"

"I told you. We're not friends," Kelly hissed.

"Talk it is."

Kim walked downstairs while Kelly remained sitting. She heard Kim doing something and went down to investigate. Kim took out a teakettle and her mother's tea box in the kitchen. She looked at it for a long moment, musing that her mother was the last to use it. Kim selected decaffeinated pumpkin spice. "Created especially for the holidays, this unique tea imparts the appeal of a tasty pumpkin pie," she read aloud.

Kelly sat at the kitchen table, scowling. Kim was not ready for conversation, so she cleaned. When the kettle whistled, she poured two cups. Finally, Kim sat at the table and asked, "Have you ever tried pumpkin spice?"

"I'm not a tea person," Kelly grumbled.

"Neither am I."

"But you're having tea now?"

"I couldn't sleep, and this is decaf."

"Hmm. I still don't trust you three."

"I understand."

"You play mind games. I hate that," Kelly hissed.

"I understand."

Kim put the teabags in the cups and stared at the water as it steeped. "I'm not just going to open up. We aren't BFFs," Kelly stated while pointing at Kim.

Kim looked up and tried to begin on a positive note, "Hey, I would—"

Clearly, a successful conversation was impossible, so Kim returned to watching the tea. A minute later, she took a sip and found the taste bland. Kim returned to looking at the tea while Kelly wondered what was happening. *I'm not drinking tea and swapping stories like a teenage slumber party,* she thought to herself, and resolved to end the conversation. "I'm going to check upstairs."

"They're both asleep."

"I'm checking anyway."

Kelly started to stand. "Relax," Kim said. "Gabe's dreaming about computers, and Emma has been asleep for an hour."

"You know that for certain?"

"I can only read Emma and Gabe at a short distance without *technology.* I can't read others unless I'm next to them."

"Gabe is dreaming about computers?" Kelly asked, and then bit her lip. "That's weird."

"Not really. It's what he's into."

"You're not mind-reading me now, are you?" Kelly demanded.

"It is a DLS policy not to read other employees."

"Never speak those letters again!"

"Sorry."

"You better be," Kelly threatened.

"Relax. I'm not in your head."

Kelly leaned back while sizing Kim up and said, "I guess we can talk. But I'm not telling you my life's story, and I don't want to discuss fashion."

"It's cool," Kim said with a smile. "We can talk about any topic you want. Besides, I know all about you."

"You read my file?"

"I had your file on my desk along with a bunch of others. I planned to read it this week, but... Well, you know."

"So, you know nothing about me?"

"The *organization* attracts a certain type. I figure you had a messed-up childhood that led to a destructive early life. From your accent, I'm guessing you grew up in the Midwest. Later, you joined the military to improve yourself, and your success led to your current employment. Now, you're upset because they made you look after us."

"Close," Kelly admitted. "The military recruiter lied when he said chicks can go on combat patrols. To get around that chauvinistic crap, I did my four years, joined the Iowa State Patrol, and helped a lot of people."

"And then you ruffled some feathers." Kim filled in the blanks.

"I got fired and then recruited."

"Where you excelled?" Kim guessed with a smile.

"There have only been three female ACOs, and I will be the best."

"I'm sure you will."

Kelly looked at Kim, took a sip, nodded, and Kim said, "My mother liked tea. This reminds me of her."

"It tastes good."

"Can I ask you what your job is like? I understand. No technical stuff."

Kelly glanced harshly at Kim and replied, "I guess we could discuss that. My job goes from months of pure boredom to coming within inches of death. But, all in all, it's rewarding."

"Have you ever met any of the– you know– *them*?" Kim wanted to know.

"I've had two encounters. Oh, plus Donna."

"I've met a few, including Donna."

"Did you– you know– speak to them? In person?"

"I did," Kim answered with a nod.

"That must have been fascinating."

"Very fascinating. I wish we could discuss it."

"I didn't speak with *them*. But I spoke with Donna many times."

"She's amazing."

"I agree."

Kelly looked hopeful for a moment and then scowled. Kim sighed and said, "I get it. They told you I helped a bunch of prisoners escape."

"True," Kelly said in a forced, calm voice.

"It's alright to be angry."

"You know how hard I work," Kelly shot back.

"I made your job a lot harder, and I'm sorry."

Kelly nodded while making intense eye contact, making Kim more depressed. Finally, she stood and turned to the refrigerator. There was a note from Emma's teacher, and Kim stared at it. It praised Emma's writing ability, and Gabe had put it on the fridge with a hamburger magnet. Kim contemplated the incident and spoke without turning around. "There's some truth to all of it."

"Did you do it?" Kelly asked with narrow eyes. "Did you betray us?"

"That depends on your perspective."

"From your perspective. Did you screw up?"

Kim looked at the magnet while deep in thought and answered, "Yeah, I messed up big-time."

"They did not provide the details."

"It's safe to say I got duped." Kim paused for a moment. "But I somehow get the feeling they did us the biggest favor ever."

"If they presented all the evidence to a jury, how would they find you?" Kelly asked.

Kim thought for a long moment and answered, "Innocent, but I still feel like I messed up. Dang! I should have seen it. I should have put it all together. I should have reacted better."

Kim covered her face, and Kelly asked, "Could you have expected the outcome?"

"I don't know. It may have been their plan from the start."

"Hmm," Kelly mused, nodded, leaned forward, and said, "A bigwig at the Iowa State Patrol was stealing drugs from the evidence room."

"And you found out about it?" Kim said.

"Yes."

"And when you told people about it?"

"I got the blame, and *he* got a promotion. Men!" Kelly said with a snort.

"Still want to do something about it?"

"Nahhh," Kelly answered with a dismissive gesture.

"You already did," Kim guessed, and Kelly smiled wickedly. Kim nodded and said, "Nice."

"About as nice as that alligator video."

"Hmm. True," Kim admitted. She sipped her tea and commented, "Needs honey."

"I like it plain. More flavor that way."

Kim took another sip and said, "I'm guessing you know all about me."

"A lot of stuff got redacted. But, yeah. I know about you three."

"Any gems?" Kim asked with a thin smile.

"Your family did a lot of drugs."

"You got that right. Gabe told me he found a bunch of hiding places. He also told me that my mother got into heroin. Plus, you know my history."

"Your family did more than that," Kelly said with a wicked smile.

"Really? What?"

"I read a school report about a teacher catching your younger brother dealing. The school accused your mother of being his supplier."

Kim looked away in disgust and put her hand on her forehead.

"Sorry," Kelly offered.

"You have nothing to be sorry about. I like your honesty." Kim turned back and asked, "Hey, enough heavy stuff. What do you do for fun?"

Kelly answered angrily, "None of your business. I told you. We aren't friends."

Kim stared at Kelly for a long moment and asked, "What's your deal?"

"I have no deal."

"Well, you're upset about something. And that something has nothing to do with this situation."

"I'm fine," Kelly hissed.

"You're not fine. Something primal is eating you up."

"I'm going to check upstairs."

"Have you told anybody?" Kim demanded.

"What?"

"That you like girls?"

Kelly looked at Kim in horror and hissed, "Stay the heck out of my head!"

"A, I wasn't in your head. And B, putting yourself under so much pressure isn't healthy."

Kelly stared at Kim with hate-filled eyes and asked, "Did you find that in my file?"

"I told you I didn't read your file."

"Then how did you know?" Kelly wanted to know.

"I knew the moment we met."

"Because you read my mind?"

"No, it's obvious," Kim answered, repressing a chuckle.

"I don't understand."

"Kelly, you're around 30? Right?"

"Twenty-three," Kelly corrected.

"The longer you wait, the more damage you will do to yourself. There's nothing wrong with the way you are. But, if you don't embrace your reality, one day, you'll eat a bullet."

Kelly turned away for a long moment while Kim finished her tea. Several minutes later, Kim poured another cup and said, "There's a subject I'd like your help with."

Without turning back, Kelly hissed, "I told you. We aren't friends."

"I know, but you are the only person I can talk to."

"Why?" Kelly asked after turning to face Kim.

"Let me start, and you'll understand."

"No promises."

"Here it is. When Gabe and I were doing all that deprogramming, we got mentally exposed to couples having sex."

"So?" Kelly asked.

"Well, here's the thing. He liked the mental view. He liked it too much."

"Gabe wants to be in the minds of people having sex?"

"I didn't think that activity would turn him on, but it did. Anyway, after all the deprogramming, I expected his desire to fade, but I occasionally catch him thinking about these encounters. The worst part is that I feel his desire to go out trolling. It's creepy."

Kelly saw Kim's concerned expression and asked, "Why are you telling me this?"

"Obviously, I cannot talk to my friends about this topic. I planned to talk to Donna, but that door is closed."

"Why her?" Kelly asked.

"She has a sharp perception."

"Hmm, I still don't get it. Why me?"

"Why not? You're honest."

Kelly leaned back for a long moment, reached forward, and held her teacup. She liked the warmth as she pondered Kim's true motives. "I still don't get it," Kelly said. "What do you want from me?"

"I enjoy discussing relationships, and I'd like somebody else's opinion."

Kelly stared at her cup and whispered, "I don't have many friends. Our organization frowns upon that."

"Well, here's your chance."

"What are you asking?" Kelly wanted to know.

"Whatever you want. There are no rules tonight."

"Hmm."

Kelly looked at her cup and then at Kim. She decided Kim wanted her honest opinion and asked, "How often does he do it?"

"I feel his thoughts a few times a week."

"Does he love you?" Kelly asked.

"He is the most devoted husband ever."

"Must be nice."

"There is no other way to say it. I'm the luckiest woman in the world."

"Are you worried?"

"That's the problem. I don't know how worried I should be. There are obviously no relationship articles about this topic."

"Have you two talked about it?" Kelly asked.

"A little. He says everything is fine."

"You've got to nip that in the bud or embrace it. There's no other choice."

"I have been trying to convince myself to confront him big-time," Kim said with a firm nod.

"Do it soon."

"Yeah."

"What are his other issues?"

Kim thought for a moment, glanced at the refrigerator, and answered, "He's in over his head with his semiconductor business. But he'll figure things out. The problem is that he holds his stress in."

"Hmm. And what about you? This psychic thing must be interesting."

"Interesting?" Kim chuckled. "Yeah, becoming telepathic was unexpected. Suddenly, I knew people's feelings, and later, I could make out words. It was a big change."

"What are the good and bad parts?"

"Oh, that's easy," Kim quickly answered. "The good part is knowing when people are lying. And the bad? All the perverted thoughts. Yuck! Sometimes, after a sick encounter, I feel like taking a year-long shower."

"Wow. Well, what else?"

"Well, the other big thing is that I cannot discuss this stuff with my friends. Aliens? Secret government divisions? Being silent is difficult for somebody like me."

"Hmm, I know what you mean. I still tell my family that I work for the state police."

"I see," Kim said with a nod.

"What do you usually talk about with your friends? Fashion?"

"That's an interesting question. When I was growing up, I only discussed fashion and celebrity relationships. This drove my parents crazy. But those subjects somehow became less relevant after that thing in Alaska. It's hard to explain.

"I guess the best way to say it is that people used to be flat, and now they are three-dimensional. The problem is that, except for Gabe, it is a one-way street, and a good fashion or relationship discussion needs two-way communication. I know that's not a great explanation.

"But, to answer your question, I discuss family and business with my friends. As far as fashion? I keep in contact with my best friend from high school, Jen. She works at a high-end clothing store, and we talk about the latest trends and celebrity news, but it is not the same as when we were teenagers."

Kim saw Kelly smile thinly and asked, "What about you? Are you going to come to grips with your sexuality?" Kelly's expression turned sour, but Kim continued. "I'm here to help. If you like, I can introduce you to a friend of mine. She's— like you and is a skilled listener."

Kelly stared at Kim and then turned away. Kim could tell that the time for conversation had come to an end. She said, "Come on. I'm still all hopped up from what happened today. Please leave the cup on the table."

Kim stood and turned out the lights as she left the kitchen. Kelly sat in the darkness, wondering about Kim's true motives. Finally, she stood and followed Kim upstairs to the exercise room. As Kim began stretching, Kelly stared at her with suspicion.

"Start by bending like this," Kim said.

"I'm not doing your flowery yoga thing!"

"Put your arms like this," Kim offered.

Though frustrated, Kelly never backed down from a challenge and stretched.

"Not so hard," Kim said. "Go easy. Your body will tell you when to stop."

"Like this?"

"Yes."

Kim took Kelly through several basic stretches. Surprisingly, Kelly enjoyed the experience. Still, ten moves later, she had had enough and stepped onto the treadmill. Kim wanted to continue, but she got on the elliptical. Fifteen minutes later, Kelly asked, "Did we do yoga?"

"Beginning yoga."

"I've never tried it," Kelly admitted.

"It helps with stress and improves concentration."

"Hmm."

When Kim became tired, she reduced the resistance and slowed down. Kelly increased the speed and began running harder.

A moment later, Kim got off the elliptical. Kelly ran for two more minutes and abruptly stopped. She stared forward for a long moment with an intense expression. "Does Gabe know about me?" Kelly asked without eye contact.

"I doubt it. He's not very intuitive with people, but he's getting better."

"Are you going to tell him?"

"It's not my secret to tell. We're not in grade school."

"Thanks."

"No problem."

Kim sat on the weight bench, looking at the blank wall. Kelly moved an exercise ball and sat on it. A few minutes later, Kim said, “Thanks for your thoughts about Gabe.”

“Sure.”

“Well, I’m going to sleep.”

“I’m also tired,” Kelly admitted.

“Look. We’ve all had a long day, and I guarantee you nothing will happen tonight. The guest bedroom is all yours.”

“I may use it,” Kelly offered.

“Good.”

Kim and Kelly stood and walked out of the room. Just before turning off the light, Kim looked at Kelly with amusement and said, “You know, it’s no accident that you’re here.”

“What do you mean?” Kelly demanded.

“Think about it. Who else would talk to you about your situation?”

“I don’t understand.”

“The organization you work for. They don’t do random.”

Kelly stared at Kim for a long moment and suddenly exclaimed, “Donna.”

“She assigned you here so I could help.”

“That’s a gigantic leap.”

“Give it some thought,” Kim said with a thin smile. “And remember, I’m here to listen, not to judge.”

Kelly looked at Kim for a long moment and said, “I may take you up on your offer.”

“That sounds good.”

“Um. You’re good at this kind of stuff.”

“Thanks.”

Kim entered her bedroom, put on her pajamas, and returned to bed. She felt good about helping Kelly and continued thinking about her day. Kim was almost asleep when she saw the door open. In the faint light, Kim watched Kelly pointing a handgun at her. “This will not help,” Kim whispered.

“You know the truth,” Kelly threatened.

“So do you.”

Kelly stared at Kim through the sights of her gun for a long moment. Then, when Kim sensed the right time, she said, “You are a good person. I know it.”

“I do bad things, and now I’m going to do another,” Kelly hissed.

“Did you do those bad things for the right reason?”

“Of course,” Kelly shot back, her eyes narrowed.

“That still makes you a good person.”

A long moment later, Kelly asked, “What will you tell the DLS?”

“Nothing.”

“Why not?”

“I told you. Your secret isn’t mine to tell.”

“I don’t believe you!” Kelly hissed.

“I keep my secrets tight. That’s who I am. And my file should prove that fact.”

Kelly stared at Kim and then slowly lowered her gun. Kim nodded and closed her eyes. She had been intensely swimming in Kelly’s mind and sensed great conflict. Kelly closed the door, and Kim heard sobbing.

<What’s her deal?> Gabe telepathically asked.

<You’re awake?>

<Of course, babe. That treadmill makes a thunderous racket.>

<Kelly’s got issues.> Kim started to feel fearful.

<I always thought something deep in her mind was at odds. It’s like she is fighting some big battle to be like everybody else.>

<Very perceptive.>

<So?> Gabe asked.

<I told her to embrace her sexuality.>

<Oh. That must have been rough,> Gabe thought.

<That’s why she pointed a gun at me.>

Gabe opened his eyes. <What the heck!>

<Relax, hon. It’ll be a long road, but she’ll get through it. She’s a tough gal.>

<Is Emma in danger?> Gabe asked.

<Hon, things will be fine. Get some rest.>

<Alright, babe. I trust you.>

<Goodnight, my love.>

<It’s always an adventure with you,> Gabe thought warmly.

# EIGHTEEN

The following morning, Gabe and Kim dressed. When they opened their bedroom door, they saw Kelly asleep in a chair, snoring loudly. Kim called her name four times, and she awoke on the fifth.

"Breakfast?" Kim asked.

"I wasn't asleep!" Kelly exclaimed.

"Do you want breakfast?"

"I guess."

"Waffles?"

"Whatever."

Kim woke Emma up and dressed her for school. They walked downstairs and met Kelly at the kitchen table. Gabe made waffles for the adults and poured Emma a bowl of applesauce. After a quiet breakfast, Gabe asked Kelly, "Do you want to meet up after work or stay with us?" Kelly looked at Gabe with an angry stare, and he continued, "It's Kim's turn to take Emma to school and stay with her. I'm heading to my work."

"I need to maintain surveillance on all three of you."

"Well, my office is about ten minutes from Emma's school. So, you can go back and forth."

Kelly frowned at Gabe. After getting ready and saying goodbye, the family walked to their two cars. Kelly got into her beat-up white SUV and closely followed Kim to preschool. Once there, Emma ran into her class to see her classmates.

In a side room, Kim used her laptop to answer emails. Several minutes later, Kelly sat across from her in silence. Kim looked up and then returned to her computer. Half an hour later, Kelly demanded, "Are you emailing Jason?"

Without looking up, Kim answered, "I told you that your secret isn't mine to tell. Plus, they made it clear not to communicate with them."

"Oh. Alright. Um, what did you tell Gabe?"

"Strange as it may seem, he kind of knew."

A few minutes later, Kelly asked, "Is it that obvious?"

"To some."

"Do you think Jason knows?"

"He suspects," Kim guessed.

"Oh."

"Come clean with yourself. And trust me, Jason only cares about the job."

Forty minutes later, Emma walked into the side room and asked, "Mommy Kim?"

"Yes, sweetie?"

"It alright if you go with lady Kelly to dry clean."

"Are you going to be comfortable without us?"

"I'm a big girl," Emma announced with pride.

Kim kneeled and sternly told her, "You remember what we talked about? No swimming without mommy or daddy. You must be on your best behavior, no matter what the other children do."

"I understand, Mommy Kim," Emma said with a big smile. "I try really hard!"

"We're proud of you."

"Thank you, Mommy Kim. I talk to lady Kelly?"

"Alright."

Emma walked over to Kelly and opened her hands, smiling. Kelly picked up Emma and set her on the table. Suddenly, Emma pointed her finger at Kelly with great intent and said in her most threatening voice, "Never show gun to mommy!"

Emma glared at Kelly, hopped off the table, and left.

"Wow!" Kelly exclaimed.

"Runs in the family."

"The reports said she cut up a man in Jamaica."

"Yup."

"Spunky little girl."

"She takes after her mother," Kim said coldly.

"I see that."

"Well, I need to go to work. Stay here, follow me, or whatever."

"I'll follow."

"May I suggest something?"

"Umm, sure."

"Take a shower," Kim whispered.

"That bad?"

"Yes."

"Sorry."

"It's fine."

Kelly drove to her apartment, bathed, packed enough clothes for two days, and met Kim at her office. She liked the efficient operation, and Kim explained that she would be "the new office helper." Kelly spent the day unenthusiastically on mild office tasks.

Kim critiqued an advertising campaign and negotiated lower equipment repair prices. Overall, she appreciated the progress her team had made in her absence. Later that afternoon, she met with Dan and Sally to discuss expanding into Tallahassee.

After the meeting, Kim took stock of her situation. She enjoyed being in control of her company and appreciated being surrounded by talented people. She had a wonderful daughter and a fantastic husband. Her business thrived, and his business would soon be profitable as well. Soon, Kelly would be out of their lives, and they could concentrate on being a normal family.

•

Gabe arrived at a KimSemi work disaster. The CEO, Gary, resigned because he hated working for a "part-time micro-manager."

To make matters worse, the test article returned from fabrication, and initial testing revealed many issues. Gabe harshly blamed himself and threw himself into understanding the problems.

Three hours later, Gabe determined that the test article had six functioning segments, which validated his overall design theories, forcing him to make a big decision: abandon the entire project or invest more money in an ill-conceived dream. After a long moment of reflection, Gabe decided not to decide. Instead, he wrote a long email to his business partners, Ken from Pacific Progressive Peripherals and Al from Silicon Serpent.

After work, the family enjoyed a takeout pizza from the same restaurant Jason had used. Gabe brightened when he learned that Emma had spent most of the day unattended at school. They were proud of her progress and asked her many questions about what she learned.

Kelly silently ate at the end of the table while watching the family. At one point, Gabe asked Kelly how her day had gone, but she did not answer. After dinner, Emma wanted to learn more about Egypt because they had discussed it in school. Gabe found an excellent YouTube video on the "History for Children" series. Then, he changed into sweats and began a yoga routine. Kelly went into the guest bedroom and closed the door with a bang.

Kim joined him five minutes later and asked, <Tough day?>

<Yes, babe.>

<Could've been worse.>

<True. Emma had a wonderful day. Plus, we didn't get shot last night.>

<Funny.>

<How did it go with Kelly?> Gabe asked

<I told everybody that I hired her to be the new office helper.>

<Oooh. I bet she liked that job with all her *training.*>

<Hey, don't be so mean.>

<I don't like it when somebody points a gun at us,> Gabe thought angrily.

<She's going through a lot. Ease up with your bend. That leg pain is telling you something.>

<Today sucked,> Gabe thought after adjusting his stance.

<Spill it.>

<What?>

<Tell me all about it,> Kim encouraged.

<It's just work.>

<Hon!>

<Babe, I'll deal with it tomorrow. This time is special. It's about us getting closer.>

<Hon,> Kim challenged him sympathetically.

Gabe took a moment to calm down, then shifted into a downward-facing dog pose. <My test article failed,> he admitted after a long contemplation.

<Did you examine all the problems?>

<I only looked at ninety percent of the faults. I couldn't even access the other ten because the design is so botched.>

<Do you know what went wrong?> Kim asked.

<We uncovered a bunch of mistakes.>

<Can you fix them?>

<I don't know.>

<Guess,> Kim encouraged.

<I think so,> Gabe replied, uncertain.

<How hard will it be?>

<I don't even know.>

<When other companies make a test article like this, do they expect this level of problems?>

<They get better results,> Gabe admitted guiltily.

<Well?>

<This entire episode invalidates KimSemi as a legitimate engineering company!> Gabe cried.

They changed positions to a cow face, held it, and Kim thought, <You told me you broke a lot of new ground.>

<A whole lot,> Gabe conceded.

<Would another company have setbacks with so many new advances?>

<I suppose.>

<You're so hard on yourself. Send out another test article,> Kim said, encouraging him.

<I'm not sure.>

<I know you. Right now, you're wound up. Later, you will think about what is going on and fix the issues. Your engineering mind won't settle for anything less.>

<I suppose,> Gabe admitted.

<Trust me. You have this.>

<Maybe.>

<What else is bugging you? That thing about losing your CEO, Gary?> Kim asked.

Gabe took a moment to answer. <How could he quit right when we needed him most?>

<Hon, they forced you to spend time in California and Alaska. It was out of your control, so stop beating yourself up.>

<I suppose.>

<Look, you loaded your team with talented people. This isn't a big deal.>

<I guess,> Gabe admitted again.

<See, that was simple.>

<I don't know.>

<Hon, think about it,> Kim encouraged.

<I guess things will work themselves out. Thanks, babe.>

<No problem. Hey, I can already feel the weight lifting in your mind.>

<Me too,> Gabe thought with relief.

They changed to a high lunge pose, and Kim thought, <I think Kelly will be here for about a month. All she needs to see is that we will not flip out.>

<I hope so.>

<Hey, stop feeling down,> Kim repeated.

<Sorry.>

<You had a minor setback. Get over it.>

<I'll try.>

<Enough. I had a wonderful day.>

<Tell me all about it. I want to hear every detail.>

Kim discussed her work, and Gabe began feeling better.

•

Gabe took Emma to school the following day and spent an hour in a side room. During this time, Kelly silently observed Gabe read his email. Ken and Al encouraged him to make more test articles. He then emailed his coworkers to see if anybody knew a manager who could take over for Gary.

When Gabe was sure Emma would be content without his presence, he drove to work with Kelly following. An hour later, a logic designer named Ted came into his office to tell him about his sister, Christine. She had a degree in business and worked at Falcon Micro Devices. Christine was vacationing in town this week, and they arranged an interview over dinner. For the rest of the day, Gabe analyzed the test article problems and devised solutions.

The family and Kelly met Christine that evening at a local Italian restaurant. She had requested financial documents and other information beforehand. Christine was in her late forties, with thinning brown hair tied in a bun, and needed to lose some weight. She wore a modest blue dress with pink stripes, which would have been more suitable for sightseeing. Kim noticed Christine applied her makeup hastily, and her shoes did not match her outfit. She also saw her confident, penetrating dark blue eyes, which missed nothing.

"Is Kelly associated with KimSemi?" Christine pleasantly asked with a grin.

"I'm an observer," Kelly coldly answered.

"Fair enough. Well, let's get started. Sorry for my attire. I had not planned an interview."

"You look great," Gabe said with a smile.

"Good. Well, as my younger brother told you, I'm a senior manager at Falcon Micro Devices and looking to advance my career."

"We're a small company, and I'm not sure we can provide a major bump."

"I've read over your financials. Not too impressive for a startup, but you have a good team."

"We all work hard."

"I can see that. Do you know why I took this meeting?"

"You want a challenge?" Gabe guessed.

"I like you. A little naïve, but I like you. No. That's not the reason at all. Let me ask you a question. Would you hire me if I led the team at Intel when they invented the microprocessor?"

"Sure. Any semiconductor company would want somebody with that rich experience."

"I read your report. You cracked it," Christine said, biting her lower lip with a nod.

"Meaning?"

"You cracked asynchronous logic, the biggest thing to hit semiconductors in the last forty years. I'm here because I want to be a part of the success. I've been waiting my whole life for an opportunity like this."

"It doesn't work yet," Gabe admitted.

"It will. Ted said the same thing. He believes in you; that's all the proof I need."

"We need to make a bunch of test articles. That will be expensive, and I don't know if it is worth the risk."

"In the grand scheme of things, not a big deal."

"Told you," Kim interrupted.

Christine observed Gabe's obvious discomfort and asked, "What gives?"

"He is down because his first attempt failed," Kim answered.

"With a project this advanced, there will be setbacks. But that's not what's important. You have a proven foundation, and once it works, every semiconductor company will require your technology, or they'll go out of business."

"What are you proposing?" Kim asked.

"KimSemi has a few issues. Gary was tackling them one by one. His most significant contribution was a well-executed advertising campaign. But he didn't push it. We need to enter new markets. Plus, you must spend big when your asynchronous processor hits the market."

"I don't want to spend wads of cash until I know the design is solid," Gabe countered.

"I agree. But once it does, the floodgates need to open. I know a guy in New York, and he can help."

"How?"

"He's a billionaire, and he owes me a huge favor. So, when you show him a working model, he'll cough up the money without a controlling interest. That's his style."

"Oh. Well, what do you want?"

Christine leaned forward and answered, "I want five percent of the company. I agree that I only get this five percent when your company is worth a billion bucks. As for my salary, I'll work for peanuts. Say one hundred grand a year. That'll cover my expenses. Additionally, I require complete control over finances, day-to-day operations, sales, and marketing. You do the technical parts and nothing else."

"That is what I am looking for," Gabe admitted.

"Two things before I commit. The first is that I need to see your agreements with Computix Systems. Second, no more trips. KimSemi must be your only priority. Next to your family, of course."

"Gabe's not going anywhere," Kelly tersely interjected. "That, I can promise you!"

"Fair enough," Christine said with a nod. "I like your moxie."

Kim and Gabe had been swimming in Christine. <She's confident,> she thought to him.

<Can she do what she is promising?>

<She thinks so. She also hates going back on her word.>

<Should I hire her?> Gabe asked, unsure.

<Hon, it's your company.>

<I don't know what to do.>

<Hon! Talk to her.>

<What should I say?>

<Ask what's in your heart. Go, go, go!> Kim pushed.

"I can show you the emails and agreements," Gabe said. "The basic deal is that Computix gets the first bite at the product— ten thousand asynchronous processors— and then we're on our own."

"Fair enough. I can tell by your expression that you still have concerns. Let's hear 'em."

"Am I that bad?"

"Yes," Kelly answered with a chuckle.

"Dang."

Emma laughed and said, "Daddy Gabe funny."

"My, my. You're speaking well."

"Thank you, lady Christine."

"Oh, I like you."

Gabe thought momentarily and said, "I'm uncomfortable turning everything over to you."

"We can have an outside person peek in from time to time."

"My marketing person, Ellen, or my business manager, Dan, can look at things," Kim suggested.

"Seems fair."

"I guess I'm out of excuses," Gabe said with a weak smile. "You're hired."

"Great. I'm looking forward to starting."

"Wonderful," Kim said. "My hubby had been stressing over this."

"His stress has just begun. Gabe, I need you to go full bore on solving all these test article problems. Get me a working unit ASAP."

"That I can do."

"See, not that hard. Kim, do you always have to twist his arm?"

Kim rolled her eyes and answered, "Every time. Every time."

•

The following day, Kim took Emma to preschool and gave her a five-minute goodbye. Then, she went to work and had a productive day.

During the week, Kelly came and went as she pleased. Occasionally, she would join Kim and Gabe for yoga, but usually ran on the treadmill for hours. Kim did not like the dirty guest bathroom, but she knew Kelly was more relaxed, which would ultimately help.

Over dinner, Kelly occasionally contributed to the conversations but was usually content to eat in silence. Kim encouraged her to consider this situation as "deep undercover work," which made her smile.

Two weeks later, Christine arrived at KimSemi and jumped right into the job. The employees were not accustomed to her direct style, but they appreciated her encouraging attitude. Gabe immediately noticed his company recovering from Gary's abrupt departure.

Christine encouraged Gabe to file the 22 patents he had been working on, and she "forced him, kicking and screaming," to develop 13 more. By the end of the month, Gabe felt confident enough to send out another test article.

The following day, Kelly informed Kim that she would no longer stay at their house and would check in once a week. Unfortunately, she did not permit the family to travel outside the city. Kim protested, wanting to visit distant dry cleaners, but Kelly refused.

Three days later, Kelly arrived unannounced at dinnertime and watched the family eat an excellent salmon fettuccine meal prepared by their housekeeper, Anna. Kim noticed she wore thin rainbow earrings. Later, Kelly pulled Kim aside and told her she'd informed the DLS of her life preferences. They accepted her admission without fanfare, and she apologized to Kim for her overreaction.

# NINETEEN

It had been a long month, and Kim organized a business appreciation event. All employees and their families attended a Miami Marlins baseball game and had a late dinner at the exclusive Versailles Restaurant.

Kim also invited Kelly and another friend who had an alternative lifestyle. Kim watched them from afar as they had a pleasant conversation and exchanged phone numbers.

During the evening, there were many toasts (Gabe and Kim had club soda), and after dinner, a few employees stayed at the bar to watch another baseball game. Kelly also sat at the bar while Gabe and Kim relaxed on a large sofa. Emma was asleep beside them, and she dreamed of riding unicorns.

<Perfect idea, babe,> Gabe thought.

<True.>

<You love compliments.>

<I do.>

<We need to do this every year.>

<I agree. You know what? I'm happy right now,> Kim admitted warmly.

<Me too.>

<This is great.>

<It is,> Gabe agreed.

<You're great.>

<Thanks, hon.>

<We're making it. It's so amazing.>

The group talked until late in the evening, and they were getting ready to leave. Suddenly, Emma woke with a jolt, looked around, yawned, and asked, in a sleepy voice, "Mommy Kim?"

"Yes, sweetheart."

"The Veronn are here."

Kim jolted upright and thought to Emma, <What?>

<Veronn talk to me. Listen.>

Kim opened her mind to feel an alien presence, and they communicated in distant thoughts, <Meet us at the identical location as our last encounter in one earth cycle.>

<Why?> Kim asked but did not get a response.

Gabe had been dozing off, but when Emma said "Veronn," he came to attention. He followed Kim's thoughts and yelled, "Kelly!"

Kelly was talking to Christine about the baseball game and looked annoyed at being interrupted. "We have to go!" Gabe said in a heightened voice.

"Why?"

"That stuff we do."

Kelly leaped off her barstool, and a water glass crashed to the floor. The family began walking out when a waiter approached and said, "The tab is still open."

This basic statement befuddled Gabe, and he handed Christine his business credit card. "Please take care of this."

"Sure. Wait, you're not leaving? Not one of your mysterious trips?"

"Unavoidable," Kelly tersely replied.

"Wait, wait, wait. That wasn't part of the deal. You promised!"

"Sorry," Kim offered. "We didn't plan this."

"But–"

The family and Kelly briskly walked out of the restaurant, and when they got to their car, Kelly asked, "What the heck?"

"The Veronn are back," Kim answered.

"The off-worlders who took you?"

"Yes."

"You don't have an onk. So how did they talk to you?" Kelly countered.

"I don't know."

"What did they say?"

"They told me to meet them tomorrow at the same spot we saw them last time."

"I must make a report."

"Do it on the drive to our house."

They drove home rapidly, with Kelly following closely behind. When the front door closed, she held a device with antennas and loudly said, "This is my voice." After repeating the phrase six times and walking around the living room, she confirmed, "We're clear. Now, spill it. What the heck is going on?"

"Like I told you," Kim answered. "The Veronn said to meet them in Alaska tomorrow evening. That's it."

"Tell them to leave!" Kelly demanded.

"I'm not in contact with them."

"Well? Contact them!"

"It doesn't work that way."

Kelly looked annoyed and said, "There is no report from the satellite warning system. U.S. Space Force said the same thing from their sensors."

"All I can tell you is what they thought to me," Kim said.

Kelly made a fist, took out her phone, dialed, and said, "Sam, we're on speaker."

"Gabe, Kim. What's all this about? Remember, this is an open line, no specifics."

"The people who took us have returned," Kim answered. "They want to meet us at the same open field in Alaska where the tourists leave personal items on the ground. You need to move the people away so there won't be an incident."

"Tell them to cease and desist."

"They're not listening."

"We'll prepare a response," Sam said coldly.

"What kind?"

"That's not your concern."

"They're expecting us there."

"What do you think will happen if you aren't?"

"No idea."

"Guess."

"You know what horrors they did before."

"True," Sam admitted. "How confident are you on this?"

"One hundred percent."

"What do you think we should do?"

"Prepare the area for their arrival. But I need a decision. Do you want us here or there?"

Sam paused and answered, "Kelly. Off speaker."

Kelly pressed an icon, listened momentarily, and said, "No, they aren't lying. Kim never lies." Kelly listened. "No, they wouldn't do that."

Another pause. "No, they wouldn't do that either." She listened again. "Yeah." There was a final pause, and then she said, "I agree."

Kelly hung up and ordered, "Pack for five days. Now!"

Gabe and Kim ran upstairs and threw clothes into two carry-on bags. Eight minutes later, they met Kelly downstairs. "Donna arranged a flight," she confirmed.

"Where are we flying to?" Gabe asked.

"Alaska. Obviously."

"Wow, I asked a stupid question. Sorry. What do you want us to do there?"

"Sam will provide instruction when you land," Kelly answered.

"He will be there?"

"That's my understanding."

"Are you going to be there?" Gabe needed to know.

"I'm to escort you to a commercial flight. We would normally use a military aircraft, but we were unable to arrange one in time. We're trusting you to make the Dallas transfer. Can we count on you?"

"Of course!" Gabe answered with a scowl.

"I guess you have proved yourself in the past. Sorry, nasty habit."

"It's fine."

"Donna had to bump three people off flights to make this trip happen. The airline is holding the plane for us, and they're big-time upset. Let's go!"

They got into Kelly's white SUV, and she drove to the airport at breakneck speed. "Gabe. Glovebox!" She ordered, and he opened the glovebox. "Yellow envelope." He opened the envelope. "Those are two FBI credentials."

"They have our pictures on them," Gabe marveled. "Special Agent Gabriel Franco and Special Agent Kimberly Clark? Franco? Really? Do I look like a Franco?"

"Yes, *Mr. Franco.* Get used to it. If there are any issues, use those identifications. After this is over, I want them back. No games."

"You had this planned all along?" Kim wanted to know.

"With all that late-night deprogramming, we had them prepared."

"These look real."

"They are real, and the FBI database lists you as agents."

"Wow!" Kim chirped.

"Don't get caught up in the moment. Gabe. Under the seat."

Gabe reached under his seat and pulled out a blue plastic container. On top, it read, "H&K." He knew it had a handgun inside.

"Take this with you," Kelly ordered.

"Understood."

"It's loaded with hollow points and is my personal property. Do not use it, and you will return it. Understood?"

"Yes."

Kelly remained silent for the rest of the trip. Finally, they entered the airport passenger area, screeching to a stop. Kelly motioned to an officer standing nearby and showed him her identification so the family could not see it. "I need to escort these three clowns to their plane," she ordered. "I will return in six minutes."

"Leave the car running. I'll drive it over there."

"Affirmative."

The family exited, with Kelly following. When they approached the security checkpoint, Kelly flashed her identification, and the guards escorted them through. Gabe noticed one guard nod, and he suspected she knew him. Kelly drove them to the gate in an electric cart with a dramatic stop. "Don't screw this up!" she yelled.

"We try hard, lady Kelly," Emma answered.

"See that you do."

Kelly nodded, and the family walked to the plane. At the door, the flight attendant greeted them and had to rearrange seating so that Emma and Kim could sit together. The aircraft door closed, and the flight attendants began their safety lecture. Gabe marveled that they did not have tickets.

When the plane took off, the family fell asleep. They awoke to a flight attendant's voice announcing the landing. The woman next to Kim was staring at her.

"Yes?" Kim asked in an annoyed voice.

"I've seen you before. Are you a model?"

"No."

"I'm sure I recognize you," the lady mused.

"I doubt it."

Emma woke and said, "Mommy Kim, I'm hungry."

Kim started to talk to Emma when the woman interrupted, "That's it. You're Kim? The Kuiu Island bear killer!"

"No. That's somebody else," Kim dismissed. "People confuse me with that Kuiu lady all the time."

"I'm not sure. You look like her."

"Trust me. I am not that girl. She's ten years younger and lives in California."

The woman continued to stare until the plane landed. Gabe exited first and waited for Kim at the door. When Kim and Emma got there, the woman said, "Gabe? I knew it. I knew it."

"We're tired," Gabe hissed. "Go away."

At that moment, an airport security officer walked up to the family and asked, "Special Agent Franco and Special Agent Clark?"

Gabe had forgotten their new identifications and looked confused. Kim picked up on the issue, cleared her throat, and said in her best authoritative voice, "My partner's tired. That's us."

"Identification?"

Gabe fished through his backpack, and the officer became concerned when he saw a gun case. He handed over the identifications. "Let's go," the security officer said.

"You're police officers?" the woman chirped. "Wow."

"Not a word!" Gabe threatened. "Not a word."

The befuddled woman walked away, and the officer asked, "What's that about?"

"She's a drunk," Kim said dismissively.

"We get that all the time."

Kim's swimming revealed that the security officer did not believe her explanation. He drove the family to their connecting flight in an electric golf cart, and after feeding Emma, the family tried to relax. The plane landed in Fairbanks, and they transferred to a smaller plane. They landed at the small Kuiu Island airport and, upon exiting, realized they should have packed warmer clothing.

A school bus drove up with General Shefford and Sam. They were dressed in thick blue jackets and looked upset. The family noticed Jason in the driver's seat. Gabe handed the gun case and the FBI identifications to him. Jason nodded and began driving. "This better not be a joke," General Shefford growled.

"No joke," Kim answered.

"What do these Veronn, as you call them, want with you three?" the general demanded.

"No idea."

"How will this play out?"

"I think we need to stand in that field and wait. I assume you got all the locals to go away."

"That took a lot of effort," Sam answered. "The conspiracy nuts are having a field day. We already have online rumors, and major media outlets are pressuring us to set up cameras. You need to finish this ASAP."

"We'll do our best," Kim said.

"We've set up a perimeter and a decontamination area," General Shefford said. His eyes narrowed. "You three will suit up. Alright?"

"We can do that," Kim answered, smiling weakly.

"When the craft lands, Sam, Gabe, and I will approach it. Then Gabe will tell them to go away."

"I don't think they want that," Kim offered.

"I don't care. We're doing it that way."

"How about Jason and Gabe make the approach?"

"Why?" Sam asked.

"Jason is trained for this situation, and I trust him to keep a cool head."

Kim noticed Jason briefly looking in the oversized rearview mirror while driving. "This incident involves a craft. That is within the Air Force domain. I need answers," General Shefford countered.

"I think this is one of those times where we might not get answers," Kim said. "Let's keep calm and see what they want."

"We're not doing it that way."

"Well, I'm going on record as saying that Jason should be the person to greet them."

"So noted," General Shefford said with a grunt.

After an awkward moment of silence, Kim asked, "Sam? What's our status?"

"Your status?"

"Yes. Our status."

"Meaning?" Sam wanted to know.

"Are we on house arrest or whatever?"

Sam was quiet for a long moment and answered, "When this is over, you'll get an answer."

"I need more."

"Is that a threat?" Sam demanded.

"We're beyond threats."

"Meaning?"

"Threats aren't necessary. We know who you are, and you know who we are."

"Then what are you asking?" Sam asked.

"We want to travel."

"Is that all?"

"That's all."

"You didn't mention working with the DLS."

"That ship has sailed," Kim admitted.

"It has."

They all stared at each other, and Sam offered, "If this goes well, I will arrange for limited travel."

"Thank you," Kim said with a smile. "Now. What happens the next time you need a little favor?"

"Little favor?" Sam asked with raised eyebrows.

"Face it. We're the only humans who can communicate with off-worlders."

"Let's cross that bridge when we come to it."

"We're not saying no," Kim offered with a big smile.

"You're not saying yes."

"Sam, look. We're on the same team and want to do what's best for Earth."

"I will discuss this matter with my superiors."

"Thank you."

A minute later, General Shefford asked, "Sam?"

"Yes."

"That thing we were talking about earlier. They're going to read about it."

"I know."

"What thing?" Kim asked.

Sam looked at Gabe, then Kim and Emma. Finally, he took a deep breath and answered, "Remember that man who messed with your lives, Sato? Yesterday, he made a deal with the district attorney. They are allowing him one hour per day of supervised computer use."

"How the heck is that possible?" Kim demanded.

"The details are being kept under tight wraps. Tight even by my standards."

"Do you know what he is doing on the computer?"

"Our experts reveal he is contacting friends to restart his smear campaign. Fortunately, nobody wants to have anything to do with him. Even his family refuses to answer his emails. He's also begging the governor for a pardon."

"What else?" Kim demanded.

"That's all we know."

"Well? What are you doing about it?"

"We have a plan."

"Do you want us to do something about it?"

Sam raised his eyebrows and answered, "Sato is in double-isolation lockdown, and they even brought in three guards from the state capitol to keep him safe. So, there isn't much that you can do."

"Not what we wanted to hear," Kim said with a frown.

"I assure you, this is not what I wanted to hear, either."

The passengers sat in awkward silence as the bus passed a security checkpoint. They arrived at the same unassuming patch of ground where a massive Veronn spacecraft had once landed. The souvenir shops were gone, and they saw additional fences. Jason directed the family to a tented area that contained environmental suits. Gabe and Kim found it interesting that they had a small suit for Emma. Kim wished she could take a picture as she put it on.

The family waited in uncomfortable chairs, and two hours later, the sun set. A man dressed in military fatigues brought the family three Meals Ready to Eat, and they consumed them without fanfare. General Shefford came by four times to ask if anything had changed. The "we do not know" answer was wearing thin.

The stars became visible an hour later, and the security guards turned on ten portable light towers. Gabe sensed the lights needed extinguishing and shared his concerns with Sam. After a discussion with General Shefford, they turned off five.

An hour later, the family saw a familiar flicker in the stars. This pattern reminded Gabe and Kim of their cruise ship experience, which sent a chill up their spines. He pointed upwards and said to Sam, "There."

"That's them?"

"I think so," Gabe answered.

"It would take something huge to block out the stars like that."

"Yes."

"Wow!" Sam exclaimed.

A minute later, Kim got an impression and asked, "Sam?"

"Yes?"

"They'll be here soon. They want us to approach the craft. Nobody else."

"Did they tell you this?" Sam needed to know.

"Not exactly."

"How do you know?"

"I'm not sure," Kim admitted.

"Now what?"

"The guys with the guns. Tell them to put them down."

"Not going to happen!" General Shefford yelled.

Gabe sighed and said, "Either they put them down, or they get evaporated."

"You know this for a fact?"

"All I can tell you is what happened before. You saw the video?"

"We studied it in great detail," Sam admitted. "It was horrific."

General Shefford raised his eyebrows. "What video?"

"We'll talk later," Sam answered.

"I'm trying to prevent something bad," Gabe continued.

"Alright."

General Shefford walked away, returned, and said, "I ordered my men to locker their weapons. You'd better be right about this. Now what?"

"Tell everybody to keep calm when they arrive. No sudden moves or angry thoughts. You play nice, and they will play nice."

"They better."

Five minutes later, the air felt electric and smelled of ozone. Gabe and Kim were both brought back to their first encounter. Kim picked up Emma and held her close. Gabe hugged them and tried his best to think encouraging thoughts. However, the intense memory of losing his family came into sharp focus. A deep hum came from above, and a large gray shape passed overhead.

<I hate this!> Kim thought to Gabe.

<It'll be fine.>

Sam removed two onks from a lead case and handed them to Gabe and Kim. "I'm going out on a limb here," he said. "You better not mess this up."

Gabe nodded, held his onk, and excited Veronn thoughts instantly came to his mind. <Where did you go?>

<I don't understand,> Gabe thought.

<We communicated with daughter Emma many times, and then she stopped. Why?>

<These guys took our onks from us,> Kim answered.

<Why?>

<We made a mistake, and they confiscated them,> Kim explained.

<Why were they given back to you at this exact moment?>

<I think they're afraid of you,> Gabe told them, with a touch of humor.

<Prepare for departure.>

<What?> Kim thought, confused.

<You get that?> Gabe asked Kim.

<Yes.>

<It looks like we're going on a trip to outer space.>

<Always an adventure, hon,> Kim thought wryly.

"They are about to land and take us somewhere," Gabe told Sam.

"No, no, no," Sam cautioned. "Your mission is to tell them to depart immediately. You cannot leave this planet. It's against the law!"

"Sam, you saw the video. They can beam us up like on *Star Trek*."

"We're coming with you," Sam warned.

"I don't think you're welcome."

"This discussion is moot!" General Shefford affirmed. "Sam and I will tell them to leave."

"We can try it your way."

"You're not going anywhere. *That I guarantee!*" General Shefford threatened.

Kim set Emma down, and all five people walked to the center of the clearing. They put on their environmental suit helmets and adjusted the airflow. While waiting, Kim felt a distant thought from her brother, Marcus. He encouraged her to succeed, which uplifted her spirits. Gabe also got similar thoughts from his deceased daughter, Victoria. When he looked at Emma, she smiled.

The air became electric, and the humming increased. The hairs on their arms stood on end, making everybody nervous. Emma gripped Kim's leg tightly and took a rapid breath. Kim now felt a deep wave of fear as the sound became louder. Then, a massive craft with an undistinguished gray shape moved overhead and descended. The five floodlight towers reflected off an uneven gray surface. Gabe found it fascinating that the craft touched the ground without a downdraft. Astonished, they all watched as a thin door opened at the base. Orange light bathed the ground as a ramp extended from the door.

Kim looked at the ramp and then at Gabe.

"Sam? General?" Gabe asked. "Are you guys ready?"

"You three first." General Shefford ordered. "Walk slowly."

"Alright."

Gabe and Kim took three steps forward, stopped, and turned around. Sam and General Shefford had not moved. Their faces wore frustrated expressions.

"Are you two frozen in that position?" Kim asked, knowing the answer.

They did not reply, and Kim said, "We'll write up a full report when we return."

Kim was turning around when she caught Jason's eye. He had been standing nearby in an environmental suit, and he nodded. Kim nodded, turned, and the family entered the massive Veronn craft. The door rapidly closed behind them, and the orange lights turned white.

On the far side of their small room was a door with hinges. The white walls looked dusty, and three gray outfits in their sizes were on a bench.

In the center of the room, a small Veronn individual stood in a similar gray outfit, wearing a large face mask that obscured his features. Kim noticed he had a holster with an earth handgun. She recognized the gun they had traded for the white rifle. The Veronn patted the handgun and pointed at her.

This individual's face had a light flesh tone, small brown eyes, a little nose, and thin lips. He stood four feet one, with no visible hair, small ear nubs, four fingers on each gloved hand, and tiny gray teeth. He thought pleasantly, <Remove your present clothing and apply the provided collective protective garments.>

<Why?> Gabe asked.

The Veronn did not respond. Not knowing what else to do, the family took off their environmental suits and began putting on the garments.

<Remove all former garments,> the Veronn thought.

<Kind of embarrassing,> Kim thought with concern. <Are you going to turn around?>

The Veronn did not respond. Its face adopted an amused expression. With some trepidation, the family removed their remaining clothing. For Gabe, the event brought back memories of his prison shower experiences. Kim did not like being naked or getting amused thoughts from the individual.

<I see daddy pee-pee stick,> Emma thought comically.

<Emma. Enough!> Kim thought harshly. <Behave yourself. Now, let me help you with this suit.>

<Yes, Mommy Kim.>

Kim put on her garment and then helped Emma. Gabe put on his garment and looked at his wife. Kim's garment stressed her shapely bust and perfect butt.

<Wow, sexy space babe!> he thought, lustfully.

<Hon!>

<Hey, that suit looks like somebody painted it on. I can't help but stare at my amazing wife.>

Kim looked at Gabe and said, <You too. Big stud!>

Gabe looked down, and the garment had perfectly adapted around his groin. He made a big gulp of embarrassment.

<Place your onks in the side receptacle,> the Veronn told them.

Gabe and Kim put on their face shields and placed their onks into a molded slot above their ear. {Interfacing with collective protective garment,} their onks thought.

Kim felt her garment working and adjusting to her breathing. She visualized a display of her vital signs and the functions of her garment. Kim began interacting with the controls and determined the suit had bladders to adjust the fit. She inflated the ones to provide dignified support for her bust and butt.

Kim's attention turned to her shoes. They felt comfortable and cushioned her feet interactively. Kim took two steps and marveled at how pleasant her feet felt and how well they gripped the floor. *These are the best shoes ever!* she thought with glee.

Gabe figured out how to adjust his garment to present a uniform groin appearance. He looked down to see Emma in tears. He knew she also wanted to adjust her garment, but did not have an onk. To his great relief, the Veronn bent down to present her with one. Emma smiled, and she looked happier than he had ever seen her.

Emma placed the onk into the mask receptacle, her garment rapidly adjusted, and she thought to Gabe intensely, <Daddy Gabe! Daddy Gabe!> He felt stunned by Emma's vivid and precise thoughts. <They gave me an onk. It is Generation 85. My own! I set it to bond with me.>

<That's wonderful.>

<It best day. It best day ever!>

<I'm happy for you.>

<We maintain a restricted schedule,> the Veronn advised them.

A green flash made their environmental suits disappear, and Gabe thought to Kim, <Hey, my watch was in that pile!>

<Hon.>

<I liked that watch. It had a black metal band. They don't sell those anymore.>

<It's a cheap Casio. I keep telling you to buy a better watch.>

<Still!>

<I have deposited your garments at the landing vicinity,> the Veronn told them with amusement. <The members are collecting them. This includes your inaccurate time-keeping device. Come.>

Gabe felt embarrassed by his mental outburst. The Veronn opened the hinged door with a twist knob, and the family followed down narrow, dimly lit hallways with low ceilings. Plastic boxes were scattered on the floor, making travel difficult.

They went to another room to see three metal enclosures, each sized for a family member. The fourth enclosure was unique and appeared to be for the Veronn.

The onks explained that these enclosures were "integrators." They would "secure their bodies during extreme acceleration." Gabe noticed there were no other doors in this room and surmised they were the only passengers on this massive craft.

<We are about—> the Veronn thoughts drifted.

Time became perplexing for the family. Events that occurred five minutes ago felt like they were happening again. They were also aware of impending events. In this future, the family left their integrators and walked off the craft.

The Veronn distantly continued in a manner that was hard to comprehend, <...to travel. Please enter the integrators. They will prepare your bodies for interstellar delivery.>

<What's going on?> Kim asked with concern, but had already leaned back into the integrator.

Gabe was still focused on his conversation with Sam, but he felt relieved because he knew the trip *was successful.*

Kim became aware that the craft had *already* entered an "accelerated inter-dimension rupture Type 218." She somehow understood that this meant they *would* go faster than the speed of light.

Gabe was intrigued by the process. His onk communicated detailed information, and he put great effort into comprehending the vast technical concepts. He understood some basics, but his limited knowledge of high-energy subatomic physics prevented him from fully comprehending how the craft operated.

Emma wanted to yell out in delight as she jumped into her integrator and enthusiastically embraced her new time-shifting reality.

A clamshell door closed on each integrator, and Kim understood through "craft status" that the Veronn had entered his integrator. He supervised the computations, and the craft applied vast amounts of energy. The integrators tightened around their suits, which constricted their bodies. Breathing became difficult, and Gabe struggled to focus on his conversation with Sam. It occurred to him that his heart had stopped beating, and his lungs no longer moved.

Kim could not blink, and she also realized her breathing had stopped. At one point, the family sensed that all thoughts had stopped, yet they could still comprehend the events. The faster-than-light travel started slowly (or rapidly, depending on the observer's perspective). They knew their bodies experienced a physical pull, and then a sudden stop. Kim could no longer communicate with her family, but she understood that Emma had tried to yell, "Faster, faster!"

Events began converging, and they felt drawn toward an inevitable conclusion. Gabe understood they were going to push away from planet Earth. He perceived a dangerous level of energy building up to a specific release point. For a single moment, they experienced intense clarity.

Gabe saw a laboratory with Bunsen burners, glassware, bench equipment, and a surprised scientist. The individual had features similar to those of Duve, and he wondered whether they were a related species. The scientist wore a white lab coat with a green stain on his left sleeve. Gabe liked seeing a pocket protector full of pens.

Kim also experienced an unexpected sight. The scientist stared at her in great disbelief. Kim wondered how many beings were staring at him and if he understood her presence. His blue pants reminded her of Homer Simpson, and his tan belt looked like leather. The image faded, and Kim tried to commit the scientist's facial features to memory.

The sequence of events reversed (or had progressed farther, depending on the perspective), and their time confusion faded. Kim knew her heart had restarted, and the tightness around her body had lessened. The clamshell door opened, and she applied great effort to stand. Kim watched in confusion as two Veronn in yellow collective protective garments assisted her in walking.

Gabe looked down to see three Veronn helping him stand. <Have we arrived?> he asked the closest Veronn. They did not answer, and he asked, <Did we travel through space?>

One of the Veronn replied, <Your status will become clear. Attempt to center yourself.>

Kim also tried to grasp her surroundings as the two Veronn led her from her integrator. As she attempted to ask a question, it occurred to her to look at Emma. She had a big smile and thought, <We here, Mommy Kim!>

<Where?>

<Veronn home world!>

<Oh.>

# TWENTY

A Veronn in a yellow collective protective garment led the family through the narrow walkway with low ceilings into an open area and down a ramp. They saw through the windows that their craft had landed in a white building with large green doors. The family continued down different hallways with several doors. They stopped before three pink doors, and each member entered alone. Gabe and Kim did not like leaving Emma, but she was comfortable being separated. Inside, they found a sterile white environment with a single bench seat, shower, toilet, and drawers. Gabe and Kim still felt disoriented when their onk thought, {Decontamination now in process. Remove your mask and make use of the provided seat.}

They followed the instructions, and Kim asked Emma, <Are you alright?>

<Yes, Mommy Kim. I take off my mask like okey-okey tell me to.>

<Alright, sweetie.>

The family relaxed for a few minutes to allow their bodies to adjust to the updated time frame. During this time, their focus sharpened, and the wooziness faded. Then Gabe noticed something odd. He stood and made a small hop. *This planet has lower gravity,* he thought. *It's like jumping on a bed.* Kim also noticed the difference in gravity and thinner air.

Several minutes later, their onks directed them to remove their collective protective garments and place them in the drawers for decontamination. Kim compared this activity to dry cleaning, which made her chuckle.

Their onks then instructed them to step into the stand-up shower and prepare for "surface cleansing." Suddenly, an articulated arm with a nozzle began sweeping around their bodies, spraying a caustic, brown liquid. This spray made their skin tingle and their eyes burn. They tried to move, but an unknown force held them in place. Then, the articulated arm rinsed off the caustic liquid and rapidly blew warm air across their bodies.

{Remain calm; phase two will be unpleasant,} their onks warned.

A thin robotic probe entered their nose and ears while spraying a caustic mist, which stung. Then, a different probe was inserted into their anus. They felt it extend and release a liquid. The probe retracted, and another entered their mouths and sprayed a foul-tasting substance, but they could not cough. It extended further and went into their stomachs. They watched a clear tube removing their partially digested Meals Ready to Eat. The probe sprayed as it retracted and then descended into their lungs.

Finally, the probe retracted, and the body hold was released. They coughed out foul-tasting brown fluid for several minutes.

Then, the mental hold returned, and a thin probe inspected every part of their bodies in great detail.

When the probes retracted, they regained complete control. Emma thought to Kim with profound confusion and shame, <Mommy, it's inside my pee-pee hole.>

<It's over, sweetie,> Kim thought with encouragement. <We sometimes must go through that. It's part of being a woman. You acted maturely, and I'm proud of you.>

<Alright, Mommy Kim,> Emma answered, embarrassed.

Gabe had been monitoring their conversation and did not like how they had treated his wife and daughter. The onks directed the family back to their seats and asked them to place their arms on a trough-shaped cushion. A needle was inserted and a blood sample was taken. Gabe and Kim were relieved that there was no pain. Their onks displayed hundreds of blood test results.

The "outbreak prevention system" began planning "antibodies, correctors, and modifiers to assist the eradication of undesirable micro-organisms." Five minutes later, the onks directed the family to place their arms in the same trough-shaped cushions. A different needle was used to inject a "custom inoculation agent." Afterward, they felt nauseous and had to lie on the bench.

For the next two hours, the family watched videos about Veronn history on their onks. Their world consisted of a single continent and a single race. As a result, they lacked class distinctions and significant conflicts (wars). Their government had been in place for 421 full cycles. Kim inquired about their culture, fashion, and politics. Emma wanted to learn what they did for fun. Of course, Gabe wanted to know all about their technology, science, and semiconductor development.

As the learning continued, the family felt an impending urge to have a bowel movement. Gabe could not believe this device looked and operated like his home toilet. He sat and had an aggressive release for several minutes. Kim and Emma had a similar experience.

A bidet spray bar was extended to clean them. Then, the family returned to learning about Veronn's history. An hour later, their onks explained how to behave during their stay. Specifically, it directed them to obey all laws and not leave their "instigator."

It was unclear who their instigator was, but they suspected he was the same Veronn who had been on their ship. They were also told that failure to comply with these rules would result in punishment and a ban on future visits. Legal counsel contact information and a lengthy explanation of their rights were provided. <Lawyers rule the universe,> Gabe thought to Kim.

<Agreed,> Kim said with a chuckle.

The family members had two smaller bowel movements and urinated twice. An hour later, their coughing had subsided, and their onks directed them to place their arms in the receptacle to draw more blood. After additional blood testing, their onks permitted a "short duration admittance."

The drawers opened, and they put on their cleaned collective protective garments. The pink doors opened a minute later, and they rejoined each other. Gabe and Kim kneeled to hug Emma.

A Veronn in a yellow collective protective garment led them down another long hallway. The walls contained posters of museums, attractions, and events. Below the pictures were words in a strange alphabet. It was clear these were entertainment advertisements.

Their onks translated, {Hear the greatest musician, Gleen.} {Visit the spectacular crashing waterfall of blue rocks.} {Family enjoyment at the park of many cultures.} {Explore the artwork of Jem, the painter.} Kim found these posters quirky and amusing.

Gabe was more interested in seeing that the posters had filament lamps, cords, and plugs connected to wall outlets. He would have expected advanced LED technology without wires.

A door opened, and they saw a bored-looking Veronn sitting at a blue desk in a yellow collective protective garment. <Purpose of your visit?> he asked Gabe.

<What?>

<Why are you visiting Veronn?>

<I don't know,> Gabe admitted with confusion.

<Let me inquire with your instigator.>

A minute later, the Veronn thought with the same bland emotion, <You are here for planet updates and status checks. What is the duration of your stay?>

<I don't know,> Gabe admitted again, with even more confusion.

<I will inquire again with your instigator. I grow weary of your lack of knowledge,> the Veronn thought, annoyed. A moment later, he thought, <The answer is one cycle. What is your political status?>

<Republican.>

<Not amusing,> the Veronn thought with mild anger. <Your Veronn political status?>

<I don't know how to answer.> Gabe wondered why this individual did not understand their situation.

The Veronn sensed Gabe's annoyance. <This conversation is no longer tolerable. In coming to our planet, you must know the basic facts behind your visit. I will inquire again. This will be my last moment of patience.>

<Look, I do not know who brought us here or why.>

<Your attitude will prevent a successful visit,> the Veronn warned.

<I'm not trying to be stubborn.>

<You will depart if I do not get satisfaction in the first order.>

<Alright,> a bewildered Gabe thought.

After a long interaction, the Veronn looked surprised and thought, <You're Gabe. This is Kim and Emma.>

<Why would we be anybody else?> Gabe asked.

<From the Earth?>

<Of course.>

<Well, this is a great cycle,> the Veronn thought joyfully. <Don't worry about all these dubious question-questions. I will take care of them in post-rapid succession.>

<Thanks,> Gabe thought with relief.

<Tell me. What is Moe Howard truly like? Is his humor always of the seventh {slapstick} type?>

<Who?>

<You must know, his best friend is his entertaining brother. They have such wonderful times.>

<I'm not following,> Gabe thought with confusion.

<You are most humorous,> the Veronn thought with wonder and kindness. <Their dear friend is Larry Fine. An amazing male. You must greet him every day.>

<Hon, do you remember what Jason told us? He's talking about *The Three Stooges*,> Kim explained with a giggle.

<Where are the teeth in my mouth? By the two rings, I'm referring to *The Three Stooges*! Such great representatives of your culture. Truly first order.>

<I guess,> Gabe replied.

<Your thoughts are reserved. By my word, you must be hiding your overjoyment because you sense how much I appreciate their comedic dancing ability. I can never keep my thoughts silent about this sincere fact.>

<Sure.>

<Ahh, denial. Most shrewd. Well, this questioning process brightened my cycle.>

<But, how do you know about *The Three Stooges?*>

<We have been monitoring Earth broadcasts for many full cycles.>

Gabe shook his head, and Kim thought, <Nice meeting you.>

<The enjoyment proceeded from my side of the desk. Remember to keep your collective protective garments on for the full visit duration. Travel through that door for important question-question.>

<Alright.> Relieved, Gabe took a long breath.

The family entered a small room and saw a serious-looking Veronn dressed in a black business jumpsuit. His appearance and stern thoughts put them on edge. They wondered why the Veronn was not wearing a collective protective garment as he waved a black box with a silver loop around them. As he studied the display, he asked intently, <Have you encountered past or future time frames during your transit?>

Gabe felt compelled to answer truthfully. <Oh, you are a time cop.>

<An overall impression. Please answer.>

<I saw the laboratory during my visit. My mental time frame got a little strange. But nothing I could consider time travel.>

<How far did your thoughts extend?>

<I guess ten to fifteen minutes. But I cannot be sure.>

<And you?>

<About the same,> Kim answered. <Maybe ten minutes.>

<And you, little being?>

<No long duration, time person.>

<I direct you never to disrupt the Veronn timeline. Any failure will incur severe punishment. Including Type 10 {immediate death}, Type 11 {eternal suspension}, or the dreaded Type 12 {soul tortured suspension}.>

<We understand,> Kim answered.

<Your instigator is waiting. Entertain a friendly visit.>

<Thank you,> Kim thought with relief.

The bewildered family walked through a door, down a hallway, and found themselves outside. Gabe immediately noticed the sun looked smaller, and the clouds looked identical. He also saw concrete sidewalks with curbs, cracks, expansion joints, and what appeared to be the contractor's name embedded. Then, a bird flew by that looked like a black seagull.

The street was lined with cars featuring black wheels, windshields, and doors. They were a mix of sedans, delivery trucks, and vans. Gabe estimated that they were sixty percent the size of Earth vehicles. Two cars parked across the street looked exactly like Honda Civics. Above them, he saw a thin street lamp and an orange fire hydrant to the right. Down the street, a traffic light had square green, yellow, and red lights.

Kim noticed grass, trees, white flowers, and plants that looked like the weeds in front of her house. The leaves on most plants were longer and greener than on Earth. One tree had a small animal that looked like a blond squirrel. She then looked at one-and-a-half-year-old Emma walking and marveled at how much her daughter was experiencing. Kim could tell without swimming that she was excited to be there.

The immediate area looked like an office district. The buildings had square, reflective windows and slogans on their sides. Kim found it hard to believe that the advanced Veronn race did not have flying cars. The sight of a car with a bumper sticker sidetracked her. It had a young Veronn in loud pink clothes making a vertical finger gesture.

Emma loved the new sights and jumped up twice to experience the lower gravity. A restaurant was across from their location, and she wondered what food they served.

In front of them, a Veronn individual waited. He stood four feet one, had thinning honey-brown hair, no facial hair, and a slim build. The individual wore a striped pattern shirt, light blue slacks, and tan shoes similar to Dockers. He wore stylish blue sunglasses with a small clip that held his onk and purple bracelets on each arm. He broadly smiled at the family and waved.

<Welcome to my home world,> the Veronn male thought with pride.

<Hello,> Gabe replied cautiously.

<We have a lot to do in this cycle.>

<What do they call you?>

<In our culture, we have single-short names. My full name is Tangellion Longeer of the family Garp. Call me Tan.>

<You traded your gun with me and brought us here?> Gabe asked, concerned.

<Correct.>

<Why?>

<You have many questions, and I will answer them by the short cycle. For now, we must be posthaste. My brother will arrive in a rented transport.>

<You rent cars with money?> Gabe asked in disbelief.

<Of course.>

<I thought money would be useless to an advanced society.>

<All worlds run on money.>

<A constant of the universe?>

<Indeed.> Tan chuckled.

A large (by Veronn standards) gray van driving on the right side of the street turned a nearby corner. It had writing on the side, and the onk translated, {Low Rate Rapid Cargo Vehicle Rental}. A Veronn male waved to them, and Kim asked Tan, <Your brother?>

<Zanger Longeer of the family Garp. Call him Zan.>

<Where did you two grow up?>

<We grew up on Alcubierre, an outpost in the Dorn region proximity.>

<Are your parents still there?>

<Tragically, our parents perished in a Type 215 craft failure,> Tan answered sadly.

<I'm sorry to hear that.>

<The Type 215 had charging grid faults.>

<May I ask how old you are? I hope that isn't a rude question.>

<By your arm, most would consider your inquiry rude. However, in the truth, I do not bother with tradition. Therefore, I am 51.23 full cycles.>

<Is that considered old?> Kim asked, curious.

<Vernon males live to an average 96.66 full cycles, and Veronn females live to 104.45 full cycles.>

<Do you have a wife?> Kim wanted to know.

<A mate?>

<Yes.>

<Lem is no longer at my side,> Tan replied, again with sadness.

<What happened, or is that subject too forward to ask?>

<For my culture, you are becoming forward, but I do not have harsh feelings. Exposure brings full closure.>

The conversation was interrupted by the van pulling up. Zan exited and opened a sliding door. He wore loose-fitting gray pants, green boots, bold red sunglasses, and a shirt with pink lettering that translated to "Why is the hand on my arm?" Gabe and Kim did not understand the statement or the constant references to body parts. The family got into the back and sat in seats made for much smaller individuals.

<Gabe. Good day, solid partner,> Zan thought cheerfully.

<Hello, Zan. Nice to meet you.>

<A grand cycle to you, Miss Kim.>

<Nice to meet you, Zan,> Kim thought with kindness.

<By the fingers on my hand. You must be Emma.>

<Hi, funny Zan!> Emma thought excitedly.

<What a great cycle. Did the decontamination clean you out?>

<It go in pee-pee hole,> Emma thought with embarrassment.

<In the fourth degree. Uncomfortable!>

The door automatically closed, and Zan began driving. Gabe could not believe the van had a steering wheel. They reached the end of the block and stopped at a red light. He found it amusing that the traffic lights had the green light at the top. Gabe even saw an indicator for pedestrians to know when it was safe to cross the street.

<What subject did Tan refer to as I arrived?> Zan thought with a smile.

<He was telling us why Lem left,> Kim replied. <But first, tell me why everybody keeps talking about their body parts.>

<Lem left because Tan did not have the snails to tell her father to stay out of their partnership. And the body parts conversation is classic Veronn culture.>

Gabe and Kim wondered what the term "snails" referred to, and their onk refused to translate.

<Zan, I'm the eldest, and I will continue my description on my personal terms,> Tan countered harshly.

<Always the old authority standing, brother. Well, continue with the fiction. Inform of the essential departing element like a full zorget {Slang for rodent}.>

Tan looked annoyed and thought, <Allow full conversation, brother. Our government uses effective screening criteria to place new families onto successful career paths. As I contained an advanced aptitude for relating individuals together, this provided wide decision-making connections. Testing confirmed my path to becoming a royal court associate.>

<A more effective translation yields that father used money-money influence to get his first son into that position,> Zan interrupted wryly. <Continue, brother.>

<Admission in full,> Tan thought with annoyance. <Money-money influence for total truth. With my life path established, I became educated in an appropriate forum and entered government service. I set certain goals to become a first prime assistant.>

<What's a first prime?> Gabe asked.

Tan thought momentarily and answered with authority, <That would be eight elder orders down from the first ring. It is the job of a first prime to oversee projects. Now tell in full truth. Are you aware of the history between your Earth and the Veronn?>

Kim hesitated. <Not really.>

<That is an important aspect of my telling. The Veronn established outposts on distant planets. Your Earth contained one called 'Spirit and Tree Retreat.' We conducted research and used this location as a point of enhanced relaxation.>

Stunned, Gabe asked, <When did they build the place?>

<Records indicate 321 full cycles ago.>

<What is this age in Earth years?>

<One Veronn full cycle translates to 0.912 Earth full cycles. Math indicates 292.752 Earth full cycles. At that stage, humans were not in proximity of the outpost.>

<Ahh. That's why you called us aliens.>

<Precisely,> Tan replied.

<That makes sense.>

<Indeed. Continuing. This outpost became popular. Visitors appreciated the clean air, added gravity, and playful wildlife. Circumstances prevailed, and your kind multiplied. We considered ending options, but ignorance overrode actions. A massive shift occurred 113 full cycles ago. Your kind instigated an attack which put down many Veronn. The overall tragedy became great.>

<I did not know,> Kim thought sadly.

<Much is the complete sorrow,> Tan thought with reserved emotions. <Continuing. A Type 7 {standard subdued} recovery team was dispatched to recover the fallen. By royal decree, we removed all remaining Veronn property posthaste, and the planet was declared a loss.

<In recent time, an exploration became undertaken to this former outpost to observe the aggressive culture. A promising new commander, Second Class Dingleen Trappen of the family Sambien, became selected to lead this mission. Upon arrival, his vessel underwent a Class 3 attack {focused optical energy} resulting in forced defense. He conducted many Type 7 {a full order of magnitude above Type 6} energy exchanges. Using great skill, his defense became complete.>

Confused, Gabe shook his head. <That makes little sense. We were there. It was a peaceful night, and something cut the ship in half.>

<Indeed, by the arm, your suspicions may be correct,> Tan answered coyly. <As his reports came into viewing, a Class 3 energy exchange seemed implausible. My first prime, Harbineer Vancoot of the family Sarper, made haste to investigate raised claims. As I had proven his trust with my supremely diligent ability, I became selected as Level 2 {one level below the supreme prime} investigator. As such, I became assigned to provide a Level 4 {senior grade} investigation with twelve assistants. Upon first arrival, I found Din prevailing in full battle. He applied dedicated energy at their highest power setting. I further observed Din applying horrific means.

Tan turned away for a moment, turned back, and thought, <At close range, Din engaged his energy projectors in their partially phased state. In our society, we deem this setting as Type 11 Punishment.>

The family sensed horrific shame. Gabe asked, <What does Type 11 do?>

<We reserve Type 11 Punishment for severe criminals,> Tan replied with deep regret. <These individuals had committed multiple death-death crimes without remorse or interfered with Veronn timelines. Such individuals serve as examples. Type 11 Punishment involves partially-phased projections. In this instance, the energy would remove the atoms while maintaining structure. The body's presence continues to exist without a physical form. The essence cannot travel long distances and cannot truly perish. Type 12 Punishment is also possible, but only used in dire circumstances. Due to Emma's young nature, I am forbidden from providing a detailed description.>

<Din subjected our families to Punishment 11?> Kim demanded.

<Regrettably, yes,> Tan admitted with great sorrow. <Upon observing this aggression, I contacted my first prime. He ordered Din to cease punishment, who complied out of obedience and presented anger.

<I engaged Din in Level 3 {prime importance} debate. The conclusion prompted investigating the human perpetrators who instigated the Type 7 energy exchange. We scoured the surrounding area for additional energy projectors and located what became known as Kim and Gabe. Upon confidence, we suspended you two from active time and subsequent travel to Veronn. Leading biologists conducted tests with excellent returns.>

Confused, Kim interrupted Tan. <Why did you take us? Why were we so special? Why not somebody else?>

<We monitored your aggressive survival efforts and concluded you would be ideal representatives. I took over the observation effort. Upon this occurrence, my foot became damaged by your metal spikes. Most humiliating.>

<Ahh, you stepped on our nails,> Gabe thought.

<Indeed. Later, you confronted me and presented mercy. To answer your challenge, I became interacted with your thoughts. By the fingers on your hand, the deep loss you experienced pulled my arm to the point of pain. Until then, we became reassured that your race did not maintain close interactions. My surprise became complete upon full comprehension of the massive error.

<With complete clarity, I used my Level 3 {under sub-prime} personal authority to terminate offensive operations. With immediate permission, I depolarized the matter stream. This action counteracted the Type 11 Punishment and allowed the suspended individual structures to collapse.>

<So they could die?> Kim asked.

<Type 11 Punishment is not within the parameters necessary to be alive. A corrected result would be to allow them to fade into non-energy.>

<When we go to that location, we can sense them,> Kim told Tan. <Other humans can also do this.>

<A residual effect. It will pass in the coming full cycles.>

<Are their bodies physically there?>

<That answer is upon your prospective reference. In a short finger, the answer is no. In a long finger, the answer is yes.>

This information confused the family, and Tan continued, <From that time reference point, we monitored Earth society and have come to appreciate the vast errors Din incurred. As such, in the posthaste, a royal court hearing occurred of the first magnitude and by the three rings. Din's arguments were of low value. His social standing reset to zero upon ruling, and his possessions dispersed. Posthaste, he now resides in restricted living address. There will be no exceptions.>

<He is a prisoner?> Gabe asked.

<Your term summarizes his condition. My extensive research concluded that you were also in restricted living?>

<You're correct,> Gabe admitted.

<For what crimes did this occur?>

<My society did not appreciate Kim's young age when we met.>

<I have a misunderstanding. You complete her? Why does your society not accept this at a full arm's length?>

<My society has complicated laws. Sometimes, they're not fair.>

<Could you not have passed the test of passion?> Tan asked.

<You mean something like kissing Kim in front of the judge?>

<Yes.>

<That would have made matters much worse.>

<Your sense of modesty is paramount,> Tan thought with sympathy.

<Tan,> Zan thought. <By the teeth in my mouth. Flubel-glob! {Slang for ridiculous.} Enough serious topics. Tell them why you did not have the snails to stand up to Lem's father.>

<Younger brother, your place!>Tan admonished.

<Tell or I will.>

<Very well. It had been no accident for Din to take charge of that mission. His pre-birth family had perished in the Earth outpost attack of so long ago. Din sought revenge of the highest order. Without my Level 3 {prime importance} direct intervention, he would have subjected your complete population with Punishment Type 11. Most horrific.

<With my reports, I presented Din's crime before the royal court. In pursuing justice, Din prevailed upon his family to circumvent my ring-appointed authority. This influence extended to my mate, Lem. She made a full honor request for me to alter the official record. As my documents were of the highest order, I refused. My reason included the royal court bond. In result, Lem became displeased. As the matter held full honor, she sided with her family. In this moment, it became my right to challenge her family's honor. I took deep regret for not acting.>

Kim felt his sorrow and thought, <Lem made her choice too. What else were you two going through?>

<A perceptive female of your species,> Tan admitted. <I worked late to impress my first prime because of intended advancement. Lem did not tolerate my extended duty as she raised Zic in solitude. It is my perception that she desired the company of another, but positive proof is lacking.>

<And thirteen cycles later, Lem found silly-boy Tip's residence!> Zan interrupted with an accusation. <Thirteen cycles, brother. Am I correct in this matter? Proof is positive. Tell me by your left arm!>

<Yes. Correct in the most astute sense,> Tan admitted. His face betrayed regret and sorrow.

<Older brother, locating a new mate is now essential. Or by the teeth in my mouth, I'm going to send a top-priority message to Bun.>

<As younger brother, you would not take that place!> Tan admonished.

<Who's Bun?> Kim asked.

<His former lead up,> Zan answered slyly. <A complete spunky-spunky. She would make a great mate for mighty-mighty like Tan.>

<Hold your place, Zan.>

<You made the priority in Lem against your own wishes.>

<An arranged marriage?> Kim asked.

<A court-appointed union,> Zan corrected.

<Lem became in line to serve a first prime when our child occurred,> Tan thought. <By law, they put off her service term until Zic lasted three full cycles.>

<I want to meet Zic,> Emma thought excitedly.

<Soon, Emma,> Tan thought.

<You know Zic?> Kim asked Emma with suspicion.

<He my best friend,> Emma answered joyfully.

<You met him through the onk?>

<Yes, Mommy Kim. We think-think often.>

<You should have discussed this with us.>

<It's alright, Mommy Kim. Zic funny,> Emma giggled.

<I see.>

<She's growing up, babe, and already has a boyfriend,> Gabe thought to Kim.

<Hmm.>

<Good-good Earth beings,> Zan thought with joy. <We're on our way.>

<Where?> Kim asked.

<We are traveling to Restricted Living Address Number 315. You are to confront Din for his crimes.>

<You want us to yell at the guy who killed our families?> Gabe asked, incredulous.

<It is your duty as a victim of the primary incident. Did Din not take the life of your former mate and two female offspring?>

<Yes, he did,> Gabe admitted, feeling his anger rising.

<Why the urgent hesitation?>

<You're right. Let's go smack him around.>

<Kim, on your word. Does Gabe always behave in the full arm position?>

Smiling, Kim replied, <Since the moment we met.>

# TWENTY-ONE

During the drive, the family got a look at the astounding city. It surprised Kim and Gabe to see lower-class districts with homeless Veronns in ratty clothing, graffiti on walls, and abandoned buildings. They also traveled through pleasant neighborhoods with big houses and green lawns. One house had Veronn children playing with balls and riding three-wheeled bicycles.

There were construction sites with workers dressed in overalls, and green school buses. Gabe even spotted a child with a shirt that read in English, "Game on." It floored Kim to see a dry cleaner, and she almost asked Zan to stop so she could look inside.

The family checked in at the front desk in the restricted living facility. The low ceiling made walking difficult. Tan and Zan remained in the lobby while two Veronn, dressed in blue security jumpsuits, escorted them to a sparse conference room with devices that resembled video cameras. They sat at a low table in small plastic seats that Kim and Gabe found uncomfortable.

Five minutes later, the door opened, and two muscular (by Veronn standards) guards escorted an individual in. They forced him to sit and remained directly behind him, their hands firmly grasping his shoulders. Gabe found it funny that they both had black hair with crew cuts.

Din appeared to be a meek individual with a shifty expression. He was dressed in a tan and bright green striped jumpsuit, which reminded Gabe of his time in prison. The onk translated the writing on his jumpsuit label, {Non-Citizen Number 7834712, Class 0, Crime: subversion of authority, Multi-kill 26.}

Din was stunned by the family's presence. The guards did not provide him with an onk, which made communications awkward. Their onks thought to the family, {Restricted communication protocol active. Interfacing with court databases. Interfacing with public disclosure archive databases. Interfacing with interested population outlets. Formally interfacing with the royal court. Proceed at communication depression level. By the royal rings, observe cautious thoughts.} Gabe and Kim did not fully understand this complex suggestion, but they interpreted it to mean, "You are being recorded and must behave."

Din looked at the family and was clearly uncomfortable in their presence.

<Hello,> Kim thought angrily.

The family felt Din's stunned emotions as he remained silent, refusing to respond. <Going to say something?> Kim demanded.

Din was still in shock and did his best to avoid eye contact.

<You're the jerk who killed my family?> Gabe asked crossly. <Aren't you? Well?>

The accusation stunned Din, and he turned away.

<Hey, idiot!> Kim thought. <They told us you would cooperate. Now talk. Say something.>

Finally, the left guard pushed Din's head forward and shook him from side to side.

<Is that a yes? Did you murder my family?> Gabe asked intently.

Din again tried to turn away, but the left guard again forced him forward, and Kim asked, <Why did you kill all those people? Why did you kill my mother?>

Din tightly closed his eyes as the left guard nudged his shoulder. A long moment later, Din answered with a forced low emotional level, <You were the first attackers. Not I.>

<Nobody attacked you,> Kim thought. <We were there. Remember? Stop lying!>

<In the before. Your forefathers massacred my pre-father and pre-mother. They offered no defense. On their passing, your race presented no regard. I state this by the length of their raised arms. The records proved it. You are a race of murderers!>

<And you think that excuse justifies your actions?> Gabe asked, struggling to control his anger.

<By the royal rings, I must indicate yes.>

<I don't care about your darn royal rings. Answer me! What gives you the right to kill my family?>

Gabe's bold statement surprised the guards. Din looked happy, opened his eyes, and answered, <I indicate satisfaction. Your insult to the rings is proof of sedition. In full. In full, I tell you!>

<Answer the question, you asshole!> an enraged Gabe thought.

<I answered your filthy question from my backside. Your disrespect for the royal rings proves my intentions were correct.>

<And revenge had nothing to do with it?> Gabe struggled not to jump out of his seat and strangle Din.

<I obtained a gratifying secondary benefit of the first order.>

<You're not hiding your thoughts,> Kim replied with narrow eyes. <It's clear that you only thought about revenge. You knew they were innocent people. Nobody attacked your ship.>

<Your world contains fools. As positive proof of the third order, they watch repetitive slogans for products of the lowest quality.>

<Don't change the subject,> Kim thought angrily. <Why'd you do it?>

<Orders surrounded my direction.>

<You vaporized children. Do you feel that? Children!> Kim harshly thought.

Din looked shocked, and he turned away.

<You kill baby!> Emma angrily thought. <Only bad man kill baby.>

The two guards looked horrified, and the right one gasped in shock. Din covered his face with his left hand and raised his right arm. The family interpreted this gesture as a request to end the conversation, but the right guard pushed his arm down.

<It's clear you weren't expecting to see us again,> Gabe confronted Din.

Din again tightly closed his eyes.

<They told us you tried to bribe your way out of jail,> Kim thought. <You're pathetic.>

Din tried to ignore Kim with maximum effort. Gabe sensed this and thought, <You don't understand what it means to be a decent individual. You're nothing but a stain on this fantastic planet.>

Gabe stood, and Kim traded one last jab. <You are by far the worst individual there has ever been. Die a cowardly death. Baby killer!>

Din began crying. Kim stood, and the family turned to leave. <You will die like bug!> Emma angrily thought. <On that day, I will be happy. All Veronn be happy.>

Din hunched over the table, and his body shook. The guards were in complete shock, and the right one turned away to avoid eye contact with the family as they left the conference room. Outside, their onks allowed normal communications, and Gabe thought to Kim with relief, <Not how I expected my day to go. I wanted to punch that guy.>

<Yeah, I felt your anger. He acted so full of himself. Obviously deluded. He still thinks he can somehow get himself out of jail.>

<What a loser,> Gabe said dismissively.

<Din know he kill good people,> Emma thought with sadness. <He like doing bad.>

<I'm sorry you had to go through that,> Kim told Emma. <Let's get out of here. This place gives me the creeps.>

Two guards escorted the family to the lobby, and Zan thought, <Wow, do you three have the snails.>

<What the heck are snails?> Kim asked quizzically. <You keep saying that.>

<Male reproducers.>

<We call them balls.>

<How fundamentally amusing.>

<I guess.> Kim chuckled at the thought.

<By your full leg, you compared Din to your digestive exit opening. The humor from that moment is of Level 7 {Two levels above intentional joking}.>

<Din tried to shift the blame. He has no heart,> Kim replied.

<To reward the cycle, Gabe used a royal ring slur. The snails he has.>

<What's the big deal?> Gabe asked.

<It's against the law to think in such terms,> Tan answered, concerned. <Fortunately, First Act 274 protects you from punishment during a cited conversation. This negative event will complicate matters when we see my first prime.>

Kim grew concerned. <We're going to see your boss?>

<He has relevant question-question about the incident,> Tan answered. <Notes must be in order.>

<How many people know about what I said? I mean, what I thought.>

<All Veronn knew of the impending incident because of the public record. An immediate first discussion is in process.>

<What is a royal ring?> Kim wanted to know.

<I have studied your culture at length. By my word of understanding, does your state of England contain a royal family?>

<Sort of. They don't actually run the government. Their rule is symbolic.>

<By my understanding. Do the royal rulers of England wear a crown to indicate authority?>

<Oh, I think I get it,> Kim surmised. <Your government is a monarchy.>

<Our king proudly wears three glorious rings of pure copper to signify his superior position.>

<Ohh. I insulted your king,> Gabe admitted, realizing his error. <I'm sorry about that.>

<Under Depression Level 3, emotional outbursts are permitted. From your thought context, it is clear that you had no aggression toward the rings. Is my statement accurate?>

<I have no aggression,> Gabe stated with certainty.

<By my teeth, this is good to understand. Now, we have a primary appointment with my first prime and an important task.>

Hesitant, Kim asked, <What's the important task?>

<Do you enjoy surprises?>

<Sometimes,> Kim admitted.

<By the fingers on my hand, you will enjoy this task.>

<Alright,> Kim thought, now smiling.

The family returned to the van, and they began driving. Along the way, Zan described his job as a party planner and said he enjoyed it. They drove over a beautiful suspension bridge and stopped on the other side to take in the city view. The colorful buildings gave it a European appearance that the family appreciated.

The scenery changed to woodland, and fifteen minutes later, they arrived at a massive circular office building. Unfortunately, the lobby greeter misunderstood the purpose of the visit. After clearing up the confusion, they walked down a narrow hallway where Gabe and Kim had to stoop while stepping side-to-side.

They came to a nondescript door with a sign, {Knowledge and Duty.} Tan knocked, and Gabe wondered why this advanced society did not have automatic doors. <Enter,> a distant thought answered.

Tan opened the door to a large, tastefully decorated office with an almond-colored wooden conference table. Gabe and Kim sat in chairs barely large enough to fit them.

The Veronn who greeted them was dressed in a well-tailored green velvet tracksuit. He had thinning gray hair, wrinkles under his eyes, a thick nose, and a bandage on his left wrist. Kim found it interesting that the Veronn wore glasses. Tan bowed and exited. Their onks thought with precision, {Official recording mode engaged. All thoughts are on record in the royal ring's first article. Begin.}

The new onk mode felt constrictive, and the male Veronn began, <As stated by the royal court, this conversation is part of the official records, Type 13 {Three levels above passive disclosure}. As such, under Article 61, with the first ring. I am first prime, Harbineer Vancoot of the family Sarper. Refer to me as Har. Do you comprehend my thought of most with Positive 278 Clarity? {15 levels above aforementioned}.>

<What is Positive 278 Clarity?> Kim asked.

<Were you not briefed to Level 234 {11 levels above Primary Seclusion}, Section 4 at the decontamination facility about your rights?> Har questioned with concern.

<We read the rules, but it was a lot to take in.>

<By coming to our society, the rings granted you limited rights. By Act 871, your thoughts are on record.>

<I guess,> Kim said.

<We will begin. By the ring, you must state all necessary details in the first order.>

<You want us to tell the truth?> Gabe guessed.

<By the state and the rings, by haste. Indeed.>

<Look, this isn't working,> Kim thought. <It does not help us when you keep referring to legal ring stuff. We understand. You need the truth.>

<By the full ring, under Article 232 of Ring Number Two, are you waiving your rights of the full prospect of numeric translation?> Har asked cautiously.

<I do not know what you mean,> Gabe admitted. <Please ask simple questions, and we will provide straightforward answers.>

Har leaned back in his small chair and thought, <Very well. Did Zan inform you about your requested presence posthaste?>

<Wow, that's much easier to understand,> Kim thought with relief. <To answer your question, you guys became concerned when we stopped using our onks. That's why we are here.>

<That is the secondary reason. By ring law, I require more information on the incident in question.>

<The attack?> Kim asked

<Yes.>

<We will tell you what we know.>

Har contemplated his next question for a long moment and asked with reserved emotions, <Are you aware of the original massacre?>

<Tan told us a little,> Gabe answered.

<Many Veronn lives were lost,> Har informed them.

<That's what he said.>

Har's eyes narrowed as he leaned forward. <Of what else, by the rings, do you know?>

<We work with some Earth government people, and they said an incident occurred in Alaska. The Earth's public is unaware that anything happened.>

<Did your government provide you with precise details?>

<No, and I do not think my government has all the information. The incident occurred a long time ago, and the records are incomplete.>

<Most unusual,> Har commented. He nodded and thought, <During the incident, many prominent Veronn were present.>

<Ahh, I get it. A lot of important Veronn got killed.> Gabe concluded with a nod.

<A tragedy of the first order.>

<And you guys are still upset by what happened?> Gabe asked with concern.

<Some are,> Har admitted with regret.

<That guy Din was angry as heck about his family dying,> Gabe said, filling in the blanks.

<By the ring, he made that apparent in the first order,> Har sadly thought.

Har was acting cagy, and Kim and Gabe got the impression that the incident had much more behind it.

Har briefly squinted as if he had picked up on their suspicion and changed the subject. <Will you confirm two facts in the most honest?>

<Of course,> Gabe replied.

<The floating vessel they stationed you two on. For what purpose did it serve?>

<It was a cruise ship for families.>

<A military transport?> Har probed.

<No. We were on vacation.>

<On what level of armaments were present?> Har asked and narrowed his eyes.

<What are you talking about? It was a pleasure ship.>

<We have detailed records of the deployed weapons.>

<Wait. Does your planet have ships? Or boats? Do those words translate?>

<We possess water floating vessels,> Har answered, confused.

<Are some for sightseeing? Or tourists? Or having fun?>

<We possess floating vessels for pleasure excursions. Our citizens may rent them upon desire.>

<How many weapons do they have?>

<None,> Har answered, befuddled and biting his upper lip.

<The same as our cruise ship.>

<This cannot be correct. Our records show that the floating vessel construction contained heat-treated iron Type 922 {basic steel}.>

<Yes, we make cruise ships with steel. But they have no weapons,> Gabe corrected, still not understanding the issue.

<You intended this floating vessel to be used for pure pleasure? No armaments?> Har asked, more confused.

<Of course not,> Gabe thought with annoyance. <Why would a cruise ship have guns?>

<Our records showed a massive energy displacement from the floating vessel. Type 7 {10.2 kilowatts per square centimeter} energy exchanges. Most dangerous to an approaching craft.>

<What are you talking about?> Gabe asked with annoyance. <There were no energy exchanges. A massive yellow flash cut the ship in half. Nothing more.>

<This cannot be proper. I have visual records. Observe.>

Their onks displayed a high-level view of the ocean. The family watched as the cruise ship lights came into view. Gabe and Kim instantly remembered that horrific night. Suddenly, pulsed green light beams shot from the smokestack of the cruise ship. From a visual perspective, the spacecraft took evasive action to avoid the energy beams. Next, numerous numbers appeared in the lower part of the screen, followed by targeting crosshairs. Finally, a confirming indicator appeared, followed by a yellow flash. Gabe and Kim painfully recalled the intense beam that cut through the ship, sending them into the water.

<As such, you have observed,> Har confidently thought. <An offensive Type 7 energy exchange. Explanation complete, by rule of visual logic.>

<Wait, wait,> Gabe thought in great confusion. <What were those silly green flashes coming from the ship's exhaust? That makes little sense.>

<Clearly observe the high-intensity focused visual energy,> Har thought annoyedly.

<Lasers?> Gabe asked.

Their onks worked on a translation, and Har thought, <Yes, 'lasers' is an appropriate description for this proper record.>

<We were on a cruise ship,> Gabe thought and raised his hands in confusion. <You are looking at stupid effects inserted into the video.>

<That is most improper. Additions to the formal record are inconceivable. Allow me to disprove. Tan!>

The door opened, and Tan entered. Har thought, <These Earth beings contradict the official records. Inform of the impossibility.>

<As stated in Paragraph 126 of the official Ring Document 89,021, in our cycle of 8,094, a post-rendered green visual anomaly was added to simulate Type 7 energy exchanges.>

Har stood and harshly thought, <What! By my left hand. By my left hand. Why is the information not presented posthaste in Magnitude 16? {Three levels above a general inquiry.} Why is this in Paragraph 126 and not Paragraph 1? Why am I learning this discrepancy in the post? In the post!>

<In the original report, I stated the anomaly in Paragraph 1.> Tan thought with forced, calm emotions.

<Who altered the official document?> Har demanded. <Strictly forbidden. Strictly forbidden!>

<Observe history,> Tan thought with confidence.

Gabe's and Kim's onks displayed large amounts of complex information loaded with unfamiliar legal jargon. A long moment later, Har leaned back in disbelief and thought, <This is the most impossible. Alteration at the highest order of the royal court. Altered records. Changed paragraphs. More altered records. Tan, I dismiss you. Posthaste, matters are to be discussed at full length.>

Tan bowed and left the office. <Never in my existence has this been of witness to upsets with official records.> Har thought in bewilderment.

<What are you going to do about it?> Kim demanded.

<This is a Magnitude 16 document. I must rectify it to remain proper.>

<Good. Everybody needs to know the truth.>

<Yes. By the most fortunate. The offending incident became halted before high death-death.>

<No, a bunch of people died!> Kim replied angrily, then quickly regretted her outburst.

<By the ring, we recorded low numbers.>

<No, no, no. Many people died— including our families!>

<A verified total of 26.>

Kim sat upright. <What are you talking about? Thirteen thousand four hundred and fifty-one people died!>

Har leaped out of his chair. <By my teeth and the length of my arm! Impossibility. Impossibility!>

<Thirteen thousand four hundred and fifty-one is the official number,> Kim repeated, annoyed with Har's denial. <Check for yourself.>

<Records cannot be altered so far. The closer number is likely 26.>

<Look. There is an easy way to settle this,> Gabe interrupted, hoping to calm the conversation. <Do you have a recent, detailed scan of the area? Or an overview? Does that translate?>

<Of course.>

Gabe's onk displayed a vision of Kuiu Island. He appreciated the superb visual clarity. Gabe figured out how to maneuver the image viewpoint, navigated to the visitor center, and thought, <Look here. See those red stone things. Each one has a bunch of names engraved on the sides. Look, here's one.>

<I see the single inscription.>

<Now, use your visual analysis tools to count the names.>

<Most negative. I will check this fantasy. Records of 26 will be confirmed.>

Their onks processed the image. Har sat up abruptly, a look of stunned defeat on his face. <Confirmation of the sum.>

<That's how many people died, including my family,> Gabe told Har.

<Show me.>

Gabe maneuvered the image to find pillar #25 and recognized the names of his family. Unfortunately, the image still had Victoria's name spelled as "Vactory," which angered him.

Har studied the image, removed his glasses, and turned away. Without turning back, he said regretfully, <In all Veronn, there has never been a tragedy of such magnitude. To compound, someone aggressively altered formal ring records. This is now a dark cycle. I must contemplate the severe nature of the recent discovery. Therefore, I terminate this inquiry to allow my emotions to settle. I dismiss you.>

<Important man Har?> Emma asked.

Har turned back, put on his glasses, and thought, <Yes, daughter Emma?>

<You not know how many people die?>

<The formal ring records were altered. In the present, I know the truth.>

<It make you sad?>

<By the rings, I am sad.>

<You going to tell others of sadness?>

<Yes, daughter Emma.>

<Why you think differently?> Emma questioned with confidence.

<What?>

<Why you want to hide numbers?>

Har was taken aback, and Kim confidently thought, <She's correct. What's the deal?>

A long moment later, Har thought, <The worst life-life loss in our recorded history had been a continent slide. Two buildings collapsed, and 832 expired.>

<You had an earthquake, and 832 died?> Kim clarified.

<In the correct.>

<And that's the worst tragedy your society has ever had?>

<On the truth.>

<Well, the attack that killed my family was a lot worse.>

<The number 13,451 is inconceivable.>

<The dead people deserve a voice.>

<Your thoughts contain truth,> Har admitted weakly.

Har turned back to the family and looked at Emma's face for a long moment. During this time, they conveyed sad emotions.

Har nodded, took a deep breath, and said, <Daughter Emma is in the proper. The fallen deserve respect. I will correct the offending official record and remove the post-rendered fantasy. As it is so. As by the three rings. As is formal by the royal record. As by my personal honor.>

<Thank you,> Kim replied, relieved.

<Your request will be of the difficult. Many royal court upsets will occur.>

<The truth means everything.>

<You will now take your leave as I contemplate the severe topic.>

<Can we count on you?> Kim needed to know.

<When the three rings get summoned, then an agreement must conclude.>

<Good.>

<I enjoyed meeting the family of Gabe. I am sorry it occurred under unfortunate circumstances,> Har regretfully thought. <After clarification, I would like to meet the family again to record more details.>

<We would like to see you again,> Kim answered warmly.

•

The family left the office and met Tan and Zan in the front lobby. Zan was in deep communication with a female Veronn. She stood three feet eight, was thin, and wore a blue shirt with slender pants. Females had longer and higher ears. These features gave her a foxlike appearance that a human would consider attractive. The two had obviously been flirting, and she appeared interested.

Zan waved goodbye to the female, and everybody got into the van. Kim asked Tan, <What happened back there? Why didn't Har know how many people had died?>

<The records were altered.>

<Why?>

<To cover up the magnitude of the event.>

<They tried to get away with covering up the real number?> Kim asked with suspicion.

<By my left foot, truth. In secret, your presence had become one primary reason for requesting your visit.>

<You need us to set the record straight?> Kim added, connecting the dots.

<To force anomaly removal.>

<I see.>

<In short passing, thank you,> Tan thought with gratitude.

<Don't thank me yet. I suspect that Har guy still wants to cover it up.>

<You provided independent visual proof of the alterations during a formal inquiry. The unaltered record will be difficult to contradict.>

<True. Where are we going now?> Kim asked.

<To my domicile,> Than answered.

<Your house?>

<My rented living quarters.>

<Your apartment?> Kim corrected.

<That is a standard translation.>

<What are we going to do?>

<My surprise will be complete.>

<Alright, we like surprises. Hon, put on your happy face.>

<Sure, babe,> Gabe thought warmly.

On the drive, they passed a power station with billowing steam plumes and farms with automated equipment. Two Veronn were repairing a tractor, and Gabe found it funny that they were dressed in wide-brimmed cowboy hats and green denim overalls. After several minutes, they arrived in a district of tall buildings. Two turns later, they entered an underground garage and parked.

Tan led the family to an elevator with low ceilings, which forced Gabe and Kim to sit. They rose 26 stories, and the doors opened into a narrow hallway. Gabe and Kim had to stoop to walk. Tan used a brass key to open a lock on a wooden door, which looked indistinguishable from Earth's. Inside, they sat on a small blue couch.

<It's permitted to take off your masks,> Zan thought warmly.

<But the warnings at the center said not to,> Kim reminded him.

<Booble-snake! {Veronn colloquialism referring to a spotted Yagum.}> Tan declared. <This is my domicile. Here, I hold the rings.>

<Won't you get in trouble or get sick?> Kim asked. <Or we could get sick.>

<Contamination procedures presented full success.>

Kim looked down, and Emma had taken off her mask. Gabe and Kim looked at each other and took off their masks. Their first breath detected the aroma of cooking. A side door opened, and a Veronn boy ran out. He stood two feet ten, dressed in black shorts and a colorful green shirt decorated with yellow triangles. He did not wear shoes, and Kim found his tiny toes cute.

"Zic!" Emma shrieked.

The boy ran over. They bumped fists, turned around twice, and hugged each other. Then, they both ran back in the same direction, and Zic shut the door.

<What the heck?> Kim thought, confused.

<My son, Zic,> Tan answered with a grin. <He has been eager to meet daughter Emma. Zic took it upon duty to guide her through the first onk introduction.>

<He taught her how to use an onk?> Kim asked.

<The event has been most distracting for his education. As it is such, children. What can you do?>

<That's funny,> Kim thought with a big grin.

<Now on to important. For this surprise segment, face shields are necessary to maintain ring law.>

<You need our masks on for the next part?>

<On point, yes.>

Kim and Gabe put on their masks. Zan brought over what they thought was a video camera and had them sit beside each other on the couch. Zan looked at the camera image and adjusted the room lights. Their onks thought, {Interacting with the public database and interested individuals. Observe full disclosure laws and proceed with all noted cautions.}

Zan sat in a chair next to them, counted from four to one, and thought, <A big friend Zanger Longeer of the family Garp. Hey, you Veronn out there in the eager comments. Full surprise. With me is—>

Zan seemed to wait for a response, and he then thought, <Think your names, human.>

<Gabe. Um. Gabriel of the family Alexander. Call me Gabe. And this is Kimberly of the family Alexander. Um, call her Kim.>

<Perfect, perfect. Now, told you two of a big surprise. This is an interview for the entire Veronn!>

<You are interviewing us for the entire planet?> Kim thought with disbelief. <In your apartment?>

<Most correct!> Zan thought with great enthusiasm.

<This is a surprise.>

<By my teeth, yes! This is the big surprise! We have important questions in full order!>

<Everybody wants to know about us?> Kim asked. <Really?>

<By my full arm and both my hands! First question. Why is Cosmo Kramer so disrespectful to his proximity friends?>

The question caught Kim by surprise. <What?>

<On joking, you.>

<I don't understand. Hon, do you get this?>

<No,> Gabe answered, just as confused. <What are you asking?>

<Earth broadcast *Seinfeld,*> Zan answered.

<The TV show?> Gabe asked.

<By my hand, yes.>

<The *Seinfeld* TV show? Do you want to know about the Kramer character?>

<In truth, correct,> Zan said with an encouraging gesture.

Incredulous, Gabe asked, <And this is the big surprise?>

<Yes!>

Gabe and Kim were shocked. They looked at each other, and Kim thought, <Well, I haven't watched much *Seinfeld*. So, I don't know what I can tell you.>

<I only watched a few episodes,> Gabe admitted with embarrassment.

<Well, by the leg, lead us to an answer. Why the constant disrespect?>

<Um. I don't know,> Kim admitted. <His character is supposed to be funny. That's all.>

<Are you telling all Veronn that humor became Cosmo Kramer's only motivation?>

<I guess.>

<See, brother, I provided the correct theory.>

Tan walked behind the sofa to be in camera view and thought, <Younger brother, you are in error. Cosmo Kramer provides more than a mild humor foil. His character served as the full learning portal to Jerry Seinfeld's character. Number Zero. Observe the eternal optimist aspect. Number One. Observe sarcastic comments over the full duration. Conclusion. Cosmo Kramer is a central character of Type 21 {superb humor foil}.>

Gabe and Kim found the conversation difficult to follow. Then Kim became sidetracked by dance music coming from Zic's room. Emma had happy thoughts and did her best to move to the music. <By the rings, I see many comments,> Zan interrupted her thoughts.

Gabe and Kim's onk displayed several lists. Zan selected Garellgion Tonnac of the family Groon, <Tan, you're most incorrect. Cosmo Kramer is a product of pure humor. Observe.>

Gabe and Kim began viewing a segment of *Seinfield*. In it, the character Kramer pretends to be a police officer who interrogates a suspect. Simultaneously, he steals items. Gar thought, <As such. Complete comedy. Jerry Seinfeld cannot be present for the scene. Your conclusion?>

Gabe had never seen this episode and neutrally responded, <That looked funny to me. Babe?>

<Seemed funny,> Kim admitted.

<Proof as positive. Next,> Zan thought and selected Giagonna Tiller of the family Dren, <Lady man. Explain in full detail.>

Gabe and Kim did not understand, and Kim asked, <What is 'lady man?'>

<You will observe.>

Their onks began displaying the television show *MASH.* In the scene, Klinger invented an excuse to fly home to see his sick father. Unfortunately, the onks provided an incorrect translation, referring to Klinger as "Lady man of Position 3" and Colonel Blake as "Boss-man 2 of Position 5."

<Wait, wait,> Gabe interrupted with confusion. <I used to be a huge *MASH* fan, and I remember this episode. First, his name is Max Klinger. Not lady man. Second, he is not of Position 3; his rank title is corporal. Now, this episode is hilarious. Klinger is trying to convince Colonel Blake that his father is dying. Then, Colonel Blake shows him all the past letters he faked.>

<Why is Corporal Max Klinger a gender perplex?> Gia asked, even more confused.

Gabe explained the show's history, plot, and characters. Gia and others asked many questions, and they were stymied because the show was fictional, but the Korean War was not. Zan explained that a show of this type would be impossible on Veronn out of respect for the dead.

The interview changed to the television show *The Dukes of Hazzard* and then *Alf.* Gabe and Kim enjoyed explaining quirky Earth television culture while clearing up the confusion. However, they found it odd that the advanced Veronn could not distinguish between actors and their characters.

The subject shifted to movies, and Gabe and Kim could not believe how popular the obscure movie *Spaced Invaders* was. Gabe barely remembered it, and Kim was unaware of its existence.

Kim asked about the types of programs the Veronn liked to watch, and the immediate answer was "Interact with Boo!" Gabe and Kim selected the most famous episode and played a clip from it. Their onks altered their visual perception, and they found themselves immersed in a three-dimensional brick room with tacky furniture. In the center, a young Veronn male stared at Gabe and Kim with comical emotions. The pair looked at each other, surprised to see their altered appearance.

Gabe appeared like a Veronn male, and Kim was a Veronn female. She wore a polka-dot suit with two fake arms attached, and he had an outlandish yellow suit with a comical blue hat. Gabe held a long green stick in his right hand, and Kim held a fake four-legged fur animal in her arms. The onk allowed them to change their view (where their eyes looked) but did not let them feel the objects or move their simulated bodies.

Boo stood in front of them. He had dressed in a white-and-black diagonally striped outfit. Boo turned around twice, looked at the pair, and asked, <Do you want me to touch my nose?>

The pair were unsure what was happening, and Kim answered with suspicion, <I guess.>

Boo spun around, swayed to the side, twisted his hands, and challenged, <I'll do it. I will.>

<It's fine,> Gabe thought. <We're not stopping you.>

<I'll touch it.>

<We're still not stopping you,> Gabe confirmed, confused.

Boo spun around again, and then he touched his nose. He then laughed with a high-pitched whine and touched his nose again. A long moment later, their vision returned, and they saw that Tan had fallen over with laughter. Gabe turned to Kim and shrugged.

Confused, Kim asked, <I don't get it. Does touching your nose have significance on your planet?>

Tan laughed even harder, struggling to breathe. Their onks showed a massive humorous reaction and wild comments. The onk summed up the comments, {The humans do not understand. Even more funny!}

<By my finger touching my nose, you experience the best double joke,> Tan thought, still chuckling.

<What?> Gabe asked.

<The first joke contained the nose, and the second is simulating a recorded broadcast,> Zan thought.

<Meaning?>

<On point! A third joke!>

<I still don't get it,> Kim thought. <We knew we were on a live show.>

<Really?> Zan asked.

<Yes, we knew we were interacting with somebody.>

<Most funny!>

Eventually, the humor died down enough for Tan to explain that asking a Veronn to touch their nose in public is outrageously forward—and therefore funny. However, Gabe and Kim did not understand why this timid act impressed anybody, especially a sophisticated society with spaceships capable of flying to distant planets.

The Veronn audience asked more questions and provided a list of other Veronn programs. Most shows were slapstick, light drama, or dramatic readings of poems. The nonfiction programs were news, documentaries, sports, and precision dancing.

One unique aspect of Veronn culture was its obsession with the stock market. Every Veronn was passionately invested in and closely watched the market. There were hundreds of commentators, information sites, and opinion forums. The Veronn were unaware that Earth also had stock markets.

Next, Gabe and Kim asked whether the Veronn population liked soap operas, reality shows, thrillers, horror, adult shows, or detective shows. Tan explained that the government restricted adult content, and the other show types were undesirable. Gabe and Kim found it odd that they had never watched a quiz show. When asked why, Tan explained, <Mastering specific knowledge is pointless.>

One dramatic show stood out. An elderly Veronn woman had spent three full cycles searching for her missing son. In the clip they watched, she discovered that her son had survived a spaceship failure, but he prevented her from finding him. The pair enjoyed the show's emotional intensity and profound sorrow. When the clip ended, Gabe and Kim knew this show would be an instant hit on Earth.

After their interview, all parties agreed that more discussions would be welcome. Tan said goodbye to the audience and turned off the video camera. Gabe and Kim looked at each other and removed their masks.

<Wow,> Kim thought with relief.

<You two pleased the masses,> Zan thought with happiness.

<We are glad they enjoyed it.>

<Enough in the present,> Tan said. <By the sense of your onk, nourishment is required. I profess I am an excellent meal preparer. Relax in the moment.>

<Need any help?> Kim asked.

<In households, males do all chores and, as such, the cooking.>

<Must be nice.>

<Your comment indicates that the roles are reversed on Earth?>

<Sometimes.>

<What of your household?>

<We both cook,> Kim answered.

<What is your favorite dish?>

<I make great lasagna.>

<The translation of the term lasagna is improper. Inform of the ingredients.>

<It has cheese, tomato sauce, big noodles, a different cheese, and cooked ground beef.>

<Cheese is the product of lactate?> Tan's eyes narrowed.

<You mean milk?>

<Yes, lactate,> Tan agreed.

<Cheese is made from lactate.>

Tan looked annoyed and thought with disapproval, <We do not consume lactate. Most distasteful.>

<We like it.>

<Very well. Are tomatoes of the vegetable domain?>

<Yes.>

<And what of beef?> Tan wanted to know.

<It's from a cow?>

<An animal?>

<Yes.>

<Most crude. Most crude!>

<Are you all vegetarians?> Kim asked.

<By the hand and the eyes, we are! It is a disgrace to embark on the consumption of flesh.>

<Hey, I understand. I have vegetarian friends. So, it's all good.>

Tan stomped into the kitchen area in a huff.

<Brother is hoody-fine over being a proper vegetarian,> Zan thought with a laugh. <In truth, some Veronn eat flesh.>

<We understand.>

<By my arm, that is good,> Zan thought.

<What happens after dinner?> Kim asked.

<You have two goals before you. Number 0. Make an entry into the Galactic Database. I will explain that procedure posthaste. Number 1. Return to the departure point.>

<We have spent so little time here,> Kim thought, disappointed.

<Rules are standard for first-time visitors. You are permitted one cycle of presence unless you have special permission. Because of proper behavior, your next trip will have time extensions.>

<I see.>

<You desired to do something else?> Zan asked.

<We have these medical issues,> Gabe explained. <Apparently, they result from our minds not being calibrated during faster-than-light travel.>

<Ahh, an Upset Dimensional Calibration Phase Disturbance Type 19 {Four levels above passive disturbance}. Most common. I was unaware you were suffering from this malady.>

<Can it be fixed?> Gabe asked.

<By the rings, yes,> Zan answered confidently.

<Can we stop by a hospital to have somebody look at us?>

Zan smiled. <By my arm, you are unaware. Your onk may correct this malady. Observe.>

Gabe and Kim were directed to the "interdimensional calibration corrections" menu. They found incomplete calibrations, and Zan guided them to a travel history menu. They were stunned to learn that they had traveled to Veronn nine times. This occurred when they were taken from Kuiu Island while unconscious. Zan showed them how to select each trip as "active" and move those records to the interdimensional calibration corrections menu. Their onks thought, {Proper calibration established. A mental adjustment will occur over the next 38 cycles.}

<You directed your onks to correct all variations,> Zan explained. <As stated, the process will require 38 cycles. Now, caution. Do not disconnect onks for the duration or incomplete results.>

<Our onks work in the background to fix the health problem?> Gabe asked excitedly.

<A correct summary,> Zan answered.

<And then we will feel better? No more headaches, twitches, or dizziness?>

<Another correct summary.>

<Thank you!> Gabe thought.

<The pleasure is on this side.>

Kim smelled something wonderful, and she asked, <What's Tan cooking?>

<Knowing older brother with such precision, he is making tuble kane {acidic Veronn meal}. Does the smell not entice?>

<It smells good.> Kim felt her stomach rumble with hungry anticipation.

<Indeed,> Zan thought.

<We heard about foods that change flavor. Is that what he is cooking?>

<Van koof? {Interactive food}. No, such edibles are prohibited on Veronn.>

<Why?> Kim asked.

<Van koof is addictive and not nutritious. Consuming such cuisine has damaged many societies.>

<Oh, I guess that makes sense. Anyway, should I get Emma and Zic ready for dinner?>

<Most wise.>

Kim walked to the door, knocked, and entered. Inside, she found a small bedroom with posters of Veronn athletes playing with a blue ball. To her, it looked exactly like her younger brother's room with his basketball posters. Emma and Zic were playing tag. <We are about to have dinner,> Kim told them.

<Sixteen subcycles,> Emma thought with annoyance.

<Now!>

<Yes, Mommy Kim.>

<Understand, Daughter Emma,> Zic thought with regret. <Sorry, lady Kim.>

<Did you get this Mommy Kim and Daddy Gabe stuff from talking to Zic?>

<Of course, Mommy Kim,> Emma answered with a giggle.

Kim rolled her eyes but smiled. <This explains a lot.>

They walked to a large green table. Emma sat in a chair, but Gabe and Kim had to sit on the floor. Gabe liked the tan/gray plates and three-prong forks, while Kim appreciated the silver holders containing pink wax candles. The door opened, and Tan walked out carrying a small black pot with a red lid. Zan and Zic looked impressed as Tan placed the pot in the center of the table. He opened the top, releasing a cloud of steam and a powerful vinegar scent.

<I can see that the smell entices you,> Tan happily thought.

Gabe and Kim nodded. Tam used a slotted spoon to scoop out cubed white vegetables. Gabe and Kim waited anxiously, anticipating what the dish would taste like, and communicated their desire to each other. Tam placed a scoop of approximately 20 cubes, each the size of a pea, on each plate, then sat.

Emma almost grabbed a cube with her hand when Zan cautioned, <Daughter Emma. We must wait. As such, the telling of thanks. I will begin posthaste. I am grateful for meeting the family of Gabe. In addition, I am grateful for the food preparation. As the next male elder, Gabe, please.>

Gabe looked around and thought, <Oh. This is like saying grace before dinner. Alright. Well, my mother always told us that our health is the most important thing. So, I am grateful for my good health and the good health of those at the table. Second, I am grateful for my wonderful family and for being here with Tan, Zic, and Zan.>

Tan thought with warm emotions, <A wonderful telling. I am grateful for the knowledge to make this food and the wonderful company. Mother Kim.>

<I am grateful to be in the presence of such wonderful individuals and this delicious food. In Jesus's name. Amen.>

<Who is Jesus?> Tam wondered.

<A man who is part of my religion. He died for our sins.>

<He died for my sins? I cannot comprehend your meaning,> Tam thought in confusion.

<It is part of the story behind my faith.>

<A resurrection component?> Tam thought with interest.

<I guess that term applies.>

<Most intriguing. We will have to explore this topic at a later date. Now, daughter Emma. What are you thankful for?>

<I am thankful for meeting Zic! I am thankful for Mommy Kim and Daddy Gabe being so nice.>

<Son Zic, what are you thankful for?>

<I am thankful for my father, Tan, the rings, and for meeting Kim and Gabe. I am also thankful for meeting cutie-cutie Emma.>

<Excellent thoughts by all.> Zan thought with warm emotions. <By my left arm, please experience tuble kane.>

Gabe used his fork to take a bite of the vegetable cube. It tasted strongly of vinegar. He swallowed with great effort. Kim and Emma had the same experience. Zic, Tan, and Zan enjoyed the food, smiling.

<Too much acid?> Tan asked with repressed emotions.

<This is not what we are used to,> Kim admitted with regret.

<I know,> Tan thought with humor.

<You know?>

<We have a full report of your stomach contents from former encounters.>

<Then why are you serving this?> Kim asked, concerned.

<In our culture, serving an unpleasant first meal is a grand custom. This creates a desire for the next.>

<You were messing with us?> Gabe smiled.

<By the rings, I served you tuble kane. The harshest Veronn dish!>

Tan, Zic, and Zan laughed.

<Alright,> Gabe thought with a chuckle. <We fell for that one. What else have you got?>

Tan smiled and returned to the kitchen. He brought out a green pot with a blue lid and opened it. The food smelled smoky and sweet with a hint of olive. Tan placed a scoop on each of their plates. It looked like creamy red apple sauce with small, round brown chunks.

Emma ate a large portion with her fork and seemed to be in heaven. Gabe took a bite and enjoyed the hearty cheese flavor with a mild, earthy nut finish. Kim took a big bite and appreciated the smoky flavor. Tan saw the joyful expressions and served another larger scoop to the family members.

<I knew they would like it,> Zan thought happily. <We call this Yarro {a cuisine from the Zalon region often served in morning meals}. The brown bits are the seed of the zean {from the daroon plant}. When we cook them, they are referred to as glen and doon {great times together}. Tan is a meal preparation master of the first order.>

In between bites, Gabe thought with pleasure, <Wow, this is wonderful. And it's made from vegetables?>

<Of course,> Tan thought with pride.

<This is the best vegetable dish I have ever had,> Kim said. <It tastes so creamy.>

<Most true.>

Tan then brought out an orange pot with a yellow lid, containing steamed green and orange vegetables. The family found it amusing that the green vegetables tasted like carrots and the orange vegetables tasted like asparagus. Everyone gobbled up the meal, and afterward they relaxed and engaged in small talk. Tan cleaned the plates and returned with purple bowls and small blue spoons. He then produced a white plastic box with pictures of a leafy plant on the side and opened it. Next, Tan placed scoops of black frozen froth into the dishes.

<This looks like ice cream,> Kim thought.

<An accurate assessment,> Tan happily thought. <Try.>

Kim took a bite and found it tasted like sweet poppy seed gelato. <Wow, this is fantastic.>

The rest of the group enjoyed dessert, and after Tan had cleared the plates, they sat on the sofa.

<On to Assignment 0,> Zan said. <It is long overdue to set your planet into the Galactic Database.>

<What's that?> Kim asked, curious.

<All participating Division 6 planets require an entry. Results will record status and development.>

<Where do we begin?>

Their onks began interfacing with the Veronn central computers, which interfaced with over a million off-world computers. They were presented with nine categories. The first concerned their planet type. The classifications considered oceans, mountains, atmosphere, gravity, size, vegetation, and animal species. From the list, Earth perfectly fit category 16.

The second category determined the "species evolution stage." This category defined the dominant species, but it was highly ambiguous. Kim reviewed all the possibilities and determined that Earth fell into evolution stage eight.

The third section recorded their level of physical development. Kim reasoned that humans lacked telepathy, genetic manipulation, advanced mental abilities, and many redundant organs, which led to category five.

The fourth section Kim addressed was society. Earth has many countries with different government types, rights, and laws. There is no central governing body, universally accepted agreements, a common currency, or shared agendas. In addition, humans have not abolished warfare. This lack of commonality and understanding resulted in category four.

Gabe reviewed the fifth section, technology. Earth scientists split atoms, developed worldwide communication, and explored the local orbiting planets. However, there were significant gaps in communication, biology, genetics, medicine, computers, and physics. Gabe found it interesting that the most extensive missing area concerned the interactions between branches of science, such as physics and biology. Four entire categories were unknown to Gabe. He drew the logical conclusion that Earth was at a technology level of three.

The last four sections were all zeros. Other than their family, no human could use an onk, and nobody on Earth had built a faster-than-light craft. Gabe did not understand anything in the "active quantum entanglement spin duration" category, and no human could make Kebos.

Once the section numbers were entered, Earth was established as a Type 2 planet (undeveloped). Additionally, the database offered other options. The first concerned their reassessment. Typically, assessments occur every 54 years; the pair considered this a reasonable interval.

Another option addressed external interaction. Gabe and Kim discussed it, and they selected "no interaction requested until a reevaluation," which seemed the most appropriate choice given the strict DLS policies on off-world non-interaction. This request included the provision of continued interaction with races that had prior contact.

# TWENTY-TWO

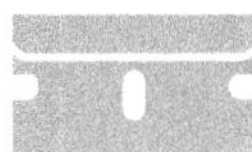

Gabe and Kim bade farewell to Zic and Tan. Emma cried and refused to stop hugging him. Zic held her with all his might, and it took several minutes to separate the two. Zan them out of the apartment while Emma continued crying. Gabe and Kim experienced her vivid, painful emotions as they rode the elevator to the parking area.

The sun had set, and the yellow streetlights were on. As Zan drove them away, the mood was somber. They took a different road, and Zan told them about the local community. Five minutes later, Emma stopped crying and looked out the window without interest. Kim held her hand as she pointed out sights. Zan drove the van to a large parking lot of what looked like a mall. The group got out, and Zan thought, <Of the too depressing. We have a brief period before departure. It is most logical that you have never experienced a Kebo through a Dotsun?>

Gabe still felt Emma's depression, and he absently answered, <No, but it sounds interesting.>

<Inside is a facility whereby we can rent a Dotsun for your body configuration.>

The group walked to the mall entrance, and inside, shops sold clothing, household items, shoes, kitchen appliances, food, and furniture. Several Veronn walked about, and one couple had a stroller. The family stopped and admired a girl who looked nearly indistinguishable from a human baby except for her ears. This encounter brightened Emma's mood.

They continued window shopping, and Gabe noticed the hardware store. He recognized pliers, wrenches, and drill bits in the front display case. It amused Gabe to see their lumber and plumbing section. Kim also enjoyed the mall and liked the impressive selection of shoes and fashionable jumpsuits. She saw three stores selling women's gloves and surmised that gloves were essential accessories. Emma brightened when she saw a toy store with fluffy stuffed animals in the display case.

Zan guided them toward the mall's center, where they came to a facility with a big sign, {Kebos and Dotsun by the subcycle. Enjoy, enjoy.} Near the entrance, a crowd of young Veronn had gathered, and they were laughing as they tossed a blue ball to each other. They looked at the family with amusement, and a female thought with great joy, <The family of Alexander!>

<Indeed, is the truth,> Zan confirmed. <Time is of low. We must proceed.>

<On point. By my finger. Party on, Garth.>

Gabe recognized the line from the popular movie *Wayne's World* and thought, <Party on, Wayne.>

Everybody except Emma laughed. Zan interfaced with a computer terminal at the entrance, which led them down a hallway to what appeared to be a locker room. Three small doors popped open from a dispenser, and Zan selected packages from each. The cardboard packaging with colorful writing reminded Gabe of a recently purchased power tool.

Zan directed the family to a room with black walls and thought, <By the by. Zan informed of human modesty. I will wait outside in the short duration. Inside is a sterile enclosure. Remove collective protective garments and replace them with Dotsun. I have selected my favorite Kebo.>

The family walked inside, and Kim closed the door. They took off their collective protective garments and opened the packages. Inside, they saw a thin, black plastic outfit with wires and devices. When they put on the suits, they interfaced with their onks.

Kim had expected a Star Trek, Holodeck-like device, where a person entered a simulated reality with music. Instead, became overwhelmed by the astounding new sensations as her body transitioned into a Veronn girl.

Kim was now able to vividly comprehend the girl's body, thoughts, emotions, smells, sounds, and tastes. Her arms felt smaller, and they moved faster. The girl had four fingers and four tiny toes. Kim felt her Veronn body breathing, pumping blood, moving her arms, walking in shoes, and her mind creating Veronn thoughts. She experimented with this reality; her fingers touched themselves, and her eyes blinked. Kim began walking on a beach with green sand and flowing waves.

Gabe also experienced this profoundly emotional moment and felt his new clothing, thoughts, body, and emotions of the keen {actress}. Gabe enjoyed her fluid thoughts and even experienced her positive wishes and uplifting desires.

As the Kebo adapted to Emma's body, she was overjoyed to be an older Veronn girl.

When the Dotsun sensed the individual had become comfortable, the routine began. Far (her name) started a well-choreographed dance routine where she "let it be known to all that this is a glorious cycle." Far's performance featured precise dance moves, singing, skillful gymnastics, clever props, cunning mental tricks, excitement, and surprise at the male guest star, "Dlu, the tactile dancer."

The Kebo uplifted the family to a new state of happiness while they appreciated Far's radiant outlook. It impressed Kim that Far choreographed her breathing and heartbeats to the musical beat.

When the routine concluded, Far thanked the viewers for enjoying her Kebo. The family continued thinking about their glorious cycle as they returned to feeling human. Then, the Kebo displayed hundreds of credits and pictures of Far practicing her routine. The family realized that Far had spent her entire life preparing for this single Kebo.

Their Dotsuns disabled their body interface. The family sat for a long moment to appreciate their experience and return to a normal frame of reference. Then, Emma jumped up and thought, <Again, again!>

<Maybe next time,> Gabe thought, smiling.

The family changed back into their environmental suits, and when they met up with Zan, Emma asked him if they could experience Zic's favorite Kebo, "Funny Ran, and his serious dance."

Zan laughed and answered, <Next time.>

<Wow, that felt amazing,> Kim thought. <It's strange getting back to being human.>

<Indeed,> Zan thought. <By the rings, I knew the experience would improve daughter Emma's feelings.>

<I feel some better,> Emma admitted.

<It's a good cycle.>

<How often do people experience Kebos?> Kim asked.

<I sense concern of the first magnitude.>

<I can see that people could get addicted to an experience like that,> Kim suggested.

<The government strictly regulates Kebo viewing numbers.>

<Do other worlds have this problem?>

<By my arm, some planets have an enormous Kebo addiction.>

Kim nodded. <I can see why.>

<You have another question?>

<Why did Far spend so much time training to make that Kebo? And what did all the other Veronn listed in the credits work on?>

<For some, making Kebos is a calling. For others, it is the glory. Still others, it is the money-money. On the other point of your question. You have failed to grasp the amount of effort to make a proper Kebo. It takes many full cycles to perfect a single performance. Technicians are involved and apply personal efforts to tingle the user. Most of the effort concerns adapting the Kebo to all body types.>

<I think I understand. But why are Kebos so important? Why are governments so protective?>

<By my toe, I do not have a complete answer in the first degree,> Zan admitted. <It is said that a Kebo is the best achievement a planet can make.>

<Do the Veronn like Kebos from other worlds?>

<Of course,> Zan quickly answered and then turned toward Gabe. <By my nose, I sense you have a personal question. Switching to direct communication mode.>

Gabe's onk displayed a menu he had not explored, allowing him to communicate only with Zan. <Oh, I didn't realize you read my thoughts. I let my mind drift. Sorry.>

<On point. Fine. Ask your question.>

<Alright. On Earth, we have lots of intimate videos,> he thought with reserved emotions. <You know. Sex. I would think sexy Kebos would be everywhere.>

<I understand your inquiry. With great sorrow, it is true. Kebos of a kissy-kissy content is present. Strictly forbidden. In the short answer, criminal-criminal permit use in seclusion. By my arm and the rings, I have no interest. Zero punishment is not worth the limited pleasure.>

<Makes sense.>

<Did you notice?> Zan asked coyly.

<Notice what?>

<Far's missing reproductive organs.>

<I wondered about that,> Gabe admitted with embarrassment.

<By primary ring law. All Kebos for public display must obfuscate the sensitive anatomy aspects.>

<That answers some questions.>

<All first-time Kebo participants inquire on that topic.>

<Thanks for the information.>

<By my knee!> Zan chuckled.

Gabe switched his onk back to normal and thought, <What now?>

<By the rings, our time has passed,> Zan answered. <It is urgent to get back to the departure point.>

<I wish we could stay longer,> Kim thought.

As they walked back to the van, Gabe had another question. <Hey, Zan?>

<Yes.>

<Did the Veronn modify Kim and me to be telepathic?>

<We applied an individual treatment to update your minds for proper understanding.>

<How did we pass that along to the people we interacted with?>

Zan looked puzzled. <Explain.>

<We passed telepathic ability to our friends when we exercised. I think it had to do with the way we used our fur-mow.>

<Most improper. I have no information on such an occurrence.>

<How did Emma become telepathic?>

<The scanning equipment at the decontamination facility revealed that a telepathic update was applied. It contained advanced methods.>

<Would you explain this?> Gabe inquired.

<Our database did not correlate information about the update.>

<Can you tell us anything else about it?>

<Another race altered her development.>

<Oh. Do you know which one?>

<By my arm, no.>

<Hey, I have a question,> Kim thought.

<Indeed,> Zan thought back.

<When we applied the calibrations to our minds to correct for the past faster-than-light travels, it said spaceships took us to your planet nine times. What's up with that?>

<Your surprise is clear, yet the answer contains no surprise. The reports I provided were of the dubious, and government officials requested confirmations.>

<You mean that your government did not believe we were just people trying to survive?>

<Your summary is of the too high level. Our officials did not conceive that your race had…> Zan paused and thought with timid emotions, <Minimum intelligence.>

<You needed nine trips to determine that? Couldn't you have done one of your scan thingies on Earth?>

<From our records, your government contains many elements. Ours is the same.>

<Oh, I get it. A bunch of bureaucrats needed convincing.>

<Indeed.>

Kim and Gabe laughed. Then, the family got into the van, and Zan pointed out more sights along the drive. They said a long goodbye at the departure point.

•

Inside, they met the same bored Veronn official. He inquired about their visit and asked several questions, including a long one about the Klinger character from the *MASH* television show. The family then proceeded to individual decontamination rooms. Fortunately, this procedure was less invasive.

Afterward, four Veronn in silky-red jumpsuits came to escort them. Kim and Gabe became concerned as they noticed weapons. The family sensed something had changed.

Their onks communicated, {Entering restricted mode, royal ring three. Outside communication suspended. Recording suspended. Proceed at security Level 15 (maximum), and observe full protocol Type 3 (no exceptions). Proceed with diligence and dignity.}

The family was unsure about these new procedures, and their onks refused to provide additional details. Finally, a door opened, and the four Veronn led the family to an elegant vehicle. It had light blue paint, six tires, and flashing green lights. Their onks refused to translate the writing on the side. Kim thought it looked like a secure limousine. Emma hopped right into a seat with a big smile, while Gabe and Kim needed to stoop. The four Veronn got in, their faces stern.

The vehicle began moving silently as Kim and Gabe wondered where they were headed. Their onk's provided a limited communication ability, so Gabe asked Kim through his mask, "Any ideas?"

"No clue. But something big is up."

"Agreed."

"Do you think we're in danger?"

"I think if we were, they would have put us in handcuffs, or at least these guys would point their guns at us," Gabe concluded.

"True. How ya doing, Emma?"

"Fine, Daddy Gabe," Emma cheerfully answered.

"This will be over soon, sweetie."

"It fine. Veronn always do right."

"Let's hope so."

Ten minutes later, the vehicle came to a gentle stop, and the left door opened. The family saw the entrance to a large, octagonal, three-story building with a grand blue-tiled entryway. The four Veronn exited the vehicle and motioned to the family to follow. They walked through several hallways with exquisite stone sculptures, nature paintings, and objects in protected cases. The sight of a well-used VHS tape of the movie *Spaced Invaders* made Gabe chuckle, and the sight of a musical instrument nearly identical to a violin impressed Kim.

The four Veronn led the family into a grand room with a large blue stone desk. A dignified Veronn male sat behind it, dressed in an immaculate red-velvet-like business jumpsuit. He looked up when they arrived and motioned to three dark-blue chairs. The Veronn male held his right hand in a grand gesture to display two large copper rings. Gabe and Kim did their best to suppress their amusement about the thrifty power symbols.

Their onks communicated, {Notice provided. You are now before the two rings holder. Entering restricted communication mode. Thoughts to be recorded for declared record. Respect and honesty is demanded.}

The Veronn male thought with calm emotions, <As proof, I present my two rings in supreme upstanding. No doubt in the first to which manifest or be admonished.>

The family did not understand, and the Veronn waited for a response. Gabe did not wish to offend this individual and looked to the other four Veronn guards for help. Kim felt the tension building and came up with a neutral response.

<Hi, ring man!> Emma joyfully interrupted. <How you doing on this fine cycle?>

The Veronn male was unsure why Emma was communicating and asked, <Of what in the supreme article by the ring prime draws my attention?>

<You funny, ring man. Mommy Kim and Daddy Gabe not going to understand formal-formal ring speak.>

<By official credo of the first?>

Gabe worried that Emma would get them arrested, while Kim appreciated Emma's shrewd ability to bridge the communication gap.

<No, ring man,> Emma answered with joy. <Mommy Kim and Daddy Gabe still did not understand. Please think normal. It alright. Your right hand will preserve rings in the first order.>

The Veronn male seemed to ponder this request for a long moment. He then thought in reserved emotions, <I am Samvral Kuler of the family Bean the Twelfth. My status is the supreme two-ring holder. You may refer to me as Samvral the Twelfth.>

<You are the king of this world?> Kim asked.

<Most is the incorrect. Older brother Pareron Kuler of the family Bean the Sixteenth is the glorious holder of the three rings. Younger brother Konifon Kuler of the family Bean the Seventeenth is the single ring holder.>

The family found the family name Bean funny. Samvral the Twelfth picked up on their amusement, and he did not understand its source. <Gabriel of the family Alexander, do you disrespect the rings?> he asked with concern.

Gabe hesitated. <This is about what I said in prison, right?>

<Indeed,> Samvral the Twelfth answered with narrow eyes.

<Hey, look. Din tried to justify his actions with lies. This ticked me off, and my outburst made it seem like I disrespected the Veronn government. That was a mistake, and I'm super sorry for my actions.>

<And by the rings, you respect our laws?>

<I don't understand your laws, but I do my best to lead an honest life.>

<Indeed.>

Samvral the Twelfth thought for a long moment. He made a fluttering gesture, and the four Veronn guards exited. <Harbineer Vancoot of the family Sarper presented an inconsistency requiring correction.>

<You want us to change the number of people who died?> Kim surmised.

<Indeed.>

<You are asking us to lie?> Kim asked with great concern.

<The record required correction.>

<It's not the truth!> Kim shot back, trying to control her anger. <Thirteen thousand people died. Including my family.>

Kim's anger frightened Gabe, and he gestured to her to calm down.

<Of what is your recommendation?> Samvral demanded.

<A Veronn ship killed a bunch of people. You cannot cover that up forever.>

<It will be done!> Samvral the Twelfth strongly responded.

Kim paused and eyed the Veronn. <Wait a minute. What's going on?>

<A Type 2 record correction.>

<No, that's not it.> Kim replied. <You ordered the attack, didn't you?>

<By the rings, I did not participate.>

<You don't lie well.>

<My thoughts are most fluid, and your accusation endangers ring solitude.>

<It's in your eyes. I can see it.>

<In my eyes?> Samvral the Twelfth asked, his thoughts apprehensive.

<Your eyes jitter when you lie.>

Samvral the Twelfth studied Kim. <Most perceptive. The reports about female Kim contained accuracy.>

<You ordered the attack?> Kim asked again.

<As second in ring order, it is my duty to coordinate our aggressors.>

<And now you want to cover it up?>

<An incorrect assessment. I require the recorded number as 26.>

<It's still a lie,> Kim reminded.

<An error.>

<My family is dead.>

<The incident increased beyond my strict parameters.>

<And the Type 11 Punishment?>

<A unverified level.>

Gabe watched Kim and Samvral the Twelfth argue. He interrupted to defuse the tension. <What are you really asking us to do?>

<The correct record,> Samvral the Twelfth answered, and touched his two rings to show authority.

<Look, we get it. You'll lock us up if we don't tell you 26.>

<How are you to uncover said knowledge?> Samvral the Twelfth asked with deep suspicion. <I guard my thoughts.>

<You guys and your thoughts. You're so used to keeping things all closed that you forget about the big picture. Now, tell us. What's going on?>

Samvral the Twelfth looked at Gabe in disbelief. He stood, walked to a nearby display of ceramic figures, and stared at them for a long moment. Samvral the Twelfth turned around and thought timidly, <My brother will take my rings.>

<That's what this is all about?> Kim asked. <You'll get in trouble?>

<Thirteen thousand, four hundred and fifty-one is too high. There can be no forgiveness for such alteration.>

<You mean you could go to jail?>

<I would be status zero. Never status zero!> Samvral the Twelfth angrily thought.

<You killed a bunch of people. They had families. I had a family. Gabe had a family. They're all dead!>

<On the truth, former distant-sister also perished,> Samvral the Twelfth shot back.

<A bunch of years ago, some human killed your relative? That's not an excuse for Type 11 Punishment.>

<Her status is of the fourteenth. The fourteenth!>

<There's a saying on Earth,> Kim confidently offered. <Two wrongs do not make a right.>

<We have a statement of equivalence.>

Gabe took a deep breath and thought, <We'll give you whatever number you want, but that doesn't solve the problem.>

<You feel that my promise of freedom is insincere?>

Gabe composed his thoughts and concluded with conviction, <I do.>

<On your honor, you said you would respect the rings.>

<This is too important,> Gabe countered.

<You may not disrespect the rings. My honor is now in question. Worst offense. Worst offense.>

<You called our honor into question when you asked us to lie,> Gabe thought angrily. <Is that your definition of honor?>

Kim thought to Gabe with great concern, <Hon, don't push him so hard. He's sheltered from reality.>

<We're fighting for our lives,> Gabe reminded Kim.

<Keep a cool head.>

<I'm trying, but this guy isn't making it easy.>

Samvral the Twelfth thought in a panic, <I can never be status zero. I forbid this possibility. As such, you will become status zero.>

<We can work this out,> Gabe thought with forced pleasant emotions.

<Twenty-six is fine,> Kim offered. <All we ask is that you don't kill us.>

<Status zero is too much.>

<Ring man, you can trust Mommy Kim and Daddy Gabe,> Emma thought confidently.

<On the truth?>

<They best,> Emma thought with a big smile.

Samvral the Twelfth looked at Emma for a long time before thinking with conviction, <Status zero is of the most unpleasant.>

The door opened, and the four Veronn guards appeared. They drew their weapons and pointed them at the family. Samvral the Twelfth looked confident and thought, <By the two rings, detain the family Alexander for inquiry. On the action of extreme ring obfuscation. In the posthaste!>

Gabe started to protest when Emma thought, <Ring man, you stop. Tell truth.>

The four guards looked stunned at the outburst. <By both of my rings, truth is a constant,> Samvral the Twelfth thought, confused.

<You tell truth!> Emma demanded.

<Truth is a constant,> Samvral the Twelfth replied weakly.

<Ring man do kissy-kissy Kebo.>

Samvral the Twelfth took two steps back and thought in a panic, <Never, in royal history has a ring holder experienced kissy-kissy Kebo.

On the word of both rings, always of the truth. Emma of the family Alexander is of the obfuscation. The full obfuscation!>

<No lie, ring man.> Emma pointed her finger at Samvral the Twelfth. <Tell the truth on kissy-kissy.>

<Of such, by the two rings. Away with the family. They are to be status zero. Posthaste. Status zero! Posthaste!>

The four guards felt fear and confusion. They looked at each other while still pointing their weapons. <Tell about kissy-kissy, or I will!> Emma again demanded.

Gabe and Kim now understood what Emma had done. Samvral the Twelfth had not been paying attention to Emma. When she entered his side thoughts about sending the family to prison, he briefly recalled a lusty bondage scene from an adult Kebo. Emma now irritated Samvral the Twelfth with her discovery, and his profound fear caused him to think about the lie.

The four Veronn guards observed Emma's discovery and were unsure of what to do. Samvral the Twelfth looked around in desperation and then ran around his desk. He began shoving Gabe toward the door. Gabe's larger size prevented the much smaller individual from moving him. He stared at Samvral the Twelfth in disbelief.

<No push daddy,> Emma angrily thought. <Ring man. You tell about kissy-kissy. You tell the truth!>

Samvral the Twelfth looked at her with wide eyes, and he stopped shoving. Taking a moment to compose himself, he ran his ringed fingers through his hair, walked to the first Veronn guard, and demanded, <Present your weapon upon inspection. By order of the two ring holder.>

The four Veronn guards looked at each other, and the left one replied shakily, <By agreement between population and the rings. Under 238 Section 19. Holder of the rings may never touch armaments. By my wrist, no exceptions.>

<On command, you will!> Samvral the Twelfth demanded.

<Forbidden by Section 19,> the left Veronn guard weakly repeated.

Samvral the Twelfth screamed, "Yar der feen koop, ongle!" {Present your weapon!}

Everybody stared at each other, and Samvral the Twelfth attempted to pull the gun from the Veronn guard. The other Veronn guards were utterly stunned by the struggle, and the rightmost guard put his weaponless hand over his mouth. The door burst open a moment later, and a vivid thought entered their minds. <Enough!>

Everybody turned to see an older Veronn walk in. He was dressed in similar red velvet, but the cut looked more dignified. The family noticed his right hand had three large copper rings. The four Veronn guards holstered their weapons and stood at attention. Pareron the Sixteenth thought, <Samvral Kuler of the family Bean the Twelfth. Have you removed your shame? You dare request armament? Of the worst!>

<On the rings they—> Samvral the Twelfth started.

<Enough!> Pareron the Sixteenth thought and showed everybody his three rings in a grand gesture.

<On the rings, I—>

<You will inform of the truth,> Pareron the Sixteenth interrupted with disgust.

<I speak the truth, by my arm.>

<By your arm? In the royal court? None of your arm speak is desired.>

<Brother—> Samvral the Twelfth pleaded.

<Holders of the rings never encounter armaments. Priority 1. Number 238. Section 19. That is the sacred agreement that all ring bearers must make with the population. We only rule with words. Always clear!>

<On the rings, I would do no such—>

<On the rings!> Pareron the Sixteenth interrupted in anger. <On the rings? On thought, I observed your request. On voice, I listened to your request. On four royal witnesses observed your request. On family Alexander observed your request. On formal ring record, recorded your thoughts. Clear as purified water. Answer posthaste. Did you request armaments?>

<Brother—>

<By the three rings, you will answer or lose your rings.>

Samvral the Twelfth thought timidly, <Misunderstanding is the result. Mistake in the first order. Armaments not requested. By my right arm. By my left arm.>

<No arm speak. Answer for the recording!> Pareron the Sixteenth thought harshly.

<I made no armament request,> Samvral the Twelfth thought, forcing pleasant emotion into each word.

<None is the formal choice?>

<By my two rings, yes,> Samvral the Twelfth again thought.

<Formal inquiry in progress. Summon the first ring holder and the alternate ring holder.>

The four Veronn guards looked at each other in shock and bowed. Samvral the Twelfth put his head down while Pareron the Sixteenth glared at him. Not knowing what else to do, the family bowed.

A minute later, two Veronn walked into the room. They were dressed in similar red velvet with less dignified cuts. The Alexanders noticed the right one wore a large copper ring.

Pareron the Sixteenth thought with great formality, <Samvral Kuler of the family Bean the Twelfth. You stand accused of violation under 238 Section 19 by your first left finger. Of present, who will witness?>

Reluctantly, each Veronn guard stepped forward, which deeply shocked the two Veronn who had entered. The Veronn without a ring gasped and put his hands over his mouth. Konifon the Seventeenth shook his head and waved his ring hand in a circle.

Pareron the Sixteenth thought with disappointment, <Samvral Kuler of the family Bean the Twelfth. On order, pass along your rings.>

<Brother?> Samvral the Twelfth pleaded.

<Brother? No brother! In the posthaste.>

Samvral the Twelfth looked at the ground for a long moment and removed his two rings. He stared at them and then stretched his arm out, still looking at the ground. Konifon the Seventeenth removed his ring and passed it to the other Veronn, who thought, <Pareron Kuler of the family Bean the Sixteenth. I accept a ring for the first time and agree to all responsibilities.>

The four guards shook their heads, and one gasped. Konifon the Seventeenth accepted the two rings, put them on, and thought, <Pareron Kuler of the family Bean the Sixteenth. I accept the two rings with all their responsibilities.>

<In the records posthaste. Prepare brother for a public inquiry.>

<I—> Samvral the Twelfth briefly thought in agony.

<Away!> Pareron the Sixteenth commanded with authority and anger.

The four guards led Samvral the Twelfth and Konifon the Seventeenth away, along with the other Veronn who held one ring.

<Most of the unpleasant.> Pareron the Sixteenth thought to the family with anger that was not directed toward them.

<Thank you,> Gabe thought with great humility.

<Records cannot be altered.>

<You knew?> Gabe asked with surprise.

<Ring influence allowed me to view the unaltered report.>

<That's why we are here?>

<I hoped younger brother would present honor.>

<This incident must have been difficult.>

<A correct statement. Now to the formality. Gabe of the family Alexander, Kim of the family Alexander, and Emma of the family Alexander. Apology in the first. Harm besieged your world. Thirteen

thousand, four hundred and fifty-one is the correct count. Punishment Type 11 was uncalled for. We will observe Veronn justice in the full.>

<Thank you, Pareron Kuler of the family Bean the Sixteenth,> Gabe thought with gratitude.

<Indeed.>

<You nice, ring man,> Emma thought with joy.

<A wise child. Tell in the primary. How did you uncover younger brother's failure?>

<He thinks kissy-kissy Kebo,> Emma replied with pride.

<Younger brother did not restrict his open thoughts?>

<I trick him.>

<Few have that ability,> Pareron the Sixteenth thought with amusement.

<Thank you, ring man.>

<Kim of the family Alexander, are you aware of how special your child is?>

<We are very proud of her. She is far more intelligent than other children.>

Emma blushed, and Pareron the Sixteenth thought, <This child is special. By my right toe, I will follow her development.>

<Thank you,> Kim thought with happiness.

<Is everything going to be alright?> Gabe asked.

<In our royal history, no ring holder ever violated Section 19. Combined with record alteration and Punishment 11, there will be no avoiding status zero.> A moment later, Pareron the Sixteenth continued with concern. <Immediate transition will be difficult.>

<Is there anything we can do to help?> Gabe asked.

<A generous offer. Perhaps a future visit will suffice.>

<I noticed you had a video of *Spaced Invaders*,> Gabe whimsically thought.

<Humor of the fourth {parody}. So vivid.>

<When we return, we could bring some other videos. I think you would like *The Simpsons*.>

<Indeed. I would also like to discuss the humor behind Cosmo Kramer.>

<We will prepare for a great discussion.>

<Time is in the short cycle. A formal hearing is in order.>

<Thank you for all your help,> Gabe thought warmly.

<A delightful experience with the family Alexander,> Pareron the Sixteenth thought pleasantly. <Most of the meeting of Emma. A safe journey.>

Pareron the Sixteenth stood, briefly bowed, and left the office. Four different Veronn guards, all wearing red collective protective garments, escorted the family to the same vehicle and drove them back to the departure point.

After another decontamination, a different Veronn male pilot led them to a spacecraft and guided them to their integrators.

Fortunately, the family now understood the importance of recording flight calibration data and interfaced their onk's with the ship's systems. They expected to see the same laboratory when the transition occurred, but the image did not appear. Soon, the craft returned to a standard time frame, and the clamshell door opened.

Standing took a minute, and the family reoriented themselves to walking. The Veronn male escorted them down the corridor, and the door opened to a dark evening. Seeing the same field they departed from brought relief.

# TWENTY-THREE

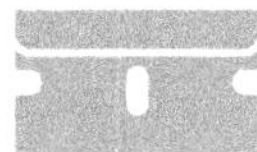

The ramp extended, and the family walked down. When they took two steps beyond, it rapidly retracted, and the ship flew away, leaving the air feeling electric and smelling of ozone. Jason stood nearby in a yellow environmental suit. He smiled when they approached and shook his head with amusement. "Nice outfits."

"Thanks," Kim replied with a grin.

Jason accompanied them to the decontamination area, where they each received a heavy dose of blue foam. A woman in a yellow environmental suit directed them to take off their collective protective garments and spray themselves with a caustic green substance that made their eyes burn.

Afterward, the family changed into the clothes they had brought and were delighted to be allowed to keep their onks. Kim laughed at the sight of Gabe reuniting with his Casio watch. Jason sealed their collective protective garments in oversized plastic biohazard bags, and then they each received two shots of a decontamination agent.

Jason motioned to a man, and he departed. The man stood six foot two with dark brown hair in a sharp crew cut. His eyes, narrowed and intense, seem to bore into Gabe's soul with unwavering focus. The man wore brown slacks and a tan shirt that had sweat stains. When they saw his expression, it was apparent that entering his mind would not be welcomed.

"Describe your recent craft timeline," the man ordered with a New York accent.

"I'm not sure how long the trip took," Gabe answered.

"Guess."

"Ten minutes?"

"Describe the timeline of your trip."

"We were in decontamination for about three hours and spent about seven hours on the planet. Mostly meetings. After that, an hour of decontamination, an hour meeting, another hour of decontamination, and back."

"Did you interact with past or future events?"

"When we were on the craft, the trip felt weird. I think we observed the past and the future at the same time."

"How far in each direction?"

"Um. I guess ten minutes?"

Their interrogator squinted at Gabe. "No other travel?" he demanded.

"No."

"Ma'am, do you agree?"

"Yes," Kim answered.

"Emma?"

"Yes, question man," she answered with a big grin.

The man studied each family member and took out a small instrument with a silver loop from his pocket. He waved it in front of each family member for several minutes. Gabe found it interesting that the device was indistinguishable from the one the Veronn individual used. Once satisfied, the man asked, "Do you know who I am?"

"Jason mentioned something about Time Cops," Kim answered. "I'm guessing that's you."

"I'm a Temporal Displacement Officer, but it's alright to call us Time Cops. One must always ask permission in writing before undertaking faster-than-light travel."

"We were not aware."

"My instrument records no timeline damage. Remember, check with me first. Understood?"

"There will be future travels?" Kim asked.

"Here's my card. If you encounter a time discrepancy, contact me immediately. Failure to comply will lead to your immediate termination."

"We understand," Gabe answered.

The man handed Gabe a card and walked away. He read, "Walter Woods, Logistics, (202) 555-0382 Walterwoods345@aol.com"

Jason returned and asked, "Hard-core? Right?"

"He seemed intense," Kim answered.

"True. Anyway, round two. Sophia, please come over here."

Jason made a gesture, and a woman in a blue pantsuit walked up to the family. Sophia was five foot six, slim, and had black hair in a tight bun. Her expression had a quiet strength that carried lots of authority. Sophia looked annoyed and asked sternly, "Did you come under any spiritual influence?"

"I don't understand," Kim answered.

"Did you take part in any religious events?"

"No."

"Did you accept any religious material?"

"Of course not."

"Did you offer any religious material or share your religious views?" Sophia demanded.

"Um, well—" Kim's voice drifted off.

"Well, what?" Sophia demanded.

"I talked a little about my beliefs."

"How many were in attendance?" Sophia again demanded.

"Three."

"Their reaction?"

"They found my beliefs odd, and I told them I would explain it later."

"Describe your interaction."

"I only said, 'In Jesus's name. Amen.' Our conversation lasted less than a minute. Not that serious."

"Are you planning future sermons?"

"Of course not. But I would share my beliefs if they brought it up."

"Now listen here. You may not share Earth's religious beliefs. There is too much at stake. Got that!"

"I don't understand," Kim said.

"Think about how many humans have died during religious conflicts. Remember the Crusades? Sharing our beliefs or bringing new beliefs to Earth will cause immense harm. Imagine a billion off-worlders taking a pilgrimage to Mecca or praying at the Wailing Wall. It would be a disaster."

"Oh, I see your point. Sorry, it will never happen again."

"Our spiritual culture is extremely fragile, and it's my job to keep radical beliefs at bay."

"Jason talked about religious police."

"We prefer Transcendent Supervisors. Here's my card. Always contact me before and after any off-world activity. Remember. Keep your beliefs to yourself!"

Sophia handed Kim a card and walked away in a huff. The card read, "Sophia Cortez, Accountant, (202) 555-0932 Sophiacortez133@yahoo.com"

Kim chuckled, and Jason said, "Normally, Sophia is a pleasant woman, but don't get her wound up. She has a lot of power at her disposal."

"What's next?" Gabe wanted to know.

Jason sighed and answered, "We are flying you to Virgilio Airfield."

"How long were we gone?"

"Just over a day."

"How much trouble are we in?" Gabe asked, not genuinely wanting to know the answer.

"You broke almost every secret law there is. So, you're going to be behind bars for a long time."

"Wow," Gabe said with a deep sigh.

"Yeah, wow."

"Are you going to read us our rights and put handcuffs on?"

"Are you going to be a pain?"

"No."

"Then no."

"Thanks," Gabe said, smiling weakly.

"No problem. One other thing."

"Sure."

"We're letting you keep your onks. This is to prevent your Veronn friends from returning. You may not communicate with them. Understood?"

"Yes," Gabe flatly answered.

"Failure to follow my instructions will have extreme consequences."

"We understand," Kim said with a sigh.

"Have a pleasant flight."

"Will we see you soon?" Kim asked.

"From what they tell me, this is the last time we will ever meet. Sorry."

"I see. Well, thanks for all your help."

"Any time."

Two security guards escorted the family to the bus and the airport. They flew a small plane to Anchorage and transferred to a six-passenger jet. As soon as they took off, the family fell asleep.

After landing at Virgilio Airfield, three guards escorted them to a decontamination room, where they were required to remove their clothes. A woman in a white protective suit sprayed them with a caustic purple liquid and then gave them three shots each.

After they showered, the guards led them to a room with three piles of clothes on the floor. Gabe immediately recognized prison outfits. There was even a little outfit for Emma. Kim wondered if there was a children's supplier or if a tailor had made it for her. Unfortunately, it was too large, and she had to hold her pants up while walking.

While changing, Kim found it difficult to fit into her undersized shirt and suspected that a perverted staff member was responsible.

Two guards escorted them to a room with medical equipment. A man in a white lab coat walked in, looked at Kim, smiled, and said, "I'm Dr. Adams. Today, I will give you three a physical."

Gabe felt his deep sexual desire and yelled, "No way. Not you! Get somebody else to examine my wife and daughter."

"You forget your place," Dr. Adams chided.

"I'll punch your lights out!" Gabe threatened.

"Hush! Or I will ask the guards to restrain you."

Dr. Adams wickedly smiled, and Gabe again threatened, "Get somebody else!"

Dr. Adams snickered. "I think not." He turned to Kim and said, "I am going to begin by taking your temperature."

Gabe felt Dr. Adams's dominant sexual desires building and did not know what to do. Kim interrupted his thoughts coldly. <Hon, take a seat.>

<I will not permit this,> Gabe thought, panicking.

<It's alright. Now, relax, and cover your eyes.>

<What?>

<This guy's a wimp. I got this.>

<I hope you know what you're doing.>

Gabe sat in a nearby chair and covered his eyes with his arm.

Perplexed, Dr. Adams asked, "What's going on?"

"Were you here when everybody got stunned?" Kim asked, narrowing her eyes.

"Of course."

"Then you know what is about to happen," Kim stated. "This time, I'm going to use Level 10."

"I don't believe you."

"Emma, cover your eyes and turn away," Kim cautioned. "This man's head is about to explode."

"I do, Mommy Kim."

Kim stared at Dr. Adams and held up her right pointer finger. Dr. Adams now had a tingling sensation in his cheeks. Kim extended her left arm, raised three fingers, and chanted, "Woo, woo, woo."

"Stop. Stop!" Dr. Adams yelled. "Alright. I will have a nurse perform the exam. Geez!"

<That was funny,> Gabe thought.

<Told you.>

<You crack me up, babe. It's taking all my self-control not to laugh.>

After their exams, the guards led the family to three cells. Kim stared daggers at the lead guard. He looked embarrassed and allowed Emma to be in Kim's cell. When the door closed with a loud clang, Kim felt a sense of crushing disappointment. Gabe accepted his familiar surroundings with an enormous sigh.

A moment later, the family received foreign thoughts with greedy emotions, <They let you keep your onks? Stupid humans. Together, we can rule this planet. How long before your forces arrive?>

<We're humans, idiot,> Kim thought harshly.

<You're still prisoners. Together we can—>

<Stop thinking,> Kim cut off the unknown individual.

<Together, we can escape.>

<Can we block the weirdos out of our thoughts?> Gabe thought to his onk.

{These beings are the Dag. A crude race that artificially advanced. The Veronn developed Filter Type 2123 to counter unwanted mental intrusions. Engaging.}

<Stop that!> A Dag protested.

<Leave us alone, and the filter will not affect you,> Gabe thought.

<Turn it off. We need to escape. This place is horrible.>

<Kim, Emma, put on Filter Type 2123. It's in the left sub-menu.>

<I already do, Daddy Gabe,> Emma thought gleefully.

<Stop that.> Another Dag mind thought intruded.

<There's nothing else to do here,> the first Dag individual angrily explained. <They make us watch the Earth show *Sesame Street*. I know how to count to ten. We need to escape.>

<I will ask them to bring you a book,> Kim snickered.

<Arrrgh,> the annoyed Dag responded.

Kim understood six Dag beings were in nearby cells, and they ceased mental communications.

•

The family settled into an unrewarding routine in their small jail cells. To occupy their time, they communicated with each other and explored the onks' endless information. Emma was allowed to be with Kim, but they were not allowed to see Gabe. The only bright spot was that Gabe commented, "The food's not bad."

Three days later, a man approached Gabe's cell with a notepad and said, "Please describe your trip. If you refuse, I will punish you."

"There is no need to threaten me. Bring a computer, and I will write a full report."

"That's not how we do it."

"I do a lot better on a computer. Give me your questions."

"I suppose it will make my job easier."

Two hours later, the man returned with an ancient laptop. It had three red-and-white stickers that read, "Contains classified material." Gabe found it comical that it ran Windows 95. There was only one app– Notepad– and he clicked on the icon and started writing. Unfortunately, this program lacked editing features, and he had to use the return key frequently because it did not automatically wrap text. Fifteen minutes later, the battery died.

Three hours later, the man returned, furious that the battery had died. An hour later, he provided a newer laptop with Windows XP and a power cord. This time, the only icon on the screen was WordPad. Gabe laughed at the absurdity of the situation and started typing.

In the next cell, Kim explained the details of their trip, and the man wrote them down. They had agreed beforehand not to reveal that they had eaten or removed their collective protective garments.

Emma told her interviewer, "We went to Veronn to meet Zic! He my best friend. We then do Kebo! Let it be known to all that this is a glorious cycle!"

When the interviewer asked for more information, Emma said sweetly, "I don't know." He tried three more times and gave up.

Gabe finished his report that evening, and the same man brought another list of questions for Gabe to answer the next day.

On the fifth morning, guards took the family to a conference room. General Shefford and Sam looked at the family angrily as they sat. "You made Earth a Type 2 society!" Sam yelled.

"Of course," Kim answered. "Earth *is* a Type 2 society."

General Shefford interrupted, "We have advanced spacecraft technology and can fake the rest. That makes us a Type 4."

"We should be a Type 3!" Sam corrected. "This is a disaster."

"What the heck are you talking about?" Gabe demanded. "We answered the questions accurately."

"I know," General Shefford hissed. "We're a Type 2. That's obvious."

Kim threw up her hands. "Then what is the issue?"

"A Type 3 or 4 planet has more options," Sam answered. "We could even apply to be on the Enlighten Council."

"I do not know what that is," Kim admitted. "Look, the Veronn explained it was imperative to answer the questions truthfully. The punishment for falsifying the answers is a forced lower status for 54 years."

"Type 2 will classify us as undeveloped for 54 years. It's the same thing," General Shefford countered.

"No, it means we can interact on our terms. Plus, we have automatic protection."

"I know you were trying to do your best, but you three screwed up big-time," Sam chided. "Our agreements clearly state that negotiations with Earth governments are required for all database entries."

"There you go again," General Shefford interrupted. "The Air Force is always out of the loop."

"We began negotiations before the Air Force involvement," Sam retorted.

"Enough," Kim interrupted. "Both of you. What's done is done. In 54 years, there will be a reevaluation."

"This is a big deal," Sam countered. "Your actions upset powerful people."

"Are you upset?"

"I told you not to go off-world," Sam reminded them. "And you had no right to update the Galactic Database. That's our job, not yours. So, yes, I'm upset."

"What will happen to us?" Kim asked.

"That's still under discussion," Sam answered. "But I know one thing. You three will be here for the rest of your lives."

"No trial?" Kim meekly asked.

"No trial!" General Shefford shot back.

"Can we at least do something productive? Gabe can do technical stuff, and I can talk with our off-world friends."

"Absolutely not," Sam answered.

Gabe took a deep breath, let it out slowly, and said, "We understand."

They all stared at each other, and then Sam said, "Alright, that topic is closed. Gabe, I would like to thank you for the comprehensive report. We learned a lot."

"You're welcome," Gabe said with a weak smile.

"Are we going to see you again?" Kim asked.

Sam took a deep breath and answered, "This is the end of the line for you three. I'm sorry."

"What about Emma?" Kim demanded. "She should not have to grow up in an Air Force jail."

"Circumstances make this action necessary."

General Shefford cleared his throat and said, "Now, here's the deal. The three of you only have one goal for the rest of your lives. Make sure your Veronn colleagues never return. Are we clear?"

"Yes," Gabe answered, deflated.

"You will not communicate with them. Correct?"

"Correct."

General Shefford paused before continuing. "One other matter. That little stunt you pulled on Captain Adams didn't please me. We planted explosives below your cells, and I have my finger on the button. The moment you communicate will be your last. Got that?"

"You're fooling yourself," Gabe said with a snort.

"I am not."

"You have explosives. That's clear. But getting Lieutenant Tiller to read our thoughts about communicating with the Vcronn is a joke."

"Were you reading me?" General Shefford demanded.

"Of course," Gabe answered with another snort.

"You violated my trust."

"You violated our trust first by putting us in prison without a trial," Kim shot back. "Plus, you put a bomb underneath us. Is that what you call trust?"

"Hmm," General Shefford mused and leaned back momentarily. "You have a point, but stunning Captain Adams with your mind was out of line."

"She can't mind stun anybody," Gabe said with a chuckle.

"Then, what did she do?"

"Tugged at his mind and acted tough. Kim's good at bluffing."

"Damn," General Shefford exclaimed.

"Besides, that deviant has no business being a doctor. I would have beaten him bloody if the guards weren't outside."

"He is a competent officer with a spotless record," General Shefford countered.

"All three of us were in his head, and he–" Gabe momentarily turned to Emma and continued, "Had uncomplimentary thoughts about Kim. Then, later that evening, he planned to make whoopee to himself while holding Kim's identification picture."

Emma laughed and said, "Doctor man play with pee-pee stick."

"Emma. Behave!" Kim admonished.

"Sorry, Mommy Kim."

General Shefford stood, walked five paces, sat, and said through gritted teeth, "There is no proof of Captain Adams's lewd actions. However, I don't tolerate such behavior. There are rows of dirty latrines, and I assure you he will be up to his ears in crap until I'm satisfied that he gets the message."

"Thank you," Kim said with a weak smile.

"And I have your word that you will not use your mental ability to cause mischief?"

"You do," Kim confirmed.

"And the three of you will not try to escape?"

"Where could we go?" Gabe asked. "The DLS has people in every corner of the world."

"You could contact somebody, and they could send a ship here."

"And leave Earth?" Kim protested. "Our lives, families, and friends are here. This is our planet. Besides, who the heck would drop everything to rescue us?"

"Makes sense. We will do our best to make your time here as pleasant as the circumstances allow."

"Thank you," Gabe said, smiling weakly.

"Is there nothing we can do to make this right?" Kim asked.

"No," Sam quickly answered.

"I see," Kim said in defeat.

"And yes, I know you were trying to do the right thing. And I know that you genuinely wanted to help. And I know you do your best to be trustworthy."

"Well, thank you for that," Kim said.

"What happened isn't personal."

"We understand."

"Good."

Sam closed his eyes momentarily, then said, "I'll try to drop in from time to time."

"We would like the company," Gabe said with a smile.

"Well, we must attend another meeting to clean up this mess."

"We hope to see you soon," Kim said.

"Likewise."

"Bye-bye boss-man Sam and General Buzz Lightyear," Emma said with a big grin.

Sam and General Shefford chuckled as the family left the conference room. When they got out of earshot, Sam said, "It's a real shame Emma has to grow up like that."

"We spared her life, and that's something."

"True."

•

The family's boring routine never let up. They ate a tasteless breakfast of powdered eggs and burned toast. The mornings became blisteringly hot, and their only relief came from fanning themselves. At noon, they ate a bologna and sharp cheese sandwich with a glass of powdered milk. They ate stale, powdered mashed potatoes with salty gravy from a can and overcooked fried chicken for dinner.

Thirty minutes later, two armed guards escorted one family member to a fenced-in courtyard with a well-used basketball but no hoop for ten minutes of "free time." Their cells became bitterly cold at night, and the thin, scratchy blanket made sleep challenging.

In the third week, guards brought them books as a reward for good behavior. A guard placed a portable DVD player outside their cell two weeks later. While the movie selection was poor, the family appreciated the distraction.

The Dag were kept in a nearby secure area. Nevertheless, they pestered the family with angry thoughts, and their onks responded with a painful buzz. The family sometimes could hear them yelling at each other in a strange language.

Kim and Gabe put in all their effort to educate and entertain Emma. Fortunately, the guards provided her with paper and a pencil. She kept a positive attitude and was content to learn from the onk and her parents. Gabe and Kim found her presence a source of strength and encouraged her to ask questions. Emma understood her role and tried her best to keep the family together.

The guards had an odd security rule about not using their names, so the family resorted to calling them One, Two, and Three. However, the worst security rule was that Gabe could not see Kim or Emma. The family learned that the logic behind it was to limit their "mental power."

The isolation, repetitive food, and the lack of seeing each other had severely affected them by week seven. After a lengthy mental discussion, Gabe and Kim decided that Emma needed a chance at everyday life, and they wrote a letter to General Shefford requesting an hour of together time per week. Unfortunately, he did not respond.

During the tenth week of their incarceration, they discussed their situation at length. Gabe concluded that the extreme security made escape impossible. Even if they escaped, they would have to walk across miles of desert. Kim knew Emma could not undertake this journey. In desperation, Gabe and Kim tried to use their onks to communicate with a spacecraft housed in a nearby hangar. They established "greetings and identities," but without a "transcode password," they could not proceed.

The extreme isolation pushed Gabe and Kim to the breaking point by week thirteen. In desperation, Kim contacted Tan through her onk. While the family's plight saddened him, he revealed the Veronn home world was in chaos.

After Samvral the Twelfth's unprecedented request for a weapon, two guards recanted their accusations. Tan and many Veronn were sure that Samvral the Twelfth had used "money-money" influence. He also informed Kim that their laws prevented interference in other cultures' legal matters. Kim thanked Tan for being honest.

This information depressed the family, and their hope faded. Gabe and Kim felt each other's sanity slipping as the days passed. Communication between them became angry and incoherent. They played mental games and practiced yoga for hours to combat the madness, but the intense interaction also made them want to spend more time apart from each other's minds.

•

The family had lost count of the days despite their onks' excellent chronograph systems. One morning, Guard Number Two came to see them. He held three paper bags and looked extremely upset. "You three!" he yelled at the top of his lungs. "Get dressed! Now. I said, now!"

The guard threw the bags down, opened their doors, and dramatically walked away. Kim cautiously walked out of her cell and opened a bag with misgivings. It contained Gabe's clothes from Alaska. <It's our clothes,> she thought with jittery emotions.

Gabe left his cell, looked around for a long time, and thought, <I don't understand. What do they want?>

<They want us to put on our clothes. Guard Two was all pissed off about something. I bet they want us to look presentable for a meeting. Or an execution. We're in more trouble than ever.>

Suspicious, Gabe demanded, <What? Who said that?>

<Take it easy. It's me,> Kim answered angrily. <You are looking right at me.>

<And?>

<We need to change clothes.>

<Is it safe?> Gabe asked, preparing himself to strike.

<I'm not sure. Be ready for anything.>

<Oh, I'll be careful. Just watch.>

Gabe took his bag back to his cell and changed. The clothes hung limply on his body because he had lost weight. Gabe cautiously walked out while holding his pants up with his left hand. Kim and Emma changed and then walked out of the cell. When they saw each other in regular clothes, their spirits lifted.

<You look nice.> Gabe said with a smile.

<You too, hon.>

The family hugged for a long moment. Then, Guard Number Two reappeared and yelled, “I told you to get going. Now!”

“Where?” Kim demanded.

Guard Two glared at them for a long moment, and they followed him through the heavy doors. Finally, the family saw the desert and walked together, feeling happy to be outside. They expected to be led to a conference room, but Guard Two led them to a six-passenger jet. They got inside and recognized the same pilots. Kim demanded to know the destination, but did not get an answer.

In the back were three clear bags containing their collective protective garments, which puzzled the family. They took their seats and wondered why the guards were not accompanying them and why they were not in handcuffs. Two minutes later, the plane’s engines started. On the flight, the family remained concerned and only glanced through the windows.

Four and a half hours later, the plane touched down at a small airport. The door opened, and the family saw Kelly beside her white SUV. From the other car’s license plates, they realized they had returned to Florida.

They cautiously exited and entered Kelly’s car. She then threw the bags holding their collective protective garments in the back. Gabe tried to question Kelly on the drive, but she remained silent with an angry scowl. Ten minutes later, he asked how long they had been in prison, and she mumbled, “One hundred twenty-one days.”

Twenty minutes later, the SUV abruptly stopped at an IHOP Restaurant near their house. “Gabe! Out! Now!” Kelly yelled.

“To do what?”

“Now!”

Still holding up his pants, Gabe exited the car and walked inside. A wall clock read 3:15 p.m., and a single customer was sitting in a booth. Gabe barely recognized the same tough biker from their previous meetings. The man wore a nice patterned shirt, a brown tie, Dockers, and stylish black shoes. He sported a trim haircut and was clean-shaven. Gabe noticed minor shaving cuts on the man’s face, and his clothes still had their factory creases.

The man looked glad to see Gabe and warmly shook his hand for an unusually long moment. “I’m happy to see you,” he began.

“Um, thanks,” Gabe mumbled, not knowing what was happening.

“My name is Wilbert Campbell.”

“Nice to meet you, Wilbert.”

"They asked me to be brief. So here it is. We are taking care of Sato once and for all."

Wilbert diabolically smiled, which frightened Gabe to his core. "What will you do to him?" he whispered.

Wilbert looked away momentarily and then twisted a napkin in front of him. A server came by, and Gabe ordered coffee without intending to drink it. She poured his cup full and left. Wilbert still seemed to ponder the question and asked, "Do you know what happens when somebody betrays a brother?"

"I would never betray the brothers!" Gabe blurted out. "Never. No matter what. You've got to believe me. Please!"

"No, I know you would never do something like that," Wilbert said warmly. "You've been in the hole, and you know what's what. Plus, you're a family man. Now, your boy Sato chose a different path."

"He blames me for ruining his life," Gabe admitted.

"He ruined a lot of lives. Ya see, Sato became invisible in the hole. Nobody cared about that little punk as he silently watched the cons do their deals while the screws turned a blind eye. Everybody figured he didn't snitch in the past and knew what would happen if he opened his piehole. Well, ya see, that's where everybody screwed up. Your boy had a plan. Every night, he wrote every scrap of information in a diary. He also made up a bunch of stuff that fit the facts.

"When our frame-up job put him in solitary, he made a deal. In exchange for testifying, he could use a computer. The screws even put him into special protective custody to keep his worthless ass alive. Then, boy-howdy did he spill his guts. He told them about every stash, deal, hit, and plan. He squealed on the cons, screws, and the outside helpers. Every group got smacked, including the brothers. He even made up stuff about the Muslims. Now, you were in the hole, and you know that nobody messes with those boys."

"I'm sorry your brothers got caught up in his rage."

"Nothing to be sorry about. Your boy knew what would happen if he betrayed the brotherhood."

"That's terrible."

"Not your fault," Wilbert said with a wicked smile.

"What did the brothers do to him?"

"We made a deal with the Nuestra Familia. Imagine that? The brothers making a deal with the Mexican mob. That is how much we all hate Sato. The guards have a trusted prisoner who delivers meals to those in protective custody. His mother has cancer, and the brothers are paying for her treatment. Even the screws are in on the act."

"Why?"

"They will get hurt the most when he testifies. No screw ever wants to be in the hole."

"That's true," Gabe said with a nod.

"Heck, it's a family affair. The Bloods provided the shiv, and the Tran Vietnamese gang passed it through security."

"Wow. I never would have thought the gangs would work together like that."

"On rare occasions, we have one-on-one deals," Wilbert informed him with a chuckle.

"Why are you telling me this?" Gabe asked.

"We promised to deal with your boy."

"Yes, but Sato betrayed the brotherhood, and you would ice him anyway. So why are you here?"

"You know what kind of person I am and what I do."

"A tough biker," Gabe firmly answered.

"I'm the real deal. A true hardened criminal. Just like the movies. My brothers and I bike, party, steal, kill, and don't care who gets hurt. But you—"

Wilbert looked away and returned to twisting his napkin. Gabe waited for Wilbert to continue. A long moment later, he looked up and said, "You roll with a dangerous crowd."

"They threatened you?"

Wilbert bit his lip, grunted, and answered, "No. The threats came later. The pain came first."

"I'm sorry. But please understand that I'm not in charge."

"Your lady friend said you don't call the shots, and your only job is to keep a low profile. Sato interfered with that."

"I see."

"I got a page ten minutes ago. It's done."

"Oh."

"We also took care of the two others who messed with you. Free of charge."

Gabe did not understand what Wilbert was referring to, and he responded neutrally, "Thanks."

Wilbert took a deep breath and said, "You have nothing to fear from the brothers. We will not contact you again unless you need a favor. Are we on good terms?"

"Sure," Gabe answered with relief.

"That is great to hear," Wilbert said with a nervous smile.

"I am glad I could help."

"Have a happy life, Gabe."

"You too, Wilbert."

Wilbert dropped a fifty-dollar bill on the table and walked away. Gabe noticed his pants still had the price tag label on the back. He returned to the car, and Kelly coldly asked, "Did they terminate the mark?"

"Wilbert told me they took care of Sato ten minutes ago. He also said he took care of the other two. I don't know what he was talking about."

"Good."

"Now, will you tell us what's going on?"

Kelly drove the family to their house in silence. Inside, they saw a tough-looking Hispanic gentleman dressed in a flawless tan suit. He stood six foot three, had jet-black hair in a sharp crew cut, and greeted them with confident brown eyes. The man had a ghastly zipper surgical scar on his right wrist and a religious tattoo on his neck. Kelly motioned for the family to sit, then began pacing.

<Do you have any idea what's happening?> Kim gravely asked Gabe.

<Kelly is beyond upset,> Gabe answered. <I've never seen her so wound up. See her hand? She is touching the outline of her gun. She wants to pull it out and shoot us.>

<This will not end well.>

<I think once she tells us what is going on, things will get better.>

<I hope so,> Kim thought.

<It's nice to be home,> Gabe thought.

<It is.>

Kelly stopped pacing and yelled, "You three. What you three did!"

"What? What did we do?" Kim asked, confused.

"We ordered you not to communicate with anybody."

"Um, well, we were going crazy being locked up in solitary. Besides, the Veronn refused to help because of their laws."

"Ha! You admit it. You broke your promise," Kelly admonished.

"We were losing our minds!" Kim exclaimed.

"The three of you! The! Three! Of! You! Cannot sit still and take your punishment. Nooo. You had to make life difficult for everybody. Couldn't sit still for another month."

"You were trying to get us out?" Kim asked, her jaw dropping.

"Of course. You three can use an onk. Do you have any flipping idea how valuable that makes you? You three are solid gold. But nooo. You had to communicate. Had to communicate!"

"Nobody told us," Kim defended.

"Of course not. We were negotiating with the Air Force bozos to set you free. The deal was to teach Lieutenant Tiller how to use an onk."

"Other humans cannot operate an onk. They need to be modified, and we don't know how to do that."

"We know that! Plus, Tiller's a dumbass. We planned to give him a hunk of plastic and say it's an onk. Then let him waste years trying to get it to work."

Gabe and Kim chuckled, and Kim asked, "I don't get it. What happened? Why are you so upset? And who's the guy over there?"

Kelly went back to pacing, and ten laps later, she answered, "From this point forward, you will refer to this man as Mr. Sanchez. He is a highly trained individual with vast experience in combat, covert operations, and firearms. Mr. Sanchez has completed his training with distinction and will be a superb ACO in the Mexican state of Jalisco. We scheduled him to return next week, but you three changed everything. Like me, he has no interest in babysitting, but your little stunt makes it necessary to have an ACO bodyguard. You are to treat Mr. Sanchez with supreme respect. Is that clear?"

"Of course," Gabe answered. "May I ask what 'stunt' you are referring to? Because we don't know what you're talking about."

In anger, Mr. Sanchez folded his arms, and Kelly returned to pacing. Six laps later, she asked, "You don't know? Really? You don't know?"

"No," Kim answered. "Please tell us."

Kelly went back to pacing while angrily touching the outline of her gun. Three laps later, she said, "I want to believe you, but I don't. I don't trust you three. I never did. You play mind games. I hate that!"

"Honestly, we don't know what you're talking about."

"You do not know that you are the ambassadors to Earth?"

"What the heck?" Kim protested. "That makes little sense."

"The Galactic Database lists you three as the formal ambassadors to Earth. It will take 54 years before we can change the entry. This is an enormous mess. You cannot comprehend what you've done!"

"What?" Kim again protested. "We're not the ambassadors of anything."

"Yes, you are."

"What? Gabe, did you know about this?"

"Of course not," Gabe answered. "Emma?"

Emma smiled and answered, "I think with Zic, and he wanted to help."

"Emma! You shouldn't have done that," Kim scolded. She got off the couch, knelt, and looked at Emma. "Tell me exactly what happened."

"Mommy Kim and Daddy Gabe were sad. I asked my best friend Zic for help, who asked leader Par."

"Emma, you should have talked to us about this."

"I do bad, Mommy Kim?"

Emma began crying, and Kim picked her up. <You were doing your best,> she soothed.

<I do bad.>

<No, sweetie,> Kim soothed.

<I had to save Mommy Kim and Daddy Gabe.>

<I know.>

<I try hard.>

<I know.>

Kim walked around holding Emma as she sniffled. Kelly looked at Mr. Sanchez in stunned disbelief. They walked to the kitchen and whispered to each other for several minutes. When Emma stopped crying, they returned.

Kim set Emma down, and Kelly said, "I keep underestimating you."

"Sorry, lady Kelly," Emma said in between sobs. "I saved Mommy Kim and Daddy Gabe."

"What does this all mean?" Gabe asked.

"Well, one thing is for sure. We don't know. But we do know that the ambassadors to Earth cannot be in prison."

"I see."

"As for the rest, we'll take it one day at a time."

"What does this mean for us?"

"For now, your lives will return to normal. Well, as normal as the circumstances allow."

"So, we go to work, and Emma goes to school?"

"Well, that's where things get more complex," Kelly answered, tilting her head to the side.

"Meaning?"

"Emma cannot attend regular school because there is no security. However, Mr. Sanchez has devised a creative solution. He knows some *individuals* who settled in Florida, and their children attend a private school."

"Wait a minute," Kim interrupted. "You are not suggesting she attend school with a bunch of drug cartel kids, are you?"

"That's the idea," Kelly said with a grin.

"No way. Never."

"Mr. Sanchez identified one family with a school facility on their secure estate. Several children from elite families also attend. A few are Emma's age, and it's an accredited program."

"But they're the drug cartel," Kim protested.

"What about all *your* crimes?"

"Oh."

"It's a suitable compromise."

"Will she be safe?" Kim demanded.

"Those people are all about safety. There are ten guards with Uzis."

"So, now what?" Gabe asked.

"In the morning, one of you will drop off Emma and check the place out."

"What about the ambassador part?" Kim asked. "Will we have to meet with dignitaries and write up treaties?"

"That is what ambassadors usually do," Kelly answered with a scowl. "Now, ground rules. First, your house does not suit our needs. We have arranged for a larger house. And yes, it used to belong to a drug dealer. And yes, you two will have to pay for it. Second, the three of you never leave our sight. And I mean never! We're working on getting another ACO to guard Emma, but that's been a little tough because–" Kelly shook her head. "Never mind. Third, from now on, you three will behave. Got it?"

"I think so," Kim answered with a huff. "Where's the house?"

"It is in an exclusive neighborhood in Southwest Ranches."

"How much is it going to cost us?"

"We negotiated a million bucks."

"What did it list for?" Gabe asked and bit his lip.

"It's on fifty acres with guest houses, garages, gardens, fast cars, secret passages, priceless furniture, and lots of security. You do the math."

"Oh."

"It's not all fun and games. To save resources, we're moving the ACO training operations there. As a result, your new house is about to become a busy place."

"I see."

"Fourth. More ground rules. You two will always carry weapons. When Emma is older, she will get one."

"I have knife," Emma interrupted, pulling a razor blade from her sock.

"Emma!" Kim yelled.

Kelly chuckled and said, "Wow. You got that through Air Force security? Impressive. Well, keep it close."

"I will, lady Kelly," Emma said with her best brave expression.

Kelly nodded and returned to pacing. Six paces later, she stopped and said, "Finally. You must respect what we do. Our jobs are tough, and you three made it a lot worse."

"Sorry, lady Kelly," Emma whispered.

"Think about the consequences next time."

"I try hard, lady Kelly."

"Thank you. Now. Unpack, dinner, and sleep."

Two hours later, Kim ordered Chinese food. They put their collective protective garments in the guest bedroom closet. Kelly took the first watch while Mr. Sanchez slept on the downstairs sofa. Kim tucked Emma in, went to her bedroom, and thought to Gabe, <What a crazy day. Ambassadors to Earth? What the heck do you think it all means?>

Kim smiled. <No idea.>

<It's nice to be with you.>

<Hey! No hanky-panky.>

<Babe, I have not even touched you in? What did she say? One hundred twenty days or something?>

<I feel your pain, and I want to jump you.>

<We can kiss?> Gabe asked.

<Soon, hon, soon. For now, hold my hand. Sound good?>

<For you, anything.>

The pair fell asleep in each other's arms.

# TWENTY-FOUR

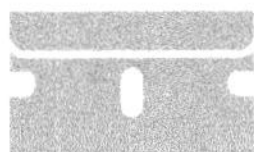

Kim, Kelly, and Emma drove to a nearby estate the following day. Three guards at the outer gate scrutinized the occupants and thoroughly searched the car. The secure school within the lavish estate had thick concrete walls with bulletproof windows. Three heavily armed security guards patrolled the compound. An administrator gave Kim the evil eye at the school entrance and double-checked her identification against their sign-in sheet.

The facility had a small playground and lunch area. Inside were three stimulating classrooms with student artwork covering the walls. Emma's class had eight children, one teacher, and a teacher's assistant. Their ages ranged from two to five. The children enjoyed having a new student, and Emma blended in.

Kim then spoke with the principal for 20 minutes about her "personal pager" and academics. Satisfied that Emma was in good hands, she drove with Kelly to her work.

Gabe and Mr. Sanchez drove to KimSemi, and he was happy to see everybody. Gabe gathered his team and began, "Sorry for being gone so long. Anyway. My family and I have gone through some, er, um, *changes*. I wish I could be more open about what's going on. Well, I guess there is no other way to say it. We have a new team member. This is Mr. Sanchez, and he is... well, he's my bodyguard. To answer your next question, you guys aren't in danger, and we would both appreciate it if you would ignore his presence. The only exception is if you see something security-related. Also, no joking around. Mr. Sanchez is a serious dude. Thanks, everyone."

Gabe went into his office, and Christine followed. They left the door open, and Mr. Sanchez stood outside.

"What the heck?" Christine asked and threw up her hands. "What the heck?"

"It's complicated," Gabe answered with a sigh.

"You bet it's complicated."

"I'm sorry. Believe me, I didn't plan for any of this."

Christine again threw up her hands and walked around the office. Gabe could see her frustration and changed the subject. "How have things been around here?"

"Sales are up, and morale is great."

"That's wonderful."

"Got any more trips planned?"

"No idea," Gabe answered, looking away.

"I don't like your answer."

"I cannot help what's going on. I wish I could."

"I see."

"Well, let's get things going. First, we must get the prototype ready for fabrication. During my absence, I thought about the problems and some new features."

"We already sent the design out," Christine said with a smirk.

"What?"

"We already got it back and tested it."

"Oh, I wish you didn't waste so much effort because I know it's got big issues. Especially in the accumulator."

"We know," Christine said with a broad grin.

"Well? Tell me. How bad was it?"

"You're so doubtful. Answer your own question."

"It worked?" Gabe asked.

"Of course! You know that."

"Where were the faults?"

"The upper accumulators return garbage, and the zero-flag conditional jump goes eight locations ahead of where it should. Oh yeah. The multipliers sometimes return the wrong value."

"Otherwise?"

"It's all good."

"All of it?" Gabe asked, standing with a surprised expression.

"All of it!"

Gabe felt conflicting emotions and asked, "What aren't you telling me?"

"You didn't ask about performance."

"Well?"

"It's fantastic."

"How much?"

"You lowballed your numbers, didn't you?"

"Um, kind of."

"It's eighty-three percent better than your calculations. We'll need rakes to pile up all the money we are about to make." Christine smiled.

Gabe lowered his gaze, embarrassed. "I know what's wrong with the accumulators."

"We located the conditional jump error and simulated the multiplier issue. How confident are you about making a functional processor?"

"I can do it in less than two months."

"We're still aiming for the low-end server market?" Christine asked. "Right?"

"That's where the bucks are."

"Good."

Christine looked at the open door and then back at Gabe. He gulped and said, "Thanks for sticking around."

"I only did it because I believed in your breakthrough."

"Well, thanks anyway. And again, I'm sorry about all this."

"So, you have a bodyguard. You don't seem like the type."

"It's complicated. Please don't discuss the subject."

"Is he on the payroll?" Christine asked.

"I'm not sure."

"Any idea how long he will be here?"

"Years," Gabe admitted with a sigh.

"You said we're not in any danger."

"Mr. Sanchez is a precaution."

"Can you tell me anything?" Christine asked.

"Sorry."

"Hmm. We need a name for your processor. Something sexy. Any ideas?"

"Veronn."

"Wow, right out of the gate. Where did you come up with that?"

•

That weekend, the family drove to the large estate that Kelly had arranged for them to move into. It had imposing black steel gates at the entrance, giving it a foreboding appearance. Inside, they walked around the main house and saw expensive furniture and extravagant artwork. With a wicked grin, Kelly revealed that "the previous occupants left in a hurry." The kitchen was large enough to prepare meals for 200 people, and the master bedroom had enough space to set up a basketball court.

Kelly explained that the family would move into guest house number two. Gabe estimated it to be over twice the size of their present house. Kim liked the decorations, and Gabe appreciated the den.

Kelly continued the tour, leading them to a home theater building, an indoor gun range, a fully stocked underground wine cellar, and a twenty-bay garage filled with expensive cars.

"First thing, all that booze goes away," Kim told Kelly.

"That space will become our high-security storage. We arranged for a liquor distributor to purchase the alcohol."

"Good."

Kelly showed them two fences surrounding the estate, multiple cameras, and several disguised "pillboxes" that would allow the guards to defend the house. In addition, every building had a panic room and an escape tunnel.

The family liked their house and moved in over the next three weeks. While packing, Kim found more evidence of her family's drug problem and divorce papers. She had been unaware that her parents were having marriage difficulties. Eight days later, Kim put her family home on the market, which was a bittersweet moment.

The DLS converted the main house of their new property into a training office, classroom, and coordination center. Gabe sat in on a few sessions and liked the many "what if" scenarios the instructors presented.

Kim inquired several times about their role as ambassadors, suspecting the DLS had not figured it out. She also asked about visiting Alaska, which Kelly implied "might occur in the distant future."

Six weeks later, Kelly announced that the family would attend a DLS meeting in France, but provided no details.

•

Tuesday, October 8, 2019, 1:18 p.m. Paris time. The six-passenger jet landed, and the door opened to a waiting tan SUV with tinted windows. Gabe found it interesting that they did not pass through customs or airport security. After a pleasant drive, the family arrived at a beautiful hotel outside Paris. Kelly instructed the family to wait, and she stood outside their door. Emma enjoyed watching *Bugs Bunny* and *The Simpsons* in French. A blue SUV took them to a nondescript government building three hours later.

Kelly led the family through heavy security, and Emma's presence surprised everybody. She wore a lovely pink dress and walked next to her parents with a confident smile. Kelly directed them to a large conference room, and they sat in the back row with Kelly between Gabe and Kim. Several people were already in attendance; some wore mesh hoods to conceal their faces.

Kim motioned to Gabe, and they passively read these unseen people. It was clear they were high-level DLS managers. Kim found it interesting that one manager was an off-worlder. He turned to the family when they passively probed him.

As more people arrived, the family watched Donna take a seat in the second row. She was dressed in a fashionable gray pantsuit and made eye contact with the family.

Kelly leaned over and whispered to Kim, "I order you three not to play mind games. But I'll never tell."

Kelly winked, and Kim found the encounter odd. Two minutes later, General Shefford walked in, glared harshly at the family, and sat in the front row.

Kelly commented, "See that guy? That's the DLS leader of Mexico. I think his name is Hector. Oh, there's China, and that's his translator. I cannot remember his name. Oh, over there is Russia, and there's Uri from Israel. I worked with him before— total badass. And there's Yasin from Saudi Arabia. Oh, look, he has a new haircut. Over there is the DLS leader of India. I don't know her name, but she runs a tight ship. There's Japan, and there's France. A tough SOB. There's Canada, and I think that guy runs Brazil."

A man in a trim black suit with a white tab collar sat in the second row. "That guy represents the Vatican," Kelly said. "I didn't think he would make it."

Gabe and Kim were unsure why they needed a Catholic church representative. Three more people arrived, including Jason, who made eye contact. A final person entered, glared daggers at the family, and sat in the back row. Kelly whispered, "That's Dexter, the head of DLS security. He hates your guts. No mind games with him. This time, I mean it!"

A minute later, Sam walked in and stood behind the lectern. He introduced himself as Phillip Hansen and began outlining the "goals for the year." Sam needed to stop his speech several times to defer questions. He then summarized the cleanup events in Alaska with vague or incorrect details. Kelly grasped Gabe and Kim's legs several times to ensure they remained silent. Kim wondered why Sam was lying to the people who should be able to handle the truth.

Sam then described a recent major incident in India. A craft landed, and the "extensive cleanup effort nearly failed." The result was three new procedures and additional training. He then deferred several questions with "I'll get back to you on that."

Emma had been confident, smiling when anybody stared at her. Eventually, her attitude became too infectious, and a nearby man interrupted, "Why the heck is this kid here?"

Sam took a deep breath and answered, "That's our next topic. As all of you know, we strive to maintain a low profile. However, we have experienced a significant change in status that you should be aware of. We have been formally recognized and–"

"What does this mean?" the same man interrupted.

"All worlds have an entry in the Galactic Database. Earth is now listed as a Type 2 society. That means we're undeveloped."

"We are Type 3!" Uri from Israel interrupted. "We must correct this error."

"The decision is sound," Sam countered as he glared at the family.

"That's not an answer," Uri countered.

"We cannot change the classification for 54 years."

"This is intolerable!" Uri yelled and threw up his hands.

"I understand your frustration, but the choice has been made. Because we were recognized, there will be more off-world interaction, but this does not change anything. All present DLS policies remain in place." Sam took a moment to focus and continued, "I predict that in less than five years, we will have this same discussion with the public. That's why I called this meeting."

The room erupted with people talking. Jason looked stunned, and Kelly covered her mouth. Kim noticed Donna briefly nod. It took Sam five minutes to calm the room. "Hold on. Hold on!" he yelled. "This is an estimated time. Right now, we need to make plans."

Several people asked questions at once, and Sam deferred answering. Then, after getting the room back in order, he said, "There is another matter that I need to share. When a planet receives a classification, an ambassador position becomes available. Essentially, the ambassador represents the Earth and all its nations. Typically, the planet's leaders submit a candidate to be evaluated. However, there is a planet called Veronn. And they have a leader named 'Pareron Kuler of the family Bean the Sixteenth.' He is a super-high-ranking political figure, and he approved our ambassador. Semom of the Quip Domain and Garonnet Tor of the Slone formalized the evaluation. Now, what does this mean? It means that the ambassador to Earth cannot change for 54 years."

The room erupted with questions, and Sam repeated, "I will get to that." He held his hand to regain order. When the questions stopped, he took a deep breath and continued, "We are fortunate to have the ambassador with us today."

Sam glared at the family. Kelly looked at Kim and then Gabe. They turned to each other and meekly stood. Gabe raised his right hand to say "hi," and Kim smiled.

Sam awkwardly cleared his throat and continued, "Um. Actually, um. There's only one ambassador and a designated backup."

"Kim will make a great ambassador," Gabe said. "She's good with people, business, and legal stuff. Everybody can count on her to do a great job."

Kim confidently smiled, and Sam became uncomfortable. "What?" Kim asked, and Sam remained silent. "Oh, of course. Gabe is well-versed in technology, which is crucial for effective negotiations. He's also good at business."

Sam continued to act awkwardly, cleared his throat, and shook his head. "What?" Kim asked. "What are you saying?"

"Um. Well, here's the thing–"

"What?" Kim demanded.

"Um."

"Not Emma. She turned two yesterday."

"Well–"

"I ambassador for all Earth," Emma interrupted. "Zic talk to Tan, and he work with Var and leader Par. He make me an ambassador to help Mommy Kim and Daddy Gabe leave jail."

The people in the room were stunned. Gabe noticed Jason nodding with a broad smile. Kelly moved to the person in front of her, tapped him on the shoulder, and whispered, "You owe me 20 bucks."

The DLS leader of China said through his interpreter, "This cannot be true. The girl is a child. Therefore, we must alter this decision."

"I'm ambassador for all Earth," Emma said with pride. "You cannot change rule. Leader Par say so."

Sam angrily tapped his forehead and said, "She's correct. Emma Alexander will serve as the ambassador to Earth for 54 years. Kim is her alternate, and Gabe is her assistant. This decision is out of our hands."

The DLS leader of Mexico yelled, "You didn't consult us. This decision is too important to be made without consultation!"

"Ohhh, I agree they didn't consult us," Sam stated as he leaned forward and stared at the family.

"How could this happen?" the Mexican DLS leader demanded. "And what's this jail incident she spoke of? Who are these people?"

"Well, we *accidentally* placed them into *protective* custody."

"We require all details if they are to represent Mexico."

"I will provide that information after the meeting. Now. Here is what will happen in the coming months. Emma and her family will travel to the planet Ton-Groon. As all of you know, the Earth is in Division 6, and the Division 6 ambassadors all meet there. Once confirmed, Emma will take on the full responsibility for all Earth diplomatic relations."

There was a collective gasp. With a grin, Emma confidently looked around and said, "Don't worry. I do good."

"That's my girl," Kim said with a warm smile.

The DLS leader of Mexico yelled, "This is unacceptable! We cannot trust the entire planet to a child."

"Look!" Kim shot back. "You need to understand that we are the only people qualified."

"How can this child be qualified?" the Mexican DLS leader demanded.

"She's correct," Sam interrupted. "For reasons I cannot fully reveal, they are the only people qualified. Also, the decision is final. And, as strange as it may seem, children often fill this role."

The Mexican DLS leader interrupted. "This is intolerable. I will not stand by as a child represents my country."

"Look, buddy!" Kim interrupted. "We didn't ask for this. It just happened this way. Plus, Emma will do a fantastic job. I know it."

"We will launch a formal protest," Mexico's DLS leader countered.

"You don't know what's going on," Kim retorted. "There are all kinds of crazy off-world guys out there. And they are coming, coming to Earth. Now, you can either deal with them or look the other way. I don't care. But the rest of us will protect the Earth. That is what the DLS stands for."

Kim and the Mexican DLS leader got into a debate about how critical the situation had become. Gabe admired his intelligent wife, and he appreciated her passion. After a sharp retort from Kim, Sam interrupted, "Look, everyone. All of this means that we have a tough job ahead of us."

"Time to behave like big girl," Emma said with pride.

A few people chuckled, and Sam made his closing remarks. Afterward, Kelly rushed the family away to avoid answering questions.

# EPILOGUE

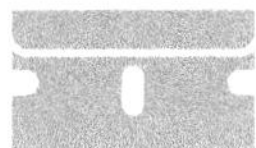

The family arrived home at 1:45 a.m. After tucking Emma in, Kim looked at Gabe and thought, <Quite a day, hon.>

<Emma did well.>

<I'm proud of her. She'll make a great ambassador.>

<What do you think will happen next?> Gabe asked.

<Sam told us we're going on a trip. What was it called?>

<Planet Ton something. Do you know anything about them?>

<No,> Kim admitted with some trepidation.

<Well, we have an interesting future ahead of us.>

<We do, husband.>

<You still enjoy calling me husband.>

<Would you have it any other way?>

<Daddy Gabe is the best father!> Emma interrupted.

<Emma!> Kim humorously thought.

# ABOUT THE AUTHOR

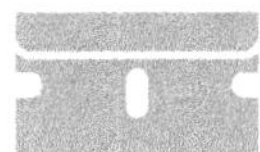

Writing books has been an enriching experience. Not only do I get to delve into the depths of my imagination and bring stories to life, but I also receive invaluable comments, questions, and feedback from my cherished readers. It's a journey filled with significant challenges, profound rewards, and epic failures. I would not miss it for the world.

Yet there is one exception to this rewarding journey: marketing. I have never been the bubbly, extroverted type who enjoys being in the public eye. Successful marketing demands putting yourself out there, taking risks, and spending a small fortune. This is something I need to work on.

Before publishing the prior book, *Pushed to the Edge of Survival*, I had already developed the basic plot for this book. This time, I wanted to explore the fascinating world of telepathy, including exploring a telepathic couple and a telepathic planet. Raising a telepathic daughter? That would be tough. How about a telepathic jury? <Of course, I robbed the bank! Whoops.> A telepathic first date? The possibilities were endless.

Yet, at its core, my story is about two parents raising their daughter during tumultuous times. Like all couples, they experience victories, confront challenges, and withstand setbacks. While offering unique advantages, their telepathic ability presents unforeseen obstacles, adding a layer of complexity to their already chaotic lives.

I used to romanticize the idea of instantly understanding another person's thoughts. However, as I delve deeper into writing about telepathy, I question the allure of such intimacy. Private thoughts are called private for a reason. My mind wanders to bizarre places, and my dreams are a whirlwind of nonsensical imagery. Would others judge me for that jumbled mess? I would expect that a telepathic society would have "thought police" who lock up wacky people like me. In fact, there would be a mental wing dedicated to my entire family.

Creating an alien race was the highlight of this book, and I avoided the outlandish science-fiction pitfalls I have seen in other works. Like us, extraterrestrial beings eat, work, have problems, and wind up with silly leaders. However, the Veronn society boasts significant differences, which I've endeavored to portray realistically. For instance, they eat different but similar-tasting food and wear jumpsuits. They do not fly cars because thousands of vehicles zooming around a big city would not be practical.

My journey as a writer is one of continuous exploration and discovery, both within the realms of imagination and the complexities of human nature. And while the road ahead may be fraught with challenges, I embrace each hurdle as an opportunity for growth and creative expression.

I recently started the next book in the series, *Pushed to The Edge of Reality*. I can reveal that the families will be tested to the limit, and there will be a fun plot twist. Stay tuned.

On to the important part. I grew up in San Diego, California, and have an Electrical Engineering degree from Worcester Polytechnic Institute with a minor in English. I will keep writing until they pry my dead fingers away from this well-used keyboard.

Bill Conrad, December 2025

# DEDICATION

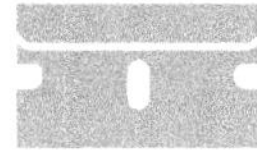

Why are book dedications always in the front? How does that location help the reader? Do they have the Oscar Award thank-you speeches at the beginning of movies? With that in mind, I put my dedication at the end.

I have been fortunate to have had two amazing parents. They were supportive, wonderful, patient beyond words, caring, and loving. Without their support, I would be nothing of consequence. My mother pushed me to keep writing and is my trustworthy beta reader. My father has authored numerous ceramics textbooks and served as an inspiration and role model.

I would also like to thank two remarkable authors. My pen pals Emily Rayven and Miriam Yvette have been encouraging, helpful, and great friends. I am lucky to have met them and read their fantastic works.

My wife, Laurie, has been immensely supportive of my writing, and without her help and love, this story would have remained hidden in my bonkers mind. And finally, I dedicate this book to my daughter, Kayla. She makes my life complete.

www.ingramcontent.com/pod-product-compliance
Lightning Source LLC
Chambersburg PA
CBHW070836260626
47170CB00007B/2396

* 9 7 8 1 7 3 4 0 3 8 7 4 3 *